BY THE SWORD

ALSO BY F. PAUL WILSON

Repairman Jack*

The Tomb	Gateways
Legacies	Crisscross
Conspiracies	Infernal
All the Rage	Harbingers
Hosts	Bloodline
The Haunted Air	

Young Adult*
Jack: Secret Histories

The Adversary Cycle*

The Keep	Reborn
The Tomb	Reprisal
The Touch	Nightworld

Other Novels

Healer	Implant
Wheels Within Wheels	Deep as the Marrow
An Enemy of the State	Mirage (with Matthew J. Costello)
Black Wind*	Nightkill (with Steven Spruill)
Dydeetown World	Masque (with Matthew J. Costello)
The Tery	The Christmas Thingy
Sibs	Sims
The Select	The Fifth Harmonic
Virgin	Midnight Mass

Short Fiction
Soft and Others
The Barrens and Others*

Editor
Freak Show
Diagnosis: Terminal

*See "The Secret History of the World" (page 349)

BY THE SWORD

A Repairman Jack Novel

F. PAUL WILSON

A TOM DOHERTY ASSOCIATES BOOK • NEW YORK

BY THE SWORD

A Forge Book
Published by Tom Doherty Associates, LLC
175 Fifth Avenue
New York, NY 10010

www.tor-forge.com

Forge® is a registered trademark of Tom Doherty Associates, LLC.

Library of Congress Cataloging-in-Publication Data

Wilson, F. Paul (Francis Paul)
    By the sword : a Repairman Jack novel / F. Paul Wilson.—1st ed.
        p. cm.
    "A Tom Doherty Associates book."
    ISBN-13: 978-0-7653-1707-0
    ISBN-10: 0-7653-1707-9
    1. Repairman Jack (Fictitious character)—Fiction. 2. Swords—Japan—Fiction. 3. New York (N.Y.)—Fiction. 4. Cults—Fiction. I. Title.

    PS3573.I45695 B9 2008
    813'.54—dc22

                                                                    2008031727

First Edition: October 2008

Printed in the United States of America

0 9 8 7 6 5 4 3 2 1

ACKNOWLEDGMENTS

Thanks to the usual crew for their efforts: Mary; Meggan; my editor, David Hartwell; Elizabeth Monteleone; Steven Spruill; and my agent, Al Zuckerman.

Many thanks to Alexis Saarela, Jodi Rosoff, Dot Lin, and head honcha Elena Stokes of Tor/Forge publicity for taking such good care of me during 2007.

Thanks also to a trio of gunnies from the repairmanjack.com forum: Biggles, Ashe, and Ken Valentine. They did their best to help solve the katana-meets-Glock question. The problem became a Gordian knot, which I finally Alexandered.

Special thanks to Tom O'Day, whose generous charitable donation earned him a violent death within.

And last, thanks to Paul Ramplin for the title. As often happens, I'll write a novel with no idea what to call it. Once again, I asked the members of the repairmanjack.com forum to help me out. Paul came up with *By the Sword*, and it stuck.

AUTHOR'S NOTE

I've always said that Repairman Jack would be a closed-end series, that I would not run him into the ground, that I had a big story to tell and would lower the curtain after telling it.

Well, we're nearing the end of that story.

And with only a few novels left in the series, I'm running into a problem. I'm no longer able to tie up each novel as neatly as I'd like. I've always kept longer story arcs running from book to book, but I used to be able to bring each installment to a satisfying conclusion. That, I'm afraid, is no longer the case.

As I move people and objects into place and set the stage for the events that will tip all of humanity into *Nightworld*, the final chapter, this sort of incremental closure has become impossible.

So I ask you to bear with me. You may have noticed that *Bloodline* didn't quite end. *By the Sword* picks up where it left off, and the next installment will pick up where this leaves off.

At most, three or four more novels remain in the series. Along the way we'll be reprinting the remainder of the Adversary Cycle, synching the releases of *The Touch, Reborn, Reprisal,* and *Nightworld* with Jack's timeline. (See "The Secret History of the World" at the end of this book for the sequence.)

More and more now, the post-*Harbingers* installments of Jack's tale are going to form what the French call a *roman-fleuve*—literally, a "river novel," with one story flowing from volume to volume. As a result, each new installment is going to feel richer, deeper, and make more sense if you've read the ones before.

Hang in there, folks. It's been a long ride, and we've still got a lot of wonder, terror, and tragedy ahead, but I promise you'll be glad you made the trip.

—F. Paul Wilson
the Jersey shore

SUNDAY

1

They weren't making muggers like they used to.

After trolling for about an hour through the unseasonably warm May night, here was the second he'd found—or rather had found him. Jack was wearing a Hard Rock Cafe sweatshirt, acid-washed jeans, and his *I ♥ New York* visor. The compleat tourist. A piece of raw steak dangling before a hungry wolf.

When he'd spotted the guy tailing him, he'd wandered off the pavement and down into this leafy glade. Off to his right the mercury-vapor glow from Central Park West backlit the trees. Over his assailant's shoulder he could make out the year-round Christmas lights on the trees that flanked the Tavern on the Green.

Jack studied the guy facing him. A hulking figure in the shadows, maybe twenty-five, about six foot, pushing two hundred pounds, giving him an inch and thirty pounds on Jack. He had stringy brown hair bleached blond on top, all combed to the side so it hung over his right eye; the left side of his head above the ear and below the part had been buzzcut down to the scalp—the Flock of Seagulls guy after a run-in with a lawn mower. Pale, pimply skin and a skull dangling on a chain from his left ear. Black boots, baggy black pants, black Polio T-shirt, fingerless black leather gloves, one of which was wrapped around the handle of a big Special Forces knife, the point angled toward Jack's belly.

"You talking to me, Rambo?" Jack said.

"Yeah." The guy's voice was nasal. He twitched and sniffed, shifting his weight from one foot to the other. "I'm talkin a you. See anybody else here?"

Jack glanced around. "No. I guess if there were, you wouldn't have stopped me."

"Gimme your wallet."

Jack looked him in the eye. This was the part he liked.

"No."

The guy jerked back as if he'd been slapped, then stared at Jack, obviously unsure of how to take that.

"What you say?"

"I said no. *En-oh*. What's the matter? You never heard that word before?"

Probably hadn't.

His voice rose. "You crazy? Gimme your wallet or I cut you. You wanna get cut?"

"No. Don't want to get cut."

"Give it or I stab you in the uterus."

What?

Fighting a laugh, Jack said, "Wouldn't want that." He reached into his pocket and pulled out a wad of cash. "I left my wallet home. Will this do?"

The guy's eyes all but bulged. His free hand darted out.

"Give it!"

Jack shoved it back into his pocket.

"Nope."

"You crazy fucker—!"

As he lunged at Jack, jabbing the blade point at his belly, Jack spun away, giving him plenty of room to miss. Not that he was worried about any surprises. Most of his type had wasted muscles and sluggish reflexes. But you had to respect that saw-toothed blade. A mean sucker.

The guy made a clumsy turn and came back, slashing face-high this time. Jack ducked, grabbed the wrist behind the knife as it went by, got a two-handed grip, and twisted.

Hard.

The guy shouted with pain as he was jerked into an armlock with his weapon flattened between his shoulder blades. He kicked backward, landing a boot heel on one of Jack's shins. Wincing with pain, Jack gritted his teeth and kicked the mugger's feet out from under him. As the guy went down on his face, he yanked the imprisoned arm back straight and rammed his right sneaker behind the shoulder, pinning him.

And then he stopped and counted to ten.

At times like these he knew he was in danger of losing it. The blackness hovered there on the edges, beckoning him, urging him to go Mongol on this guy, to take out all his accumulated anger, frustration, rage on this one pathetic jerk.

Plenty accumulated during his day-to-day life. And every day it seemed to get a little worse.

He knew now the origin of that blackness, where it hid in his cells. But that didn't make it go away or any easier to handle. So when one of these knuckle draggers got within reach, like this doughy lump of dung, he wanted to stomp him into the earth, leaving nothing but a wet stain.

A thin wire here, one he Wallenda'd along, trying not to fall off on the wrong side. Spend too much time there and you became like this jerk.

He did a ten count and willed that blackness back down to wherever it lived. Let out his breath and looked down.

"Hey, man," Polio fan whined. "Can't you take a joke? I was only—"

"Drop the knife."

"Sure, sure."

The bare fingers opened, the big blade's handle slipped from the gloved palm and clattered to the earth.

"Okay? I dropped it, okay? Now lemme up."

Jack released the arm but kept a foot on his back.

"Empty your pockets."

"Hey, what—?"

Jack increased the pressure of his foot. *"Empty them."*

"Okay! Okay!"

He reached back and pulled a ragged cloth wallet from his hip pocket, then slid it across the dirt.

"Keep going," Jack said. "Everything."

The guy pulled a couple of crumpled wads of bills from his front pockets, and dumped them by the wallet.

"You a cop?"

"You should be so lucky."

Jack squatted beside him and went through the small pile. About a hundred in cash, a half dozen credit cards, a gold high school ring. The wallet held a couple of twenties, three singles, and no ID.

"I see you've been busy tonight."

"Early bird catches the worm."

"Yeah? Consider yourself a nightcrawler. This all you got?"

"Aw, you ain't gonna jack me, are ya?"

"Interesting choice of words."

"Hey, I need that scratch."

"Your *jones* needs that scratch."

Actually, the Little League needed that scratch.

Every year about this time the kids from the local teams that played here in the park would come knocking, looking for donations toward uniforms and equipment. Jack had made it a tradition to help them out by taking up nocturnal collections in the park.

The Annual Repairman Jack Park-a-thon.

Seemed only fair that the oxygen wasters who prowled the place at night should make donations to the kids who used it during the day. At least Jack thought so.

"Let me see those hands." He'd noticed an increasingly lower class of mugger over the past few years. Like this guy. Nothing on his fingers but a cheap pewter skull-faced pinky ring with red glass eyes. "How come no gold?" Jack pulled down the back of his collar. "No chains? You're pathetic, you know that? Where's your sense of style?"

The previous donor had been better heeled.

"I'm a working man," the guy said, rolling a little and looking up at Jack. "No frills."

"Yeah. What do you work at?"

"This!"

The guy lunged for his knife, grabbed the handle, and stabbed up at Jack's groin—maybe thinking he'd find a uterus there? Jack rolled away to his left and kicked him in the face as he lunged again. The guy went down and Jack was on him once more with the knife arm yanked high and his sneaker back in its former spot on his back.

"We've already played this scene once," he said through his teeth as the blackness rose again.

"Hey, listen!" the guy said into the dirt. "You can have the dough!"

"No kidding."

Jack yanked off the glove and looked at the hand within. No surprise at the tattoo in the thumb web.

These guys were starting to pollute the city.

"So you're a Kicker, eh."

"Yeah, man. Totally dissimilated. You too? You seem like—"

He screamed as Jack shifted his foot into the rear of his shoulder and kicked down while giving the arm a sharp twist. The shoulder dislocated with a muffled pop, nearly drowned out by the high-pitched wail.

He hadn't wanted him to finish that sentence.

The Rambo knife dropped from suddenly limp fingers. Jack kicked it away and released the arm.

"Don't know about the rest of you, but that arm is definitely dissimilated."

As the guy retched and writhed in the dirt, Jack scooped up the cash and rings. He emptied the wallet and dropped it onto the guy's back, then headed for the lights.

He debated whether to troll for a third donor or call it a night. He mentally calculated that he had donations of about three hundred or so in cash and maybe an equal amount in pawnable gold. He'd set the goal of this year's Park-a-thon at twelve hundred dollars. Didn't look like he was going to make that without some extra effort. Which meant he'd have to come back tomorrow night and bag a couple more.

And exhort them to give.

Give till it hurt.

2

As he was coming up the slope toward Central Park West he saw an elderly, bearded gent dressed in an expensive-looking blue blazer and gray slacks trudging with a cane along the park side of the street.

And about a dozen feet to Jack's left, a skinny guy in dirty Levi's and a frayed Hawaiian shirt burst from the bushes at a dead run. At first Jack thought he was running from someone, but noticed that he never glanced behind him. Which meant he was running *toward* something. He realized the guy was making a beeline for the old man.

Jack paused a second. The smart part of him said to turn and walk back down the slope. It hated when he got involved in things like this, and reminded him of other times he'd played good Samaritan and landed in hot water. Besides, the area here was too open, too exposed. If Jack got involved he could be mistaken for the Hawaiian shirt's partner, a description would start circulating, and life would get more complicated than it already was.

Butt out.

Sure. Sit back while this galloping glob of park scum bowled the old guy over, kicked him a few times, grabbed his wallet, then hightailed it back into the brush. Jack wasn't sure he could stand by and let something like that happen right in front of him.

A wise man he'd hung with during his early years in the city had advised him time and time again to walk away from a fight whenever possible. Then he'd always add: "But there are certain things I will not abide in my sight."

This looked to be something Jack could not abide in his sight.

Besides, he was feeling kind of mean tonight.

He spurted into a dash of his own toward the old gent. No way he was going to beat the aloha guy with the lead he had, but he could get there right after him and maybe disable him before he did any real damage. Nothing elaborate. Hit him in the back with both feet, break a few ribs and give his spine a whiplash he'd remember the rest of his life. Make sure Aloha was down to stay, then keep right on sprinting across Central Park West into yuppieville.

Aloha was closing with his target, arms stretched out for the big shove, when the old guy stepped aside and stuck out his cane. Aloha went down on his belly and skidded face-first along the sidewalk, screaming curses all the way. When he stopped his slide, he began to roll to his feet.

But the old guy was there, holding the bottom end of his cane in a two-handed grip like a golf club. He didn't yell "Fore!" as he swung the metal handle around in a smooth, wide arc. Jack heard the crack when it landed against the side of Aloha's skull. The mugger stiffened, then flopped back like a sack of flour.

Jack stopped dead and stared, then began to laugh. He pumped a fist in the old guy's direction.

"Nice!"

"I needed that," the old dude said.

Jack knew exactly how he felt. Still smiling, he broke into an easy jog, intending to give the old dude a wide berth on his way by. The fellow eyed him as he neared.

"No worry," Jack said, raising his empty palms. "I'm on your side."

The old guy had his cane by the handle again; he nonchalantly stepped over Aloha like he was so much refuse. The guy had style.

"I know that, Jack."

Jack nearly tripped as he stuttered to a halt and turned.

"Why'd you call me Jack?"

The old man came abreast of him and stopped. Gray hair and beard, a wrinkled face, pale eyes.

"Because that's your name."

Jack scrutinized the man. Even though slightly stooped, he was still taller than Jack. Big guy. Old, but big. And a complete stranger. Jack didn't like being recognized. Put him on edge. But he found something appealing about that half smile playing about the old dude's lips.

"Do I know you?"

"No. My name's Veilleur, by the way." He offered his hand. "And I've wanted to meet you again for some time now."

"Again? When did we ever meet?"

"In your youth."

"But I don't—"

"It's not important. I'm sure it will come back to you. What's important is now and getting reacquainted. I came out here tonight for just that purpose."

Jack shook his hand, baffled. "But who—?" And then a sixty-watter lit in his head. "You don't happen to own a homburg, do you?"

His smile broadened. "As a matter of fact I do. But it's such a beautiful night I left it home."

For months now Jack had intermittently spotted a bearded old man in a homburg standing outside his apartment or Gia's place. But no matter what he'd tried he'd never been able to catch or even get near the guy.

And now here he was, chatting away as casually as could be.

"Why have you been watching me?"

"Trying to decide the right time to connect with you. Because it is time we joined forces. Past time, I'd say."

"Why didn't you just knock on my door? Why all the cat-and-mouse stuff?"

"I doubt very much you like people knowing the location of your door, let alone knocking on it."

Jack had to admit he had that right.

"And besides," Veilleur added, "you had more than enough on your plate at the time."

Jack sighed as the events of the past few months swirled around him. "True that. But—?"

"Let's walk, shall we?"

They crossed Central Park West and headed toward Columbus Avenue in silence. Though they'd just met, Jack found something about the old guy that he couldn't help liking and trusting. On a very deep, very basic, very primitive level he didn't understand, he sensed a solidarity with Veilleur, a subliminal bond, as if they were kindred spirits.

But when and where had they met before?

"Want to tell me what's going on?"

Veilleur didn't hesitate. "The end of life as we know it."

Somehow, Jack wasn't surprised. He'd heard this before. He felt an enormous weight descend on him.

"It's coming, isn't it."

He nodded. "Relentlessly moving our way. But the key fact to remember is it hasn't arrived yet. Relentlessness does not confer inevitability. Look at your run-in with the rakoshi. What's more relentless than a rakosh? Yet you defeated a shipload of them."

Jack stopped and grabbed Veilleur's arm.

"Wait a sec. Wait a sec. What do you know about rakoshi? And *how* do you know?"

"I'm sensitive to certain things. I sensed their arrival. But I was more acutely aware of the necklaces worn by Kusum Bahkti and his sister."

Jack felt slightly numb. The only other people who knew about the rakoshi and the necklaces were the two most important people in his world— Gia and Vicky—plus two others: Abe and . . .

"Did Kolabati send you?"

"No. I wish I knew where she was. We may have need of her before long, but we have other concerns right now."

" 'We'?"

"Yes. We."

Jack stared at Veilleur. "You're him, aren't you. You're the one Herta told me about. You're Glae—"

The old man raised a hand. "I am Veilleur—Glenn Veilleur. That is the only name I answer to now. It is best it remains that way lest the other name is overheard."

"Gotcha," Jack said, though he didn't.

So this was Glaeken, the Ally's point man on Earth—or *former* point man, rather. Jack had thought he'd be more impressive—taller, younger.

"We must speak of other things, Jack. Many things."

There was an understatement. But where?

Of course.

"You like beer?"

3

"An interesting turn of phrase," Veilleur said, pointing.

Jack glanced up at Julio's FREE BEER TOMORROW . . . sign over the bar. It had hung there so long, Jack no longer noticed it

"Yeah. Gets him in trouble sometimes with people who don't get it."

They were each halfway through their first brew—a Yuengling lager for Jack, a Murphy's Stout for Veilleur. In the light now Jack could see that Veilleur's eyes were a bright, sparkling blue—almost as striking as Gia's—in odd contrast to his craggy olive skin. He watched him pour more of the dark brown liquid into his glass and hold it up for inspection.

"All these years and I still don't understand why the bubbles sink instead of rise."

Jack knew the answer—someone had explained the simple physics of the phenomenon to him once—but he didn't want to get into it now. No sidebars, no amusing anecdotes. Time to get to the point.

Julio's was relatively quiet tonight, leaving Jack and the old guy with the rear section pretty much to themselves. An arrangement Jack preferred on most occasions, but especially tonight.

Probably best to conduct discussions about the end of the world—or at least the end of life as anyone knew it—without an audience.

He glanced around the bar with its regulars and its drop-ins, drinking, talking, laughing, posing, making moves, all blissfully unaware of the endless war raging around them.

Jack envied them, wishing he could return to the days, a little over a year ago, when he had shared their ignorance, when he thought he was captain of his life, navigator of his destiny.

No longer. No more coincidences, he'd been told. Instead of steering his own course, he was being pushed this way and that to serve the purposes of two vast, unimaginable, unknowable cosmic . . . what? Forces? Entities? Beings? If they had names, no one knew them. Nothing so simple as Good and Evil. More like neutral and inimical. Forces that humans in the know had dubbed the Ally and the Otherness—although Jack's dealings with the Ally had caused him only pain and loss. He'd learned he could trust it as an Ally only so far as his purposes were in tune with its agenda. If their purposes diverged, he'd be dropped like last week's *Village Voice*, or crushed like a fly against a cosmic windshield.

The man on the far side of the table had answers Jack desperately needed.

"So you're the one I'm supposed to replace."

Veilleur shrugged. "Should the need arise, someone is going to replace me. You aren't the only candidate."

"I'm not?" Dare he hope? "Could've fooled me."

"You are a prime candidate—perhaps *the* prime candidate—but there are backups out there."

"Swell. I sound like a replacement part."

"In a very real sense you are. Don't think of yourself as anything more than a tool. You're not. But you became a tool that stood out among the other tools when you caused the death of the Twins."

Jack closed his eyes, remembering the gaping hole in the Earth that had swallowed a house and a pair of very strange men.

"I was only defending myself. It was them or me. I even tried to save them at the end."

"But you were the proximate cause, and that shifted the mantle of heir apparent to you."

"But I don't want it."

"No sane man would. But only a certain type of man qualifies. He must have a sense of duty and honor and—"

Jack snorted. "Considering my lifestyle, I think I'd have a permanent spot on the bottom of the list."

"You may be what your society considers a career criminal, someone it would lock away if it knew you existed, but I gather you must be someone who does not easily turn his back on problems, and who finishes what he starts."

"What do you mean, 'must be'?"

Veilleur shrugged again. "Though I don't know you all that well, those are the qualities the Ally requires, so I must assume you possess them."

Yeah, well, maybe he did, maybe he didn't. Navel gazing wasn't his thing. And even if it were, who had time?

Jack leaned forward. "What's it like being the Ally's point man? Does it change you?"

"You mean physically? Of course you're changed, but you feel the same as you ever did. The only difference is you stop aging. If you get sick, you beat the infection quicker than anyone else; if wounded, you heal faster."

"Immortal." The word tasted bitter.

Veilleur nodded. "So to speak. But not indestructible. You can die, but it takes a lot to kill you. An awful lot. But it's the living on and on that changes you. Watching your loved ones age and die while you stay fit, young, and vital." Flashes of infinite hurt danced in his eyes. "Friends, lovers, children, family after family dying while you live on. Watching their wonder turn to hurt as you stay young while they grow old, stay well as they sicken; the hurt turning to anger as you refuse to grow old with them; and sometimes the anger turns to hate as they come to view your agelessness as betrayal."

He sighed and sipped his Murphy's in silence while Jack put himself in those immortal shoes . . . watching Gia age while he didn't . . . watching Vicky grow until she was physically his contemporary while her mother moved on through middle age and beyond . . . burying Gia . . . burying Vicky . . .

The prospect made him ill.

Veilleur broke the silence. "Maybe it *is* a betrayal of sorts not to tell them from the start that you'll go on and they won't, but I've tried it that way and it doesn't work. First off, your lover doesn't believe you, or perhaps concludes you're slightly daft and accepts that. Because in the heat of new passion, her lips may acknowledge what you've told her, but her heart and mind do not embrace the possibility of it being true . . . until bitter, sad experience confirms that it is." He shook his head. "Either way, it nearly always ends badly."

Jack saw a bleak landscape stretching before him—possibly.

"So that's what I've got to look forward to."

"Not necessarily. If the Adversary has his way, you and I and the rest of humanity will have a very short future."

"About a year or so, from what I've gathered."

"Yes . . . next spring if all goes according to his plans. But that's only if his way is unimpeded. That's if we don't interfere with his plans."

"But if Ra—"

Veilleur held up a hand. "I assume you've been warned about saying his name."

Jack nodded. "Seems weird but, yes, I've been warned."

He'd been told on a number of occasions over the past year never to utter the name Rasalom, to refer to him instead as the Adversary. Rasalom allowed no one to call him by his name or even speak it—although he used anagrams of it for himself. Say the real thing and somehow he knew—and came looking for you.

Jack had witnessed what happened when Rasalom caught up to someone who'd been using his name. Not pretty.

"How old is this Adversary?"

Veilleur pursed his lips. "It's hard to be sure, what with the fall and rise of civilizations, each keeping track of time in different ways. Counting from his first birth, he's a few years older than I am—about fourteen, perhaps fifteen thousand years."

Jack sat in stunned silence. He'd expected him to be old, but . . .

"Wait . . . you said 'first' birth?"

"Yes. He's hard to kill. I helped bring about his demise on our first meeting, but he didn't stay dead. I thought I had finished him for good—so had the Ally—on the eve of World War Two. In fact, the Ally was so sure he was gone it freed me and allowed me to start aging."

"But wrong again."

"Unfortunately, yes."

"But the Twins—where did they come in?"

"They were created to watch over things in the aftermath of the Adversary's supposed death and my return to mortality. The Adversary was gone, but the Otherness was very much alive, so they restarted the yeniçeri to—"

"The yeniçeri . . ." Jack ran a hand across his face. "Oh, man. What a nightmare. Wish I'd never heard of them."

"I'm sure the feeling is mutual. They answered to me until the fifteenth century when I locked the Adversary away—for good, I thought. After that, their numbers dwindled until the Twins resurrected them."

Jack pounded a fist on the table—once.

"And if the Twins were still around, they'd be taking care of business and I wouldn't be involved in any of this, and you and I wouldn't be having this conversation."

He wanted to kick himself, but pushed back the regrets. *If only* was a futile game, and since he couldn't exactly call Peabody and Sherman and have them crank up the Wayback machine, he'd have to play the hand he'd drawn.

"Take it two steps further backward: If a German army patrol hadn't breached a wall in the Adversary's prison, he'd still be there. Or just one step back: If the Adversary had died back in 1941, as thought, even the Twins would have been redundant. By a quirk of fate—and this I believe was a true coincidence—his essence found a home in a man of, shall we say, unique origins. But though he was undetectable, he was also trapped and powerless. Until that man fathered a child. Then he was able to move into that child—*become* that child."

"When was this?"

"Early in 1968."

Jack did a quick calculation: He'd been born in January of 1969, which meant . . .

"Early 1968? Hey, *I* was conceived in sixty-eight."

"Not a coincidence. Once the Adversary merged with the fetus, the secret was out. Plans were set into motion. You were one of them."

Jack leaned back and stared at the wall. "So I was part of this even before I was born."

Some things he'd learned as a kid suddenly made sense.

Veilleur nodded. "Perhaps I was too."

"Why all this cloak-and-dagger crap? Why don't the Ally and the Otherness duke it out mano a mano—or cosmo a cosmo, or whatever they are?"

"Because that's not how the game is played. And though it's a life-or-death struggle for us, to them it's something of a game."

"And we're the pieces they move around."

"Reluctant pieces in our case. Not so the Adversary. We're still fully human, but he's something else now. That's what happens when you align yourself with a power that is inimical to everything we consider good and decent and rational. He became the agent provocateur for the Otherness. He gains strength from all that is dark and hateful within humanity, feeding on human viciousness and depravity."

"And he's gaining momentum, isn't he?"

Veilleur leaned closer. "Why do you say that?"

"I can feel it. Can't you?"

He sighed. "Yes . . . yes, I can. The pieces of his endgame are falling into place, I fear. Some of them I can't identify, but I can feel when they fit together."

"So where's the Ally? Why isn't it fitting its own pieces into place?"

Veilleur paused a moment before speaking. "I can't say for sure, but my sense of it is that after I appeared to have ended the Adversary's existence, the Ally retreated in a way—downgraded its surveillance of our corner of reality. An infinitesimal speck of it is still watching, still acting, but in a limited capacity. I don't think it senses any imminent danger, so it's maintaining a state of readiness or preparedness and little more."

"It should be making countermoves."

"Against what? The Adversary is playing this very carefully, keeping his hand out of sight as he strengthens it. Part of the reason for that is me."

"You? You've been riffed."

"But he doesn't know that. He thinks I'm the same hale and hearty being who pierced his gut with a sword that sucked the life from him and spit it out. He has no idea that I'm an old man in a creaking body or that the sword is long gone. He fears if he tips his hand, I'll come looking for him, and this time he might not be so lucky."

"Instead, *you're* hiding from *him*."

He nodded. "Not so much for myself—I've lived longer than I ever wanted to, and quite frankly, I'm tired—but for my wife and the rest of you. If he learns the truth about me, he'll feel free to act openly, and he'll waste no time stealing our world from the Ally."

"But how? Won't that set off cosmic alarm bells?"

"So one would think. But he must have a way—or thinks he does. And something between now and next spring will trigger his plans." Veilleur's expression grew bleak. "The only thing I can think of is that he'll discover my weakened, mortal state."

"Then you'd better stay damn well hidden. But maybe it's something else, something he's cooking up, something we can stop. Any idea what he's been doing behind the scenes?"

"Well, the latest is this so-called Kicker movement and—"

That pricked up Jack's ears. "Whoa. 'So-called' Kicker movement? Why do you say that?"

"Because its leader has no idea what he has tapped into, nor what he might unleash."

"Hank Thompson. I've met him. Definitely trouble. What *has* he tapped into?"

Veilleur glanced at his watch. "A long story . . . one I've no time for tonight."

"How long a story?"

"It begins fifteen thousand or so years ago."

Frustration clamped down on Jack's shoulders. "You can't waltz off and leave me with just that."

"My time is not my own. I've a sick wife at home."

"Give me *some*thing."

He sighed. "Very well. It's courting disaster to concentrate so many Taints in such a relatively small area."

" 'Taints'? What are you talking about?"

"Taints is what we called them millennia ago, before the Taint in their blood became diluted enough that they were no longer a threat. Now their distant progeny are becoming aware of their Taint, and calling themselves Kickers."

"Yeah. Idiotic name, but—"

Veilleur shook his head. "Not so idiotic if you're aware of the story behind it, but that's part of the secret history of the world, so virtually no one knows it."

Secret history of the world . . . jeez, did that ever ring a bell.

"You're making me crazy." But something else he'd said had struck too close to home, sending a wave of uneasiness through Jack's gut. "This Taint in the blood . . ."

"A contaminant from the Otherness."

Just what Jack had suspected . . . and the last thing he wanted to hear.

"Some folks have another name for it: oDNA."

Veilleur frowned. "Never heard of it."

"It's part of what's considered junk DNA, and if I may echo you: Virtually no one knows of it."

"But you do?"

"I was told by an expert." Dr. Aaron Levy had told him a lot—way more than he cared to know. "And I guess it's only right that I know, since I'm loaded with it."

Veilleur gave Jack a long, cool stare, then said, "In a way, that makes a perverse sort of sense. The Ally is trading in the only Taint-free human on Earth for one who is heavily tainted. Maybe it thinks it can turn the Taint against its source."

"There's only one Taint-free human, and you're it?"

Veilleur nodded. "I predate the Taint. The Adversary would be untainted as well, but he was reborn into tainted flesh."

That meant Gia carried this Taint. And Vicky.

No.

"Wait-wait. You said Thompson was courting disaster by concentrating so many Taints in such a small area. You mean Manhattan? Because if we're all Taints, then this town is about as concentrated as you're gonna get."

Veilleur shook his head. "Simply carrying the Taint doesn't make you a Taint. You must carry enough to influence your behavior, enough to taint your relationship with the world around you."

"So . . . the greater the Taint, the greater the . . . what? Potential for violence?"

"The greater the potential for making this place more to the Adversary's liking, and pushing it closer to the Otherness."

"Do you know for sure the Kickers are Taints?"

He gave Jack a perplexed look. "I can smell them."

"Then I must stink."

"Oddly enough, you don't."

A flash of hope. "Then maybe I don't—"

A quick shake of Veilleur's head. "Oh, you do. It's just that somehow you've learned how to compartmentalize it—or perhaps you were born with that ability. That talent, or knack, or whatever it is, allows you to bottle up the brutish tendencies so common to Taints, and set them free when you need them."

"Sometimes they set themselves free."

Veilleur stared at him, nodding slowly. "I imagine they do. What's that like?"

"Scary. And yet . . ."

"An exhilarating high? A dark joy?"

"Yeah. 'Dark joy' pretty much nails it."

"Perhaps that ability to compartmentalize was why you were chosen."

"But where's this Taint come from?"

Another glance at his watch. "Too long a history lesson for now." He rose. "Thank you for the beer, but I must be going. See you here again soon."

Jack wanted to shove him back into his chair and duct-tape him there till he'd told the whole story. Instead he settled for grabbing his arm.

"Wait. So you think the Adversary's got a hand in this Kicker thing?"

"The Adversary or the Otherness itself. That image—the Kicker Man—
on the cover of his book and graffiti'd all over town makes me suspect the
Otherness. This Thompson couldn't have discovered it on his own. It must
have been implanted."

"What's it mean?"

"No time. But I can tell you it's a lure of sorts. Taints respond to it. They
see it on the cover of his book and the Otherness within them reaches for it.
They can't get it out of their heads, so they tattoo it on their skin and paint it
on walls. And they are drawn to others who feel the same way. This Thompson has no idea what he's tapped into."

He slipped his arm free and started for the door.

"Just one more thing," Jack said. "What would be the purpose of creating a super-tainted child?"

Veilleur stopped and turned. "Super tainted?"

"Yeah. Back in the seventies a guy went to a lot of trouble to father
heavily tainted children to mate and produce a super-tainted child."

"Did he succeed?"

"Don't know. The child hasn't been born yet and I don't know where its
mother is. But I'm sure you've seen her picture."

He frowned. "She wouldn't be the one on those ubiquitous flyers, would
she?"

"You got it."

"And she's carrying a super-tainted fetus?"

"Could be—no one knows what the child's made of yet."

"Do you know the name of the man who did this?"

"Started it all? That would be her grandfather—Jonah Stevens. Or so
I've been told."

Jack wasn't sure what to believe anymore.

Veilleur's eyes widened. "Really. Jonah Stevens. That's very . . . interesting."

Then he turned and left Julio's.

4

"The katana! It is near! It awaits!"

Toru Akechi started at the high-pitched wail. He hadn't been expecting it so soon.

Through the eyeholes of his silk mask he watched the legless monk, naked but for his mask and fundoshi, writhing on the rumpled futon in the Sighting room. He had drunk the Sighting elixir twenty minutes ago and it was starting to take effect.

The windows to the Sighting room had been sealed during the old building's renovation. The darkness was virtually complete but for the glow of the four candles placed at the corners of the futon, wanly limning the dozen figures, robed and hooded in dark blue, encircling the Seer. Some of those figures stood, some sat, and the ones without limbs lay on the floor.

Toru knew them all by the designs on their silk masks and the shapes of their bodies. Some were missing limbs, showed empty sockets through their masks. Those lacking ears and tongues and noses were less obvious.

With his arms jerking back and forth, his torso twisting, the Seer appeared to be suffering an agony of sorts. His empty eye sockets could offer no sign of pain or distress, but his body gave full testament. Suddenly he lay still. All present held their breath, listening.

And then the Seer sat up and swiveled his masked, eyeless face back and forth. Toru knew he wasn't seeing the Sighting room. He was seeing somewhere, some*when* else.

"The katana!" he wailed. "It is near! It awaits!"

We know all about the missing sword, Toru wanted to scream. You told us during the last sighting and the sighting before that. Say something new.

"It waits where, my brother?" he said in an even tone.

"Here! In this city! I see it!"

"Where do you see it?"

"In a dark place!'"

"And where is this dark place?"

"Here! In this city!"

Toru ground his teeth as the Seer went on, presenting nothing new.

"The sacred scrolls! They have returned to our Order! But that is not enough! The katana! The Order must possess the katana that once sealed its doom! When the Order controls the katana, it will control its future, and its future will be assured for a thousand years!"

"Will we succeed?" Toru asked, as he always did.

"Only if we persevere!"

All eyes in the room turned toward him. He had been assigned the task of finding the sacred scrolls, stolen from their Order—the Kakureta Kao— in the last days of World II, plus the katana that had destroyed the Order by fulfilling a prophecy of doom.

He had succeeded in finding the scrolls, but the katana eluded him, slipping through his fingers. He now had a plan in motion to secure it.

"If the Order does not control the katana," the Seer screamed, "it will again destroy us! It will slay the last surviving member!"

Toru swallowed. The last surviving member . . . the Seer was talking about the death of everyone in this room, in this building. No equivocation there. They were all going to die if they didn't find and hold that benighted blade.

"The Order came to this place to destroy this city! And the saced scrolls will provide the Order with the means to do so!"

Yes, they would. Toru had his students scouring the city for the ingredi- ents to create a Kuroikaze—a Black Wind.

"But the Order will itself be destroyed if it does not possess the katana!" He turned his sightless sockets on Toru and pounded the futon. "The katana! The katana!"

Toru's fellow monks, all still staring at him, took up the chant.

"THE KATANA! THE KATANA! THE KATANA! . . ."

5

Jack watched the door swing closed behind Veilleur. He could follow him, but to what end? Force his way into his home and quiz him while he tended to his sick wife—assuming he really had a sick wife.

Nah. The guy wanted contact—had initiated it. He'd be back. Meanwhile, Jack had a lot to digest.

Like the Kicker Man, for instance.

. . . it's a lure of sorts. Taints respond to it . . .

He remembered the first time he'd seen the figure—in Dr. Buhmann's while standing next to the stroked-out professor. Remembered the odd twinge of familiarity it triggered, and the feeling that something long dormant within had stirred.

But he hadn't noticed any desire for a Kicker Man tattoo, or a compulsion to grab a can of spray paint and start tagging walls.

Maybe because his Taint was, as Veilleur had said, compartmentalized.

The Taint . . . where had it come from? The Otherness, sure, but how had it seeped into humanity's bloodstream?

But the biggest surprise of the night had been meeting Glaeken, the man whose shoes he might have to step into—would definitely have to step into if Rasalom made his move.

Glaeken and Rasalom . . . two ancient enemies, each thousands of years old . . . Jack had met both now, and felt like a punk . . . far, far out of their league.

Rasalom . . . looked as human as the next guy until he lowered his guard and allowed a peek into his eyes—twin black holes of hunger with no hint of mercy or regard. Total self-absorption.

Glaeken—better get used to calling him Veilleur—was still a man, a regular guy. Or at least he seemed to be. Thousands of years old, yet hurrying home to his sick wife—the first wife he'd grown old with. Was that why she was so precious to him?

Jack had never felt further out of his depth.

At least he'd been able to tell Veilleur something he didn't already know—he'd seemed genuinely surprised to hear the name Jonah Stevens. Seemed to have recognized it.

But Jack was more interested in Jonah Stevens's granddaughter and great-grandchild—Dawn Pickering and the unborn, super-tainted baby she carried.

Almost a month now since Dawn had disappeared. Where the hell could she be? Her mother was dead, she had no family. Hank Thompson and his Kickers were looking for her too, and the fresh posters with Dawn's picture going up almost daily, asking HAVE YOU SEEN THIS GIRL? were proof of sorts that they'd yet to find her.

Which meant she had to be hiding. But where?

Jack had met her once, and then only for a minute or so when he'd handed her an envelope while pretending to be a delivery man. A slightly overweight, seemingly natural blonde with a round face and puggish nose, not a wowzer but not a bowzer either. Good grades, accepted to Colgate, but it seemed unlikely she'd be going if she didn't finish her senior year of high school.

Eighteen years old and alone and pregnant in the city. Or maybe not in the city. Her Jeep was gone too, so she could be anywhere.

Jack assumed officialdom was looking for her as well. After all, her mother's death was a suspected murder, and with both her and her boyfriend—more like manfriend—Jerry Bethlehem pulling a disappearing act, the hunt would be on.

Except she wasn't with Jerry, she was hiding from him. Someone needed to get word to her that the father of her baby, the man she'd known as Jerry Bethlehem, was dead, thanks to Jack. But the irony of it all was he'd done it in a way that had left the man with little or none of his skin, thus virtually ensuring that he'd never be identified.

But being the object of a manhunt—womanhunt?—meant Dawn couldn't use her credit or ATM cards without leaving a financial trail.

So where was she? Jack hated the thought of her sleeping in her Jeep, or staying in some flop motel until her cash ran out.

Poor kid.

6

Dawn closed her eyes and totally luxuriated in the caress of the bubbles as they rose through the hot tub's steaming water.

Extending her legs, she let herself float to the surface and peeked at her body. Not bad for almost two months pregnant. You'd never know. Those weeks of morning sickness had had a silver lining: She'd dropped some of her blubber. *Much* of her blubber, in fact. Check out that flat ab—well, almost flat—and those sleek thighs. They didn't do total justice to the flowered Shan bikini, but didn't totally insult it.

She raised her head and gazed through the green-tinted glass walls at the towers of the El Dorado building over on Central Park West. She wished she were farther downtown where she could be looking at the Ghostbusters building, or maybe at the Dakota, but she'd be like a total dumbass to complain about this view. Below, out of sight at this angle, lay Central Park.

The bubbler cycled off as it hit the twenty-minute mark. As Dawn reached over to reset it, she heard the gym door open behind her. She sighed. She knew who it was.

Gilda.

Right on time, carrying a white terrycloth robe.

Did she have her own timer? Or was she like a dog and the bubbler signal was like the sound of a can opener? No matter where she was, did she hear it and hurry over?

"Did miss enjoy her soak?" she said in her accented English.

She came from somewhere in Eastern Europe but Dawn had totally forgotten where. Thick-bodied, graying, bunned-up hair, dark eyes, and a gap-toothy smile.

"I was just beginning to. I could stay here for hours."

"Tut-tut-tut. You know the rules, you can read the signs: Twenty minutes is all you are allowed."

"But another five minutes—"

"Any longer might hurt your baby."

"It's not a baby—it's a *thing* inside me and I want it out. Can't anybody here get that through their heads?"

"The Master said—"

"It's not his body, it's mine, and I want it back. Totally."

Gilda held up the robe by the collar and jiggled it. "Come-come. I bring your nice soft robe. I will help you." Another jiggle. "Come."

Pissed, Dawn rose and stepped over the edge of the tub. She noticed Gilda giving her wet body a careful up-and-down. Looking for signs of pregnancy? Or just . . . looking. As a housekeeper, Gilda seemed totally efficient and not a bad cook either. Totally no-nonsense but always cheerful. Seemed devoted to her job, but every so often Dawn would catch her looking at her in a way that she found just plain creepy.

She slipped her arms into the robe—God, it had to be an inch thick—and folded it around her. As she knotted the belt she stepped to the glass wall and stared down at Jackie-O Lake.

"Why do you call him Master?"

"Because he is the Master of the house."

"Yes, but—"

"And because he wishes us to."

That didn't surprise Dawn. Mr. Osala had a commanding air, like he was totally used to being in charge. But hearing him called "the Master" all the time made her feel like she was in Dracula's castle or something. All he needed was a red-lined cape.

The Master this, the Master that . . .

Screw the Master.

Who was he, anyway? He said he'd been hired by her mom before she died—hired to protect her from Jerry—or Jerome, as Mr. Osala had called him on the night he'd interrupted her planned dive off the Queensboro Bridge.

That had been a bad time—the low point of her life. Mom dead, killed by Jerry who'd tried to make it look like a suicide.

A lump rose in her throat as she thought about it. Her fault. If she hadn't got involved with that creep, whatever his real name was.

Nowadays Mr. Osala just called him Bethlehem.

Mr. Osala didn't seem to have a first name, at least not one that he used, but he was rich, no doubt about that. A Fifth Avenue duplex with its own penthouse health club. No way Dawn could complain about her treatment here. She had a bedroom with a breathtaking view of Central Park. She could order totally anything she wanted to eat, and if Gilda couldn't make it, they'd have it delivered. Anything she wanted she got. She'd asked for a swimsuit for the pool and hot tub, and a few hours later this Shan bikini arrived—just her size. Yeah, she could have anything she wanted.

Except an abortion.

And a walk outside.

She so wanted to get out of here, even if only for an hour or so, but Mr. Osala—the fucking Master—said no. Too risky.

Who was he anyway to tell her what to do? Just because Mom hired him as some sort of bodyguard didn't mean Dawn had to listen to him. Trouble was, she had no choice. He had key-only deadbolts on the doors and wouldn't let her out. Too dangerous, he said.

Like being in prison. Okay, maybe that was pushing it. More like a birdcage—velvet lined, with solid gold bars, but a cage just the same.

"I need to get out of here," she said to no one in particular.

"Oh, but miss, you can't. That man might see you."

That man . . .

Jerry Bethlehem, or whatever his real name was. Yeah, Jerry was out there looking for her. Looking real hard, she'd bet. Totally. Because he wanted his kid—wanted it like crazy. Insanely.

The Key to the Future, he'd called it.

Mr. Osala's reasoning was that as long as she remained pregnant, she'd be safe from harm by Jerry, because hurting her could hurt his child. But if he ever caught up to her and learned she'd had an abortion, her life wouldn't be worth two cents.

Last month she'd wanted to die, had been ready to jump off a bridge. That had passed. Now she wanted to live, but this wasn't the kind of living she had in mind.

Mr. Osala didn't seem to want anything from her beyond cooperation in keeping safe. She wound up with proof of that when she told him she'd left her Jeep parked in a garage near the 59th Street Bridge. He'd taken her ticket and "relocated it to a safer place."

And then he'd handed her an envelope containing a quarter of a million dollars.

Her quarter mil. Or rather her mom's.

Either Mr. Osala was so honest that he wasn't tempted by any amount of money, or so totally rich that a quarter mil was pocket change. Or both.

Fine. But what good was any amount of money if she wasn't allowed to spend it?

"Jerry's one man and there's a zillion people in this city. What are the chances of the two of us running into each other? Like almost totally zero."

"But you have everything here." Gilda pointed through the glass at the rooftop garden. "You have trees and flowers right outside."

"How about shopping? I want to go shopping."

"Why? Anything you want, you have only to ask and it is brought to you."

She turned and faced Gilda. Didn't she get it?

"I'm talking about shopping—s-h-o-p-p-i-n-g. You know: walking up and down aisles, looking at things, touching things, trying stuff on. *Shopping.*"

Gilda looked genuinely puzzled. "I do not understand. Why should you want to go out when everything can be brought in?"

A scream rose in Dawn's throat. She started to suppress it, then figured, what the hell, let it all out.

And she did— a formless screech that echoed off the glass walls.

Gilda paled and backed up a step.

"Miss—?"

Dawn kept the volume cranked up. "I'm going *crazy* here! Can't you see that? If I don't get out for a while I'm going to climb that fence out there and jump off!"

Gilda backed up another step. "I'll get Henry."

"Get your fucking Master!"

"He's away, searching for your Mister Bethlehem. Henry will know what to do."

As Dawn watched her bustle off, she thought, Probably thinks I'm a spoiled brat.

But she wasn't. Mom had seen to that. Even went so far as to make her get a job waiting tables in the Tower Diner. Not a bad job, and the tips had been decent. Mom never would have stood for a tantrum like the one she'd just thrown.

Her throat tightened, her eyes filled. Aw, Mom. Why didn't I listen to you? Why didn't I appreciate you while you were here? I miss you.

She swallowed and blinked back the tears. Had to stay tough. Spoiled brats didn't whimper, they screamed and threw tantrums. And if that was what it took to get somebody to listen around here, then this place was about to become Tantrum City.

Totally.

7

"Gilda tells me there's a problem, miss?"

Dawn looked up and saw Henry standing in the entry to the great room. As usual, he wore his chauffeur's black livery. Reed thin with a tall frame—six-four if an inch—that made him look even thinner. His angular, dark-eyed, thin-lipped face never smiled, at least not when Dawn was looking. Mr. Osala didn't seem to have a first name; Henry didn't seem to have a last.

She hadn't changed out of her bikini and robe, electing to sit in the glass-and-chrome great room and wait for Henry to show his face. She'd turned on the gigonda plasma-screen TV and pretended to be watching.

She rose and faced him. Normally she'd never have the guts to confront someone like this, but she was playing a part now—the bitch brat.

"I want out of here."

"I'm afraid that is out of the question." His stiff posture and faint British accent gave him a snooty air, but she heard no hesitation in his voice. "The Master won't allow it."

"He can't keep me prisoner!"

"His promise to your mother was to keep you safe, and he is doing so."

"I'm sure she didn't want me totally isolated like I am."

"You have the television, you have a computer—"

"Yeah, one that's fixed so I can't IM or send e-mail."

She still couldn't believe that AOL, Yahoo, Hotmail, Gmail, and all the rest were blocked to her. She could surf anywhere, even MySpace, but couldn't message anyone.

"That was done for the same reason the telephone is coded: to prevent you from accidentally revealing your location. We are sure your friends are being watched, and one or two of them might even have had their computers hacked and monitored."

"That's crazy. How could Jerry do that?"

He wagged a finger at her. "You can't be too careful these days."

"This is crazy." She felt herself filling up. She would *not* cry. But she felt so totally helpless. "I'm a prisoner."

To her amazement, Henry's features softened—just a bit.

"I know it seems that way, miss, but you must resign yourself to the fact that you cannot risk showing your face. He might see you."

"And then what? Grab me and drag me kicking and screaming down the street?" She felt a spark of rage begin to glow. "You ever think maybe he should be worried about *me*? Like maybe if I saw him first I'd be on him like a cat, scratching his eyes out of his head?"

"Now, miss, I know how you feel—"

"No, you don't!" The rage flared. "You haven't a *clue* how I feel! You can't *begin* to know how I feel!"

"Allow me to rephrase: I cannot imagine how you must feel, but you must not reveal yourself. Not yet."

She felt herself cooling. Would she really have the nerve to attack that bastard? She wanted him hurt, but she didn't know if she had it in her to do it. Maybe some day she'd find out.

"What if I wore a disguise—like a brown wig and big sunglasses?"

He shook his head. "Still too dodgy, I fear."

That hadn't been a flat no. Was he softening?

And then it hit her—the perfect solution to the whole problem.

8

Jack let himself into his third-floor apartment but didn't turn on the lights. He didn't need light. He emptied tonight's proceeds from the Park-a-Thon onto the round oak table in the front room. He knew a fence who'd turn the gold chains and rings and medallions into cash tomorrow morning, then he'd give everything to Gia who'd make the official donation to the Little League.

He dropped into a chair and stared out at the night. Not much to see, just other brownstones like his across the street. No famous Manhattan skyline visible from here, just an occasional tree.

No need to keep an eye out for the mysterious watcher tonight. He'd just had a beer with him and he was home with his sick wife.

Or so he said.

Jack didn't know what to believe anymore. Everything he'd believed about himself and his family and the world around them all had been shot to hell in the last couple of years. Nothing was what it seemed.

And to top it off, his relationship with Gia was starting to feel a little strained.

His fault.

He'd withdrawn from her and Vicky. Not completely, but after moving in and living with them during the months they'd needed to recuperate from the accident, returning to his own apartment must have seemed like a form of abandonment.

But he hadn't abandoned them. He still saw them on a daily basis, but it wasn't the same. Things had changed—not them, nor his feelings for them. But his feelings about himself . . . those had changed when he'd learned about the measure of Otherness he carried in his blood.

The Taint.

What a perfect name for the perfectly awful.

Knowing the truth had, well, tainted his relationship with them. He felt the need for some distance. Rationally he knew he couldn't contaminate them any more than they already were—he'd been assured everybody carried a little oDNA—but something deep in his subconscious wasn't so sure. Sex with Gia, so sweet and sweaty and wonderful . . . he couldn't escape a hazy image of him injecting her with bits of Otherness.

Crazy, yes. They'd been together almost two years. But knowing . . . knowing colored everything.

He shook himself. Had to get over this. And he would. Just going to take some time, was all.

But he felt so alone. He'd always been able to be alone without being lonely, but this was different. He felt like a Stylite monk standing on an infinitely tall pinnacle. Everyone he cared about waited far below, forever out of reach as he faced the swirling cosmos alone.

He smiled and shook his head. Look at me: drama queen.

Buck up and shut up.

He rose and stepped over to his computer. Needed a distraction.

He logged onto repairmanjack.com and checked the Web mail there, deleting the predictable inquiries about appliance repairs until he came to one with "*Stolen—help please*" in the subject line.

He knew what that meant: Something indeed had been stolen, but the victim could not report the theft to the cops because the item was either illegal or ill-gotten. That was where private eyes came in. But if it was very, very illegal or major-felony ill-gotten . . . that was where Jack came in.

This sounded promising. He opened the file.

> *Dear Jack Mr. Repairman Jack—*
> *I was given your name and told you might help me find a lost object. The authorities cannot help. I am praying you can help.*
> *—N*

Concise and to the point—Jack liked that. *The authorities cannot help*—liked that too. Implied he couldn't go to them. But "authorities" . . . who still called them "authorities"?

He pulled one of his TracFones from a drawer and punched in the number. After two rings he heard a male voice say, "Hai," and rattle off a string of syllables that sounded Japanese.

Surprised, Jack hesitated, then said, "Um, did you recently leave a message at a certain Web site?"

The voice switched to accented English. "Repairman Jack? You are Repairman Jack?"

Jack hated admitting it—never fond of that name. Abe had stuck him with it and now it followed him around like a bad debt.

"Yeah, that's me. What's up?"

"A family heirloom was stolen last month from my home. Please, I must have it back."

"Where's home?"

"Maui."

Well, that put an end to this job-to-be.

"Maui as in Hawaii? Sorry. No Maui. It's got to be within an easy drive. Better luck—"

"No-no! You do not understand. It was stolen in Maui and brought here to New York City."

"You know that for sure?"

"Reasonably sure."

Reasonably was close enough.

"Just what is this heirloom?"

"I would rather not say right now. I have pictures I can show."

"Is it big?"

"It is not small, but can easily be carried with one hand."

Good. Liked to hear that. One more, then he'd quit the twenty questions. Jack liked to know how a customer found him.

"Where did you hear about me?"

"From friend of friend on Maui."

Jack frowned. Did he know anyone out there? Didn't think so.

"Name?"

"I prefer not to speak names on phone. Where can we meet? I will tell you everything then."

Jack couldn't argue about keeping mum but the meeting place was a good question. He'd been overusing Julio's lately and couldn't risk becoming a creature of too much habit. Someplace public . . . far from Julio's . . . that served beer, of course.

"Okay. We'll meet tomorrow at—"

"Can we not meet tonight?"

"Tomorrow. Three P.M. at the Ear. It's on Spring between Washington and Greenwich."

"The *Ear*? This is a true name?"

"Believe it. It's a pub."

"It does not sound appetizing."

"You eat sushi?"

"Of course."

"Well, don't expect to find any there. See you at three. If you're late, I'm gone."

MONDAY

1

Hank Thompson lay blinking in the dark, just awakened from a dream.

But not the usual dream. Not the dream of the Kicker Man protectively cradling a baby—Dawn's baby, Hank was sure—in his four arms. This one involved the Kicker Man, yes, but instead of holding a baby he was swinging a Japanese sword—one of those long, curved samurai numbers—whipping it back and forth. And then he dropped it and faded away.

But the sword remained, allowing Hank a closer look.

A real piece of crap—no handle and its blade eaten away in spots up and down its length.

But maybe it only *looked* like a piece of crap. Its appearance with the Kicker Man meant it was important. Somehow it figured into the future of the movement—or "Kicker evolution," as he was calling it.

A few months ago Hank would have been asking, *How? Why?* Now he knew better. Somewhere along the way he'd become a sort of antenna for signals from . . . where? *Out there* was all he could say, although where that was and what was out there he had no idea. His daddy had told him about "Others" on the outside that wanted to be on the inside, and that Daddy and Hank and his sibs had special blood that would put them in great favor if they helped the Others cross over.

Daddy's talk had sounded crazy at times, but he had a way of saying things that made you *believe*. That dead eye of his could see places and things no one else could. Or so he said.

But a couple years ago Hank had started having dreams of the Kicker

Man, and the man had shown him things . . . things he'd put into a book that had sold like crazy, making him famous—or maybe *notorious* was a better word—and attracting a following from all levels of society, especially people living on the fringe.

Yeah, *Kick* was zooming toward its two-millionth copy sold, with no signs of slowing. He was rich.

Hank glanced at the glowing face of his clock radio: 2:13 A.M. He pushed himself out of bed and wandered to his room's single window. He looked out at the Lower East Side block, just off Allen Street, one story below.

Funny, he didn't feel rich. Not living in this single room in the Septimus Lodge. But he had to keep up appearances, had to live like his peeps. Get into conspicuous consumption and he might lose them—and that meant losing their donations. He had a few whales giving big bucks to the Kicker clubs, but most donations were small. But they added up because there were so many of them.

Well, he was used to living lean. No biggie. He could hang out until the Change came and the Others arrived. Then he'd be rewarded. But there might be no change and no Others arriving if he didn't help open the door. And to do that he needed the Key.

Had to find Dawn, damn it. Her baby was, as Daddy liked to say, the Key to the Future.

But what about that ratty sword? Where did that fit in?

He'd have to put that on the Kicker BOLO list.

2

Hideo Takita stood in Kaze Group's Tokyo office looking down at the Marunouchi district's gridlocked streets. Even in early afternoon—jammed.

He lifted his gaze beyond the skyscrapers to the Imperial Palace squatting low and graceful among its flanking gardens, but the sight of it offered no peace.

He wiped his sweating palms on the pants of his gray suit. A systems analyst such as Hideo was not invited to the office of Sasaki-san, the chairman of the board, simply for idle chatter. Idle was not a word one would associate with Kaze Group.

The reception area offered little reassurance—literally and figuratively. Bare walls of polished steel, black ceiling, gleaming floor, and floor-to-ceiling windows looking out on the city. A brushed-steel desk and chair were the room's only furnishings, and not meant for visitors. One must not be comfortable if one is idle at Kaze Group.

Kaze . . . a fitting name.

Although ostensibly a simple holding company, Kaze Group was more powerful than the largest of the *keiretsus*, the giant vertical and horizontal conglomerates that ruled Japanese business.

Formed shortly after World War II, it had slowly woven itself into the fabric of Japan's economy. Today, through a web of dummy corporations, it owned controlling interest in Japan's "Big Six" keiretsus and most of the major corporations. The keiretsus were like icebergs—their small, uppermost portion visible, the vast bulk looming hidden beneath the surface.

But what determined the path of icebergs through the sea? The currents. And what dictated the currents?

The wind.

Kaze.

Not satisfied with Japan alone, Kaze Group had branched out, extending its reach in all directions. Although it produced nothing itself, it had a hand in the manufacture of everything of importance produced around the globe.

"Takita-san?"

Hideo whirled and saw that the slight, business-suited receptionist had returned and was standing behind the desk. Hideo tried to look relaxed and confident as he approached.

"Sasaki-san will see me now?"

The receptionist's lips twisted. Hideo realized with a spike of embarrassment that he was suppressing a laugh.

"You will not be seeing the chairman today."

Hideo imagined him adding, *nor any other day.*

The receptionist handed Hideo a thumb-size flash drive.

"On this you will find scans of a shipping tube taken at Kahului Airport on Maui. In that tube you will see the image of a damaged katana. The item was checked through to Kennedy International in New York. The passenger's name was listed as Eddie Cordero. That, however, is an alias. The chairman wishes you to go to New York and find that katana." The receptionist gave him a knowing look. "If you deliver this katana to him, he will be most grateful."

Hideo knew what that meant. But . . .

"The chairman wants me to find a damaged sword?"

"You question the chairman's desire?"

"No, of course not. I did not mean that. I meant, why me? I have no special skills."

"The chairman thinks you do, and the chairman is wise." The receptionist paused, as if embarrassed, then added, "The chairman knows it is a difficult task. But he believes you will be especially diligent and expend extra effort because success will go a long way toward restoring your brother's honor."

Hideo hung his head. Yoshio, what happened to you? Who killed you? He looked up and nodded to the receptionist.

"I will go. I will find the chairman's katana."

"It is not the chairman's, but he wishes it to be. However, it may not be the katana he wants. It must meet certain criteria, all of which will be explained on the drive." The receptionist glanced at his watch. "Your flight leaves in two hours. You had better hurry."

Hideo made a quick bow and started toward the door.

"Oh, and one more thing," the receptionist said, "you will not be traveling alone."

Hideo eyed him. "Oh? Who—?"

"Your three travel companions will meet you at the airport. They will be along to aid you should you need their sort of help. The chairman doesn't want you to end up like your brother."

Hideo shuddered. Neither did he.

3

"Well, what do you think?" Gia said.

Jack stared at the little wooden sculpture—although why it wasn't called a carving, he had no idea. But nomenclature aside, he liked it. A lot.

"It's beautiful."

He looked at Gia. For a while she'd let her blond hair grow out, but last week she'd shown up with it cut short again. He liked it short, with its little unruly wings curving into the air.

She'd dragged him down to this SoHo art gallery, saying he just had to see the latest Sylvia. Jack had no idea what a Sylvia was, but he'd come along. And was glad he had.

According to the brochure, some artist who signed her work simply as "Sylvia" was famous for her faux bonsai trees, laser sculpted from a model of the real thing. And Jack could see why. Her latest was a mix of bonsai and topiary—a boxwood with a curved trunk, its roots snaking over a rock and into the soil of its pot. But the rock wasn't a rock, the soil wasn't soil, and the tray wasn't clay. The whole thing was a solid block of laminated oak. Interesting enough, but the tiny boxwood leaves had been teased and coaxed and trimmed into the shape of a skyscraper. Jack knew that shape: the tapering spire, the scalloped crown, the eagle heads jutting from the uppermost setback. Of course their size didn't allow the details of a bird's head, but Jack knew what those tiny protruding branches represented.

Gia fixed him with her clear blue eyes. Her smile was dazzling. "Knowing how you love the Chrysler building, I figured this should be added to your must-see list."

Jack walked around its pedestal, leaning over the velvet ropes that kept him from getting too close. Someone—Sylvia?—had hand-painted it, mimicking its natural colors. The leaves and moss were green, the tray and clasped stone different shades of gray, the trunk left the natural shade of the original oak.

Jack stepped back. "From a distance it looks alive."

"Isn't it just fabulous?" said a soft male voice behind him.

Jack turned and saw a slim, middle-aged guy wearing a sailor shirt and white duck pants. His little name tag said GARY and his black hair was perfect.

"Fleet Week's not quite here yet," Jack said.

Gary grinned. "I know. I can't wait. But as I said"—he gestured to the tree—"isn't it fabulous?"

"Yeah. Fabulous." A word misused and overused, but here it fit.

"And it doesn't just *look* alive, it's so very *much* alive in the way all true art lives. And best of all, it requires no pruning, no wiring, no watering, and yet it remains perfect. Forever."

"I like the low-maintenance idea. Always wanted a bonsai, but I have a brown thumb."

"Maintenance is not an issue. This is a work of art, and so much more than a bonsai. This is a subtle melding of the man-made and the natural, a brilliant use of the latest in modern technology to preserve an ancient art form."

Seemed like Gary had memorized the brochure.

"How much do you want for it?"

"It's not a matter of how much *I* want," he said, reaching into a pocket. "If I had my way it would stay on display here forever." He pulled out a card and pen and scribbled. "But alas, that won't pay the rent."

Alas?

He handed Jack the card. He'd written a number on it.

Jack couldn't help laughing. "Twenty thousand dollars?"

Gary cooled. "Each of Sylvia's trees are fashioned in strictly limited editions of one hundred, signed and numbered by the artist herself."

"And people actually pay twenty K apiece?"

"Each edition sells out almost immediately. Our gallery was consigned only one. We put it out this morning. It will be sold by closing."

What a crazy world.

Just then a jewel-dripping thirty-something blonde strolled up, clutching the arm of her Armani'd, sixty-something sugar daddy.

"Oh, look, honey. Isn't that a Sylvia? Alana has a Sylvia and I want one too. Can we get it?"

The words leaped from Jack's mouth before he could stop them.

"I'll take it."

"Jack!" Gia said, giving him a wide-eyed stare.

"It's only money."

"Are you serious?"

He shrugged. "I've got all this moolah socked away—you know that. For what? You won't let me spend it on you and Vicky." Spend it? He'd tried to give it all to her back in December when he thought he'd be leaving on a forever trip. "So I might as well blow it on something like this."

"I can assure you it will only appreciate in value," Gary said. "Some of Sylvia's early trees are selling for triple what you're paying."

"See?" he said to Gia. "It's an investment." He turned to Gary. "You accept gold?"

"The AmEx Gold Card? Of course."

That wasn't what Jack had meant, but . . .

"Okay. Wrap her up to travel."

"I suggest you let us deliver it. It's very valuable and you don't want to risk someone stealing it."

Jack smiled, aware of the weight of the Glock 19 nestled in the small of his back. But it was Gia who spoke through a wry smile.

"Oh, I don't think we'll have to worry about that."

4

"Nobody likes to hear of an artist hitting a big payday more than I," Gia said. "But—"

"Speaking of art, what about yours?"

They were walking up Greene Street toward Houston, passing the grave of the Soho Kitchen & Bar. Whenever Jack had been in the neighborhood, he'd made a point of stopping in for a draft pint of Pilsner Urqell. Another goddamn boutique occupied the space now.

"I'm back to work—three dust jacket assignments and some paperbacks on the way."

"Yeah, but that's work done to order. That's not you. What about the stuff you're doing for yourself?"

She shook her head. "Told you: not happy with it."

"Still?"

"Still."

"When are you going to let me see it?"

A shrug. "Maybe never. I may just take them somewhere and burn them."

Jack stopped and gripped her arm. "Don't even joke about that. Anything by you is valuable to me."

"Not these. Trust me, not these."

"They can't be that bad."

"Oh, yes, they can. I don't like them and I don't want to show work I don't like."

"Even to me?"

"Especially to you." She tapped the box under his arm. "Frugalman Jack, spending twenty thousand on a sculpted tree . . . I don't know what to say."

Obviously she wanted a change of topic, so he let it go. For now.

"I've been frugal because I've always wanted to be able to retire early." He could have added, *while I'm still alive*, but didn't.

"Granted, it's a stunning piece of work, but twenty thousand?"

"Better than letting some bimbo blonde—"

"Ahem."

"What?"

She pointed to her hair. "What color is this?"

Oh, hell.

"But you're not a bimbo. And yours doesn't come from a bottle."

"It gets help from a bottle."

"You know what I mean. Anyway, I didn't want that . . . *person* to get her grubby mitts on it."

Gia stopped and laughed. "You've *got* to be kidding! You spent twenty thousand just for spite?"

"Not spite. I may not be an artist"—he placed a hand over his heart—"but I have the soul of one." He tapped the box under his arm. "And this—what's the art-speak phrase?—this *speaks* to me."

Gia demonstrated the unofficial ASL sign for *Gag me with a spoon*.

He put on his best offended expression. "Well, it does."

Truth was, it *had* spoken to him by appealing to something deep within. He'd wanted it from the first instant he'd set eyes on it. He'd bought it not so much to save it from the bimbo as to possess it—to put it someplace where he'd see it every day.

"Really? And just what does it say?"

They'd reached Houston, the wide, bustling thoroughfare that linked the East and West Sides down here, the street responsible for SoHo's name—south of Houston. Jack raised his free arm to flag a cab.

"As you can see, it's all wrapped up at the moment, so I can't hear it. But back in the gallery it said, 'Please don't let me go home with that bling-bedizened beotch.' It really did."

Gia laughed and leaned against him. "I love you."

"I love you too."

"And I'd like to *make* love to you again sometime before I die."

Uh-oh.

A cab lurched to a halt before them.

"You and me both."

"Then why—?"

He handed her the box with the tree. "Take this back for me, will you?"

Concern tightened her features. "You're not coming?"

"Got some bidness down here."

She eased herself into the backseat of the cab and looked up at him.

"Is something wrong?"

"No . . . it's just that I've become involved in a situation that could be dangerous to you."

"Like what?"

"It's too complicated to get into here and now."

The cabby looked like a Hotel Rwanda bellhop. Jack handed him a twenty and said, "Sutton Square."

The guy nodded. Did that mean he knew where it was? Too many cabbies didn't know zilch about the city anymore. At least he had a GPS.

Gia was still looking up at him. "When, then?"

"When what?"

"When can we get into it?"

He leaned in and kissed her on the lips.

"Soon, Gia. Soon. I promise."

"I'm back on the pill, if that's what you're worried about, and I'm never going off it again."

That wasn't it. Or maybe it was. He wished he knew.

"I'll talk to you later."

Then he closed the door and the cab took off. Gia's puzzled face in the rear window felt like seppuku—without a second to deliver the coup de grâce.

5

It took Henry until two o'clock to track down what Dawn had requested. He finally returned with a box labeled with Arabic script.

"I suppose this would have been easy to find if I'd known where to look," he said, handing her the box, "but I didn't. I believe this is what you want."

Dawn tore it open and found a large blue silk scarf within. But not just any scarf. This one had a veil attached. She'd Googled Muslim clothing last night and came across this whack Muslima fashion site that featured something called a *pak chadar*. It had looked perfect. This morning Henry had gone in search of one.

She pulled it out and stepped into the powder room for a look. After draping it over her head and shoulders she checked herself in the mirror. Not bad. The color intensified the blue of her eyes. She pulled the top front lower to hide her blond hair, then draped the long end of the scarf over her opposite shoulder. Now for the final touch: the veil.

She stretched it across her nose and her lower face and fastened it on the other side.

Well, it was totally stupid looking but it did the job. The only things visible were her eyes. On the one-in-a-zillion chance Jerry saw her, he would so not recognize her. He'd think, there's a weird, blue-eyed, white-bread Muslim chick, but that would be it.

But what if he recognized her eyes? Simple fix: sunglasses.

She hurried back to her room where she slipped on the wraparound Ray-Bans provided for sunbathing on the roof.

Another inspection, this time in the bedroom mirror, and wow—totally unrecognizable.

Am I smart or am I smart?

Her glee slipped into sad wonder when she remembered facts from her comparative religions course—aced like most of her courses—in social studies. Hundreds of millions of women around the world were totally forced to dress like this. What was wrong with seeing a woman's face or hair? What sort of asshole came up with this bullshit? Could only be a guy, most likely one hung like a light switch. She didn't know why women put up with it. Oh, yeah. Because if they didn't they got stoned to death or something. Nice religion.

People said the world was getting totally crazy, but truth was, it had *always* been crazy—at least where women were concerned.

She ground her teeth. Mom had never talked feminism. She didn't have to—she'd lived it. Completely self-sufficient, without a man or even a family to lean on, she'd built a life for herself and Dawn through sheer guts and determination.

God, I miss her.

She shook off the melancholy and hurried back into the great room where Henry waited.

"Okay. What do you think?"

He nodded. "Even your own mother wouldn't recog—oh, I'm sorry."

"It's all right." She was getting out of here and nothing was going to bring her down. But Henry's expression turned grave. "Really, Henry, it's all right. You don't have to—"

"It's not that," he said. "I believe I'm having second thoughts."

"About what?"

"About letting you leave the apartment."

Dawn stiffened and thought her heart had stopped. No! He couldn't change his mind now. Not when she was so totally mad stoked about getting out.

"You can't be serious."

"The Master would be quite upset if he found out. I'll lose my job. Or worse."

Worse?

"He's so never going to find out. Not from me, at least. And you're not going to tell him. So . . . ?"

"There is Gilda."

"Today's her afternoon off. No way she can know."

"Still, I should check with the Master first."

No-no-no! That downer bastard would totally say no.

"But you can't find him. And anyway, no one's gonna know. Please, Henry, please. I'm dying here and we've got a perfect solution worked out. Come on, Henry. *Please!*"

The word hung between them, then Henry sighed and shrugged.

"But only for a little while—a *very* little while. I do not want Gilda to come home to an empty apartment. She will be very upset."

"Deal. Anything you say, just get me out of here." She wanted to be on the move before he changed his mind again. "Let's go."

He gestured to her legs. "That doesn't look very Muslimish."

She looked down at her bare legs and tight training shorts.

"Christ."

"He's not part of this equation."

Dawn had to laugh, and looked to see if Henry was smiling. But no. Deadpan as ever.

She rushed back to her room for something a little more modest.

6

Jack stood in a doorway of the Wyeth building near the western end of Spring Street, catty-corner from the Ear Inn's block, just a couple of hundred yards from where SoHo morphed into TriBeCa. He held a lit cigarette and pretended to be an exiled smoker—a ubiquitous fixture around the city—as he watched the entrance to the Ear.

Not the easiest place to find. It sat—quite literally—over the eastern end of the Holland Tunnel. The unlit neon sign jutting over the sidewalk was no help during the day. If you squinted you could see that the tubing said BAR and nothing else. A different story at night when it was lit: They'd blacked out the right half of the "B," enabling the sign to proclaim the place's name.

But in daylight you had to be standing before the front window to see the discreet EAR INN on the glass. Used to be a fisherman's hang back in the nineteenth century, right on the waterfront—not much west of the Ear back then but the Hudson River. Now the Hudson lay on the far side of the concrete lanes of the West Side Highway.

Midafternoon was a traditionally slow time for bars—the lunchers gone, the happy-hour crowd yet to arrive—and the Ear was no exception. Though only a couple of blocks from Hudson Street, this dead-end warehouse area, dominated by a huge UPS depot, was about as far in spirit from touristy as imaginable. No weary shoppers passing by and stopping in for a cold one. You had to know about the Ear and come looking for it.

At a few minutes to three a taxi pulled to a stop before the door and out stepped a slim Asian in a black suit, white shirt, striped tie, and fedora. Could have been Kurosawa's undertaker.

He stood looking at the Ear's front window, then turned back to the taxi and said something to the driver. Jack figured he was asking if this was really the place. Finally he forked over some cash and stepped toward the door. After a few seconds' hesitation, he pushed inside.

Jack waited a few more minutes to see if anyone followed him in, but the street remained clear. He crushed out his cigarette and headed for the Ear.

Inside he found the guy standing alone near the front end of the half-occupied bar, looking around with a confused expression. He stood out among this half hipster, half middle-manager crowd like a Hasid at a Taliban wedding.

Jack tapped him on the shoulder. He spun, a startled look in his face.

"You the fellow who lost something and wants it back?"

"Yes-yes. You are Repairman Jack?"

"Just Jack will do. Let's get a table."

As if on cue, a smiling, strawberry-blond waitress with an Irish accent appeared and asked if they wanted a table for two. Jack pointed to an empty one in the far corner of the front room with a good view of the entrance and easy access to the door to the kitchen.

She led them past the warped and scarred bar with its old-fashioned, four-legged, vinyl-topped stools. Two old-wood gables hung over the bottle racks on the wall, separated by a high shelf jammed with old empty bottles of all imaginable shapes and sizes. The front window said the place had been established in 1817. That might have been the last time those bottles had been dusted.

Jack seated himself in the corner near the huge ear mounted on the wall. He put his back against a three-sheet poster offering a graphic, organ-by-organ lesson on the ruinous effects of alcohol on the human body. The wall to his left sported portholes with either seascapes or stern-looking portrait faces gazing into the room.

Once they were seated, the guy removed his hat and placed it in his lap, revealing jet-black hair combed down over the left side of the forehead, all the way to the eyebrow. He appeared to be somewhere in his forties and had an ascetic look—hollow cheeks and intense dark eyes peering from deep orbits. Eyes that never quite made contact with Jack's. Before he adjusted his jacket cuffs, Jack caught a glimpse of a black tattoo above his right wrist—some sort of polygon.

"You know my name," Jack said. "Time to hear yours."

He dipped his head in a quick bow. "Nakanaori Okumo Slater."

"Whoa."

A quick smile. "I am called Naka."

"Naka it is. But Slater doesn't sound very Japanese."

"My father was American."

Jack couldn't detect any Caucasian in Naka's looks, so he either favored his mother's side—a lot—or his father was Japanese-American.

The strawberry-blond waitress came over, pad in hand, and handed them menus. When Jack ordered a pint draft Hoegaarden, she smiled.

"Hey, you pronounced it right. Don't hear that too often. You Belgian?"

Jack smiled back. "No, Jerseyan."

When Naka ordered water, he found Jack and the waitress giving him looks.

"I do not drink spirits."

As the waitress sighed and walked away, W. C. Fields's warning wafted through Jack's brain: *Never trust a man who doesn't drink.*

Jack picked up a menu. "The burgers here are outstanding."

"I do not eat flesh."

Jack looked at him. "I bet you don't get invited to too many parties, either."

"Parties?" He looked puzzled. "No."

"Yeah, well, neither do I. The Ear burger is really good."

The guy made a face. "You devour something's ear?"

"Only kidding."

But he wished someone in the place would find the cojones to list their big, eight-ounce sirloin burger as an Ear Burger. That would be too cool.

"I did not come here to eat. I came here to talk."

"I can do both—I'm a multitasker." Jack dropped the menu. No contest. He'd decided on the burger. "So tell me again how you found me—and name names this time."

"When an object was stolen—"

"From your home on Maui, I assume."

He nodded. "Yes. I own a plantation."

"What do you grow?"

He looked flustered. "Why do you wish to know?"

"Call me curious."

"Papaya, sugar cane, macadamia—"

"Okay. So the 'object' was stolen from your Maui plantation. What then?"

"I . . . I hired detective."

"Why not go to the cops?"

"I wish to be discreet."

"Because . . . ?"

Naka hesitated, then sighed. "Because ownership would be, how shall I say, called into question if existence of object become public."

Knew it.

Couldn't report the theft of a stolen object.

"And your detective blew it, I assume."

He nodded. "He discover name of thief but thief escape on plane to New York."

Now the pieces were fitting.

Naka's water and Jack's Hoegaarden arrived. The brew had a thin half-slice of lemon floating in the foam. He was not a fan of *witbieren,* but Hoegaarden was a treat if found on tap. Jack ordered the burger with cheese, bacon, and sautéed onions. Naka broke down and chose a salad.

As the waitress bustled off, Jack sipped his brew. Good. A light lemony flavor, great for summer or when he didn't want to feel logged down. Not on tap in many places around the city. Another reason to seek out the Ear.

He noticed another Asian—this one too looked Japanese—come in and sit two tables away. He glanced at them once, then studied the menu.

Jack turned to Naka. "So, with the thief in New York you needed some-one local."

Naka nodded. "Yes, but I have no idea where to turn. I was discussing my problem with artist I know—I buy his sculpture and we become friends. He say his consort used to live in New York and might be able to help."

First, "alas" from Gary. Now, "consort." What gives?

"What's this artist's name?"

"Moki."

"Never heard of him. How about his 'consort'? What's hers?"

"I do not know. I never meet her. We speak only on phone. She give me your name and how to reach you. She call you a *ronin* and say I should not lie to you, that you are a good man who can be trusted but who can also be not nice at times."

"'Not nice'? She said that?"

"Yes. Her exact words."

Who the hell . . . ?

"You're taking her advice, of course."

"All I am telling you is true."

Jack put aside wondering about the mystery woman until later.

"Good. So, your detective at least learned the identity of your thief."

Naka further averted his gaze. "Unfortunately, we have since learned that he was traveling under false identity."

"Which was?"

"Eddie Cordero."

Jack leaned back. Why did that name sound familiar? He was sure he'd never heard it, but something about it set off a chime.

"So what did he steal?"

"A sword. A katana. I must have it back."

"And what's so special about this sword? What's it worth?"

"That is puzzle. It is terribly damaged and of no use or value to anyone but my family."

"And why's it valuable to you?"

"One might call it heirloom. It belonged to dear friend of my father. He is deceased and sword was all my father had left of him. When my father died he made me promise to keep sword in family. I must keep promise to my father."

Okay. Jack understood that. But odd the thief would take a worthless heirloom back to New York. Unless . . .

"Maybe it's worth more than you think."

Naka shook his head. "I think not." From an inside pocket in his suit jacket he pulled a pair of photos and handed them across the table. "See for yourself."

The first showed a long, slim sword, its naked, curved blade lying atop a wooden stand, cutting edge facing up. The long, tapered tang was exposed—someone had removed the handle. The blade looked strangely mottled. The next photo was closer in and slightly blurred, revealing the mottling as a random pattern of irregular holes in the steel. The cutting edge was perfectly preserved, but the rest was Swiss-cheesed.

"A samurai sword?"

"Yes," Naka said. "A katana."

"No offense, but it looks like a piece of junk."

"In very real sense, it is. But to my family it is priceless. Therefore it make no sense for someone to steal unless they mean to ransom back to us."

Jack looked again at the moth-eaten blade and agreed: no sense at all.

"And you've received no demand?"

"Nothing. And thief has fled islands."

This didn't make a whole lot of sense. Jack felt some key element was missing—or being withheld.

"Aren't some of these swords valuable?"

Naka nodded. "*Nihontō* fashioned by ancient swordsmiths such as Masamune and Muramasa—especially those signed by Masamune—are rare and of most extreme value."

Most of what Jack had just heard was meaningless.

"*Nihontō?*"

"Only swords forged in Japan can be called *nihontō*. Foreign-made imitations cannot."

"And I take it this blade isn't signed by Moonimalaya or whoever."

"No one. Especially not Masamune." He pronounced the name with exaggerated clarity, as if speaking to a five-year-old. "A Masamune sword would never corrode as this one did."

Jack squinted at the photo and spotted a tiny figure carved into the steel of the tang:

外人

He turned the photo toward Naka and pointed. "Someone's signed something there."

Naka glanced at it and nodded. "Yes. The two characters separately mean 'outside' and 'person.' Together they mean 'foreigner.'"

That tripped a memory.

"Oh. *Gaijin.*"

Naka blinked. "You know this word?"

"I know a few words. *Arigato* and all that."

In truth he'd picked up "gaijin" reading Clavell's *Shogun*, but no need to let this guy know.

Naka pointed to the engraving and looked at him directly for the first time. "Does this mean anything to you?"

Jack shrugged. "Only that I'd be a *gaijin* in your country just as you are in mine."

"Yes." Naka sounded relieved and averted his gaze again. "That is what it should mean."

What's that all about? Jack wondered.

He decided to push a little.

"So if I want to get this sword back for you, all I have to do is go around asking about a rotted-out blade with *gaijin* written on the hasp."

Naka's seat jump was almost comical.

"No-no-no! You must not. Such inquiries could reach wrong ears."

"So it *is* valuable."

"No. It is not. As I tell you, original owner might hear. It would want back."

"It?"

"A museum in Japan."

Good. He could handle a museum. Jack didn't want some kind of Zatōichi coming after him.

The food arrived then. The burger came open-face style. Jack assembled it and took a big chomp—heaven—while Naka started to poke at his salad.

After a couple of bites, Jack forced himself to speak. He would much rather have wallowed in the ground sirloin until it was gone.

"And why would this sword have been in a museum?"

"Because it is old. It was but minor part of much larger collection, but if museum hear, it will want back."

"Gotcha."

Naka looked at him again, a plea in his eyes. "You can do this?"

"I can only promise to try."

"No. You must succeed! Moki's consort said—"

"I don't know who this lady is, but if she said I could guarantee success, she's wrong. No guarantees in this business."

Naka was silent a moment, then nodded. "That is fair, I suppose. I am glad you are being honest with me." Another pause, then, "What is your fee?"

Jack was tempted to pull a Gary: Write down the dollar amount and hand it to him. But he didn't have cards, so he pulled out a pen and wrote it on the white butcher paper that served as a tablecloth here.

Naka blinked. "That is very much money for no guarantee."

Yeah, it was stiff. Jack had upped his price since the Dawn Pickering job. His intention was to cut back. One way to do that was to be very choosy about the fix-its he took on. The other was to price himself out of certain markets.

This Naka guy owned a plantation on Maui. He could afford Jack's price, no sweat.

"Didn't your artist friend Moki's 'consort' tell you that?"

"I asked but she did not know."

Not know? That meant she wasn't a former customer. A puzzlement.

"Well, it's not as bad as it sounds. Half up front, and the rest when I deliver the goods."

"And if you do not? What happen to first half?"

"That stays with me."

"But how am I to know you have not simply taken my money and done nothing?"

Instead of answering, Jack took another bite of the burger and chewed at a slow, deliberate pace. Something about this guy bugged him. Maybe because he sensed Naka was giving him only part of the story. Then again, he couldn't expect full disclosure from someone who wanted him to steal back a stolen object.

As for the job itself, it could prove relatively easy if the thief was trying to sell the sword, but damn near impossible if he intended to keep it for himself.

Jack had set the photos on the table. He took another bite and studied the close-up of the ruined blade.

Who'd pay for a piece of junk like that?

Finally he swallowed and said, "It's called trust. You have a reference—granted, it's from a woman neither of us knows, but you trusted the source enough to get in touch with me."

"Yes, but—"

Jack held up a hand. "No buts. You either trust me or you don't. You know my price, so you either come across or you don't. I don't bargain, haggle, dicker. Make up your mind."

Naka sighed. "I do not see that I have much choice."

"Of course you do. You're dealing with maybe the last vestige of the free market, which means you can walk out the door you came in with no hard feelings—at least on my part."

Jack expected some lengthy rumination on Naka's part. Instead he surprised him by giving a curt nod and saying, "Yes, it shall be done. I shall pay you cash."

"Yes, you will. Although we accept Krugerrands as well."

"When can you start looking?"

"As soon as I have the money."

Jack had learned over the years that certain customers had to believe they were dealing with a no-nonsense, hard-ass mercenary. He sensed Naka-whatever Slater was one of those.

"I shall make call and someone shall deliver it to you within hour. Where—?"

"Right here will do fine."

No sense in burning another meeting place.

"One last thing," Jack added. "How did the break-in occur?"

Naka frowned. "I do not understand."

"Was a door pried open or its lock picked? Was an alarm system by-passed? How did he gain entry?"

"Through bedroom window."

"With you there?"

"No. Out to dinner."

"No alarm?"

"Yes, for rest of house, but my wife like to sleep with open window. Our system bypass those windows."

"No motion detectors?"

"In rest of house, yes, but he turn off alarm system from bedroom. I do not know how."

Jack did. Inside info: a cleaning girl, or maybe even someone at the alarm company.

Good. This gave him an idea of the burglar's skill set, always useful in tracking someone.

Naka rose and reached into his pocket. Jack waved him off.

"On me. I'll be running a tab." He pointed to the photos. "Got anything better than these?"

Naka shook his head. "Sorry. Those are best. My father never felt need of taking picture. He had sword in place of honor where he could see every day. Why take many picture?"

Made sense.

Naka put on his hat, bowed, and hustled out the door. Jack settled into finishing his burger, considering ordering another Hoegaarden and maybe even another burger, and thinking how this was the kind of fix-it Gia liked him to take.

Retrieving a decrepit old sword . . . really . . . how risky could that be?

7

Toru Akechi was sitting with his favorite student, Shiro Kobayashi, the fourth son of a fisherman in the Ishikawa prefecture, in one of the few rooms in the Order's temple that had remained a classroom. Most others had been converted into dormitory-like quarters for the monks, acolytes, and guards. A few of the larger rooms had been renovated for Sightings and for surgery.

Tadasu burst in. Toru sensed restrained excitement in the man as he bowed.

"The mercenary has agreed to search for the katana, *sensei*."

Toru regarded him through the eyeholes of his mask. Tadasu Fumihiro was forty-two, a former student. He had watched Tadasu grow since his teen years, mentoring him through the levels of the Kakureta Kao as it struggled back from extinction. He had earned the position of temple guard but showed promise of so much more, which was why Toru had selected him for a mission so critical to the future of the Order.

"You must stay close to this. The Order is depending on you to guarantee its future. If this man finds it . . . you know what must be done."

"I do, *sensei*. I shall not fail."

"I have faith in you. And good news for you. Shiro has located the final ingredient for the *ekisu*."

After regaining the sacred scrolls, Toru had sent out the Order's acolytes and any guards who could be spared—and who could show their faces—to scour the city for the ingredients to make the elixir that would create the Kuroikaze—the Black Wind.

Tadasu grinned and bowed to the acolyte half his age. "Most excellent!"

Shiro returned the bow. "I am honored to be of service."

Tadasu's hair was longer than Shiro's, but the two were so similar they could have been father and son.

Tadasu said, "This means that the Order can once again wield the Kuroikaze!"

Toru hoped so. He knew of only one way to be sure.

"Yes. Even as we speak, the *ekisu* is being prepared in accordance with the instructions in the scrolls. We must test it as soon as possible. For that we will need a *shoten*. The two of you go, search the city. Find someone sickly, someone with low vitality, and—most important of all—someone who will not be missed."

He followed the pair out of the classroom and returned to his quarters. He locked the door and removed the embroidered red silk mask from the folds of skin the surgeons had created in the four corners of his face. This had been done when he'd entered the Fifth Circle of the Kakureta Kao and took the Vow of the Hidden Face. No one ever again would see his face.

The Fifth Circle . . . where he had gained the folds and lost his testicles. A small price to pay, hardly a price at all, especially considering how long ago he had sworn off pleasures of the flesh.

As a *sensei*, he would not be allowed to progress beyond the Fifth Circle for many years to come. He needed all of his senses to be an effective teacher.

He stepped to the open window and let the breeze caress his face. Even though it carried a faint, sour tang of garbage, it felt refreshing. Yes, he'd made the vow, but sometimes he became weary of looking at the world through two eyeholes.

He stared across the flat lowlands and highways to the huge mounds of the Fresh Kills landfill surrounding the Order's temple.

Temple . . . a term used loosely in this case. Toru had seen photos of the beautiful five-story pagoda in the heart of Tokyo that served as home to the Kakureta Kao until the World War II fire bombings. People high and low had feared and venerated the Order. And then it had been destroyed.

Even after all these years, the Order remained a mere shell of its former self. This old, boxy, two-story schoolhouse on condemned ground was all it could afford. The toxins supposedly had been cleared but still no one wanted to live here. But the Order cared naught about toxins, and the building's bargain price was all their depleted coffers could afford.

How the mighty had fallen.

But the Kakureta Kao would regain its former status. The Seers said so. And they said that New York City was where its resurgence would begin.

Toru hated this barbaric country whose commercialism had reached across an ocean and tainted his homeland's culture. But he believed the Seers. As did the Elders. And so here the Order would stay.

But the Seers had said the Kakureta Kao would not rise unless it regained the scrolls and the blade that had caused their downfall. The scrolls they had, but they must control the blade if they were ever to regain their ancient status.

8

Blume's.

Dawn was in total heaven—six floors of paradise on Fifth Avenue. She'd spent the entire afternoon here. She'd never been able to afford Blume's on her allowance and what she'd earned at the diner.

With Henry never far away, she'd touched, caressed, tried on, and bought—on Mr. Osala's dime, of course. She'd even gone to the designer floor, intending to see how far she could push this free ride—to find the limit of Mr. Osala's largesse. A sales clerk named Rolf had shown her around, but when she saw the prices, she'd lost her nerve.

The things she'd ordered would be delivered.

She also enjoyed the sidelong glances from the other shoppers at her *pak chadar*. Kind of cool, in a way, like playing hide and seek, or spying. She could see their expressions but they couldn't see hers. She'd totally stuck her tongue out at a couple of old biddies and they hadn't a clue.

Better fun was raising a ton of eyebrows when she'd picked out a skimpy scarlet teddiette and taken it to a dressing room. Not like she'd had any intention of trying it on, let alone buying it; she'd just wanted to set tongues a-wagging. And she had. She'd heard the sales desk buzzing as she headed for the changing area.

She dragged Henry up to Fifty-seventh for a late-afternoon snack—totally tricky with the veil.

After that Henry informed her that it was time to go.

Bummer.

As they waited for the car—Henry had been adamant about using it instead of a cab for the short trip—Dawn saw a scruffy-looking man pasting a Day-Glo orange flyer on a nearby wall. The bold black letters caught her eye.

HAVE YOU SEEN THIS GIRL?

She stepped closer and saw someone was offering a five-thousand-dollar reward. It listed an 800 number.

And then she saw the name: DAWN PICKERING.

And then she saw the picture: hers.

"Oh, my God!"

The guy turned and gave her a quick up-and-down inspection. He had scraggly hair and needed a shave. He squinted at her, scowling. A button in his shirt read, ASK ME ABOUT THE KICKER EVOLUTION.

"Yo. You mean, 'Oh, my Allah,' right?"

Fighting waves of shock and nausea, Dawn pointed a trembling finger at the flyer. "Wh-who's looking for that girl?"

The guy's eyes narrowed. "Why? You know her?"

With no thought on her part, a reply leaped from her lips. "No. No, of course not. It's just . . ." Think, Dawn. "Was she . . . was she like kidnapped or something?"

"Or something. All we know is she's gone. She's out there alone and afraid and we want to help her."

That sounded memorized. "Who's 'we'?"

"Why, the Kickers, of course." He held up the back of his hand to show her the little stick figure tattooed on the thumb web. "We're out here just doing our part."

Dawn stifled a gasp. Jerry had had one of those.

"What are you going to do when you find her?"

"Return her to her home and protect her."

"From what?"

"From anything that wants to hurt her and her baby."

Her baby . . .

Dawn felt the sidewalk tilt under her. She swayed.

The guy stared at her, his expression suspicious. "You okay?" He reached toward her veil. "Let's see what you look like under that."

Suddenly he was sailing backward. He slammed against the fender of a parked car.

"You will not touch her, sir." Henry's voice.

The Kicker's face twisted into a snarl, then relaxed into a sneer when he looked up and saw Henry.

"Not like I care 'bout no Mohammed-humping ho anyhow."

Dawn would never have guessed Henry had such strength. He hid it well. As the Kicker started to turn away, Henry pointed to the stack of flyers in his backpack.

"May I have one of those?"

The man hesitated, squinting at them, then handed over half a dozen.

"Sure. Spread 'em around. The more people see 'em, the quicker we find her."

Still dazed, Dawn felt Henry grip her arm and lead her to the car. He ushered her into the backseat, closed the door after her, and soon they were rolling.

Through the rear window she saw the Kicker writing something on the back of one of his flyers.

They headed east, then uptown on Madison. And everywhere she looked she saw the flyers. She'd taken passing notice of them on the way to the store, but flyers were so common around the city, especially around construction sites, that she'd paid them no mind. But now, knowing what they said, each flash of orange was a cramp in her gut.

Forcing herself to move, she leaned over the back of the front seat and retrieved one of the flyers. She stared at it.

Where had they got this picture? She didn't remember it. It looked fairly recent, but before she'd lost the weight.

"Do you see?" Henry said. "This is why the Master does not want you out. *Now* do you understand?"

She waggled the flyer. "About these?"

"Yes. They mean far more than just one man is looking for you. There's a whole network of people. And through these flyers and the reward they're offering, they're enlisting a host of allies. You simply cannot show your face in public."

Dawn stared at the flyer. "I need to call this number."

"I do not believe that would be wise."

"Just stop at a pay phone. No one will know it's me." She had to call. She just had to. "*Please*, Henry."

For a moment he said nothing. Then, without taking his eyes off the street, he offered a cell phone over his shoulder.

"Use this. It's safe. But be very careful what you say."

Her throat tightened at his unexpected gesture. "Thank you, Henry. You're a friend. And I'll be *very* careful."

Her finger trembled as she punched in the number. A male voice answered on the second ring.

"Dawn hot line."

Dawn hot line . . . oh, God.

"Hel—" She swallowed. "Hello? I'm calling about the girl on the flyer."

"You think you've spotted her, right?" His tone was like, Yeah-yeah, tell me another one. *"Where'd you see her?"*

"You don't sound like you believe me."

He sighed. *"Sorry. We've had so many false leads and—"*

"Who are you people and why are you looking for her? I mean, you're not the police, so—"

"We're private, and we've taken an interest in her case . . . her disappearance. Have you seen Dawn? Do you know where she is?"

"Who's in charge there? Who's behind this?"

"He's not here right now. But if you haven't seen her, can you help us, give us any hint of where she might be?"

"I'm not saying another word until I speak to whoever's behind this."

"I'm sorry, he's not available right now."

"Is his name Jerry? Tell—"

A long-fingered hand snatched the phone away and snapped it shut.

"Quite enough," Henry said. "I let you call for one reason: To make clear to you that your ex-lover is conducting a very organized hunt for you. Do you understand now?"

Ex-*lover*? If he only knew the rest of it.

"I understand."

Did she ever.

9

"Still fighting chopsticks, I see," Jack said.

The Isher Sports Shop was officially closed, its narrow, cluttered aisles dark except for the rearmost section where Abe perched on a stool behind the scarred counter. The air reeked of garlic from the take-out kimchi he was forking into his mouth.

He raised his free hand and waggled his stubby, chubby fingers.

"These look made for eating with sticks?"

"You could learn."

"Why for I should learn? For westerners, chopsticks are an affectation. I don't do affectations."

No argument there, Jack thought, taking in Abe's customary white half-sleeve shirt and black trousers, strained by his bulging belly and stained by the day's parade of edibles.

"Well, for one thing, they might slow down your eating."

"I should eat slow? Why?"

"Slow eaters tend to eat less."

"You're not going to start, are you?"

Jack shook his head. "Not tonight."

He knew his own eating habits—except when Gia cooked for him—were anything but healthy. One of these days he'd get his cholesterol checked. But at least he was active. Abe spent most of his time on that stool, eating. Jack didn't like to think of his closest friend as a cardiac arrest waiting to happen.

But he was getting tired of being a nag, especially since it hadn't changed anything. The guy was fatter than ever, and didn't seem to care. With his wife long dead, his daughter barely speaking to him . . . food and reading newspapers—usually simultaneously—were his joys in life.

Abe said, "And kimchi, I'll have you know, is diet food. Fermented cabbage. More low-cal is hard to find." He pushed the container toward Jack. "You want?"

Jack shook his head. The two burgers at the Ear would hold him the rest of the night.

"Thanks, no. I didn't think any of the Korean places around here delivered."

"I picked it up on my way back from the hospice."

Jack knew why Abe had gone there.

"How's the professor doing?"

Abe shook his head. "Not good. The chemo and radiation are slowing down the cancer, but his right side is still useless from the stroke."

"And the numbers?"

A sigh. "Still with the numbers."

Peter Buhmann, Ph.D., Abe's old professor from his university days, had suffered a stroke last month while paging through the *Compendium of Srem*. Turned out to be a hemorrhage into a metastatic brain tumor from kidney cancer. The weirdest part was that he'd stopped speaking words and begun speaking numbers. Exclusively. And not random numbers—only primes multiplied by seven. Strange and sad, because the cancer was all through his body.

"How long?"

Another shrug. "Could be weeks, could be months." He burped kimchi.

"And how long before that stuff hits your colon? I would like to be out of here before then."

Abe smiled. "Why do you think I stock those NBC masks?"

"You'll let me know if I need to run downstairs and grab one, won't you?"

"Of course. But my guess is you didn't come here at this hour to ask about the professor or *tshepen* me about what I eat and the way I eat it. Nu?"

Jack told him about his meeting with Naka Slater.

"So, a second-story man you're looking for."

"Seems like it. Used the name Eddie Cordero, which rings some sort of bell with me, but apparently it's an aka."

Abe frowned. "A bell for me too. Who, I wonder . . . ?" He shrugged. "Maybe it will come. Meanwhile, we need to find a second-story *ganef* who was away for a while and has a tan maybe."

"And looking to unload a rotted-out katana."

Abe twirled his finger next to his head. "He's a little *farblondjet*, maybe?"

"Maybe." Damn, this was weird—but that made it interesting. "Anyway, you put out the word to your people, I'll talk to mine."

"You know who else you should talk to? Tom O'Day."

The name sounded familiar.

"The knife guy?"

"Yes, and a fence he'll be should the opportunity arise. Runs an East Side specialty shop called Bladeville. Sells anything and everything that cuts—from scimitars to steak knives."

"Good thought. I'll check with him tomorrow. Never met him, so could you give him a call to loosen him up?"

"Sure, but don't expect much looseness. A shmoozer he's not."

"Might be if I say I'm looking to buy it. If he knows of it, he can dip his beak as middleman."

"Good luck." Abe rubbed his belly and shifted in his seat. "Uh-oh. Fortz coming."

Jack spun and beat it toward the door.

"Bye."

10

"And you have no clue where she was calling from?"

Menck shook his head. "Tried to squeeze her—gentle, I swear—but suddenly she hung up."

Hank Thompson ground his teeth as he and Menck stood to the side of the phone bank he'd set up in the Lodge's basement. Ten phones manned by a rotating cadre of volunteers, collecting one false lead after another.

"And you didn't do anything to scare her off?"

"You've asked me that three times now and the answer's still no. Fuck no. Matter of fact, she already sounded scared when she got on the line."

"Scared how?"

Menck shrugged. "Dunno. Can't be sure but she sounded surprised. Like she'd just seen the flyer for the first time."

How could that be? They were all over the five boroughs.

Unless she'd been out of town for a couple of weeks.

"You're sure she asked for 'Jerry'?"

"Absolutely. Who's Jerry?"

Hank almost shouted, *My brother, you asshole,* but realized Menck had no way of knowing that. Only a handful of people knew he had a brother—half brother, actually—and they weren't talking.

The world knew that Jeremy Bolton was dead, but didn't know Hank's connection. It had been a big story last month when his body was found and identified by DNA. Dawn had known him as Jerry Bethlehem—still presumed alive—but the rest of the world knew him as Jeremy Bolton, the famous Atlanta Abortionist Killer from almost twenty years ago. Only the same handful of people who knew the brother relationship knew that Jeremy had been living as Jerry.

Hank was pretty sure he knew who was behind his death.

Mr. Everyman: mid-thirties, average height, average build, average-length brown hair, average nose, nothing-special brown eyes, dressed in nondescript clothing. He'd dogged Hank's trail, pretending to be a reporter, even mugged him in broad daylight.

Jeremy had described a guy just like him worming into the edges of his life.

An agent of what his father had called the Enemy. That had sounded a little bit crazy to Hank, a little bit paranoid. But then Daddy had disappeared.

Now Hank believed: They were out to ruin Daddy's Plan to change the world. Dawn's baby was the key to the Plan, and the Enemy was out to kill it. Kill it. Hank had to find Dawn first.

That had been Dawn on the phone. Had to be.

Is his name Jerry?

She was the only one who'd connect those flyers with Jerry.

Which meant she didn't know he was dead. Maybe he could use that . . .

And maybe not.

"Oh, here's Darryl," Menck said, pointing to a lean, scruffy Kicker waiting by the stairs. "He wants to talk to you. Says it might be important."

"Yeah?" Hank knew Darryl. One of his flyer posters. "Send him over."

Darryl approached and squinted at him. He always squinted, even at night.

"Hey, man. A little weirdness happened today. Might be somethin, might be nothin."

"Shoot."

"I was hangin this flyer by Blume's when this Arab chick comes over and starts asking me about it."

"Arab?"

"Well, she was wearing that veil thing they wear."

Hank nodded. He didn't know much about rag heads, but knew the veil meant Muslim, not necessarily Arab.

"What was her problem?"

"Well, for one thing, she was all shook up. I mean, her hands were shaking, man. Asking all sorts of questions about who was looking for her and what we intended to do with her if we found her."

Hank felt his insides begin to tighten.

"What she look like?"

Darryl shrugged. "Well, with the veil thing with that big scarf wrapped all around her head and shoulders, who could tell?"

"You must have seen her eyes. What color were they?"

Darryl shook his head. "Wearin shades, man. The only thing I could see was her forehead and her hands."

"What color—dark or light?"

"See, that's the thing that got me curious. Arabs got dark skin, right? Hers was real pale."

Hank felt his saliva evaporating. "Did you see any of her hair?"

"Like I said, she was covered up pretty good, but I was suspicious, so I went to take a peek under her veil and some guy dressed like a chauffeur pushed me away. Told me not to touch her. Even called me 'sir.'"

"Chauffeur?" Oh, hell, could it be the Enemy? "What'd he look like? Brown hair and eyes, average height?"

Darryl shook his head. "Nah. Tall and skinny, but a no-nonsense type. I wasn't gonna raise no ruckus with him."

"Chauffeur means a car. Did you—?"

"Scope the plates?" Darryl grinned and pulled a folded flyer from his pocket. "Sure did. Big black Mercedes. Number's right there."

Hank let out a breath he hadn't realized he'd been holding. Here was their first break.

"What time was this?"

Darryl shrugged. "Around four, maybe?"

He turned to Menck. "When did that call come in?"

Menck checked a sheet in his hand. "Four-oh-seven."

Dawn. She thought Jerry was still alive so she'd worn a Muslim veil to hide from him. After leaving Darryl, she'd called here.

Yeah, it was her.

But a chauffeur?

He clapped Darryl on the shoulder. "Good work, my man."

Darryl grinned and squinted, then headed for the door.

Hank turned to Menck, who was in charge of the Be-on-the-Lookout sheet that every Kicker was supposed to carry in his or her back pocket. Only one thing on the sheet now: a picture of Dawn.

"We need an updated BOLO list. Add that everyone should be on the lookout for a pale-skinned girl in a Muslim veil. They see her, don't get near, just tail her."

Menck nodded. "Got it."

Hank pulled a piece of paper from his shirt pocket. "And find a way to add this."

He handed him a crude drawing of the dream blade—the best he could manage from memory, but it gave the general idea. He'd written "sword blade" below it.

Menck looked at him. "What the—?"

"Just do it. And put down that if anyone sees it, bring it to me. And if you can't bring it, tell me about it. I want it."

A long shot—*very* long—but who knew? One of his Kickers might be passing a junk store or antique shop and see it in the window. Worth a try.

As Menck moved off, Hank felt his elation fade. Dawn's shock at seeing the flyer meant one thing: She'd been out of town the past few weeks.

He looked around at the phone bank and wondered if maybe all this was a huge waste of time. If she'd just got back into town, where from? Had the Enemy gotten her an abortion? Had she been spending the time recovering?

Hank wanted to scream. If she killed the kid, she killed the Plan. And for that, he'd kill her. It wouldn't bring the baby back, but it would be the right thing to do. And he'd enjoy it. Oh, how he'd enjoy it.

11

Hideo Takita sat in first class and stared at his laptop screen. The face staring back looked very much like his.

Yoshio, his twin, had flown this same route less than two years ago. Sent by the board to investigate the mysteries surrounding someone named Ronald Clayton, a man who had died in the crash of JAL Flight 27 on his way to meet personally with Sasaki-san and the entire Kaze board.

Nobody met with the entire Kaze board.

But rumor had it that Clayton had developed a world-changing technology so revolutionary that the country—or company—controlling it could call the tune to which every other nation around the globe would have to dance.

Yoshio's failure caused Hideo loss of face within the company. Had he succeeded he might have raised Japan to first among nations and Kaze to first among economic powers.

Hideo switched to another face, one of a number of photos Yoshio had sent back during his investigation. This one had Arabic features. Hideo knew his name: Kemel Muhallal. He also knew he was dead.

He clicked the arrow to proceed with his grim slide show. The next face was Caucasian: Sam Baker, an American mercenary. Also dead, his corpse found along with Muhallal's and three other bodies in the rear of a panel truck abandoned in the Catskill mountains. Two of those other bodies were mercenaries hired by Baker.

The fifth had been Yoshio, the victim of a bullet into the back of his head.

Another click and up popped a blurred photo of the mystery man. Yoshio hadn't known his name, but had labeled him "*ronin*." The *ronin* was missing. Perhaps he was dead too. And perhaps he was alive, the one responsible for executing Yoshio.

Execution . . . the manner of his death showed that he had allowed himself to be captured alive. And that meant he might have talked. Hideo knew that no form of torture could make Yoshio give up Kaze secrets, but still . . . *bushido* lived on in Kaze Group.

Hideo stared at what he could see of the face. The photo had been shot at an angle and the focus was poor. A very forgettable face. Not the face of a killer. But what then did a killer look like? Yoshio had killed in the service of Kaze. And Yoshio and Hideo, while not identical twins, had often been mistaken for each other.

Which means I wear the face of a killer.

Hideo shook his head. He could never kill anyone. Yes, he worked in the espionage wing of Kaze Group's corporate intelligence, where he spied on companies, traced money trails, hacked systems and intranets. But the only things he killed were worms and viruses and trojans.

Killing a human? Unthinkable. He hesitated killing a fly unless it became especially bothersome.

Sasaki-san obviously knew of his lack of aggression, why else would he have assigned three hoodlums as Hideo's traveling companions? Why then had he chosen Hideo of all people to chase down this ruined katana? Was it because of his computer skills? Or his language skills? He'd begun learning English as a child. He could say "Lulu loves lollipops" as well as any American.

Futile questions.

He again accessed the flash drive and stared at the scan: a cardboard shipping tube packed with foam popcorn and a bubble-wrapped katana, stark white against the surrounding grayness, measuring ninety centimeters from the tip of its blade to the butt of its naked tang. But a ruined katana, its blade filigreed with perhaps one hundred small holes of varying sizes and configurations.

He had heard that Sasaki-san collected katana. But why would the chairman, who could afford the finest blade ever made by Masamune—could probably resurrect Masamune-san himself and force him to make a new, custom blade—want this unsigned piece of junk?

And the inscription:

外人

Gaijin . . . what was the significance of that?

Questions, questions. Maybe he'd learn the answers. But more importantly, he prayed a Takita would not let down the chairman again.

He returned to the photo of the *ronin*.

I will be looking for you, he thought.

He glanced at the yakuza dozing beside him, and then at the two others seated ahead of him. If he found the *ronin* and established that he had killed Yoshio, he personally would do nothing. But he foresaw no problem in convincing his travel companions to take decisive action. They'd no doubt enjoy it.

TUESDAY

1

Bladeville lived up to its name.

Jack stood on a Madison Avenue sidewalk and stared at the display on the far side of the front window. Claymores, cutlasses, krisses, kukri, katanas, cleavers, and carvers; sabers, scimitars, and survival knives; paring, chopping, and filetting knives; daggers and dirks, Bowies and broadswords, rapiers and axes and on and on.

And swinging back and forth over them all, a model of the blade from Poe's *The Pit and the Pendulum*.

The steel security shutter had been rolled up, lights were on inside, and Jack caught glimpses of someone moving about, but the front door remained locked. The sign in the lower right corner of the window said it opened daily at ten. Almost that now.

Jack wanted to be the first customer of the day.

Finally, the snap of a latch and the squeak of an opening door.

"Coming in?"

Jack had been expecting someone who looked like Abe. This guy couldn't have been more opposite. Very tall, lean, sixties maybe, with gray in his brown hair and a bent lamp—his blue eyes didn't line up. He wore a dark blue Izod and khakis. Jack stepped forward, extending his hand.

"Tom O'Day?"

O'Day had long arms and a firm grip. "Who wants to know?"

"Name's Jack. Abe Grossman said you might be able to give me a little help with something I'm looking for."

His smile broadened. "Oh, yeah. He called. How is he? Trim as ever?"

"Trimmer."

"What are you looking for?"

O'Day's right eye kept looking over Jack's shoulder; he had to stop himself from turning to see what was so interesting.

"A katana."

"Well, you've come to the right place." He motioned Jack through the doorway. "I got a million of 'em."

At the threshold Jack did a quick scan of the walls and ceiling and spotted a security camera in the far, upper right corner. He'd worn a Yankees cap today—just for variety—and so he adjusted the beak lower over his face. A bell chimed as they stepped through.

The rest of Bladeville was like the front window, only more so. A knife-filled glass display case ran the length of the store; every kind of edged weapon imaginable festooned the wall behind it.

Bladeville. No kidding.

He motioned Jack to follow and led him through a door at the rear marked NO ADMITTANCE. He flipped a switch and the lights came on, illuminating row upon row of Japanese swords—long, short, medium—all racked on the wall in scabbards.

Jack glanced up and around. No security cam in here. A quick look over his shoulder showed no second cam in the retail area.

"My collection—Masamune, Murasama, Chogi, Kanemitsu, whoever. You name a classic swordsmith, I've probably got one."

"This is a special katana, Mister O'Day."

"Call me Tom."

"Okay, Tom. This katana was stolen recently and I'm trying to get it back for the owner."

O'Day's eyes narrowed. "You a cop?"

"Would Abe send a cop? I'm private. Just wondering if anyone's tried to sell you a damaged katana recently."

O'Day flipped off the light and they returned to the store section. He stepped behind the counter and began Windexing the glass top. Jack positioned himself with his back to the cam.

"Can't imagine anyone buying damaged when you can get them in pristine shape. Unless it's a signed Masamune or Murasama."

"Not signed by anyone, I'm afraid. And it's sort of moth eaten."

His hand paused—just a second—in mid-wipe, then continued polishing.

Jack wondered if O'Day had seen it or been offered it. If so, a good bet he might know who had it. But he said nothing. Better to approach from an angle.

"You mean rusted out in spots?"

"The owner says it's not rust, just defects."

Now the polishing stopped as O'Day looked at him. "You wouldn't happen to have a picture of this katana."

"Sure do." Jack pulled the photos out of the breast pocket of his shirt and slid them across the counter. "Not great quality, but they give you an idea."

O'Day looked, froze, then snatched them up. His hands shook. Without taking his eyes off the photos he reached behind him, found a four-legged stool, and dropped onto it.

He let out a barely audible, "Oh, shit!"

"What's wrong? You've seen it?"

"The Gaijin," he said to himself. "The fucking Gaijin."

Interesting . . .

"Yeah. That's what I'm told those doodles mean, but what's the big deal?"

He glanced up at Jack. "The fucking Gaijin Masamune, my man. This is the fucking Gaijin Masamune!"

"Is 'fucking' really part of its name?"

"This sword is legendary. And it all makes sense now. It all makes sense . . ."

"Well, that makes one of us. Has anyone approached you about—?"

"The story goes that early in the fourteenth century a wandering *gaijin* warrior commissioned Masamune to refashion his heavy dirk into a *kodachi*—a kind of short sword. He said the metal in the dirk had fallen from the sky in a blaze of light and he wanted it transformed into something more graceful. He left, saying he would be back. When Masamune began to work with the metal, he found it the strongest steel he'd ever encountered. He made a *kodachi* with an edge like no other."

Jack didn't care about where it had been in the past; he wanted to know where it was now.

"Yeah, but—"

O'Day went on like he hadn't heard Jack. Maybe he hadn't. Jack had a feeling the only way he could shut him up was blunt-force trauma.

"Masamune waited years for the *gaijin* to return but he never did. Thinking him dead, Masamune melted down the *kodachi* and added more steel—

his finest steel—but the two metals never fully mixed. The katana that resulted had a mottled finish. Though its blade was beautifully resilient, and took an edge like no katana he had ever seen, its finish embarrassed him."

"Fine. He was embarrassed. I'm sorry for him. Now——"

"Because he was so embarrassed, he didn't sign it on the *nakago* as he often did——"

"The what?"

"The tang, the butt end inside the handle. Instead he engraved it with '*gaijin.*'" O'Day pointed to the ideogram in the close-up photo. "He locked it away and prayed the *gaijin* wouldn't return. Finally, as he neared the end of his life, he gave it to a samurai who'd done him a service. No one ever knew who that samurai was and the so-called 'Gaijin Masamune' became something of a legend—supposedly stronger and sharper than anything Masamune had ever made. The story was known only to experts and collectors, and a lot of them thought it was a just that—a story. That all changed in 1955."

Jack had to admit he was interested now.

"What happened?"

"The Peace Memorial Museum opened in Hiroshima. And on display was this naked katana blade. Its *tsuka*—handle—was missing and the blade was riddled with holes. It had been found at ground zero, right where the Aioi Bridge used to be. It had the *gaijin* ideogram engraved on its tang."

"Could have been a fake."

O'Day scowled. "Aren't you listening? It was found at ground zero. It should have melted. But it didn't. Only some of it melted—the regular steel that Masamune had added to the *gaijin*'s. The *gaijin*'s steel resisted the heat. Remember the part about the blade's mottled finish? That was because the Earth steel, instead of blending with the steel that had 'fallen from the sky,' formed discrete pockets. So when it melted away, the remaining *gaijin* steel was left riddled with defects."

Despite knowing the answer, Jack said, "I gather it's no longer in the museum."

"No. The place opened in August, the sword was gone by mid-September."

Jack now knew what museum Naka was hiding from. But he couldn't have stolen it—not unless he was a lot older than he looked. Must have been his father.

"That brings us back to the reason I'm here." How to put this? "Look, you're known in certain circles as a guy who provides a service for goods of uncertain origin."

Well, that was better than just coming out and calling the guy a fence.

O'Day gave him a mean look. "What are you saying?"

Jack held up his hands: peace. "Look, I'm in those circles, and I even do a little myself. Thing is, you're also known as an expert on swords. So, if I was burdened with a katana that I wanted to be rid of, you'd be the guy I'd call."

O'Day said nothing, simply sat and glared.

Jack cleared his throat. "Well? Heard anything?"

Finally O'Day shook his head. "Nothing."

Lie. He hadn't heard about the Masamune Gaijin—his shock had been too genuine—but he'd heard something. What?

"Too bad. Look, you hear anything, you call Abe. There's a finder's fee in this for you."

He smiled. "If I find it, better hope the guy doesn't know what he's holding, because if he does, he's either not going to part with it, or he's going to want a ton."

"So it's worth a lot?"

"Ohhhhhh, yeah. I hear from him, I'll point him toward you—and expect a fat finder's fee."

"And if he doesn't know what he's got?"

"Hell, I'm going to buy it from him."

"Then what? Sell it back to my guy?"

"Yep. Hope he's got deep pockets."

"He might."

"He'd better."

Jack sensed a lie. This guy was a katana-collecting Gollum, and the Gaijin Masamune was his Precious. If he got his mitts on it, no way was he letting it go. Not for any amount. At least not now. Maybe he'd part with it down the road—cash in and be able to brag to his katana-collecting buddies that he once owned the Gaijin Masamune.

Jack couldn't wait around. If O'Day got to the blade first, Jack might be forced to play rough and gank it. An iffy and dangerous proposition he wished to avoid. The best solution here was to find this Eddie Cordero before O'Day did, and hope for the same: That he didn't know what he had.

Jack turned and headed for the door. "You hear anything, you'll call Abe, right?"

"Absolutely."

Suuuuuure.

2

Hideo leaned close to the computer screen as he ran through the tape from the security camera focused on carousel seven at Kennedy International. He'd arrived, gone straight to the Waverly Place mansion—one of a number around the city owned by Kaze Group—and set up shop.

He hadn't had to ask how the baggage scan had made its way to Sasaki-san. Kaze Group had a hand, in one form or another, in the production of almost every piece of electronic equipment in the world. The chairman had no doubt ordered an image of the sword embedded in the pattern-recognition software. When that image passed through the scanner, it was automatically forwarded to the chairman.

And since Kaze had a hand in most of the world's security systems and surveillance cams, Hideo had easily hacked into JFK's network.

The tube had been loaded onto Northwest Flight 804 out of Kahului Airport, then transferred to Delta Flight 30 in Seattle. Flight 30 had arrived on time at 3:36. Hideo fast-forwarded ahead to 3:45 on the day in question and watched the passengers crowd around the carousel. He watched the baggage start to slide down the chute. The tube appeared at 3:58 and was picked up by a stocky, dark-haired man who had already picked out a suitcase. As he turned and walked toward the cam, Hideo executed a number of freeze frames, enhancing and downloading each to the server in the basement.

He was glad this was streaming video rather than a three- or five-second refresh. He might well have missed the opportunity for a close-up.

The man was traveling as Eddie Cordero. Hideo would soon learn his true name.

Then he switched to the exit cam, advanced it to 3:58, and waited for the man with the tube and the rolling suitcase. He appeared and walked over to the taxi area and waited in line for his turn. Hideo downloaded enhanced frames of the taxi's license plates and the medallion number on its roof light.

He leaned back and smiled. All he had to do was track down those plates and medallion number, pass a little cash, and he'd know where that particular cab had dropped off the passenger picked up that day shortly after four P.M. at JFK.

He was beginning to understand why the chairman had chosen him: His computer skills made finding the man easy.

As easy as brewing tea.

3

Dawn stroked against the jets in the endless lap pool in Mr. Osala's private rooftop health club. She'd always liked swimming and now she could swim as long and as far as she wanted without ever having to make a turn. She'd read it was the best exercise of all, and knew it was toning her body.

She'd hoped the repetitive activity would totally numb her brain, act like a physical meditation mantra, but just the opposite. It cleared her head of everything but what she needed a break from.

Those posters.

Her mind wouldn't let go of what they meant: Jerry wasn't the only one looking for her. She'd thought she was in a bad situation before, but now she knew it was worse. It had ruined her day out—everything had been super up till then. But at least now she knew what she was up against.

She stopped swimming and stood panting in the warm flow from the jets. What to do?

She was a virtual prisoner here, but if Jerry found her, she'd be a total prisoner until she gave birth. And that would be, what, like January? Like next year? She shuddered. No way.

Here at least she had tons of comfort and Mr. Osala would cut her loose as soon as he'd tracked Jerry down and dealt with him.

What did he plan to do with Jerry once he found him? He always said "deal with him." But what did that mean?

God help her, she hoped he meant totally kill him. After what Jerry had done to Mom, she wanted him dead—he *deserved* to be dead. God himself should strike him dead.

A sob broke free.

And this *thing* inside her . . . every day it got a day older. Right now she could think of it as a thing. But what if it got to the point where she could feel it kicking and turning inside her? When did that happen? It wouldn't be a *thing* then. It would be a *baby*. Even with the total grossness of what it was and how it got there, she sensed she'd get to a point where she couldn't kill it.

So despite what Mr. Osala said about the thing being like an insurance policy, she totally had to get it out of her ASAP. Even if that meant running the risk of Jerry killing her if he caught her and found out.

And she thought she might have a way. It would be tricky, but if it worked she might have her cake and eat it too, so to speak.

4

"You say Eddie Cordero is his AK? You know that for sure?"

Jack sat in an inside booth at the Highwater Diner, perched on the west side of the West Side Highway, practically in the Hudson. Reaching it was real-life Frogger, but worth the risk.

Teddy "Bobblehead" Crenshaw slouched on the far side of the table, slurping iced coffee through a straw. Atop his pencil neck sat a size-eight skull that tended to wobble back and forth as he walked. Nobody called him Bobblehead to his face—he got testy about that. But no one referred to him as Teddy behind his back. When out of sight, he was Bobblehead all the way.

A half-eaten BLT and a hundred-dollar bill sat between them on the

Formica tabletop, the latter weighted down by a salt shaker. Teddy's head was steady now as he sat and sipped and kept glancing at the Ben.

"For sure," Jack said. "What I don't know is his real name and where to find him."

Bobble seemed to think on this, then took a big bite of his sandwich and spoke around it. "The Man ain't involved, right?"

Bits of bacon and mayo sprayed the tabletop and the c-note. Eating with this guy was like sitting front-row center at a Gallagher concert.

"Not at all."

"Because I already feel like a snitch as it is. Things've been kinda tight lately, y'know? But if fingering him is gonna bring real heat down on this guy . . ."

Jack wanted to shake him but knew he had to let Bobble run through his guilt trip.

"I understand. Reason my guy came to me is because he doesn't want the police involved. And there's a good chance 'Eddie' might make something on the deal."

"What if he doesn't want to deal?"

Jack shrugged. "That's his choice. I've been hired to get something he stole back into the hands of the previous owner. There's an easy way, and there's a hard way. I prefer the easy way, and so should your friend, 'Eddie.' Especially since my guy might be willing to pay a ransom. A little cooperation and it can be a win-win-win-win situation."

Bobble frowned. "Huh?"

"You get money, 'Eddie' gets money, I get my fee, and the guy gets his property back. We all walk away happy."

Bobblehead nodded. He seemed to like that spin.

"And if he's not who you're looking for?"

Jack tapped the bill, right on Ben Franklin's forehead. "Like I said: If I think your info's in good faith, you get this to keep. If it's the right guy, you get another."

He sighed and stuffed the end of the BLT into his mouth before speaking. "All right. Here's how it goes: When I heard you was looking for a second-story man going under Eddie Cordero, Hugh Gerrish popped into my head right away. He's a major possibility."

"Possibility? So this is a guess? You don't *know* this guy uses that AK?"

Jack wasn't looking for guesses. Guesses could send him chasing ghosts.

"No. Don't know for sure, but dig: Gerrish is a second-story man who loves the ponies, especially the thoroughbreds. Take two of the greatest jockeys in history, mash their names together, and you come up with Eddie Cordero."

Jack leaned back, as much to avoid the Sledge-o-Matic effect from Bobblehead as to think. *That* was why the name had rung a bell. Jack had worked a racetrack scam in his younger days. Didn't care for the sport, but anyone who knew anything about the ponies knew the names Eddie Arcaro and Angel Cordero.

"Did he disappear for a while and come back with a tan?"

"No tan, but he disappears for a couple weeks and then he pops up again, and he's buying rounds, saying what a sweet job he pulled."

"No details?"

"He's smarter'n that."

Jack mulled this a bit. Definite possibilities here.

"Okay, he sounds worth a shot. Where's he live?"

He shrugged, setting his head to bobbling. "Don't know him well enough for that. We both just tend to end up at the Fifth Quarter down on St. Mark's. But you can find out easily enough."

"Yeah?"

"He's out at Belmont most every day during the season—'cept Mondays and Tuesdays when it's dark. And since this is the season, all you gotta do is find him and follow him home."

"Great. But I don't know what he looks like."

"He's forty-something, real skinny, brown hair—dollars to donuts he dyes the gray—and . . ."

His voice trailed off as he saw Jack's face. Must have reflected the disappointment and frustration he felt. Wasted time.

"You know how many guys at the track look like that? Next you'll tell me he wears a Yankees cap—"

"Naw-naw, he's a Mets fan."

"I need a Capone scar, I need an Aaron Neville mole. And if he hasn't got anything like that, I need a photo."

Jack slipped the Ben from beneath the salt shaker and began to slide it toward his side of the table.

"Hey, wait."

"Good story, Teddy. But no address? No picture? No deal."

Bobble grabbed his wrist. "Wait! Wait! I ran into him last Saturday during the Fifth Quarter's Preakness party, just a couple days after he showed up from his 'sweet job.' Bastard won big too."

"So?"

"So Suzy the bartender was taking pictures with her phone when we were celebrating. I think she got one of me with Gerrish and some other guy. If we're lucky, maybe she hasn't erased them."

Jack rose and shoved the hundred into his pocket.

"Looks like we're heading for the East Village."

5

It hadn't taken Hideo long to single out Kenji as the smartest of the yakuza assigned to him. And although he seemed the oldest of the three, he could not be much past twenty-seven or twenty-eight.

He was the only one to exhibit any signs of intellectual curiosity. His two fellow hoodlums, Goro and Ryo, seemed to have no interests beyond smoking, drinking, watching TV, and playing cards.

Hideo didn't understand the need for Kaze Group's alliance with various yakuza groups. More powerful than all of them combined, it could crush them in a matter of days if it so wished. Yet it maintained ties. Why? Because it required a buffer between it and certain activities?

He had noticed that once out of sight of his fellows, Kenji dropped his swagger and confrontational demeanor and became a sponge for any knowledge or information to be had.

"What do we do now, Takita-san?" he said in English.

Good for you, Hideo thought.

Of the three, Kenji spoke the best English, and was obviously trying to hone whatever fluency he had.

The taxi trail had led to a dead end. Hideo had gone to the cab company and paid off the dispatcher to let him check the fare records of the vehicle in question. Yes, it had picked up a passenger at Kennedy at shortly after four P.M. that day, but had dropped him off at Belmont raceway. Hideo doubted the mystery man lived at the racetrack, so he'd have to find another way.

Sitting at his workstation, he called up one of the close-ups he'd culled from the surveillance tapes.

"I'm going to run this through our latest facial recognition program, map the landmarks of his features, and create a mathematical faceprint."

As he started the programs, a series of dots of varying colors began to appear on the face, connected by multicolored lines. Then numbers popped up as calculations were completed.

Kenji pointed to the screen. "You can no longer see his face."

But Hideo's gaze was drawn from the screen to Kenji's hand. The tip of his left little finger was missing, cut off at the first joint. Hideo knew what this meant: *yubitsume*. Kenji must have made a mistake somewhere along the line and, by way of apology for his wrongdoing, cut off the tip and sent it to his *kumicho*, begging forgiveness.

Apparently he was forgiven, or he wouldn't be here. Hideo hadn't noticed it during the trip because he'd worn a fake fingertip to divert suspicion. Traveling yakuza often became targets of increased scrutiny.

Kenji's cuff had slipped back, revealing the lower end of an intricately patterned sleeve tattoo. Hideo had never seen these yakuza unclothed, but he would bet Kenji and Goro and Ryo were covered with them, head to toe. Yakuza tradition demanded it.

"Takita-san?"

Hideo snapped his attention back to the screen. What had Kenji said? Oh, about not seeing the face.

"Yes, but the computer will use that numeric formula to create a template to which it will match other faces."

"But where—?"

"One Police Plaza will be our first stop."

According to information on the flash drive, the sword had been stolen from the Hiroshima Peace Memorial Museum over fifty years ago.

"We can go to the police?"

"Not physically, but we can visit without leaving these seats. The man we are looking for was transporting a stolen object. He may not know the history of its original theft, but I believe he knows that what he carries was not legally obtained. That makes him a criminal. And most criminals at one time or another are arrested. And when they are arrested, they are photographed. And those photographs are stored . . ."

He paused to allow Kenji to finish for him.

"In their computer, of course." He smiled and nodded. "You very smart man."

The recognition program beeped, signaling it had finished.

"No, the very smart man here is the one who designed the software. I simply use the tools he has provided me."

Hideo didn't bother going into how the algorithms and templates would work in sequence through Police Plaza's database.

He entered the database—Kaze kept easy-open access to most of the city's major databases, mostly for tracking markets for advance warning on economic and currency trends. He set up the templates and let them loose.

"How long?" Kenji said.

"This could take very long. Why don't you check on Goro and Ryo and get some rest. I want to be able to move quickly should we get any hits."

Kenji gave a quick bow, and left. Hideo watched him go, thinking how that kid could go places—if he lived long enough.

When he was alone again, he popped another photo onto the screen: the *ronin*. It was only a three-quarter shot but often that was enough. He'd made positive IDs with less.

He started the recognition program and watched as dots and lines and numbers blotted out the stranger's face. Yoshio's notes had said he suspected the man he had dubbed *"ronin"* of being some sort of mercenary hired by Ronald Clayton's daughter for protection. If that was the case, then he too might have run afoul of the New York City authorities—weapons possession, perhaps. And if so, then his photo would be in the database as well.

He stared at the jumble of colors and numbers.

I will find you, *ronin*. And when I do I will ask you questions. And you will answer. Kenji, Goro, and Ryo will see to that.

6

Dawn paced the penthouse's great room.

"I neeeeeed to go shopping again, Henry. Come on!"

Instead of easing her restlessness, her brief taste of freedom yesterday had left her totally wanting more. Despite the size of Mr. Osala's place, it seemed smaller than ever.

Henry shook his head. "I'm afraid I dare not, miss. It was a terrible risk allowing you out yesterday without the Master's permission. I don't wish to push my luck."

"Well, then, *get* his permission. Or better yet, let me talk to him. I'll get him to come around."

Fat chance of that. Mr. Osala didn't strike her as the type she could move with a crying jag. But she'd give it the good old college try.

"As I told you, he is not always accessible."

"But you know where he is, right?"

"I know he's in North Carolina, but that isn't exactly pinpointing his location."

"I thought you said he was out hunting Jerry."

"I'm sure he has other concerns besides you. He called earlier to ask how you were faring and happened to mention that he was heading for North Carolina."

"What's he doing *there*?"

"He does not offer details of his activities and I do not ask. All he told me was he is doing research and 'setting the stage' for an extended project beginning in September."

"You must have an emergency number you can call."

He nodded. "I do. But the operative term there is *emergency*. A shopping trip hardly qualifies as an emergency."

"It does to me! Totally!"

He shook his head. "I'm sorry. I can't risk it again."

Dawn fumed as she watched him turn and walk away. She so wanted to kill him right now. But she wasn't through yet. She'd find a way to get him to take her out again.

And this time she wouldn't come back.

7

"I have found the perfect *shoten, sensei*," Tadasu said.

Shiro Kobayashi knew that was not quite accurate. Shiro had found him. But he didn't begrudge Tadasu the credit. He had been the leader, and if they had failed, the shame would have fallen on him.

Besides, for years Tadasu had instructed him in the use of the tanto, the katana, the bo, and nunchaku. He had been stern but seemed to care only that Shiro learned well. And Shiro had. He was now almost as good as Tadasu.

Akechi-*sensei* nodded from where he stood by the classroom window, staring out at the day.

"Is he, as I instructed, in a weakened state?"

"Yes, *sensei*. We have him locked in an empty storeroom. Do you wish to see?"

Akechi-*sensei* turned and faced them. Only his eyes were visible through his silk mask, which puffed slightly as he spoke.

"I do indeed wish to see this fortunate soul who shall be privileged to serve the Hidden Face."

The Hidden Face . . . seeing it was the focus, the ultimate goal of every member of the Kakureta Kao. Yet to achieve that goal, one had to pass through the Inner Circles of the Order. That took dedication, resolve, will . . . and sacrifice. Eventually, the ultimate sacrifice for the ultimate reward.

Shiro greatly admired his teacher, and would sacrifice his life for the Order. But he was not so sure—at least not as sure as he had been in his younger days—that he wished to progress beyond the Fourth Circle. Because that was when the surgeries began: the flaps, the castration, losing limbs and senses one by one until . . .

Until all contact with the world except the air in the lungs was severed. Only then could one see the Hidden Face and, joining it in death, know everything.

Shiro yearned to see the Hidden Face at death, but was more than willing to wait before joining it in the Eternal Void. He had just recently passed his twenty-second birthday and was hoping to ascend from acolyte to temple guard.

If so, he intended to spend many years in loyal service at that post. Perhaps in his later years—much later years—he would ascend to the Inner Circles, but for now he wished to preserve all his senses and body parts.

He and Tadasu led their teacher to the storeroom. Along the way they passed one of Shiro's fellow acolytes wheeling a wooden cart holding a masked monk in a blue robe. He had no legs and no eyes. Shiro knew him as the Seer.

When they reached the storeroom, Shiro opened the door and the odor slapped him in the face. The man sprawled on the floor smelled as if he had not bathed since the Tokugawa Shogunate. They had brought him here from his cardboard house under a Brooklyn overpass. Although he had traveled in the trunk of one of the Order's cars, his presence had fouled the air of the passenger area. They had been forced to drive with the windows open.

The man was a bearded Caucasian of indeterminate age, but he was quite content where he was. Shiro and Tadasu had provided him with a large bottle of Jack Daniel's. He had already consumed half of it.

He studied Akechi-*sensei* with bleary eyes, then grinned, showing rotted teeth.

"Is it Halloween already? I dig the mask." He lifted the bottle in a mock toast. "Trick or treat!"

"We have done well, *sensei*?"

At least he said "we" this time.

Akechi-*sensei* nodded as Shiro gratefully closed the door. "He will make a good trial *shoten*. We want a small Kuroikaze for our test. He will not survive the strain for long."

The Kuroikaze . . . the Black Wind. Shiro had heard of it since childhood when his father had handed him over to the monks of the Kakureta Kao. But no one alive had actually seen one, so it remained a formless legend. A legend he knew by heart.

In the sixteenth century, the shoguns imprisoned the Emperor in Kyoto while they ruled as they wished. After Nobunaga took control he began killing off all who supported the Emperor. He made a special target of the Order, which had been agitating for restoration of the Imperial Line. According to legend, Susanoo, the Sword God, the direct ancestor of the Emperor, created the Kakureta Kao in the time of Jimmu, the first Emperor, and charged it with the mission of protecting the Son of Heaven, and preserving His power in the world.

Nobunaga's armies marched throughout Honshu, razing each of the Order's monasteries after slaughtering all the monks. Finally, only the oldest, largest, and best fortified monastery—in Nanao on Honshu's west coast—remained. Under siege, the remnants of the Kakureta Kao delved into the cache of ancient lore that was their legacy from the God of Swords, and found a means to defend themselves.

As the shogun's armies neared the gates of the monastery, a darkness descended and a mystical wind rose up around the temple. Some called it The-Wind-That-Bends-Not-the-Trees, some said it was another *Kamikaze*, or "Divine Wind" like the one that sank Kubla Khan's invading fleet at the end of the thirteenth century. But those in the Order knew it as the *Kuroikaze*—the "Black Wind." The legends didn't say exactly what happened, but when the Kuroikaze was done, half of the shogunate's army lay dead on the field, with the rest in retreat.

Nobunaga left the Kakureta Kao alone after that.

But the Order never fully recovered. It consolidated into a single temple in Tokyo not far from the Imperial Palace. During the Second World War it once again used the Black Wind against the Emperor's enemies, and might have changed the course of the war had it not made the fatal error of relocating to Hiroshima.

"Tomorrow night we shall test the *ekisu*. I have found the perfect place, right here on this island, almost within sight of our ultimate target."

Shiro asked, "Why New York City, *sensei*? Why not Washington?"

Recently he had explored the city in search of the compounds necessary for the *ekisu*. During his travels he had become enamored of Manhattan—so full of life and motion. He felt energized whenever he set foot there.

"Washington may be the seat of the American government, but New York City is its engine. It is the heart that pumps economic life throughout the rest of the country, and even into the rest of the world. Kill New York City and not only do we drive this foul nation to its economic knees, but we deal a death blow to its spirit."

Shiro was not so sure about that, but who was he to doubt his sensei?

Tadasu said, "Pardon, *sensei,* but will we truly be able to level Manhattan using such a miserable excuse for a human being as a *shoten*?"

Shiro saw the skin around Akechi-*sensei*'s eyes crinkle behind his mask holes, a sign he'd come to recognize as a smile. "We once thought the *ekisu* effective only when used with a child. We have since learned that any living human, no matter how miserable, can serve as a *shoten*. And as for Manhattan, we shall not level it. The Kuroikaze will do much worse. Tomorrow night you shall see."

8

From outside, the Fifth Quarter looked pretty much like every other Irish pub Jack had seen. Inside, two steps down from street level, it looked pretty much like every other sports bar he'd seen: oval bar in the center, a ring of wide-screen TVs above it, high pub tables and stools near the bar, regular tables and chairs farther out, booths along the walls. And more TV screens in every corner.

Each and every screen was running the Mets game—they were leading the Phillies four-zip. Jack had been a Phillies fan as a kid. Now it was Go Mets.

"There she is," Bobblehead said, pointing toward the twenty-something teased blonde behind the bar. "Thank God it's her shift."

He hurried ahead of Jack, demonstrating—in case anyone might have forgotten—the origin of his street name.

By the time Jack reached the bar, Suzy had her phone out and was doing a two-thumb tap dance on the keypad.

"I kept somma them," she said in a thick Nassau County accent. "Most was so blurry I ditched them right off."

Bobble glanced ceilingward with a *please-please-please* look.

"Hope you kept some of me," he said, turning back to Suzy. "My mother wants to see a recent picture, and I think the best kind to send her is one of me having fun with my friends. Hey, y'got one of me and Hughie? He was in rare form Saturday."

Suzy grinned. "Should've been. He picked the winner." More button pressing. "Let's see here. Hey, here's you and Artie."

"Nah. Where's the one with me and Hughie?"

"Here's you with Joey from Ohio."

"You must be one photogenic guy," Jack said. "Everyone wants a picture with you."

"Yeah, I'm a photo ho. Look, Suze—"

"Here's the last one of you—with Laurie this time."

Bobble glanced at it with a disappointed expression, started to look away, then grabbed the phone for a closer look.

"Hey!" Suzy said.

He handed it back. "Sorry. Any way I can get a copy of that?"

"I can send it to your cell phone."

"Ain't got a cell phone."

She looked at him as if a third eye had just appeared in his forehead. "You're kidding, right?"

"Wish I were." He turned to Jack. "You?"

"Yeah, but you sure you want a picture of you and this Laurie?"

"Oh, yeah." He lowered his voice. "And so do you."

"Great," Suzy said. "I'll zap it to you now."

Jack pulled out one of his trusty old TracFones. "Never done that. How's it work?"

Suzy launched into a wire-head word salad about texting and attaching the photo file to a text message, then sending the message to Jack's phone, blah-blah-blah. It left him feeling like he was standing on a platform watching the technology train pull out of the station.

He held up his phone. "All I do with this is make calls."

She took it, looked it over, grimaced as if she'd just picked up a handful of spoiled meat, then quickly handed it back.

"That's about all you *can* do with that dinosaur. You need an emergency upgrade." To Bobble: "I'll have to e-mail it to your computer instead." She stopped. "You *do* have a computer, don't you?"

Bobble shook his head and turned to Jack again. "You?"

"Yeah. Send it to: r-p-r-m-n-j-c-k at yahoo."

Suzy gave a wry smile as she tapped it into her phone. "Not only a computer but an e-mail address too. Wow. I'll upload it to the photo site and forward it to you later." Her tone made it sound as if she'd been asked to use a rotary phone.

Bet I can whip your butt in DNA Wars.

"You can't do it now?" Bobble said.

"Need to get to a computer for that."

Jack nudged Bobble. "I'll print it out so you can send it to your mother."

Actually, he'd have to have Russ print it out since Jack had never bothered to buy a printer. What for?

"Or if you want, I can send it straight to your mom."

"Thanks but she, um, doesn't have a computer either."

Suzy rolled her eyes. "Where's she live?"

"Um, Toronto."

Jack could tell he'd pulled that one out of the air.

She laughed. "Toronto! I've been there! I love Toronto! It's like another country."

A few heartbeats of silence, then Bobble said, "Oooooookay. We'll be going now, Suze. Don't forget to send that picture to my man, here."

"Right. See you here for the Belmont party? Or are you going out to the track?"

"I'm here, Suze."

She gave him a thumbs-up.

"Wow," Bobble said as they hit the street. "Another *country*? She knows all that techie stuff but doesn't know Toronto's in Michigan? I mean, people are so stupid these days."

Jack let it go.

"So why do we want a photo of you and this gal Laurie?"

Bobble grinned. "Because guess who's in the background, staring straight at the camera?"

"Our man Hughie?"

"None other."

Things were looking up.

"Neat," Jack said. "Old Hughie got Zaprudered."

Bobble said, "Zapwha?"

"Never mind."

9

Hideo knocked on the door a third time. It needed painting. In fact, the whole apartment building needed a makeover. He shook off the thought. His need for orderliness sometimes distracted him from the matter at hand.

And what mattered here was getting past this door.

He heard movement on the other side. The three yakuza flanked the doorframe, out of range of the peephole. Though dressed in suits and ties, they looked anything but respectable. Yakuza . . . the word meant "good for nothing," and that quality shone through. Each might as well have had another tattoo on the forehead announcing "hoodlum."

But Hideo had no idea what he'd run into on the far side of the door, and so was glad to have them along.

The facial recognition software had done its job half well. In the NYPD database it had found mug shots of a brown-haired man named Hugh Gerrish, arrested for breaking and entering two years ago. They matched perfectly the face on the security cam. Gerrish had pleaded out to an illegal-trespass charge and been given probation with no jail time. The file listed this apartment in Brooklyn's Greenpoint area as his address.

The software had not, however, found the *ronin*. Rather, it had found too many of them. One hundred twenty-seven hits, each of them resembling the *ronin*. Either his features were very common, or the only existing photo was not detailed enough for an accurate search. Perhaps both. Hideo would have to work on a way to narrow the selection.

"I'm coming, I'm coming," said an old woman's voice from within. Her accent was Spanish. A few seconds later the peephole darkened and he heard: "Who are you?"

Gerrish's mother, perhaps? Hideo was prepared for this.

"Police, ma'am," he said, holding a gold NYPD detective's badge up to the peephole. "We need to speak to you about your son."

"Madre de Dios!"

A chain rattled, the knob turned, and the door opened. A wizened, gray-haired old woman in a stained housedress looked up at him with frightened eyes.

"Mi Julio! What has happened?"

Hideo had a sudden bad feeling about this. Hugh Gerrish hadn't looked the least bit Hispanic. He pushed open the door and motioned the yakuza inside. The old woman backed up a step and opened her mouth to scream but Hideo pressed a finger firmly against her lips.

"Silence, please. We mean you no harm." When she took a breath as if to scream anyway, he held up his other hand in a stop sign. "Please."

She stayed silent.

Beyond, in the tiny apartment, Hideo heard a cacophony of doors and drawers opening and closing. It lasted less than a minute, and then Kenji was beside him.

"Empty, Takita-san," he said in Japanese. "And no katana."

"How many bedrooms?"

"One."

Hideo nodded as a sinking feeling dragged on his gut.

"The closets—any men's clothes?"

He shook his head. "Only woman's. And not much of that."

Goro and Ryo appeared, the latter holding up a framed photograph. Hideo took it and saw the old woman with her cheek pressed against that of a dark-haired, dark-skinned young man who looked nothing like Hugh Gerrish. He showed it to her.

"Who is this?"

She snatched it from him. *"Mi Julio."* Tears rimmed her eyes. "What has happened to him?"

"Nothing. He is fine. We have made a mistake."

"Mistake?" she said, her tone and expression growing indignant. "You break into my home and frighten—"

"How long have you lived here?"

"Since September."

Eight months. Gerrish must have moved out last summer. Hideo suppressed a curse and masked his frustration as he pulled a wad of bills from his pocket.

"We have disturbed you and wasted five minutes of your time." He peeled off five hundred-dollar bills and pressed them into her hands. "I trust this will help you forgive us."

She gazed at the bills as if he'd given her a fortune. Perhaps to her it was. To him it was merely an expense he would charge to Kaze.

What had seemed so straightforward and easy yesterday was proving digressive and difficult. He had run into obstacles, but none he could not surmount.

As Americans liked to say: Back to the drawing board.

10

Shouldn't be too hard to spot, Jack thought, studying the face in the photo as he walked west along East 96th Street.

He'd just left Russ Tuit, his go-to guy for all things computer. Russ had downloaded the photo, cropped out Bobblehead and the inebriated-looking Laurie, sharpened and enlarged the guy behind them, and printed it out. Still kind of blurry, but serviceable.

Hugh Gerrish had a round, florid face topped by wavy brown hair that scooped down into a sharp widow's peak. The outstanding feature was a big diamond stud stuck in his left earlobe. Jack wished he had more of a view of his body to help spot him from a distance, but this would work.

He'd checked the post time at Belmont: first race one o'clock except Fridays when it moved to three P.M. The track was closed today so he'd have to wait till tomorrow.

"Jack?"

A woman's voice. He looked around and saw a slim blonde in her midtwenties, looking much younger because of her pigtails and her getup. She wore a white oxford shirt with a loose, askew tie, a plaid pleated miniskirt, white knee socks, and high-heel Mary Janes. Only a few of the shirt buttons were fastened, exposing her diamond-studded navel.

Jack stared, dumbfounded. "Do I—?"

She smiled and batted her heavily mascaraed, blue-shadowed eyes. "It's me. Junie. Junie Moon. We met—"

"Right-right. Gia's friend. How are you?"

They'd met last summer when Junie had been a guest at a Brooklyn party celebrating a big sale of one of her paintings. But she hadn't looked like jailbait then.

"Fine. Things have cooled down a little, but still better than I'd ever dreamed."

Nathan Lane had bought one of her paintings and publicly raved about it and suddenly her canvases were going for twenty K apiece. Jack had never seen any of her work but Gia said she was good.

"You're looking . . . different."

"Like it?" She struck a pose. "Marketing. All marketing." She stepped closer. "I saw Gia last week."

"You did?"

"She didn't tell you?"

"No."

Jack wondered why not.

"Must've forgot. I finally got the nerve to stop by. I'm such a slut of a friend. I mean, here she's been like my big sister for years, but I couldn't bring myself to stop by after the accident. I just couldn't stand seeing her hurt."

"She's pretty much back to normal now."

Junie shook her head. "Not really."

Jack felt a sinking sensation. "What do you mean?"

"Her art, my brotha. Her paintings. They're . . ."

"She showed you?"

"Well, ya-ah. We're both artists, you know. Why wouldn't she?"

It stung knowing Gia would share them with someone else but not him. Maybe the artist connection explained it, but still . . .

"I haven't seen them."

"Oh, shit. You two aren't on the outs, are you? Because if you've hurt her—"

"Never in a million years. She just doesn't want me to see them."

"Yeah, well, maybe I can see why."

"Want to give me a hint?"

"They're not her."

"What's that supposed to mean?"

"They're not like anything she's ever painted. They're . . . dark. You know how Gia's stuff has always been sunny, with all that Hopperesque bright light and shadow. Now it's mostly shadow. I think that accident changed her, Jack. I mean, you talk to her, she seems the same, but those paintings . . ." She looked uncomfortable. "They aren't from the Gia I knew."

They chatted awhile longer, with Junie monologuing and Jack monosyllabling, barely hearing what she said.

Those paintings . . . he had to get a look at Gia's paintings.

11

"Glenn! Glenn!"

Glaeken stood at the living room window, watching the stretched shadow of his building inch across Central Park's Sheep Meadow.

Glenn . . . he was glad Magda had forgotten his real name. Wouldn't do to have her calling "Glaeken!" a thousand times a day. Glenn, Glaeken, Veilleur, and all the other names he'd adopted down through the ages. Sometimes he lost track of who he was supposed to be.

Used to be he could always return to "Glaeken," but no longer. In his mind these days he'd become simply *Veilleur*.

"Coming, my dear."

The voice had come from the kitchen, as were sounds of rattling cookware now. He headed that way and found Magda standing by the granite-topped island, staring at the open cabinets in confusion.

Her white hair was neatly combed, thanks to the visiting homemaker who had just left. Her weight loss over the past few years or so accentuated the stoop of her shoulders. She wore a sweater as usual, because she was always cold.

"My kitchen!" she cried, her Hungarian accent thicker than before the decline had begun. "Glenn, what's happened to my kitchen?"

"Nothing, Magda. It's just as it always is."

A vision of a younger Magda took shape before him. Soft, smooth skin; long, chestnut hair; dark, gleaming eyes so full of wit and intelligence. That Magda was gone, but his love for her remained. He heard echoes of her voice as she sang, of her mandolin as she played, the sight of her bent over her typewriter as she wrote.

Another vision . . . Magda facing down the greatest evil . . . defying everything Rasalom could throw at her . . . terrified, horrified, repulsed, yet holding out, blocking his way until Glaeken could gather strength enough to take her place.

The memory of her courage and her unyielding trust that he would not let her down constricted his throat—now as much as then.

But two years ago her memory began to fail. She noticed it first. Then he noticed her making notes about the simplest things. He knew what it meant. And it crushed him.

The one woman across his eons with whom he could grow old was failing, becoming less and less the woman he'd fallen in love with. He refused to allow the splendid life they'd lived, the glowing love they'd shared to be tainted by her decline. He would never leave her, never give up on her. He would be with her until the end.

And perhaps that end was not too far off.

For both of them.

For everyone.

"But how can I cook dinner?"

He stepped to her side. "We've already had dinner."

She looked at him. "No! We couldn't. I'm still hungry."

"We had lamb chops, roasted red potatoes, and string beans. You cleaned your plate."

"No, I—"

"I cut your meat for you, remember?"

She closed her eyes and took a deep, shuddering breath. They were moist when she opened them.

"I do remember." She squeezed his forearm. "Oh, Glenn, I'm making it so hard on you."

He patted her hand. "Not at all, my love."

"But why am I still hungry?"

"Perhaps you didn't eat enough."

Her eating habits had become bizarre. She would be famished after a big meal, and then go most of the following day without eating anything—needing to be talked into sitting down for dinner.

"How about some ice cream? We have chocolate, your favorite."

She shook her head. "I need something more . . . more . . ." She frowned, searching for the word.

"Substantial?"

"Yes!" She brightened. "I'll have Miranda fix me some scrambled eggs."

Miranda had been their housekeeper six years ago.

"Miranda's not here, but I'll fix them."

She clapped her hands like a delighted child. "Wonderful! And you'll fix them the way I like them?"

He nodded. "With grated asiago. Of course."

He pulled out a frying pan and began melting a pat of butter. He'd cooked countless meals down the seemingly endless years and had become skilled at it.

He knew if Magda followed her usual pattern, her appetite would be gone by the time the eggs were ready. And then he'd eat them. He'd have to. He'd been hungry too many times, sagging against death's door more than once from starvation, ever to throw away food.

But that was all right. He made excellent scrambled eggs.

12

What the—?

It had happened again.

Jack sat at his round oak table and stared at the page he'd bookmarked in the *Compendium of Srem*. Nobody knew the book's age. He'd heard it was from the First Age, but no one could prove that, and the people with the credentials to do some sort of backgrounding on it believed it was a myth. After all, only one copy existed, and Jack had it. He'd been told it was indestructible, that Grand Inquisitor Torquemada had tried everything—fire, sword, ax, and anything else he could think of—but had been unable to destroy it. Finally he'd given up and buried it beneath a monastery. But it hadn't stayed buried.

All very odd, but the oddest thing about the *Compendium* was that everyone who opened it found it written in his or her native tongue.

Jack had bookmarked the section on the Seven Infernals the other day and decided tonight would be a good time to check out a weird-looking contraption he'd seen there that looked oddly familiar . . . displayed in a sideshow, long ago. But now, when he opened to the page, he found himself in another section.

Impossible that someone could have moved the bookmark, because he was the only one in the apartment, the only one for weeks.

He started paging through, looking for the Infernals again, but could find no trace of them. Instead he found pages he'd never seen before. He'd read a lot of the book—understanding little—and had flipped through it a number of times, but now he was finding whole sections he'd never even glimpsed before.

This wasn't the first time. What was this thing? Could it be sentient?

He slapped the book closed and pushed it to the center of the table. Damn thing was heavy.

He leaned back and tried to let his mind go blank, but an aching need popped Gia into his head. He saw her . . . he heard her . . . the sounds she made when they were in bed. She wasn't a wailer, not a screamer, not an oh-godder . . . just soft little moans, almost like whimpers, from way back in her throat. He felt her nails raking his back when he was in her, heard the rasp of those nails as they raked the sheets when he was down on her.

He had to go back. He couldn't stay away any longer.

WEDNESDAY

1

Usually Gia avoided mention of Emma and rarely visited her at St. Ann's. But every once in a while she felt the need to stand over her daughter's grave and speak a few words to her.

Jack understood that—all too well. What he'd never understood was why she had insisted on this particular cemetery. St. Ann's was in Bayside, way out in the far eastern hinterlands of Queens. Practically in Nassau County. The reasons had been cryptic: Because Emma had communicated during Gia's coma that she wanted a view of the water . . . and wanted to be here to comfort someone. Who that someone might be, Gia couldn't say, because Emma had never told her.

And now Gia had forgotten the dreams and that she'd ever said those things. The memories were gone but Emma would remain at St. Ann's till whenever.

Other memories . . . of the burial . . . crashed around him. The snow-covered grass, the hard-frozen ground, the cutting wind, the tiny white coffin . . .

And no Gia. Although she and Vicky were recovering from their comas and injuries at what every doctor and nurse in New York Hospital had called "a miraculous pace," they remained in the trauma unit. Emma needed burial but no way could they venture out of intensive care. Which left all the funeral arrangements to Jack.

Looking back now he recalled little of his meeting with the undertaker, or arranging the burial plot out here in Bayside. He'd been too numb. He vaguely remembered Abe, Julio, Alicia Clayton, Lyle Kenton, and a few others at the graveside. Father Edward Halloran had somehow heard about Emma and showed up, insisting on saying a few words over the grave.

And so whenever Gia wanted to visit, Jack would take her. Because he needed a visit now and again too, and didn't like the idea of her alone in a cemetery.

He'd been planning to call her this morning when the phone rang and there she was, asking if he'd drive her.

Perfect.

She sat on the ground now, running her hand through the new grass over Emma's grave. Her lips were moving in silence. Jack wondered what she was saying to her unborn child, the daughter she'd known only from within her.

To give her some space, he wandered off across the grass with no particular destination. St. Ann's Cemetery was small and old, crowded with headstones dating back a hundred years or more. As he wound among them, reading the inscriptions, he heard a male voice cursing in Spanish. He'd never studied Spanish, but a few years working for a local landscaper had taught him how to curse and swear in the language.

He headed in that direction and found a gardener kicking at the dirt of a bare patch near the high stone wall. When the man realized he had an audience, he stopped and flashed Jack a sheepish, gold-flecked grin.

"Excuse my words, *señor*." He gestured at the headstones. "Especially here among the dead."

Jack shrugged. "I haven't heard any complaints. What were you kicking there?"

"This ground . . . nothing will grow on it. I mix in the finest topsoil, I seed it, I water it, yet no grass will grow. I put sod down, it dies. I become very angry."

"I saw that. Ever think of trying some ground cover?"

"I have planted periwinkle, pachysandra, and ivy. They all die. I think the soil is poisoned, so I dig down six inches, bring in new earth. Still the same. Nothing will live here. Not plants, not even ants. Nothing."

Jack stared down at the four-foot oblong patch of bare ground. It looked like normal topsoil. The grass around it was in beautiful shape. Just this one patch . . .

He spotted a beetle scurrying through the grass toward the bald spot. He watched it veer left just before it reached it. The bug walked around to the far side of the patch, then continued on its way.

A chill ran over Jack's skin. What the hell was wrong with that patch of ground that even bugs wouldn't cross it? Had something been spilled there? Or more unsettling, was something buried there?

"I've got your solution," Jack said. "Astroturf."

The gardener shook his head. "No. I shall win. This dirt will not beat me."

Jack waved and headed back toward Gia and Emma. "Good luck."

He found Gia waiting for him on a rise.

"Ready?"

She took a deep shuddering breath and nodded. "Why?"

"Why what?"

"Why do I have to come here to be with her? Why isn't she with me? Why did this have to happen?"

"I wish I could tell you, Gia."

And that was true to the extent that Jack found himself unable to speak the words that would answer her question.

He still hadn't found the right time to tell her the truth. Maybe he'd never find the right time to say, *Because of me, because of your importance to me, because some cosmic something beyond knowing thought it could better use me if you and Vicky and Emma weren't around.*

As he took her hand and they started back toward the car, he remembered how Gia had said the dream-Emma wanted to be here at St. Ann's "to comfort someone."

He looked back at the gardener raking up the soil of the bare spot.

Could it be . . . ?

Nah.

"I want to come home with you, Gi. Vicky's at school so I was hoping maybe we could . . ."

"Talk?"

"Yes. Talk. And do other stuff."

"Other stuff?"

"Other stuff."

"I am in need of other stuff, Jack. Especially after being here. I need to lose myself for a little while."

"Me too."

She smiled that smile. "Goody."

2

Hideo had wanted to search further through the police database last night but the need for sleep and the time zone change had caught up with him. He'd awakened late this morning fully refreshed and ready for the next step.

His target was anyone connected with Hugh Gerrish. First was to search for a list of "known associates," but he could find no such list. Perhaps because Gerrish had never been a fugitive. He had served no jail time, so there was no cellmate Hideo could look up.

He went back to the crime itself and found the arrest record. His spirits lifted as he read through it: Gerrish had not been alone on the break and enter. He'd been captured along with a man named Alonzo Cooter.

Hideo searched the database for that name and found the mug shot. A beefy, surly black face stared back at him. Not a cooperative face. The belligerence in his eyes said he was not a man who would frighten easily.

But that was what the yakuza were for.

He called for Kenji, then hit the print button. While he was waiting, Hideo found Cooter's last known address—he hoped it was good—and printed that screen too. Then he scanned through Kaze Group's properties in the five boroughs. Cooter lived in the South Bronx. Kaze owned a boarded-up building awaiting demolition near Yankee Stadium. Cooter lived less than a mile away.

"Takita-san," Kenji said with a quick bow upon arrival.

Hideo wrote the building's address on one of the printouts, then handed him the sheets.

"Find this man. Bring him to this address. Then call me."

Another quick bow and Kenji was gone.

Hideo nodded. Complications had been encountered and overcome. Soon he would be talking to Hugh Gerrish.

Now . . . if only he could find the *ronin*.

He called up the mystery man's photo and stared at it, trying to devise a way to track him down.

And he would. Hideo was sure of it.

3

"As nice as that was, it's not an explanation."

Gia lay to his left on the bed, head on hand, propped on an elbow, gazing at him as she trailed fingers through his chest hair.

Jack laughed. "Nice? *Nice*? It was fantastic. At least for me."

He wasn't kidding. He loved pleasuring her with his fingertips, his lips, his tongue, and she'd experienced a couple of little deaths along the way, but after they'd fitted themselves together, Gia had taken over with an uncharacteristic hunger that left him feeling as if he'd been dissected organ by organ and then reassembled.

She smiled. "Okay, it was fantastic for me too."

"What did you do to me?"

"I'm not sure. It's kind of fuzzy now."

"Whatever it was, I think I'm going to need a walker to get out of here."

"Sorry. No walkers around. Only Nellie's old cane."

"I'll take it."

He closed his eyes relishing the touch of her fingers on his chest. He felt wiped out.

"Well?"

He looked at her and saw her expectant expression. No way out of this. He'd have to tell her something, and it had to be the truth. He wasn't going to start lying to her.

He glanced at the clock. He wanted to get to Belmont noonish. Still plenty of time, so he couldn't use that as an excuse.

He raised a finger and began tracing concentric circles on her left breast, languidly gyring toward the nipple.

"A rosy-tipped breast, as the novels like to say."

She pushed his hand away. "That tickles. And if you're trying to distract me, it might work, so stop it and tell what's been going on."

Jack sighed. Where to begin?

"Last month I learned that I have big chunks of bad DNA floating around my chromosomes." He didn't mention that she and Vicky carried a little of it too. That everyone did to varying degrees.

She frowned. "'Bad'? What's wrong with it?"

"It's not normal. It gives people . . . violent tendencies."

There. He'd laid it on the table.

Gia's expression remained neutral, registering neither shock nor fear nor revulsion.

"Oh."

"And I've got a lot of it."

"Oh."

After a silence that seemed to last forever she took a breath. "Well, I guess that explains some things—at least it's a hint as to why you're good at what you do—but it doesn't explain your gentleness around here. You're a pussycat with Vicky."

"She owns me."

"And you've never once raised your voice against me, let alone your hand, so why have you—?"

"It feels like a ticking bomb."

"You can *feel* it?"

"No, but just knowing it's there, inside me . . ." At a loss for words, he shrugged. "I don't know."

"But I think I do. You're afraid it will hurt us?"

"No. I seem to be able to control it—most times. I have no doubt that you're safe. But anyone who threatens that safety . . ." He thought of all the dead yeniçeri back in January. "They're on the endangered species list."

Her brow furrowed. "Then what? You can't infect us with it."

"No, but I just injected you with some."

She looked puzzled for a few heartbeats, then, "Oh." Her eyes widened. "*Oh*. Emma."

"Yeah. Emma."

"You think she inherited some of this bad DNA?"

"How could she not? She was half me."

Another long silence, then, "Well, it's kind of scary, but it's moot, isn't it. Emma's gone and I don't want to—I can't go through that again. I'd get my tubes tied if it mattered."

"Why doesn't it matter? Because of those coma dreams?"

She nodded.

She'd come out of the coma this way, sure that the future was short—very short. Veilleur had mentioned something along those lines, and someone he knew who said he could see the future had told him next spring ended in darkness.

When Gia had been on death's threshold, had she peeked through and seen what was coming?

Did that mean Rasalom was going to win?

He shook it off.

"Look, if anyone's getting tubes tied it's going to be me."

She smiled. "That's sweet, but it doesn't matter."

"Please stop saying that."

"Well, it's true, but I'll stop saying it."

She rose from the bed. Jack stared at her. He loved Gia's body—the breasts that fit his hands so perfectly, the curve of her hips, the slight swell of her belly. He wanted to reach out and grab her and pull her back.

She'd taken it well. Seemed like he'd been worried about nothing. But a vasectomy . . . that was a thought. He didn't want his oDNA going any further.

He glanced at the clock. Time was moving.

"Hey, Gi? How should I dress for my day at the races?"

4

Gia had thought he should dress down, and suggested his construction worker look: worn jeans, flannel shirt, work boots, Mets cap, dollar-store sunglasses.

He drove the Long Island Expressway the entire length of Queens and crossed the border into Nassau County where Belmont Park occupies a large chunk of Elmont. He arrived a little past noon. Post time for the first race wasn't until one o'clock, so he had time to settle in. He decided against valet parking, and chose the preferred lots instead, in case he needed his car in a hurry.

His big problem—besides having nothing more than a blurry photo of his quarry—was not knowing where Gerrish was coming from, or how. The Long Island Railroad's Bellerose stop was only a short distance away. If Gerrish didn't have a car, that might be the way he'd come and go.

From the outside, the patriotic bunting–bedecked grandstand was pretty much like he remembered it from the old days, except the ivy had spread farther across the brick walls and around the big arched windows.

He bought a clubhouse admission and a program, and strolled the flagstone floors, checking out the Neiman manqué paintings on the walls as he refamiliarized himself with the place.

He took the escalator up to the second floor and found a Sbarro's. That hadn't been here before.

He ordered a slice of pepperoni pie and hung at the counter where he could keep watch on the traffic at the betting windows. Jack was betting on Gerrish being a clubhouse kind of guy—if he was as flush as he'd told folks, he wouldn't hang outside with the hoi polloi. That meant sooner or later he'd show up here.

Melancholy seeped into his mood as he watched the thin, drab, sad-looking crowd, mostly middle age or older, go through the motions. No zip, no vim or vigor. He seemed to remember a livelier crowd, Runyonesque flashy dressers with style and attitude. But memories are unreliable, tending to be colored by wishful thinking. Maybe it had never been like he thought he remembered. But either way, these folks had more in common with Willie Loman than Sky Masterson and Nathan Detroit.

Around 12:45, after doing flybys to check out a couple of guys who turned out to be almost-but-not-quites, Jack spotted a likely candidate lining up at a window. He had a round, florid face and wore dark blue nylon warm-up pants with white stripes under a loud Hawaiian shirt acrawl with birds of paradise. Brown, wavy hair stuck out below the edge of his Rangers cap.

Could be.

Jack slipped the photo from his pocket and gave it a quick look.

Yeah. A definite possibility. Even had the big diamond stud earring. Trouble was, he wore wraparound shades and had his cap pulled down almost to his eyebrows. The Hugh Gerrish in the photo had a wicked widow's peak, but this guy's hat was obscuring his hairline. Jack needed a way to sneak a peek at the peak.

He hurried over and slipped behind him in the betting line.

"Rangers fan, huh?"

The guy turned and looked at him. "You got a problem with that? You gonna give me some Islander shit?"

The Islanders had just won the Stanley Cup and Ranger fans were not happy.

Jack smiled. "Hey, easy. I'm a Ranger guy too." Lie. Jack hated hockey. He hated high fives almost as much, but held up his hand for one. "Next year the cup is ours."

The guy smiled and gave Jack's raised palm a good-natured slap.

"From your lips to God's ear."

Jack made a point of staring at his cap. "That's a nice one. Where'd you get it? The Garden?"

He nodded. "Cost an arm and a leg but worth every penny."

"Yeah. Nice quality. Wonder who made it. Mind if I see the label?"

"Sure."

The guy took it off, revealing a huge widow's peak. Jack couldn't help staring at it.

Lily, call Herman—we've found Eddie.

"I thought you wanted to see it."

Jack shook himself and took the proffered hat, pretended to look at the label, then handed it back.

"Cool. Thanks. Gotta get me one. You live in the city?"

A suspicious light sparked in his eyes as he fit the cap back on his head. "Why you wanna know?"

Jack put on a flustered look. "No particular reason. Just wish I could get into the Garden more. Get me one of those hats."

The suspicious light faded. "I'm in Jamaica. The train takes me right into Penn."

"Yeah?" Jack's mind raced. "I'm in Jamaica too. Briarwood, actually. Put everything I had into a tiny two-bedroom ranch nine years ago and am I ever glad."

Gerrish nodded. "You must be sitting pretty. But, hey. It's just as easy for you to get to the Garden as me."

Jack shook his head. "Not at night . . . the wife don't like me going out at night."

He snorted a laugh. "Been there, done that. That's why she's now my *ex-wife*."

They shared a manly *heh-heh-heh* and then came Gerrish's turn at the window.

Jack leaned close to listen in, planning to bet the same horse. Gerrish supposedly knew his ponies, and winning would give Jack a chance to reconnect with him at the payout. But a glance over the bird of paradise on his shoulder gave him a shock. No human being at the window. Some sort of cash register sat there instead.

When did this happen?

He watched in dismay as Gerrish worked the thing like an accountant on an adding machine, then took the ticket that popped out and started to walk away.

"Luck to you," Jack said.

Gerrish didn't turn. "Yeah. Same."

As Gerrish moved off, Jack stepped up to the machine and studied it for a few seconds. He had no idea what to do, and no time to figure it out, so he faked working it, then walked off in the same general direction as Gerrish.

5

Dawn sat chin deep in the hot tub and stared at Henry.

"You mean you still haven't changed your mind?"

"It's not a matter of changing my mind, miss. It's simply that I have not been able to reach the Master and do not have permission. I would help if I could but I cannot risk it again. I break out in a sweat just thinking about what could have happened."

What was it with this guy? Didn't he have any balls?

Balls . . . there was a thought. Henry seemed like totally sexless. She never caught him looking at her. Not once.

What would stiff-and-staid Henry do if she totally came on to him? He looked to be like fifty—like two and a half times her age. But big deal. She'd been living with a pervo twice her age and doing him every night.

She bit back a surge of acid as her stomach tried to hurl. Don't think about that. You've got that perv's baby inside you and the only way you're going to get rid of it is to get out of this place.

She could do Henry. If she could do that perv she could do anyone. And it would only be once. She'd let him think it would be a regular thing, but no way.

How did that phrase go? Quid pro quo? Yeah. She hadn't gotten straight A's at Benedictine Academy without paying attention in Latin class.

If she did something for him, he'd have to do something for her if he wanted a replay. But no replay. This time if she got out she would be so not coming back.

Did she dare? She'd feel like such a loser if he turned her down. But she had to risk it. She had this awful feeling that her future depended on it.

She opened her mouth to speak but no words of seduction would come.

Hey. Maybe she could seduce him with money. She had a quarter of a million in cash in her room.

"Henry? What if I paid you for a shopping trip?"

"I beg your pardon?"

"What if I totally paid you ten thousand dollars to take me out for an hour?"

He looked offended. "You insult me, miss. I am *not* for sale."

She was about to double the offer but saw in his steely eyes that it would be a waste of time.

Okay. Time to bite the bullet, as it were.

Keeping her chin at water level, she reached behind her and unhooked the top of her bikini. She slipped out of it, releasing the girls, and pushed it under her. Next came the bottom.

Now . . . the big moment.

She rose to her feet and stood thigh deep in the bubbling water, facing Henry. She glanced down at her girls. The wet mounds glistened in the sunlight streaming through the windows. She could see the nipples rising in the chill room air. Maybe she was a little too thick in the waist, a little too wide in the hips, but she had great skin and she was like totally sure that hers was the best bod Henry had seen in a long, long time. She couldn't see her pubes right now but knew they looked sort of funny. Pervo Jerry had made her shave. Well, didn't force her, exactly. All he'd had to do was ask and she'd done it—like she'd done other things he'd asked. The hair was growing back now, looking like a three-day stubble.

She'd never asked herself why he'd wanted her bare there. Thought it was just some simple kink. Maybe even a hygiene thing, though he'd never shaved himself.

But knowing what she knew now, it was probably a way to make her look more like a child.

Her gorge rose again but she forced it back.

Focus, Dawnie. Focus.

She looked at Henry and saw that his jaw had totally dropped. The offended look in his eyes had given away to a sort of wonder and awe.

"Like what you see?"

Henry continued to stare in silence, his expression frozen.

She stepped toward him, trying to make her movements languid and sexy, hiding the urgency bubbling inside. If this was going to work, if this was even going to get done, it had to get started soon and end quickly. Before Gilda arrived to make sure Dawn didn't soak beyond her allotted twenty minutes.

She climbed the two steps up to floor level and stopped before him, dripping.

And still Henry said nothing. Maybe he'd been dreaming of sex with an eighteen-year-old. Maybe even younger.

"You got a problem with young stuff, Henry? If not, I'm about to make you a very happy man."

Ugh. That sounded awful. Still . . . she'd gotten her message across and he hadn't backed off. Hadn't moved toward her either.

Okay . . . looked like it was going to be all up to her.

She knelt before him and reached for his fly, hoping this wouldn't be too gross.

She felt a bulge behind the fabric as she tugged on the zipper.

Henry didn't move to stop her.

6

Gerrish had a seat in the clubhouse's reserved section but Jack had a good view of him from his spot. The guy bet on every race. Jack decided to keep his distance. He studied his copy of *Post Parade Magazine* and made a few mental bets of his own, but lost every single one—even when they were favorites.

He hoped he had better luck bird-dogging Gerrish home.

Jack made it a policy to follow Gerrish to the windows. He often collected wads of cash. Either the guy was dating Tyche on the side or really knew his ponies. After the next-to-last race he skipped the windows and headed for the exits.

Giving him a good lead, Jack followed him to the LIRR Bellerose station. He stayed out of sight until a westbound train pulled in. He waited for Gerrish to board, then hopped on two cars ahead of him. The train was fairly empty, so Jack moved back a car and sat where he could take an occasional peek at his quarry.

Gerrish got out at the Jamaica stop and walked east. With the sun still bright, Jack had no shadows to hide in, so he hopped out and walked behind a trio of chattering Ecuadorians, using them as a shield until they hit the street.

He allowed Gerrish a full block lead. The guy was a fast walker. Maybe these treks back and forth were the only exercise he got, so he made the most of them. A dozen quick blocks on Jamaica Avenue, then a left on Merrick past an old and gloriously ornate building called the Tabernacle of Prayer. Looked like a converted movie theater. Finally he stopped outside a six-story building—a beauty parlor and a Duane Reade drugstore on the first floor, and what looked like apartments above.

He watched Gerrish enter the building. By the time Jack reached the door he was gone. He peeked through the glass and saw rows of mailboxes. Excellent.

He waited around until an elderly black woman in a matching green jacket and skirt came by, lugging two plastic sacks of groceries. She put them down to take out her key. When she'd unlocked the door, Jack grabbed the handle and held it open for her.

She gave him a suspicious look. "You live here?"

He smiled. "Nah. Just waiting on a friend." He pointed to the bags. "Want help with those?"

"I can handle them."

"Well, at least let me get the other door."

He slipped into the foyer and held the inner door for her. She kept an eye on him, as if expecting him to jump her. She watched until the inner door had closed behind her, then headed for the elevator.

"You're welcome," Jack said.

He checked out the mailboxes, noted that 4D was labeled GERRISH.

Perfect.

He'd return after dark and pay ol' Hughie a visit. Find out if he still had the sword. If sold, he'd find out the name of the buyer. If not, he'd offer to buy it. If Hugh wasn't selling, Jack would take it.

Either way, like it or not, Hugh Gerrish would wake up tomorrow morning as the former owner of that sword.

As Jack stepped out onto the street he glanced back and saw the old woman watching him. He smiled and waved.

7

"Remember, miss. Only an hour."

"Sure, Henry."

Not.

Doing him had been kind of rough but not totally unbearable. Like maybe if you didn't look up or didn't think about who it was—like make believe it was someone you liked—you could get through. Even get into it maybe. Except Dawn didn't have anyone she really liked in that way—not anymore—so no way she'd been able to get into it.

But she'd gotten through it. That was what counted.

He'd never said a word. Just stood there like a statue through the whole thing. The only good thing—if anything good could be said about it—was that it hadn't taken long at all, like he was a guy who hadn't gotten any in a long time. The only sounds he'd made were some grunts at the end. And when he'd squirted all over her, at least it didn't mess up any clothes. After it was over he'd zipped up while she was still on her knees, turned, and left.

She got a little satisfaction out of seeing his legs wobble as he'd walked out, but otherwise she felt crushed. She'd made a whore of herself for nothing.

So she washed up—crying in the shower—and dressed, and was combing out her wet hair when he'd knocked on her door and said Gilda had left to go shopping. If Dawn wanted to go out, they had a window of two hours, so it had to be now. She'd stuffed her quarter mil in a shoulder bag and headed for the door.

She was surprised at how calm she was feeling about the whole thing. A little dirty, yeah, but it was over and done with now, and considering who she'd been having sex with before this, Henry was like a hot soapy shower.

Yeah, Henry . . . a total prince. No leering remarks, no familiar touching. Acted like it never happened. He was doing such a convincing job, she could almost make herself believe it hadn't.

Kind of a shame she was going to have to screw him in a totally different way this afternoon.

She'd had him drive her down to SoHo and cruise lower Broadway. Along the way she'd bargained—reasonably, she thought—to define the "hour" on the town as an hour of shopping, transit time not included. He'd reluctantly agreed. But when she tried to convince him to drop her off at one of the boutiques, he totally wouldn't.

"For your well-being—and that of my job—I cannot let you out of my sight."

She gazed out at the shopping bag–carrying throngs crowding the sidewalks and said, "Are they like giving stuff away?"

"It's the dollar, miss. Very cheap these days, which makes visiting the States and shopping here a real bargain."

Mixed among the foreigners—they didn't carry signs saying so but their clothing styles screamed *Not from here!*—were clusters of bridge-and-tunnel folks from the burbs and Jersey.

She didn't care where they came from, as long as there were lots of them. The more the merrier, and the easier it would be to disappear into their ranks.

When Henry pulled into a parking lot, she waited behind the tinted glass, adjusting her *pak chadar* while he took a ticket from the attendant. She put on her sunglasses and stepped from the car. A quick glance at her reflection in the window confirmed that no one, not even her mother, would recognize her in this getup.

She led Henry through the crowd, noticing the curious looks from the B-and-T types but not the Euros. She guessed they were more used to seeing covered Islamic women. One scruffy type was totally staring at her—or squinting, rather. With a start she recognized him as the guy with the flyers from Monday.

Her chest tightened. Why the interest? Did he recognize her from outside Blume's? Maybe that was it. No way he could match her to the girl on his flyers.

She could feel his gaze on her back after she'd passed him.

She shook it off and focused on the stores. She was looking for a certain type of layout. She stepped into one after another. The first three had their dressing rooms in the rear. But the fourth had situated them mid-store.

Just what she was looking for.

Dawn had a plan.

You can do this, she told herself as she wandered the aisles, examining overpriced T-shirts and ugly, rhinestone-studded belts and designer jeans.

Some of the sales folk were eyeing her, probably wondering why a fundamentalist chick would be interested in this stuff. Let them wonder.

She wandered to the rear of the store, hoping Henry would trail her, but he lingered at the front, people watching through the big front windows when he wasn't watching her.

She had to get him back here. So the next time he glanced her way she waved and signaled him to join her. When he arrived, she pulled a sundress off a rack and held it up before her.

"What do you think?"

His face remained expressionless. "Not my size."

She laughed. "No, silly. For me."

"It's not very Islamic."

She smiled at him. "Neither am I. Wait here while I try it on, then I want your opinion."

He glanced around. "Do you think that's wise? It's very out of character."

"Don't worry." She tugged on her veil. "I'll keep this on the whole time."

Before he could say any more she hurried forward to the changing room. As soon as she was inside she ripped off the *pak chadar* and turned to the squat Hispanic attendant busy arranging items that had been tried on but not purchased.

"I need your help," she said in a low voice.

The woman looked up at her. "You don't want that, just leave it here."

"No. There's a man following me."

"So? Call the cops."

"I don't want to cause a scene."

Totally true. She could have reported Henry to the police at any time, said she'd never seen him before and that he was following her, harassing her. Maybe while they were questioning him, she could slip away. And maybe not. She'd most likely have to identify herself, and then someone would make the connection between her and the girl on the flyers. And even if she could slip away before identifying herself, that kind of activity would draw a crowd, put her at the center of attention, attract stares. All things that were so not what she wanted.

No, she needed to do this quietly. Slip out onto the street and totally fade away

The woman gave her a bewildered look. "What can I do? Call the manager?"

"No. Look—just take a look. Is there a tall guy in a gray suit hanging around the sundresses?"

The woman peeked through a slit in the curtains, then nodded. "Is that him?"

"Yeah. Look, I have an idea. Let me help you carry these back into the store. We'll head toward the front, drop them off, then I'll escape to the street."

She gave Dawn a suspicious look. "I don't know . . ." she said slowly.

Dawn had totally expected this and had come prepared. She pulled a hundred-dollar bill from a side pocket of her shoulder bag and handed it to her.

"Please? He really creeps me out."

The woman's eyes bulged when she saw the zeroes. She quickly shoved it into a pocket.

"Okay. How we do this?"

Dawn pulled a green linen table napkin she'd snared from the penthouse and knotted it around her head do-rag style. Then she looked around and spotted another sundress, a light blue flowered print, in the pile the woman had been arranging. She grabbed that along with a couple of others and held them high by their hangers—high enough to obscure her head and torso. If she kept the dresses between her and Henry, he'd never see her.

Or so she hoped.

Her stomach totally cramped. This so had to work. If she blew it she'd never get another chance.

Do it.

"You lead the way," she said.

The woman nodded, filled her arms with clothing, and darted between the curtains.

"Ándale!"

Dawn followed, dresses held high, gliding toward the front in the woman's wake. As she reached the checkout area she tossed the dresses on a counter and kept going—out the door, onto the sidewalk, and into the ambling crowd.

This was dangerous, she knew, as she wove through the throng. Yeah, she had her hair covered, wore sunglasses, and was holding her hand across her mouth, hiding most of her lower face, but someone still might recognize her. Wouldn't be easy to do, but with the way her luck had been running lately, she couldn't take anything for granted.

She risked a look back as she turned the first corner she came to. No sign of Henry.

Relieved, she pressed on. He probably didn't even realize she was gone, and when he finally did, he'd be looking for someone wearing a *pak chadar*. But he wouldn't find one, or if he did, someone else would be wearing it. And if he asked anyone if they'd seen a woman wearing a veil, whoever they'd seen wouldn't be Dawn.

The sidewalks here on Spring Street were narrower than Broadway, slowing her progress. She resisted the urge to step off the curb and walk in the street. She wanted to avoid anything that would separate her from the pack.

She looked around and saw a cab but it was occupied. She didn't want to stand in the street signaling for one. She wanted *off* the street and sidewalk.

She'd been shopping in SoHo tons of times, sometimes with her mother, sometimes with friends. The closest subway stops were each two blocks away, but both too near Broadway. She might run into Henry. She continued along Spring. She knew of another straight ahead on Sixth Avenue.

Time to get totally lost in New York.

8

I must be living right, Darryl thought as he followed the girl through the crowd.

Or maybe it was because he was dissimilated. Hank had always said good things would start to happen once you dissimilated yourself. Darryl had memorized his words:

The time has come to separate yourselves from the herd. You don't belong with the herd. Come out of hiding Step away from the crowd. Let the dissimilation begin!

Darryl had done just that. One of the guys on the line with him at the Ford plant in Dearborn had handed him a copy of *Kick* during a break and told him to read it. Said it had changed his life and would do the same for Darryl. Well, he'd never been much of a reader, but one look at that spidery black figure on the yellow cover and he'd had to know what was inside.

He'd read it. Then he'd read it again. And again. And when he checked Hank Thompson's Web site and learned that he was speaking in New York City, he'd headed east.

And after he'd heard him in person, he never went back. What for? Back to his dead-end job? Back to an ex-wife who hated him, and a kid who barely knew who he was? Fat chance, baby.

So he'd declared himself dissimilated and stuck around, earning room and board playing gopher for Hank, and grooving to the whole Kicker Evolution thing. For the first time in his life he felt like he belonged. His brother and sister Kickers were like the family he'd never had.

He had no idea why Hank wanted Dawn Pickering found, but that didn't matter. She was going to make Darryl a star among Kickers. The five-grand reward in his pocket wouldn't hurt neither.

He couldn't believe his luck. He'd got up this morning, scrounged some breakfast, and got out and wandered. That had been his pattern since Hank had put up that reward for finding her. Some days he'd go uptown, some days down, subwaying as far up as the Bronx and all the way down to the Battery, and everywhere between. But ever since Monday, after seeing that chick with the Arab thing around her head outside Blume's, he'd been sticking to the shopping areas. Hank had thought she was the girl he was looking for, and that was good enough for Darryl. He had Dawn's face branded on his brain, but he was also keeping an eye peeled for anyone wearing a veil.

So today he'd landed on Broadway in SoHo. Why not? Blume's had another store down here. And what does he see—the same chick in the same veil thing. But with that chauffeur guy again. Darryl wasn't gonna mess with him. His back still hurt a little from where he'd landed against that car. Guy was stronger than he looked. A lot stronger.

But no way he was letting her out of his sight. He'd followed from a distance, watching the two of them go in and out of one store after another. So he'd been hanging across the street from the fourth store, killing time, when all of a sudden this blonde with a green dishrag or napkin or whatever tied around her head comes rushing out. It took him a second or two to realize it was the girl from the flyer—without her veil.

He had a frozen, what-the-fuck? moment, and then he'd started to move—cautiously, expecting her driver guy to pop out behind her. But he didn't show.

Darryl was hanging well back. Good thing too, because she kept looking over her shoulder, like she was on the run from someone. Her driver? That didn't make sense.

Whatever, she was easy to track with that dumb green thing on her head. Sure, it hid most of her blond hair, and she wore these big sunglasses, and she kept her hand clapped over her mouth, but none of that had been enough to fool old Darryl.

He wished to hell he had a cell phone so he could call Hank and get some backup. If she jumped into a cab and he couldn't find another one in time, he could kiss that reward good-bye.

He followed her along Spring until she headed down the steps of a subway station.

Darryl pumped his fist. You *are* living right!

9

Alonzo Cooter glared defiantly up at them from his chair.

"You slopes think I'm scared of you? Think again."

Hideo looked down at the man's angry black face. Most people would be terrified and begging for release or at least an explanation. This man radiated defiance. Hideo had seen that in his photo and so had prepared this building for . . . persuasion.

Cooter-san had not been hard to find, but he had been difficult to isolate. He pumped gas at a Lukoil station on Tenth Avenue in Manhattan and was not accessible at work. After work he spent some time at a Ninth Avenue bar with two of his coworkers. Then he took the subway to the Bronx. Kenji, Ryo, and Goro accosted him outside his apartment building and shoved him into a van where Kenji asked him a question that an average man would have been frightened enough to answer without hesitation. But Cooter-san had refused and so the yakuza brought him to this abandoned building, duct-taped his wrists and ankles to the arms and legs of a sturdy wooden chair, and called Hideo.

"It's a simple question, Mister Cooter. Where does Hugh Gerrish live?"

"Fuck off. Never heard of him."

"Do not lie, Mister Cooter. You were arrested with him during an attempted robbery. You do know him. And obviously you are loyal to him. That is admirable and honorable. And I am being equally honorable with you when I say that we wish him no harm. In fact, we intend to make him rich by purchasing an item he holds."

Cooter-san surprised him by grinning. "Look at me, chinky boy. Do I look like I just popped out of my momma's pussy? I got nothing to say to you."

Hideo heaved a dramatic sigh. "I was afraid of this." He nodded to Goro. "You may begin."

Goro grinned and pulled off his shirt, revealing his yakuza *irezumi*. The tattoos were so extensive that he appeared to be wearing a long-sleeve body-suit. Hideo had heard of the yakuza tradition of tattoos, of course, and had seen photos, but never before had he seen them in the flesh. A pair of carp swam in different directions across Goro's chest; from his back a tiger attacked with extended claws. Waves and hillsides and cherry blossoms filled the spaces between and wound down his arms.

Cooter-san stared in awe, speechless.

The prisoner's wrists were already secure, so Ryo began taping the fingers of his left hand to the arm of the chair—all except the little one.

Cooter-san found his voice. "The fuck you think you're doing?"

Hideo stepped away from the table, leaving the stage to the yakuza. In a very real way, it was a stage. For they were each playing a part, carefully worked out in advance.

"In my country," Kenji said in a matter-of-fact tone, "members of our organizations have a ritual known as *yubitsume*. When we offend a superior, or make a mistake that costs the organization, we make amends by *yubitsume*."

"Yeah? Well, you can bitsume my big black dick."

"The word means 'finger cutting.' We use a tanto—that is a certain kind of knife—and cut off the tip of a finger, usually the smallest, which we then send to our superior."

"I'll bet he's real tickled about that. What's he do with it? Shove it up his ass?"

Kenji didn't miss a beat. "You have offended our superior by not honoring his simple request for information. Therefore we have decided to perform *yubitsume* on you."

Hideo knew how far outside true yakuza tradition this was, but Cooter-san would not know that.

The man's expression lost some of its belligerence.

"Yeah?" He looked down at his left hand, where his little finger had been taped flat and straight along the arm of the chair. "You're kidding, right?"

Kenji gave his head a slow, solemn shake. "I do not know this 'kidding.' My associate will perform the *yubitsume*. We do not have a tanto available, so we have had to make do with what is available."

As if by magic, a meat cleaver appeared in Goro's hand. He tested the edge with his thumb.

"Oh, yeah," Cooter-san said, his air of bravado returning. "Gotta admit you put on a good show with this finger business. But I notice all you guys got your pinkies. I'm supposed to believe you guys've never screwed up? That's a laugh."

Goro frowned and shot Kenji a questioning look. Cooter-san's English had been too rapid for him. Kenji translated.

Goro smiled and tucked the cleaver under an armpit. He spread the fingers of his left hand. Then he grasped the tip of the fifth and pulled it off.

Cooter-san's shocked gasp echoed through the room.

And then Ryo revealed his stump, and finally Kenji.

As the still-smiling Goro grasped the cleaver again by its handle, Cooter-san began writhing and thrashing about in his chair.

"Wait a minute! Wait-wait-wait a fucking minute!"

The cleaver was all for show. All three of the yakuza carried tantos, but a meat cleaver caused a more visceral reaction—at least in Hideo. And, from the looks of it, in Cooter-san as well.

Hideo had given strict orders not to harm the man, merely frighten him. He was sure the sight of the tattoos and the cleaver—and now the foreshortened fingers—along with Goro's merciless black eyes would be more than enough.

Hideo admitted to some qualms about putting the cleaver into Goro's hands. He had a feral quality about him, a sense that violence lurked very close to the surface, no deeper than his tattoos. That increased the level of threat, but also increased the chances of Cooter-san suffering injury.

Goro stepped forward and positioned the cleaver over the last joint on Cooter-san's little finger.

Kenji said, "I will give you until the count of three. One . . ."

Goro smiled at Cooter-san and Hideo couldn't remember a more chilling sight.

"Two . . ."

Still smiling, Goro raised the cleaver.

"Th—"

"All right, all right, all *right*! He lives in Jamaica!"

Hideo's burst of elation at Cooter-san's capitulation died in midflash.

"Jamaica? He lives in Jamaica?"

"That's what I said. Now get this guy away from me."

"Why did he leave the country?"

Cooter-san laughed. "Leave the country? You dickwad! Jamaica, *Queens*!"

Relief flooded Hideo. Queens . . . he knew where Queens was . . . and he would find this Jamaica in Queens.

Cooter-san, defeated now, gave his friend's street address without argument or further duress.

As Hideo reached for his PDA to key in the data, he heard a *thunk* and a man's scream. He looked up in time to see a small dark object tumble through the air, trailing a fine thread of blood. Goro's hand darted out and caught it in midflight.

Hideo looked at Cooter-san and saw him writhing in agony as blood flowed from the stub end of his little finger. His stomach turned.

"What—what did you do?" he cried in Japanese.

Goro gave him a flat look. *"Yubitsume."*

"You weren't supposed to hurt him! I told you that!"

"I know."

And then he popped the fingertip into his mouth and swallowed it whole.

Hideo couldn't believe his eyes. "What—?"

Goro smiled and said, "So they can't sew it back on."

"But you were not supposed to hurt him!"

"He should not have informed on his friend."

Furious, confused, frustrated, Hideo turned to Kenji. "Stop his bleeding and return him to his home."

Then he hurried from the building. He did not want to be sick in front of the yakuza.

10

Hank couldn't believe it, so he made Darryl say it again.

"I found the bitch. She's in the Milford Plaza."

"You're sure? You're absolutely sure?"

"Hey, man, ain't I been lookin at her face all day, every day for weeks?"

Yeah, he had. Hank's gut tingled with triumph, but he was afraid to celebrate. All along he'd put on a confident face, but in his heart he hadn't truly believed he'd ever find her. The flyers had been a long shot but, ironically, in the end it had been one of his own Kickers who'd come through.

If it was really her. He had to ask again.

"No question in your mind?"

"She looks thinner than in the picture, but it's her. She was in that same Arab getup at first, and then she took it off. It's her all right. Followed her on the C from SoHo to the Deuce, in and out of a Duane Reade, and into the Milford Plaza."

Milford Plaza? What was she doing there? No sign of her for weeks and weeks, and then she shows up in a theater-district tourist trap. What was going on?

"She with that chauffeur you mentioned the other day?"

"That's the weird part. He was following her in and out of these stores like a bodyguard, like stink on shit, but then she comes tearing out of the last store and he's nowhere to be seen. Almost like she was ditching him."

None of this made any sense. Had she had a falling-out with whoever had been hiding her?

He realized it didn't matter. She'd come out of hiding and gone to ground again. But now he knew where.

"You're sure she's still there?"

"I watched her check in—paid cash. Watched her take an elevator. I'm calling from the lobby where I can see the elevators. She ain't come out."

"Good man, good man. Any chance you got her room number?"

"Naw. Didn't want to get too close. She seen me twice now."

Good old Darryl was smarter than he looked.

Be nice to know the room number, but they didn't need it. After all, not as if they could march in, bundle her up, and carry her out. No, they'd have to play a waiting game. She couldn't hole up there forever. Sooner or later she'd have to hit the street. And then they'd have her.

"Say," Darryl said, "um, when do I get my reward?"

"Soon as she's in this building, standing right here in front of me. But for now you stay right where you are with your eyeballs glued to those elevators. Got it?"

"Got it."

"I'll send you some relief ASAP." A question popped into his head. "Any idea what she bought in Duane's?"

He could sense Darryl's shrug.

"Dunno. Like in the hotel, I didn't want to get too close, so I stayed across the street. She went in empty-handed and came out carrying a little white bag. Maybe she's on the rag."

Hank wanted to say, *She's pregnant, you idiot,* but bit it back. Darryl had done good work. No upside to insulting him.

Still, he wondered what had been important enough to make her detour on the way to a new hiding place.

And then he thought he knew.

Of course.

11

Standing in the deepening dusk outside Gerrish's apartment building, Tom O'Day punched his number into his cell phone and waited for him to pick up.

"Hello?"

"I'm here."

A sigh, then, *"Okay."*

Not a lot of enthusiasm there.

The buzzer sounded, unlatching the door. Tom yanked it open and stepped inside. Halfway through the inner door he stopped.

His nape was tingling. And why not? It should be. He was standing in the same building as the fucking Gaijin Masamune.

He shook it off and headed for the elevator, cursing himself for being such a jerk when Gerrish called him the other day, offering the sword. He'd moved a little hot merch for him a couple of times in the past and now he was looking to unload the sword. When he'd described the condition, Tom had told him forget it—sell it for scrap metal.

Idiot! How could he have been so fucking stupid?

But how could he have known?

So as soon as that guy Jack had left the store yesterday he'd looked back through his phone's call history and found Gerrish's number. He'd been

calling him for two fucking days now. Finally he'd got through late this afternoon. Apparently the jerk hardly ever charged his phone.

But worse: Gerrish was no longer in a selling mood. Said he'd changed
his mind and wanted to keep it. At least he still had it. If he'd sold it to
someone else . . .

Tom didn't want to think about that.

After much wheedling—humiliating as all hell—he brought Gerrish
around to the point where he'd allow him to examine the sword.

When the door to 4D opened, Tom offered his hand.

"Hugh, thanks so much. I really appreciate this."

Gerrish's handshake was as limp as his tone. "Yeah, well, I hope you
don't think you can talk me into selling."

When he stepped through the door the tingle in his neck spread down
his back. He was in the same room as the fucking Gaijin Masamune.

"Like I told you on the phone, I just want to see it." He'd worked up this
story earlier in the day. "You said it was rusted out in spots, and that makes
it pretty much worthless. But then I got to thinking that maybe it wasn't rust.
Maybe it was some kind of design in the steel that hadn't been reported before. I need a look."

"Okay. You can look, you can touch, but you can't have."

"Sure. Fine. But a few days ago you were itching to sell. What made you
change your mind?"

Gerrish's expression wavered from resolute to uncertain. "I'm not really
sure."

"You sound pretty sure."

"When I . . . when it came into my possession, I had a feeling it was
special . . . that I could, you know, move it for some decent change."

"So you called me."

"Yeah, but you turned me down."

"That I did." Schmuck that I am.

"Turned out I was glad you did. Because the thing's kinda been growing
on me. I decided to keep it."

"Interesting. Where is it now?"

Gerrish motioned Tom down the short hallway to the main room where
he made a flourish toward the coffee table.

"Ta-daaa!"

Tom stopped and stared. The room could have been made of solid gold
and lined with the proverbial seventy-two naked virgins. Who cared? Tom
had eyes for only one thing.

At first glance, with its Swiss-cheesed blade, it indeed looked like a piece of junk. As he bent and ran a finger along the random pattern of pocks and holes, every square millimeter of his skin began to tingle. He lifted it and rested it on his palms. These weren't rusted out or eaten out—these had been melted out.

He raised it and peeked through one of the holes. He experienced an instant of vertigo as he seemed to be standing on a low bridge looking out at a bustling city filled with rough-clad Asian men and kimonoed women. Then it all disappeared in a blinding flash as bright as the sun.

He snatched the blade away from his face and stood blinking at the purple afterimage.

"What's the matter?" Gerrish said.

Tom took another quick peek. This time all he saw was Gerrish.

"Nothing."

He lowered the blade again for a closer look. The *jihada*—the steel of the cutting edge—was unmarred. The swordsmith must have concentrated the best steel there. The *hamon*—the temper line—undulated like a series of gentle waves on a placid lake.

Tom moved down to the naked tang. This was where the swordsmith traditionally carved his *mei*—his signature. No signature here, only a Kanji symbol:

$$外人$$

This was it—the Gaijin Masamune. He was holding the fucking Gaijin Masamune.

He noticed his hands starting to shake so he put it down. Not an easy thing to do. Maybe the hardest thing he'd ever done.

"I—" He swallowed around a dry tongue. "I was right the first time out: It's a piece of junk, good only for sentimental value."

"But it's so sharp," Gerrish said. "Watch this."

He stepped into the kitchen and returned with an apple. He lifted the sword by the tang and dropped the apple onto the upturned edge. A whole apple hit the blade. Two halves bounced onto the table.

"Yeah. Sharp."

Tom wanted to say, What else would you expect from a Masamune blade, especially one tempered in ground-zero atomic fire? But he held his tongue. This asshole had no idea what he had. Cutting an apple—like using a CO_2 laser to make a paper doll. Christ.

He saw the smear of apple juice on the blade and wanted to scream at Gerrish to wipe it off.

No way was he walking out of here without that blade. Like leaving a small child alone with a pedophile. Uh-uh. Not gonna happen.

He pulled a Ziploc bag from his pocket.

"Brought you a present. Since you're gonna keep this piece of junk, it might as well have a handle—what the Japs call a *tsuka*."

He sat on the couch, pushed the apple halves aside, and dumped the contents on to the table next to the sword. Two pieces of halved bamboo, a bamboo peg, a piece of cloth, and strips of tightly wound silk.

"You don't really—"

"Sure I do. My way of saying thanks for letting me see it, even if it is junk." He held up the two pieces of bamboo. "These make up the *ho*."

He fitted them around the tang, noting how they obscured the *gaijin* symbol. He shook his head in wonder, thinking, You could own this thing all your damn life and never know you had the fucking Gaijin Masamune.

He picked up the bamboo peg.

"This is the *mekugi* and it fits through the holes in the *ho* and the tang to hold everything together."

That done, he wrapped the red cloth around the *ho* and began winding the silk cord around the cloth in a crude approximation of the traditional diamond pattern *tsuka-ito*. Once the sword was his, he'd fashion a suitably magnificent *tsuka*. But for now, this was all he had time for. He'd even skipped installing a hilt—the round, ornate *tsuba*. He wouldn't need one for what he had planned.

Finally he was done. To his collector's eye the job looked like crap. But to Gerrish . . .

"Hey, you're really something." He reached for it. "Thanks a lot."

Tom shook his head. Holding the katana handle with two hands now, he rose and faced Gerrish, pointing the blade at his chest.

"I'm taking this."

Gerrish's expression hardened. "No way. That's mine, O'Day."

"We both know it's not, or you wouldn't have come to me to fence it."

Gerrish stepped forward, reaching, but backed off when Tom gave the blade a couple of back-and-forth swings.

"Uh-uh. Look, I'm not out to steal it. I'll give you a good price for it. A damn good price."

Gerrish's eyes narrowed. "So it's not as worthless as you said."

"It's junk, but it's unique junk. I want it for my collection."

"No—"

"Hughie, babes, listen to me." He briefly freed a hand from the grip to fish a wad of hundreds from his pocket. He tossed it on the table. "A thousand bucks. Yours."

"It's not for sale."

What was wrong with this jerk? He was a small-time burglar in a crummy apartment. A cool thousand in cash sitting before him for the taking and he was turning it down?

What gives?

"Look, one way or another I'm walking out the door with this katana. You try to stop me"—he swung the blade in a quick horizontal arc—"off with your head."

He smiled as he said it. A joke. But something happened during that swing. His already long arms seemed to stretch even farther of their own accord just as Gerrish took a step forward.

At first he thought nothing had happened. A bowel-wrenching near miss. Gerrish stopped cold, a puzzled look on his face. Then Tom noticed a thin red line appear across the front of his throat. Gerrish's hands fluttered like uncertain butterflies toward his neck just as the wound burst open and spewed blood in all directions.

Gerrish stood there with a dumbfounded expression, a human fire hydrant with a sprinkler cap, his mouth working but only bubbling gurgles issuing from the slash. He pressed his hands over the wound, trying to close it, trying to stanch the flow.

Tom backed away, his stomach threatening to toss up the Big Mac he'd gobbled on his way over. He glanced down at the blade. Not a drop of blood along the tip. The slice had been so clean he hadn't felt the slightest tug of resistance.

"Hey, man, I didn't mean . . ." The words clogged in his throat. What could he say?

He looked back at Gerrish and saw blood still spurting from between his fingers. He began to sway as his arms dropped and hung limp at his sides. Then he keeled over, tilting to his right in slow motion like a falling tree. He landed on his side, then flopped onto his back.

Tom dropped the katana and hurried over to him. Gerrish's eyes were fixed on the ceiling with a glazed, dead stare. Blood continued to pump weakly from his throat. Finally that stopped too.

Tom's knees weakened and he would have collapsed onto the body had his hand not found the arm of the sofa.

Oh man, oh shit, oh fuck, he'd killed him. Hadn't meant to. Almost seemed the blade had done it by itself. But here was Gerrish, horribly dead. And who was gonna believe it was an accident? Tom had already been through the system on possession of stolen property. He had a record. They'd say he was trying to steal the sword and Gerrish caught him. He was cooked, he was fried, he was—

Wait. Whoever found the body wouldn't know about the sword, and neither would the cops—not if the sword wasn't here when they arrived. No murder weapon—that would mess up the investigation. No one had seen him go into the apartment. If no one saw him go out . . .

But he couldn't simply stroll out of here carrying a katana. He stepped back to the front hall. Hadn't he seen—?

Yes. A short runner. Perfect. Now, if he could just remember everything he touched and wipe it down . . .

He just might be able to walk away from this.

12

Hideo watched the street while Kenji worked on the front door lock to Gerrish's apartment building. Goro and Ryo crowded around him, shielding his actions from passing eyes.

They had blindfolded Cooter-san and dropped him near a hospital, then gone back to the Kaze house to await darkness. He used the time to write up a report on Goro, detailing his disobedience. Goro would lose another joint on his little finger as a result.

When he'd finished he read it over and realized that the incident was as much a failure of command as a failure of discipline. He deleted it.

Hearing a grunt of satisfaction from Kenji, Hideo turned and saw the door swing open.

"Excellent work," he said as Kenji used a toothpick to jam the latch. "You three wait nearby. I will call you if I need you."

The three nodded and moved off as Hideo entered the vestibule.

He had decided to do this on his own. Not simply because he could not trust the yakuza to restrain themselves, but the mere sight of them would certainly frighten Gerrish. If the man would not open his door, how could Hideo persuade him to sell his katana?

And he would sell it. Whatever his asking price, Hideo would meet it. He had one hundred thousand in cash in his briefcase. He would bring more if need be. He didn't care. It wasn't his money. And Sasaki-san would pay anything. One hundred, two hundred, three hundred thousand—a mere pittance to the chairman. Not even an hour's interest on his holdings.

The elevator deposited him on the fourth floor. To his left, across the hall, he saw a door marked 4D.

The moment had arrived. Soon—perhaps tomorrow, if all went smoothly—he would be on his way back home with Sasaki-san's precious katana safely stowed in his luggage.

13

Jack came in through the fire escape. He'd donned a goth look for the night: sneakers, ripped jeans, a hoodie, and leather gloves—all black. He'd used a bump key on a back door of the adjoining building, come across the roof, and down the fire escape to what he figured to be 4D. Behind him, across a fairly broad alley, loomed the blank wall of the Tabernacle of Prayer.

The window opened into a darkened bedroom. It was locked but old and he easily popped the latch with the screwdriver he'd brought along for just such a purpose.

He eased up the sash and listened. Quiet as a coffin. No sign of life. Gerrish was probably out. This might prove easier than he'd expected.

He slipped into the bedroom and headed for the hall. Best-case scenario: He'd toss the place, find the katana, say sayonara, and be gone before Gerrish came back.

If he didn't find it, that could mean either that Gerrish had hidden it really well or, worse, sold it. In that case he'd have to settle in and wait for the man's return.

Jack stopped in the hallway, his senses tingling with alarm. Why? The place was dead. And then he recognized the smell.

Blood.

He pulled out a penlight and flashed it around until the beam found the corpse. Blood everywhere, especially the corpse—its entire front was saturated with it.

He stepped closer and recognized Gerrish. His throat had been slashed. Looked like the work of a straight razor.

Or a katana.

Jack knew right then he wouldn't find the sword here. Could be a lot of reasons for Gerrish's offing, but Jack's gut told him it was the sword. Someone else had wanted it badly enough to kill for it—maybe even used it to do the deed.

Time to go.

He turned back to the bedroom and saw red-and-blue flashes through the window. He stuck his head out and saw a pair of NYPD cruisers in the alley, and four cops talking to a couple of kids.

Shit.

Three choices: Climb back to the roof now and risk being spotted, wait them out, or leave by the front door. The third offered more chances to be seen by one of the neighbors, but he needed out of this crime scene. *Now.*

If he put on a pair of shades and pulled up his hood, he figured he'd be all right. He was doing just that on his way to the front door, carefully avoiding the blood splatters, when he heard a knock. He looked up and saw the door starting to swing open.

A voice said, "Mister Gerrish?"

Who—?

Didn't matter. Couldn't be caught here. He spun and dashed back to the bedroom. He was about to dive out onto the fire escape when the window lit up, then faded.

A peek out showed the two kids cuffed and bent over a car hood. One of the cops was flashing his car's searchlight back and forth over the building's outer wall. Another was using his light on the Tabernacle. Jack didn't know what they were looking for but they'd sure as hell spot him if he tried to escape.

"Mister Gerrish?" the voice repeated from the front room.

Only one thing to do.

He backed into the bedroom closet, pulled his Glock, and closed the door—the damn hinges gave out a faint squeak. He measured his breathing and waited, hoping it was anyone but a cop.

Anyone but a cop.

14

Upon approaching, Hideo had noticed that the door to apartment 4D was unlatched. He'd knocked anyway but the door had swung open under the gentle impacts.

Only darkness within.

"Mister Gerrish?"

He pushed the door open wider.

"Mister Gerrish? Are you here?"

He was concluding that Gerrish-san had left without fully latching his door, when he heard a high-pitched whisper of sound from within. He stepped across the threshold and fumbled along the wall for a light switch. He found one and flipped it.

Hideo found himself in a short hallway looking into the apartment's front room. A dozen feet away a body lay sprawled on the floor in a pool of blood. The sight drove him back against the door, slamming it shut. He dropped the briefcase and fumbled for his phone. He speed-dialed Kenji's number.

"Get up here now! All of you!"

He leaned against the wall, closed his eyes, and conjured visions of Omi-shima, the tranquil Inland Sea island he'd visited last summer. He needed to calm himself. He couldn't allow the yakuza to see him like this.

By the time they arrived, he was standing by the body, briefcase in hand, looking calm and composed, although his gut was churning with nausea at the smell of all that blood.

The yakuza, on the other hand, took everything in stride, with no more reaction than if they'd found a dead animal along the side of a road. If a stick had been lying nearby, he was sure one of them would have picked it up and poked the poor man.

Gerrish. No question in Hideo's mind, and confirmed when Kenji pulled the wallet from his pocket and checked his ID. He checked the throat wound that gaped like a second bloody mouth.

"A very sharp knife."

Hideo met his gaze—better than looking at that wound. "Or katana?"

He nodded. "Or katana. But you have shown me the X-ray. Such a rotted old blade could not have the edge to make this wound."

Hideo had a feeling it very well could. Sasaki-san was not a junk collector.

He felt his dream of heading home to Japan tomorrow shatter around him. The sword was gone. It had been used to kill its owner. He might never find it now.

Yet despite that leaden certainty, he could not leave without being sure he had turned over every rock in this garden of death.

"Search the place. Look everywhere—behind furniture, behind appliances, everywhere. Leave no corner uninspected."

15

Jack heard two voices chattering in what sounded like Japanese. Naka Slater, maybe? Didn't sound like him but, then again, he'd never heard him speak Japanese. What was he doing here? Had he—?

Footsteps approached, passing the bedroom door, heading for the kitchen. He heard furniture moving in the living room, and then someone stepped into the bedroom.

How the hell many were they?

He heard drawers being opened and slammed shut, heard the bed moved, the mattress pulled off. The closet would be next. Inevitable.

He raised the Glock, depressed the trigger safety, and waited.

Seconds later, as the door flew open, Jack thrust the muzzle against the forehead of a stocky Japanese guy in a dark suit.

"Not a word," he whispered.

Maybe the guy didn't understand English, maybe he didn't care. Whatever, he started shouting gibberish, and a heartbeat later two other young suits darted into the room with silenced pistols raised. The cold eyes sighting down on him behind those barrels said they wouldn't hesitate to shoot if they had the chance.

He'd seen enough Kitano movies to know what they were: yakuza.

But Jack had already ducked behind his prisoner and twisted him into a half nelson. He had the Glock's muzzle pressed against his lower spine.

"Hair trigger here," he said, grinding the muzzle against the big guy's back. "You know what that means?"

"I know what it means," said a voice from the doorway. Uzi-fire Japanese followed.

Christ, a fourth. How many more?

The new guy was older and wore a lighter suit—business gray. He looked upset.

The boss?

"Good," Jack said, hoping what followed would sound worse than dying. "Then know this too. I pull this trigger, your pal never walks again. He'll be piloting a three-wheel scooter around Tokyo the rest of his life."

The newcomer either translated or gave instructions.

"Also," Jack added, "mine's not silenced like yours. One shot will bring those cops running up from the alley."

The new guy glanced at the window and saw the flashes. His mouth tightened as he turned back to Jack.

"We want only the sword. We will pay you handsomely. Give it to me and you can go."

The sword? These guys wanted the sword too? That meant three parties looking for it. What did these guys want with it? Didn't strike him as the collecting types.

What had he got himself into now?

Never mind. Needed to figure out how best to play this. Dumb seemed a good way to go.

"What sword?"

"The one you stole from Mister Gerrish."

"Do I look like I have a sword on me?"

"But you must—"

"I don't. I came looking for Gerrish and found him dead, just like you did. Feel him. He's cold. I wouldn't still be hanging around if I'd killed him."

Jack didn't know if the body was really cold, but it had looked cold.

He gave Jack an odd look. "Do I know you? Have we met?"

Jack stared at him. Come to think of it, he looked kind of familiar.

"I don't think so."

He seemed to shake it off. "What was your business with Mister Gerrish, if not the sword?"

"Owes me money. Make that *owed* me money. Looks like I'm out my dough and you're out your sword."

He tightened his grip on his prisoner's neck and started pushing him toward his pals.

"Let's move this party down the road a piece. I'll let your guy go and you can watch me walk out the door without a sword, or even a bread knife."

The leader guy said something in Japanese and the three of them began backing away. Jack wished he knew what he'd said. Desperate, he tossed off the only Japanese he knew to throw them off balance—maybe.

"*Arigato. Konichiwa.* Kyu Sakamoto. Gojira. Gamera. Rodan."

When they were all out in the hall between the front room and the kitchen, Jack's prisoner began spewing angry Japanese.

The older suit protested but one of the younger pair shook his head and began speaking in English.

"We will move no farther." He raised his pistol and aimed it at Jack's eye where he peeked out from behind the thick neck. "We will dishonor our brother if we allow you to leave."

Funny, they didn't look like brothers.

"You want him crippled?"

"He will not live as a cripple."

Jack got the message. He sensed something building, something stupid and unnecessarily bloody and surely deadly.

"Okay. Let's be calm and figure what we can do here so we all go our way with our honor intact."

"You must release our brother and surrender to us."

Didn't like the sound of that.

"I don't think so."

The tension in the air increased. These crazies were going to start shooting, and if their brother went down in the crossfire, so be it.

The older guy obviously was against this and had been arguing in a placating tone. Suddenly his eyes met Jack's and bulged like a Bob Clampett character.

Now he was pointing and yammering in a high-pitched voice, repeating the word *ronin* over and over. But the two cold-eyed mooks weren't listening. Maybe he wasn't their boss.

Only thing to do was duck and let the big guy take the first shots, then shove him toward them and start blasting away.

Shit-shit-shit! What was the point? Everybody was going to lose. Every—

And then a sound, a high-pitched howl of rage from the front door as a big black guy came charging in with a raised baseball bat. Jack noticed a bloody bandage on his left little finger. He looked like an enraged grizzly and he had murder in his eyes.

What the—?

The three of them whirled. The two gunners hesitated half a second, then began firing. Without thinking, Jack pushed his prisoner toward the melee, tripping him along the way, and ducked back into the bedroom.

As he dove for the window a *phut-phut-phut-phut* sound echoed behind him. He heard something heavy thump to the floor back there, and still the *phut-phut* barrage continued. He hauled himself onto the fire escape and began climbing as fast as he could. Screw the noise, screw the cops, he had to make the roof before Tojo and company reached the window.

16

"Stop!" Hideo shouted. "Stop now!"

Finally they listened and stepped away from Cooter-san's bullet-riddled body. They began loading fresh magazines into their pistols.

Hideo's mind reeled. Two dead! All because of a broken-down katana.

Was it cursed? And then he saw Goro pushing himself up from the floor, with no one behind him.

"The *ronin!*"

Kenji clicked a magazine into the grip of his pistol and gave him a puzzled look. *"Ronin?"*

Kenji and Ryo had been so intent on killing their attacker that they'd forgotten the *ronin.*

Hideo pointed toward the bedroom. "The man! He's escaping!"

Goro swung around and charged through the bedroom doorway, Kenji and Ryo on his heels. Hideo followed, but knew what they'd find.

An empty bedroom.

Goro grabbed his pistol from the floor and barreled toward the window, still lit by red and blue flashes.

"No!" Hideo cried. "The police!"

Goro wasn't listening but Kenji and Ryo had enough presence of mind to pull him back.

"We must go," Hideo said. "Now. We cannot be seen."

Goro struggled free of their grasp, then nodded.

"The stairs," Kenji said. "That will be the safest."

They slipped past the two corpses and paused at the door. Kenji peered into the hallway, then gave the signal to follow. The four of them rushed to the stairwell and hurried down.

Hideo brought up the rear thinking about the man in the apartment. He'd looked familiar at once, but he'd been unable to place him until he caught a look at his face from an angle similar to the photo.

Yoshio's mysterious *ronin.*

His mind whirled. What were the odds of winding up in the same apartment with that man? Astronomical.

And yet . . .

He said he'd been looking for owed money, but that could have been a lie. He too might have been looking for the sword. If so, he did not have it, for he'd been bargaining to walk out of the apartment without it.

What a strange, strange day this had been.

When they reached the street, Hideo studied the traffic lights at the nearby corner, looking for—

There! A traffic security camera, trained on the corner, but pointed his way. Its angle might—he prayed to his ancestors that it be so—include this doorway. Where there was one cam there would be others. He could search them out through the police grid and review their recordings.

If he was lucky, he might see the *ronin* and gain a clue as to where he could find him.

If he was *very* lucky he might see a man carrying a katana. But no one could be that lucky.

17

Jack swayed and rocked as he rode the mostly empty Manhattan-bound train, but his thoughts remained in Jamaica.

That Japanese guy seemed to know him, and Jack had to admit he looked a little familiar. Obviously they'd met at some time. But where? Jack didn't know many Asians and they rarely came to him as customers. They had their own extralegal ways of solving problems. So where—?

He straightened in his seat. The Japanese guy in the Catskills—Yoshio. This guy looked like him. But he couldn't be him. He'd been executed by Sam Baker. As cold-blooded an act as Jack had ever seen. One Baker had paid for.

This new guy looked enough like him to be his brother. Maybe he was. But even so, how did he know Jack?

He shook his head. Be glad when this was over. And he had a feeling it would be over soon. Because he had a pretty good idea who had the sword now.

Never would have pegged O'Day as a killer. Just went to show the lengths a collector would go to.

Gollum had found his Precious.

"You're looking for a sword," said a woman's voice behind him. "You should be looking for the baby as well."

He turned and saw a twenty-something girl dressed in black like him, with bright burgundy hair and heavily kohled eyes. She sported a slew of ear, nostril, eyebrow, and lip piercings. A pit bull stared up at him from the end of the leash clutched in her hand.

"You're one of them," he said.

She nodded.

"Prove it."

She lifted the front of her Sandman T-shirt to reveal a deep depression just to the right of her navel.

She smiled. "Need a closer look?"

Jack shook his head. He knew it went clean through and exited in the small of her back.

Women with dogs had been walking in and out of his life, each knowing more than they should about him and what was going on.

"I'd love to find the baby—and its mother. Where's Dawn?"

She shrugged. "Sometimes I know and other times I don't. She appears and disappears. But her baby . . ."

"What about it?"

"It is important."

"How?"

"I wish I knew. Like the katana you seek—unique among swords—the baby is unique among mortals. It has the potential to be used for immense good or terrible ill. Whoever controls that baby may well control the future." She frowned. "Or not."

"Thanks for clearing that up."

"There's nothing clear about it."

"I promised to protect Dawn, but not her baby. If she wants to get an abortion—and she has every reason to—should I stop her?"

The girl's expression looked almost pained. "I wish I could say. Perhaps it would be for the best. It is a wild card that could provide the Adversary with an unbeatable hand. Then again . . . it may allow us to trump him."

Jack sighed. "You're a big help."

"I wish I could tell you more. That is all I know. We are in uncharted waters." As the train stopped, she said, "I get off here."

Jack didn't want to see her go. So many questions . . .

"There's nothing more you can tell me?"

She shook her head. "When I know more, I shall come to you. Until then . . ."

She stepped out onto the platform and let the dog lead her away. Jack knew better than to follow.

18

"The hireling has not yet found the katana, *sensei*."

Toru, sitting in his darkened room, did not turn at Tadasu's voice, but kept his face to his window, gazing out at the night.

"He is truly searching? You have followed him?"

"He is difficult to follow, but I believe so, *sensei*."

"You think he is an honorable man, then?"

"I do, *sensei*."

"Will that make it more difficult for you to do what must be done when the time comes?" Toru sensed an instant's hesitation. "Well . . . will it?"

"No, *sensei*. Nothing will deter me from my duty to the Order."

"Good." He waved a hand. "Prepare the *shoten* for me. We leave within the hour."

The door closed, cutting off the light from the hallway and plunging the room into darkness. Toru did not move. He sat and thought, and his thoughts were not happy. Instead of handling this matter on its own, the Order had been forced to depend on a *gaijin* mercenary. Humiliating.

But the Kakureta Kao would rise again. The Seer had promised.

He went to the small wooden bureau that held his worldly belongings and withdrew a small case of sturdy ebony, its top inlaid with ivory. He removed the top and examined the *doku-ippen* within: two dozen slivers of wood, each saturated with a different mix of herbs and extracts, rested in individual grooves. The ones ringed with blue caused mere unconsciousness. The others were soaked with deadly toxins: Those marked with black were employed for instant effect, those marked with varying shades of red conferred a delayed death. All were untraceable.

He would need one of the reds tonight.

So many needs in his life now . . .

The Order needed the katana, so that its future might be measured in millennia.

The Order also needed a successful test of the *ekisu* tonight so that New York City's future might be measured in days.

19

Hideo's ancestors answered his prayers.

A fair number of traffic cams around the city were fakes, installed on the principle that if one thinks one is being watched, one will behave accordingly. But the cam near Gerrish-san's apartment was of the functioning variety and—bless his ancestors—showed the building's entrance in the far upper left corner of the frame.

Kenji sat with him, absorbing all Hideo was doing. So difficult to reconcile this young, eager-to-learn face now with his cold-blooded expression while pumping round after round into Cooter-san.

Hideo turned to him. "How long do you think Gerrish-san was dead when we found him?"

The answer was important. He needed to know how far back in the recording to go. He had no idea of how to judge a death, but he sensed Kenji had seen his share of corpses.

He answered in English: "From way blood was only part"—he looked to Hideo for help—"thicked?"

"Clotted."

He nodded. "Yes, clotted. I say one hour."

To be safe, Hideo began reviewing at a point ninety minutes before their arrival at the apartment. He showed Kenji how to fast-forward, then leaned back and concentrated on the screen. The entrance was not terribly busy, so he did not have to stop Kenji often.

The onscreen clock read 19:52 when he saw a man step out of the entrance carrying an oblong object.

"Stop."

Kenji did so and Hideo took over the controls. He enhanced and enlarged the image. The object under the man's arm appeared to be a rolled-up rug. He estimated its length at approximately ninety to one hundred centimeters. Long enough to hide the katana they sought.

The man was moving north. If he walked any faster he would have been trotting. One might even think he was escaping from something. A murder scene, perhaps?

Unfortunately he kept his face straight ahead, providing only a high-angle profile that Hideo doubted would provide sufficient mapping points for the facial recognition program.

Hideo called up the map of traffic cams in Jamaica and found one two blocks north. He prayed again to his ancestors, begging them to go back in time and guide this man on a straight path to this intersection. Then he accessed the new cam and began his review at 19:52. He did not fast-forward but waited patiently, praying for the man to appear. If he had turned left or right at the preceding intersection, Hideo might never find him again.

Finally, miraculously, he appeared. Hideo closed his eyes and breathed a sigh of relief and thanks, then focused on the man with the rug. He crossed the intersection heading north, then turned west and waited for the green.

"Look up," Hideo said aloud, earning a puzzled look from Kenji. "Look up and check the traffic signal. Look *up!*"

And then, almost as if he'd heard him, the man looked up, almost directly into the camera. Hideo froze the frame, enlarged, enhanced, and saved. He would enter it into the facial recognition program later. But first . . .

He returned to the view of the entrance to Gerrish's apartment building and watched until he saw himself and the three yakuza exit. He let the recording run even longer, but no sign of Yoshio's *ronin*.

He sighed. He didn't see any way of finding him. But he should be grateful. At least he'd secured a picture of the current owner of Sasaki-san's katana. That was the important thing. Of course it would all come to nothing if he had never been arrested and entered into the system. But Hideo had a feeling that a man who would slit another's throat to acquire a sword would have to have been arrested at some point during his adult life. And if he had, Hideo would find him.

The *ronin*, however . . . the odds were high against his ever having another chance at that man.

But Hideo had a feeling that, with the help of his ancestors, he might
beat those odds.

20

Stupid! Stupid! Stupid!

Someone had seen her. She totally knew it.

All right, she didn't *know* it, but how could someone *not* have seen her?
She'd got on the C without knowing where she was going, but that had been
okay. What had counted was being off the street. Then she'd looked around
the subway car and seen her face on half a dozen flyers.

She'd kept her head down, her mind screaming for a solution. Finally it
hit her: tourists.

Totally.

Native New Yorkers would have her face burned on their brains by now,
but tourists came and went. And tourists usually spent their time gawking at
the sights and gazing up at the skyscrapers and such, not studying posters.
So where could she find the most tourists? In the Times Square/theater district, of course.

Tons of tourists.

She'd ducked out of the C at 42nd Street. The Port Authority had
tempted her—hop a bus to New Jersey where Jerry would never find her.
But she knew nothing about Jersey, and figured she'd probably need a car
there. She didn't know if they even did abortions in Jersey.

No, better to stay where she knew her way around. At least for now. Lots
of abortion clinics in the city. Once that was over she could think about relocating.

She'd wound through the crowds on Eighth toward the theaters. When she saw a bunch of men wearing John Deere caps and string ties come out of the Milford Plaza, she knew that was the place for her.

But checking in hadn't been easy. They'd been totally suspicious about her wanting to pay cash, but she had no choice. She couldn't use a credit card—someone watching her account would know exactly where she was. They'd wanted ID and she had to show her driver's license. That put her real name on the register.

And then the room. A single. Dawn could so not believe how small it was. A postage stamp with like four feet between the walls and the king-size bed. Even the mirrored wall couldn't make it look bigger. Plus the bathroom had fixtures that looked fifty years old.

All for the bargain price of $326 a night.

She guessed she could have chosen a better grade, but that meant more money and she wanted to conserve as much of her cash as possible. She had no idea of how long it would last.

So for the time being this would be home.

Gross.

She went to the window and looked out at the night. She couldn't see the street, only rooftops and the glow from all the lighted marquees on 45th Street directly below. Was someone down there in the crowds, watching the hotel, waiting for her to come out? Waiting so he could collect his reward?

She couldn't leave, couldn't even risk going to the hotel restaurant. She'd have to order room service and hope the delivery guy didn't recognize her.

She felt just as trapped as she had at Mr. Osala's, but at least there she'd been safe. Here . . .

This was a nightmare.

Why not just call Henry and have him pick her up? But then she'd be back where she started.

She couldn't take it. She'd been ready to end it all before but had let Mr. Osala talk her out of it. Why not finish the job now? Get it done this time.

She tried to open the window but it wouldn't budge. She picked up the room's one chair and slammed it against the glass. It bounced back. She tried it again with the same result. Some sort of safety glass.

She dropped onto the bed and began to cry.

She had to find a way out of this. She'd formed the beginnings of a plan on the subway. Maybe she should go with that.

She pulled herself together, grabbed the bag of stuff she'd bought at the drugstore, and headed for the bathroom.

21

Using his flashlight sparingly, Shiro rushed back through the dark woods to his teacher, praying the news he brought would not cause him to abort the test.

"*Sensei*, there are people in the little cabin there!"

Akechi-*sensei*, a faintly limned shadow in the starlight, nodded. "All the better. Proceed."

"But what if they interfere?"

"They will not." He pointed back toward the woods. "Go. Hurry."

Shiro obeyed, returning to where Tadasu waited with the *shoten*. The chosen site lay half a mile north of a golf course and barely more than half a mile from any dwelling, yet here among the silent trees, civilization could have been a thousand miles away.

That changed as he neared the rotting cabin in a tiny forgotten clearing.

Not completely forgotten, obviously. Four teenagers—two couples—had driven a battered Jeep to the cabin and begun an impromptu party. They had beer and were playing loud music.

He found Tadasu about fifty yards from the cabin. The *shoten* lay bound and gagged on the ground before him.

"*Sensei* says to proceed," he said when he arrived.

Tadasu nodded, then knelt next to the *shoten*. He pulled a blue vial from his pocket.

"Hold his head and remove the gag," he said.

Shiro did as he was told and the *shoten* began cursing.

"What the fuck you sonabitches—"

"Drink this," Tadasu said, forcing the mouth of the vial between his lips.

The old drunk apparently never refused anything to drink because he swallowed it in one gulp. Then he made a face.

"Shit! What is that shit?"

Shiro reapplied the gag, then stepped away. Tadasu remained kneeling. "Now we wait."

The *shoten*'s muffled protests and struggles against his bonds slowed, then ceased. When he lay quiet, Tadasu removed the gag and then produced a red-striped wooden sliver.

"A *doku-ippen?*" Shiro said.

"Akechi-*sensei*'s idea. Just to be safe." He pricked the *shoten*'s neck with it, then rose and stepped over him. "Back to *sensei*. Quickly. We don't know how soon it takes effect."

Shiro led the way, and soon the three of them were standing together next to their car on an empty side road, staring in the general direction of the *shoten*.

Suspense gripped Shiro like a vise. His breath felt trapped in his chest. "What will happen, *sensei?*"

"Something wonderful, Shiro. No one alive has seen a Kuroikaze. We shall be the first in a generation."

"Why did we use a *doku-ippen?*"

"The *ekisu* causes the one who drinks it to become a focus for the Kuroikaze. The Black Wind will last as long as the *shoten* survives. Because this is an experiment to test the *ekisu*, I do not want large-scale death. We will save that for later. I had you choose a sickly *shoten* because, while the Kuroikaze is sapping the life from all it touches, it is also diminishing the life of the *shoten*. The longer the *shoten* survives, the more fierce the wind, the greater the radius of death. The particular *doku-ippen* used will bring death shortly after it is introduced into the body. So even if this wasted *shoten* taps into some hidden reserves of strength, he won't survive long enough to raise a full-fledged Kuroikaze."

"There!" Tadasu cried, pointing. "Something is happening!"

Shiro strained to see, but the starlight was dim, and the trees dark.

And then he saw it—a layer of blackness overspreading an area of trees . . . a cloud, blacker than Shiro had ever seen . . . so black it didn't reflect the meager starlight, but rather seemed to absorb it . . . devour it.

The way it oozed across the treetops made Shiro's gut crawl. This was evil, and he didn't like to think of the Order to which he had devoted his life as dealing with evil. But then, this was certainly no more evil than the atomic bombs that killed so many in Hiroshima and Nagasaki.

Yes, if he thought of it that way, he could accept.

He watched and waited, expecting to see the inexorable flow of the blackness slow and then begin to ebb. But it continued to expand, coming their way.

"*Sensei*? Shouldn't it be stopping now?"

Akechi-*sensei* turned to Tadasu. "You are sure the point pierced his skin?"

"I saw blood, *sensei*."

"Then he should die any minute."

But the blackness showed no sign of slowing, let alone retreating.

"Perhaps we had better move farther way," Tadasu said.

"No," said their teacher. "If you did your duty, we have nothing to fear."

Shiro felt he had a lot to fear. That blackness . . . it made him want to run, and hide, find his mother and cower behind her.

Abruptly the blackness changed. Instead of spreading toward them, it began expanding upward, shooting a towering ebony column into the sky, reaching toward the stars.

And then it was gone, and the blackness over the trees evaporated like smoke in a gale.

"Quickly," Akechi-*sensei* said. "Into the woods. We must see what it has done."

Shiro led the way, directing his flashlight beam ahead of him. He moved cautiously at first because he didn't know what to expect. But then, seeing no trace of the blackness, he picked up speed . . .

Until he came upon the dead vegetation—like crossing a line of death where everything on one side thrived and everything on the other was dead. Every leaf on every tree and bush was wilted and brown, every needle on every pine was brown, even the weeds were dead. Nothing moved. No owls hooted, no crickets chirped, no mosquitoes bit.

All this death . . . from the Kuroikaze?

He came upon the *shoten*. The flashlight beam revealed a shrunken cadaver that looked as if it had been dead for weeks.

Shiro backed away, then approached the shack. Entering, he found the structure intact but its inhabitants . . . he had to look away.

He had only glimpsed them before the Kuroikaze, so he didn't know how they had changed. They looked shrunken, though not so much as the *shoten*. But what Shiro found most disturbing was their expressions. Each open-eyed, openmouthed face carried the same look: a great sadness, an unfathomable hopelessness.

"And this is how it will be."

Shiro started and turned at the sound of his *sensei*'s voice. He found him gesturing to the corpses and to the shack around them.

"They firebombed Tokyo, atom-bombed Hiroshima and Nagasaki, but worst of all, they humiliated the Son of Heaven, made Him bow to them, made Him surrender. Now it is their turn. We will set up strong, vital *shotens* around the city. We will feed them the *ekisu* and we will *not* pierce them with a *doku-ippen*. Then the clouds will rise and merge, creating such a Kuroikaze as has never been seen. It will leave the entire city like this. Millions dead, yet the buildings untouched. Imagine, the entire city silent, unmoving. All the structures intact, unmarred, just as they had been before the Kuroikaze, but filled with the dead, millions and millions of dead."

THURSDAY

1

O'Day . . . the man's name was Thomas O'Day.

It had taken Hideo a while to find him in the police database. Due to the poor light in the captured still, the face recognition program had been unable to create a sufficiently specific map to pin down the man he sought. The result was dozens of hits, followed by the wearisome task of tracing the current whereabouts of each one of them. Some were dead, some were still incarcerated, and some were free and gainfully employed.

One was the owner of a shop specializing in knives and swords. He had been arrested for possession of stolen property with intent to sell. He had lived free for a number of years now without another arrest.

But a man who had sold stolen goods in the past might have reverted to his old ways. If Gerrish had wished to sell the stolen katana, who better to seek out than a fence who knew all about swords?

It was not a sure thing, but it was the best he had. In fact, the only thing he had. He decided to pursue it.

His instincts said to wait until nightfall, especially considering the Madison Avenue address of this Bladeville store. But he reminded himself that he had waited until dark to visit Mr. Gerrish and had regretted it. He would not make that mistake again.

He called out to Kenji to gather his yakuza brothers and prepare to move.

2

Dawn checked herself in the mirror.

She'd had a totally terrible night and looked it. Hardly slept at all. Kept hearing people outside her door and worrying they were coming for her. She had the security bar in place and even had wedged the chair against the knob, but still she worried.

And then the phone had rung. Just one ring and then stopped. She'd stared at it, waiting for another, but none came. Finally she mustered the nerve to pick up the receiver and listen.

Nothing but a dial tone.

Probably just some electronic glitch in the system. Under normal circumstances she wouldn't have given it a second thought. But last night she'd stayed on tenterhooks for hours, wondering if it would ring again.

Paranoia was so not fun.

The bags under her red eyes made her look like she'd been partying all night. They went right along with the rotten haircut and dye job she'd given herself.

But at least she looked way different from the girl who'd walked in here yesterday. She'd used the scissors and brown hair-coloring kit she'd bought at the drugstore to give herself a makeover. The shoulder-length blond hair had become short and brown, barely covering her ears.

She put on her big sunglasses and turned this way and that. She looked nothing like the girl on the flyer. No way anyone would recognize her.

That made her feel somewhat better. Especially since she was leaving the hotel today on an important errand—a visit to an abortion clinic on West 63rd this afternoon. She'd called first thing this morning and they'd given her a three-thirty appointment.

She paced the tiny open area near the window. What to do till then? She had no choice but the tube. She turned on the set and found nothing but news. Something had happened last night.

Please not another terrorist attack, she thought. First the trade towers, then LaGuardia, now what?

She stopped to watch and listen to a talking head . . .

"The news from Staten Island just got worse, I'm afraid. Five bodies have been found in the dead area—an adult male and four teenagers. They have not yet been identified. For those of you who have just awakened, here is the breaking story: A half-mile-wide circle of Staten Island died during the night."

An aerial view of a wooded area filled the screen, green except for a circle of brown at its center. It looked like a lawn where someone had spilled weed killer. Dawn felt her neck tighten and crawl when she realized how *perfectly* round it was. The newscaster spoke over the image.

"People on the island, and even some in Brooklyn, reported a strange meteorological phenomenon—a vertical black cloud by most accounts—that lasted only seconds, but seemed to originate in the area some have begun calling the 'kill zone.' Everything is dead. The floor of the wooded area is littered with the bodies of birds, squirrels, mice, moles, and chipmunks. Every single bit of vegetation is brown and wilted. Nothing was spared."

Chilled, Dawn switched to the next station where she encountered a talking head described as a "cereologist."

". . . obvious that since their crop circle warnings were at best ignored or at worst ridiculed, they've progressed to the next level. Now, instead of merely knocking down vegetation, they've started killing it . . ."

Next she came to someone labeled a "chemical warfare expert."

"Look, we know it's not an infestation—first off because parasites don't kill overnight, and secondly because too many species of plants died. And a parasite won't explain the dead birds. No, it has to be a toxin—herbicidal, but toxic to birds and mammals as well. Frankly, I've never heard of such an agent, but obviously it exists, because that's the only way to explain the across-the-board lethality and the confined location."

Another channel showed a man-on-the-street interview with an old codger who looked to be in his eighties.

"What about you, sir. Are you scared? Could it be terrorists?"

"Could be. I saw something like this back in the Pacific theater during war. We called it a 'wilt' back then, and it was always associated with a black cloud. Atolls and whole islands would get hit, leaving nothing alive—even

the fish would be dead. And if any of our guys were there, they'd be dead too, all with these awful looks on their faces. It was a Jap secret weapon then, and it stayed secret from us. But it looks like someone else's got hold of it now."

Dawn turned off the set. This was creeping her out. She turned her thoughts to her appointment at the clinic.

She had all her moves planned: Out the front entrance and into one of the waiting cabs, up to the clinic for her interview, examination, and blood work, then call a cab to bring her straight back here. She estimated her maximum exposure on the street at less than two minutes. That sounded totally safe and doable.

So why then did she feel like she'd be entering a combat zone?

3

Jack timed his arrival at Bladeville for a few minutes after ten A.M. Maybe he was wrong, but his gut told him otherwise.

As he stepped through the door—keeping the beak of his hat between his face and the security cam—the chime sounded and Tom O'Day stepped in from the private area at the rear. He stopped in his tracks with a startled expression.

"Um . . . Jack, right?"

Jack nodded. He'd gone over all the possible approaches and had decided on balls-to-the-wall directness.

"We've got a problem."

What little openness there'd been in O'Day's expression shut down like the security shutter on his store.

"Really?"

"Yeah. The guy who stole the Gaijin Masamune is dead, his throat slit by the katana in question."

Jack didn't know that for sure, but figured it was a safe assumption. O'Day's sudden pallor went a long way toward confirming that.

"Wh-what do you mean? How do you know?"

"I arrived at his place shortly after it happened."

O'Day quickly regained his composure. He gave Jack a narrowed-eyed stare.

"How do I know you didn't do it?"

"Because you got caught on the lobby camera entering and leaving around the time of death."

O'Day blanched. "Bullshit!"

Which was right on the money. Jack hadn't even seen the lobby, and had no idea whether it was fitted with a security cam or not. But he had a feeling O'Day wasn't anywhere near as aware of them as Jack was, so it was a good bet he'd never noticed either way.

Jack shrugged. "After I found the body I broke into the security office and ran a quick review off the hard drive there." He smiled. "It's not much more than a glorified TiVo, y'know. Watched you walk in empty-handed, then a little later, not so empty-handed—a long, wrapped object under your arm."

No way would O'Day walk out carrying a sword for all to see. He'd have it wrapped in something—a towel, a sheet, a rug. Jack had no idea which, so he'd kept it vague.

O'Day looked weak. Sweat beaded his face.

"Hey," Jack said in his most reassuring tone, "Told you: I'm not a cop. Too bad about Gerrish. Never knew the guy, and there are probably worse ways to die, but that's between you and him. What's between you and me is the matter of the sword. I'm ready to do you a favor and take it off your hands for a nice price."

O'Day shook his head as if to clear it. "Favor?"

"Sure. Once the cops see that tape, you'll become what they like to call 'a person of interest.' When they find you—and that's *when*, not *if*—they'll learn about your trade and your collection, and when that happens you'll graduate from person of interest to suspect *numero uno*."

"And selling to you's gonna help?"

"Sure. You've got a murder weapon hidden away. Gerrish may have shown it to a friend. It's pretty distinctive, and if they find it on you, you're cooked. But sell it to my guy and he'll sneak it back overseas where he came from. You'll have big bucks, he'll have his sword back, and I'll have my fee. Win-win-win."

O'Day chewed his lower lip in silence for a moment, then gave a quick nod.

"For the record, I found Gerrish dead, just like you did. The katana was lying next to him. Since he wouldn't be having any more use for it, I decided to give it a good home."

Riiiight.

"Like I said: Never knew Gerrish. What happened between you and him stays between you and him. Like Vegas. What do you want for the blade?"

"A hundred grand."

Jack blinked. "Whoa. I don't know if he wants it back *that* badly."

O'Day gave him a sour smile. "Well, we'll never know if we don't ask, will we."

"I getcha. Where is it?"

He didn't want to be responsible for involving his customer in some low-rent scam.

"In the back. Wanna see?"

"I think I should, don't you."

He shrugged. "I guess so." He started toward the front of the store. "But first . . ." He went to the door and pulled down the security shutter, closing them in behind a wall of corrugated steel. "Like a fishbowl in here. Can't be too careful."

"We could've just gone back there."

"Don't want anyone wandering in."

Jack felt an uneasy tingle in his gut. Something askew here.

As he watched O'Day stride toward the back room, he wondered if he'd bought the security cam bit. If he hadn't, then Jack was the only person who could connect O'Day to Gerrish, and it would be in O'Day's best interest to eliminate that link.

He pulled his Glock from the small of his back and turned sideways, shielding it behind his right thigh.

O'Day returned balancing the katana on his palms. The blade was riddled with pocks and holes, just like in the photos. Jack noticed that he'd done some fixing up.

"You put a handle on it."

"It's called a *tsuka*. Yeah. I spent half the night getting the wrapping right." He pushed the sword closer to Jack. "Wanna closer look?"

"That's okay."

A little farther out. "C'mon."

"I can see what I need to see. Okay, I'll tell my guy—"

O'Day was fast for his age. In a flash he had the katana raised in a one-handed grip and swinging toward Jack's head. With a choice between getting off a shot or being scalped, he ducked and raised the Glock to ward off the blade. It struck the pistol with almost enough force to knock it free. As it was, the blow pulled his finger against the trigger and fired off the chambered round. Jack rolled and pulled the trigger again.

Nothing.

He glanced at the Glock and saw only half a pistol. The blade had sliced through the plastic frame just forward of the trigger guard, then through the spring and guide rod and—hell, it had cut through the barrel as well. The slide had been knocked free, exposing the chamber. He could see the next round waiting to be chambered.

What the—?

He leaned back as the katana made another slice at his head—the guy had one hell of a reach. He heard the whisper of lacerated air and felt the breeze in its wake.

O'Day had a two-handed grip now and was already making another swing for the bleachers. Jack flung the remnant of the Glock, bouncing it off his forehead. O'Day grunted in pain and his swing went wide.

With that, Jack vaulted over the counter, grabbed a dagger off the wall, and flung it. O'Day knocked it away in midair with the blade. He grinned, confident. He knew how to handle a katana.

And now Jack knew it too.

He grabbed another knife—a heavy dirk—threw it, and reached for his Kel-Tec in its ankle holster. But the dirk went wide and the katana smashed into the display case inches from Jack's head, showering him with glittering shards of glass.

He forgot about his backup for an instant as he rolled away from the glass and O'Day's follow-up swing. Then O'Day climbed over what was left of that section of the display case and charged, the katana held high with both hands, his mouth wide in a scream of rage. Looked like he'd had enough and wanted to end this here and now.

On the floor, with no room for lateral movement in the narrow lane behind the cases, Jack scrabbled away on hands and knees. In desperation he grabbed a wavy bladed kris from a case as he passed and winged it over his shoulder. He heard O'Day's scream choke off but he didn't slow. Without looking back he dove onto the display cabinet and rolled to the other side. As soon as he hit the floor, he rolled again, yanking his backup free along the way. He leaped to his feet, aiming the Kel-Tec P-11 at O'Day's center of mass.

But didn't fire.

O'Day stood behind the counter, leaning against the wall. He'd lowered the katana, though he hadn't dropped it. His eyes were glazed as blood poured from his mouth. Somehow, the kris had landed point first in his open mouth, piercing the rear of his throat. The wavy blade protruded at an angle, and began to bob as he made a slow turn and staggered toward the rear of the store.

Jack heard a clattering clank and figured he'd finally lost his grip on the sword. He made it to the NO ADMITTANCE door before collapsing face-first onto the floor. The dead-weight impact of the floor against the pommel of the kris drove its blade deeper into his throat and out the back of his neck. His legs spas-kicked a couple of times, then he lay still.

Jack watched it all and felt nothing.

Bye-bye, Tom O'Day. Maybe Hugh Gerrish will be waiting for you on the other side. Should be an interesting conversation.

He hurried around to the back of the counter and lifted the katana, careful to avoid its cutting edge. He felt a strange sensation run through him as he touched the blade. Couldn't identify it—at once thrilled and repulsed. He gripped it by the handle and had to fight off a mad urge to swing it in a decapitating arc.

Was that what had happened between Gerrish and O'Day?

No matter. He wasn't going to keep it . . .

Or was he?

Jack felt this mad rush of desire to take it and hang it on his wall and shred anybody who tried to take it from him.

He shook it off. Three people dead now because of it—at least he assumed the bat-wielding guy who had charged into Gerrish's apartment had left the living. Three that he knew of. Who knew how many it had killed since Masamune had made it? He couldn't see how it could be worth it.

Time to get out of here. He needed something to wrap it in, and then he'd be gone. He looked around . . .

And his gaze settled on the security cam.

Shit!

Despite his hat, with all that dodging and weaving and rolling over the counter, no way his face hadn't been exposed. Had to find that tape or disk or hard drive or whatever and trash it.

He dragged a chair over to the corner and was climbing toward the cam when a rattling racket came from the front of the store. Someone was banging on the security shutter.

"Mister O'Day?" a voice called. "Are you in there? You are supposed to be open by now."

That sounded like the yakuzas' boss from last night. The same guys? Could it be possible?

Didn't matter. Couldn't be caught here.

He hopped down and pulled on the NO ADMITTANCE door, but it wouldn't budge because O'Day's corpse was slumped against it. Jack was trying to slide him out of the way when he heard the steel curtain begin to roll up. No time to get out, so he darted toward the counter. On the way he spotted the pieces of his ruined Glock on the floor. He snatched up everything in sight and ducked behind the display cases. Beneath them he spotted wooden doors. He slid one open and found a near-empty space occupied by a few stilettos and folding knives. A tight fit but . . .

He put the katana in first, making sure its cutting edge was facing away. He followed it, folding his knees against his chest and sliding the door closed. He waited, listening, Kel-Tec ready.

4

Hideo had noticed that the security shutter was unlocked, so he instructed Goro to raise it. The lights were on within. He pushed on the door and it swung open.

"Mister O'Day?" he called again. "Are you in there?"

No answer.

Kenji slipped past him and entered the store. He took two steps and stopped. He glanced back with a surprised and concerned expression, then hurried forward. The two other yakuza followed. Hideo hesitantly brought up the rear, sensing that something bad waited ahead.

He was right. One quick look at Mr. O'Day, a flash of the hilt of a dagger distorting his mouth and the bloody point of its wavy blade jutting from the back of his neck, was all he could take. He turned away and struggled to hold down his breakfast of *natto, nori,* and miso soup.

He succeeded, then managed to say, "The katana—does anyone see the katana?"

As they began looking, Hideo noticed people passing on the street. No one glanced in, but sooner or later someone would.

"Hurry!"

Goro and Ryo rolled the body away from the rear door. Kenji stepped through and turned on the lights.

"Takita-san! Come see!"

Hideo gingerly stepped over the corpse and peeked in the room. He gasped at the dozens of gleaming blades racked on the walls. He knew little about katana, but sensed this was a magnificent collection.

Unfortunately each blade appeared to be in perfect condition. And there on the floor lay the rug he had seen O'Day carrying from Gerrish's apartment building—empty.

He glanced again at the front of the store. Madison Avenue was becoming busier and busier. Only a matter of time before someone stopped in for a look.

The katana was not here. O'Day had killed Gerrish to get it, and now someone had killed O'Day. This blade was leaving a trail of corpses in its blood-soaked wake. How was he going to find this latest killer?

Wait. Hadn't he seen a security camera on one of the walls? He stepped back in to the front area and yes—a camera mounted near the ceiling. A chair sat conveniently in place below it. He climbed upon it to get an idea of where the wire might go. He tugged on it and—

It came free.

Only a gentle tug to pop it out of the wall. Hideo found himself looking at the clean-cut end of a coaxial cable, devoid of any connector.

No! A prop!

In a fit of rage he tore the fake cam from the wall and hurled it across the store, spewing curses as it flew.

Hideo hated O'Day then. He deserved to be dead. He had left Hideo with no record of what had transpired here.

He jumped to the floor and hurried to the front door where he scanned the street. No traffic cams in sight. He cursed again, this time under his breath.

Then he turned to Goro. "Turn out the lights inside and lower the shutter." To Kenji: "Call the car."

As he waited he reviewed his options but saw no way to rescue this. He must find one. *Must.* His own honor as well as Yoshio's depended on it. He could not return to Tokyo and report failure to Sasaki-san.

5

Hearing the security shutter clang shut and the store go silent, Jack eased open the sliding door and unfolded himself from the cabinet. Good thing he wasn't claustrophobic.

He reholstered his Kel-Tec and fitted the pieces of the Glock into his pockets. Even though it was ruined, he couldn't very well leave it behind. He looked around to see what had caused the crash and the cursing. In the dim light seeping around the edges of the shutter he noticed the security cam lying smashed on the floor. When he stepped closer and saw the dead-end cable, he understood.

O'Day . . . scamming to the end . . . everybody, including Jack.

Okay. Alive and in possession of the katana. All he had left to do was get out of here and return the sword to its rightful owner. No, wait—that would be the museum in Hiroshima. Then again, the rightful owner would be the family of the man who had owned it last—probably vaporized in the A-bomb blast.

A torturous provenance. He'd go with the Hirohito he knew.

He began a search for something to wrap around the sword. In the back room he found a dusty throw rug that did the trick. But first he used it to wipe the kris's handle, and anything else he had touched.

He slipped up to the front door and peeked through a quarter-inch gap between the wall and the shutter track just in time to see the boss man and his three yakuza pals getting into a black Lincoln Town Car.

Jack waited until it had moved off, then adjusted his cap and shades for maximum coverage before lifting the shutter just enough to allow him through. He straightened and let it drop again. A quick look around showed nobody particularly interested in him. It also showed the Lincoln waiting to make a left onto 29th Street.

He stood watching it, wondering who the hell they were.

The light changed and the car started to turn, but stopped halfway. For a second Jack thought one of them had spotted him, then realized it had stopped because it couldn't go any farther. Twenty-ninth was backed up.

As he watched it inch around the corner, he realized a pedestrian could run circles around them. Hell, an arthritic snail could leave them in the dust.

If traffic stayed jammed, maybe . . . just maybe he could follow them to whatever they were calling home.

He gave them a lead of half a block or better, then followed. Cautiously. They were crossing the lower end of Murray Hill and he didn't see many places to hide. Whenever the car stopped—and that was often—he did the same and found a doorway or used an unloading van as a screen.

When they finally reached Fifth Avenue, Jack saw the problem: mini gridlock. On the far side of Fifth, the street opened up, but the avenue itself was backed up. Could be an accident, or construction, or simply the daily perversities and vicissitudes of Manhattan traffic. Didn't matter. Once their car crossed Fifth, they'd be gone.

But wonder of wonders, the left-turn blinker came on. Hope sparked. This might work out after all.

Staying out of sight on Fifth was easy—more lanes of traffic, more pedestrians. The Town Car stayed in the center fire lane as it made its downtown crawl, which told Jack that it wasn't intending to turn for a while.

After more than twenty slow blocks, they came to Washington Square Park. The car seemed aimed to pass through the famous arch when it flowed right onto Waverly Place. The car stopped before a massive, granite-fronted townhouse where the four got out and hurried up the front steps through a columned portico. They entered as if they owned the place.

He had a feeling they didn't, but maybe their employer did. He wondered who that might be. Some sort of Japanese crime organization? How else to explain the yakuza? Seemed that someone in that deep-pocketed organization—had to have elbow-deep pockets to afford a place like the one on Waverly—was a katana collector as well, and had somehow learned that Gerrish had stolen the Gaijin Masamune.

Jack was sure Abe could learn who owned it. He'd ask him to find out.

Just for curiosity's sake.

Because Jack had no intention of seeing any of that crew again. He'd contact Naka Slater ASAP, hand over the sword, collect his fee, and then it would be *arigato, sayonara,* and good riddance to the cursed thing.

6

Darryl's eyes burned in the bright midday sunlight but he kept constant watch on the comings and goings at the Milford entrance.

Even though his shift didn't start again till midnight, and he needed some shut-eye real bad, he couldn't stay away from the hotel.

With good reason: He had a big investment here.

Hank had set up two twelve-hour shifts of three guys each in a side-door panel truck, noon to midnight, and midnight to noon. They'd found a parking space across from the front entrance and camped there. The plan was to spot her and follow her and one way or another pull her into the van without being seen. In the event they were spotted and reported, the van had been fitted with stolen license plates.

Darryl had taken the first red-eye shift with two other Kickers. Hank had told them that Dawn would probably dye her hair, so give *every* chick in her age group—not just the blondes—a close look.

And just to make sure she was really registered, he'd called the hotel and asked for Dawn Pickering. Darryl had figured she'd register under a phony name but Hank had said no way. Maybe before 9/11, but not since. The hotel wouldn't tell him the room number but had put him through to Dawn Pickering's phone. He'd hung up just as it started to ring.

Yeah, she was there, all right.

Smart guy, that Hank.

He scratched his left shin. Been itching him since last night. Had something bit him?

He pulled up his pants leg for a look and saw a purplish blotch on his skin. He tried to rub it off but it was *in* his skin. Weird. And ugly. Must have bumped it in the truck. He'd spent twelve hours straight in that thing watching the entrance with no sign of Dawn. And even though he'd been relieved a couple of hours ago, he couldn't seem to let go.

He didn't know the guys on the noon shift, didn't know how sharp an eye they'd keep out for the girl. After all, what did they care. Yeah, Hank said she was important to the future of the Kicker Evolution, but what did that mean in everyday terms? Not much.

If she slipped by them they'd be like, Oh well, fucked up, we'll get her next time.

Different for Darryl. That babe meant five grand in his pocket. He wasn't about to let her slip away.

7

Hideo was having no luck. He wanted to grab his keyboard and bat it against the desk until it shattered into a thousand pieces, but he resisted that dubious pleasure. He must appear to be in control of himself and the situation—the rapidly deteriorating situation.

Despite his best efforts, he had been unable to find a traffic cam with a view of the Bladeville doorway. He also had searched the Manhattan Web-cam sites available on the Internet but still no luck.

So he decided to go to the source: Check police records on the Hawaiian Islands for a report of a stolen sword. That would lead to the owner and give Hideo a starting point.

But no such report existed on any of the islands. The possibility of a thief like Gerrish buying it seemed too remote to consider. Which left Hideo with a number of unpleasant prospects: The owner was either dead, or did not know the sword was missing, or did not legally own it.

He rubbed his sweaty palms on his trousers. What was he going to do? He had to report back to Sasaki-san's office within the next twelve hours. What was he going to say? Certainly not that he had hit a dead end. Certainly not that he had run into a man who matched one of the pictures his brother had sent back—that would only remind them of Yoshio's failure and perhaps wonder if this brother might not be headed along the same path.

No, he must sound optimistic: Through his diligence he had already had two near encounters with the katana. Perhaps add that he had missed it by scant minutes each time and hint at how he wished he had been assigned this mission sooner. Had he arrived in New York even half a day earlier, he would have the katana by now and be flying it home. He believed this to be true, and hoped it might mitigate any ire in the home office about his lack of success to this point.

What he dared not say was that he had run out of leads. The two men he had connected to the blade were dead. His encounter with Yoshio's *ronin* had been a one-in-a-million chance coincidence. He could not count on another.

All he could do was ask his ancestors for help and guidance, and pray that they or fate would drop something in his lap.

Until that happened, he must appear to be in control and homing in on the katana. The only course open to him at the moment was to find the previous owner—the one from whom Gerrish had most likely stolen it.

That meant tracing Gerrish's movements from the time he landed on the Hawaiian Islands until the time he boarded Northwest flight 804 out of Maui.

At least then he would have a goal. He could look busy, *be* busy, all the while knowing he'd set himself a nearly impossible goal.

And then two seemingly unrelated facts collided and clung: If the previous owner of the katana had no legal claim to it, might he not have followed the blade to New York and hired a local to find it? Yoshio had termed the mystery man a *ronin*—and *ronin* had been known to sell their services.

He straightened in his seat. Here was another avenue of inquiry—a daunting task but one he must pursue: Seek out someone in this city who hired out to solve problems that needed to remain hidden from the authorities.

An urban *ronin*.

8

Delivery was scheduled for ten o'clock tonight. Naka Slater did not want to take possession of the katana in a public place. Said he needed to examine the blade before he forked over the rest of Jack's fee.

Fair enough. Were positions reversed, Jack would have demanded the same.

He'd decided on the alley next to Julio's. It was convenient, he was familiar with it, and meeting there wouldn't necessarily connect him to the bar.

After cutting the call, he stood in his front room staring at the rolled-up rug lying on his round oak table. It seemed to call to him.

Shrugging, he unwrapped it and took a two-handed grip on the handle. He knew next to nothing about swords, but the katana's balance was so perfect it seemed to want to move of its own accord. He carried it to the center of the room where he lurched into an improvised sword kata that probably looked a lot more like John Belushi than Toshiro Mifune.

He felt a twinge of regret that he'd called Naka Slater. It felt good in his hands, so good that he didn't want to set it down. Heirloom or not, collector's item or not, object of murderous desire or not, he wanted this on *his* wall, not some rich plantation owner's. He could give back the advance . . .

He forced himself to put down the sword, telling himself not to start down that slippery slope. He'd made a deal to find and return it. He'd accomplished the first half, now to complete the job.

He stared down at the sword where it lay on the dirty old rug. Something entrancing about the pattern of holes in its blade. Almost hypnotizing.

What the hell.

He picked it up and began swinging it again.

9

"He has the katana, *sensei!*" The familiar voice was bursting with joy. "He will deliver it tonight!"

Only a supreme effort of will prevented Toru from leaping to his feet and shouting *Banzai!* For once the meaning would be literal—possession of the katana guaranteed the Kakureta Kao a thousand years.

But the Order did not yet possess it.

Controlling his voice, Toru said, "You have done well, but two tasks remain: Take possession of the katana, and see that no one can connect you or the Order to it."

"Yes, *sensei.*"

Toru studied the younger man through the eyeholes of his silk mask.

"You have been trained in the fighting arts, and you are so proficient that you have trained others. But you have never used them for anything like this. Are you capable of killing?" He raised a hand as Tadasu opened his mouth. "Think well on this. It is crucial. If you are not sure, I will send someone along to see it is done."

His dark eyes flashed. "I will need no help, *sensei.* I can do this."

Toru studied his determined expression for a few heartbeats, then nodded.

"I believe that you can and that you will."

He bowed. "It will be an honor to so serve the Order."

10

Darryl checked his watch—4:40. Man, he was tired. Had to give it up and catch some Z's. Needed to be rested for the red-eye shift at midnight.

Okay. Give it another twenty and quit at five, grab a couple of brews and hit the hay.

He watched a cab pull up, saw the door open and a gal get out. Seemed the right age, short brown hair, shades. He was about to write her off when he took another look. Something familiar about those shades. Just like the ones Dawn had been wearing—he knew 'cause he'd got a couple of close looks when he'd seen her in that Arab getup. He took a closer look at her face and—

Fuck me! It's her!

He watched in shock as she kept her head down and hurried inside. He shook it off and checked the cab as it passed, memorizing its number. Then he hurried over to the van. He was going to give the guys inside a bit of pure hell. And then who did he see standing there, leaning in the window, but Hank himself.

Perfect.

Hank smiled at him as he came up to the van.

"Hey, Darryl. What's—?"

"She got out!" He pointed to the guys in the van. "She got past them! Me too!"

Hank's smile vanished. "What are you talking about?"

"I just saw her get out of a cab and go inside."

"Bullshit!" said one of the guys in the van—Darryl didn't know his name. "We been watching like hawks."

"Yeah? Well, your hawks need glasses because I just saw her. Lucky for us she was going back in. But that means she was out, 'cause you can't go in 'less you been out."

"You're crazy!" said another one of the van guys.

"Whoa! Whoa!" Hank said. He was staring at Darryl. "You're sure?"

"Sure, I'm sure. You were right about her changing her hair color, Hank. But she cut it too. It's short now—kinda spiky and dykey, if you know what I'm saying."

Hank looked worried. In fact his face had gone dead white. "How'd she look?"

"I just told you."

"No, I mean her health. Did she look well?"

What was he getting at?

"How so?"

"I mean, did she look like she'd just had surgery or something?"

"No. She was moving pretty good."

He looked relieved. "Okay. But where could she have gone?"

"I've got the cab number, if that's of any use."

Hank laughed and clapped him on the shoulder. "Darryl, my man, you're invaluable!"

Darryl felt a warm glow envelop him. Hank Thompson thought he was invaluable. How great was that?

He shrugged. "Just trying to help the evolution."

"Well, you're doing a great job." He pulled a small notepad from one pocket and a ballpoint from another. "Here. Write it down. I'll have Menck grease the driver's palm with a few bucks and we'll know where she came from."

Darryl wondered why that was so important and what Hank was worried about, and then it hit: the baby. Was he worried she'd gone out and had an abortion?

Darryl was about to ask just that when he realized Hank was staring at him again.

"It just occurred to me, Darryl—what are you doing here?"

"Keeping watch."

"You had any sleep since your shift?"

"No, I—"

"You're supposed to be resting up for your next shift."

"But—"

Hank raised a hand. "I appreciate the heads-up you've just given us, but you're gonna be no damn good on your own shift if you don't get some shut-eye."

"But she got by these guys."

"She got by you too—on her way out. And she'll get by you again if you're not sharp." His expression turned stern. "Now get off the street and get some rack time. We know what she looks like now, so she won't give us the slip again. But if I see you around here during your off hours, I'm cutting you from the surveillance detail."

Darryl waved his hands. "Okay, okay. Just trying to help you out."

Hank gave him a thin smile. "We both know who you're helping, but that's okay. I'd be the same in your place. Now get out of here."

Darryl did just that. But he didn't like it.

11

"May I see it now?"

Jack looked down at the trembling fingers of Naka Slater's outstretched hands . . . and hesitated.

Again that strange urge to keep it for himself.

Setting his jaw he pushed the rolled rug into Naka's hands and felt a pang of loss tinged with relief to be rid of it.

"All yours."

Naka took it and dropped into a crouch with the bundle across his thighs. His hands shook as he unrolled the rug. He gasped when he saw the sword.

"It's true! You have found it!" He caressed the hilt. "And I see someone has added a *tsuka* and a *tsuba*." He looked up at Jack. "You?"

Jack gathered he meant O'Day's handiwork. He shook his head.

"That was done by the previous owner. Now—"

"Perfect!" Naka said, gripping the handle as he rose. He dragged the fingertips of his free hand across the filigree of holes. "It is just as they said it would be."

"They?"

An alarm bell rang in Jack's brain. Naka was acting like this was the first time he'd ever seen the katana.

The guy didn't answer. Instead, he gripped the handle with his second hand and swung the sword in a vicious arc.

Jack was already backing away, already reaching for his replacement Glock. Now he leaped away, but the tip of the blade caught his left deltoid. He knew he'd been cut—felt the edge part skin and muscle—but felt no pain.

When he looked up Naka was already into another swipe. Jack raised the Glock as he fell backward. No time to aim so he pointed the barrel in Naka's general vicinity and pulled the trigger. The shot caught the bastard in his outer thigh.

As Jack landed on his back he saw Naka spin and lurch away toward the street. He raised the pistol for another shot but decided against it. This was hardly an ideal shooting stance, and if he missed just as a car was passing . . .

What was this? Try-to-kill-Jack-with-the-Gaijin-Katana Day?

He rolled to his feet—and *now* he felt the pain. His left deltoid felt as if it had been sliced open. He looked. Yeah, it had. Only now he was feeling it.

God *damn*, that hurt.

And then from the street he heard a horn blare and tires screech, and a heavy *thump*—like a body against sheet metal.

12

Damnedest thing Darryl had ever seen.

Tired as he was, he hadn't been able to sleep. So he'd gone out wandering the city, hoping he'd eventually need to crash, but that hadn't happened. Somehow he'd wound up in the West Eighties outside this bar he'd never heard of. Why this particular bar, he didn't know. Almost as if he was on a string and the place had reeled him here.

So there he was, checking it out as maybe a good place to grab a brew and trying to figure out those dead plants in the window. He was just reaching for the door when he heard this loud *bang!* Darryl had done some hunting in his day and knew a gunshot when he heard one. And he'd just heard one.

And then this chinky guy comes stumble-running out of the alley next to the bar, crosses the sidewalk, and keeps on going between two parked cars right smack into the path of a delivery truck. The driver tried to stop, but he was clipping pretty good, so no way. Even if he'd been going slower—no way. The chink tried to stop but, again, no way.

Ba-boom!

As the chink went flying, his arms flapping at crazy angles, something flew out of his hand—long, metallic, propellering through the air. It landed point first with a *shoonk!* on the hood of a nearby Volvo wagon. No, not on the hood—*through* the hood and into the engine compartment.

Darryl took a few steps to check it out.

Be damned. A sword. And obviously a sharp one. What kind of blade can cut through a steel car hood like it was paper? One of those Jap swords like in the samurai movies, only this one—

"Fuck me!"

This one's blade was all crudded up with little holes, just like the drawing Hank had shown him.

. . . if anyone sees it, bring it to me . . . I want it.

He glanced around. All eyes were on the scene of the accident, and the folks who weren't just standing and gawking were rushing to help.

Great.

Just as he yanked it from the hood he saw a guy step out of the alley and check out the accident. He was holding his left shoulder and something dark was seeping between his fingers. Had he taken the bullet? And was he looking for the sword?

Keeping a tight grip on the handle, Darryl did a quick turn, positioning the blade along the length of his body to shield it from the guy. Then he began quick-walking east toward the park, unbuttoning his outer shirt and pulling it around the sword. It didn't hide it completely, but at least he didn't look like some nutcase ready to start chopping up pedestrians.

He'd duck into the park, wrap it in his shirt, then hightail it downtown to show the boss man what he'd found.

What was going on with his luck? Maybe not luck. Almost seemed like something was guiding him.

How cool was that?

The high point of his life since his dissimilation had been the praise and backclaps he'd received from Hank for finding his precious Dawn Pickering. He'd thought it couldn't get any better than that, but maybe the best was yet to come. He couldn't wait to see the look on the boss man's face when Darryl handed him this sword.

Oh, yeah. Hank was gonna be tickled as all hell.

13

Jack washed down a couple of Vicodins with a Yuengling to ease the throb in his shoulder. It had taken Doc Hargus nearly an hour to sew the wound closed, inside and out. But he'd stopped the flow of blood and now Jack had to deal only with the seepage.

Doc had given him some antibiotic tabs and a tetanus shot, leaving Jack covered against pretty much any complication. He'd told him to keep it in a sling. Jack had bought one on the way home but didn't know how much he'd wear it. Gave him a trussed-up feeling.

All through the repair, Hargus kept saying, "You sure this wasn't done by a scalpel? I've only seen this clean a laceration from a scalpel."

He'd scoffed when Jack told him it had been made by a centuries-old, rotted-out sword. Doc thought every one of his patients embellished the stories behind their wounds. Even Jack. Hell, Jack might have scoffed too if he hadn't been there.

He shook his head. Two days of legwork, a lot of miles, a trio of corpses, and a customer on the way to the hospital.

And what did he have to show for it? Half a fee and a neatly sliced shoulder.

And no sword. The katana had disappeared. Like magic.

Well, not like magic. Jack hadn't been able to hunt for it, bleeding as he was. He'd sent Julio and a couple of the regulars out, but they'd all come up empty. The only possibility he could think of was some passerby picking it up and running.

But why? It looked like junk.

He shook his head again. The rule of the city: What's not nailed down or protected is fair game—as good as mine.

Well, good riddance. He'd been attacked twice with it today. He wasn't angling for a three-peat.

Thing was, why had Naka Slater attacked him? Jack understood O'Day's motive, but what gave with Slater? To save the rest of the fee? That didn't make sense, considering how he owned a plantation on Maui and how fast he'd come up with the first half.

Or maybe it was a bridge-burning deal—sever his only connection to the katana. Jack couldn't fathom why he'd think that necessary, but he'd never been comfortable with the way some people's heads worked.

He glanced over at his computer and realized he was overdue to check the Web site. Hadn't logged on in a couple of days. His in box was probably clogged with spam.

He entered his user name and password on the Web mail page and—yup—welcome to Spamopolis. After deleting the come-ons for Cialis and stock tips and home loans, then the appliance repair questions, he came to a subject line that read: *Need to find lost object.*

"Just been there, just done that," he muttered, moving the pointer toward the DELETE button. Then he thought, what the hell. See what's lost before deleting.

> *Dear Repairman Jack—*
> *I hope I have the right person. Someone gave me your name and said you might help. I have it on good authority that a very valuable object stolen from my home has been brought to New York. For various reasons, I'd rather not involve the police. If I have the right person, please call ASAP. I have only a few days before I must return to Hawaii.*
> *N.S.*

Jack stared dumbfounded at the screen.

Stolen object brought to New York . . . no police . . . Hawaii.

And the initials: *N.S.* Naka Slater?

What the hell?

He grabbed one of his TracFones and punched in the number. A male voice said, "Hello," after the first ring.

Jack asked his usual opening question about whether this someone had recently left a message at a certain Web site.

"Yes, I did," the voice said in perfect English. "Is this the man called Repairman Jack?"

"Yeah. Is this Naka Slater?"

Dead silence on the other end, then a nervous laugh. "Oh, I see. Your friend must have called to give you a heads-up."

"What friend would that be?"

"I . . . I don't know her name. She's a friend of a friend."

"An artist friend?"

"Yes. Then you know who I mean."

Jack hadn't a clue, but he let it ride.

"You need something found?"

"Yes. Very much. A family heirloom that was stolen from my home. Can we meet soon?"

Oh, yeah, Jack thought. We'll meet soon. He rolled his shoulder and felt a jab of pain. Not tonight, but definitely tomorrow. No way was he going to miss this. Not for the world.

He set up a meet for an early lunch at eleven and gave him directions to the Ear Inn.

Yeah. The Ear. If déjà vu was going to be the order of the day, might as well push it to the limit.

He hung up, leaned back, and said, "What the hell?"

It was becoming a litany.

FRIDAY

1

Jack started to turn the knob on the door to Gia's third-floor studio and stopped. This felt wrong. Whatever waited on the other side belonged to Gia. If she didn't want him to see them, then he should respect that. And he wanted to respect that. And it would have been easy to respect that, if only . . .

. . . they're not her . . .

If only he hadn't run into Junie. And if only she hadn't told him about the paintings. And if only Gia hadn't left him here alone while she went off to one of her final occupational therapy sessions.

He twisted the knob a little farther. Should he?

Oh, hell, why kid himself? Showing the paintings to Junie had ruptured their protective seal, so he was going to peek through that break.

He pushed the door open and stepped inside. Indirect light from the skylights illuminated the room but he flipped the light switch anyway. Leaving the door open behind him, he looked around at the large canvases leaning against the walls. One canvas, its back to him, rested on an easel in the center of the room.

He moved to his right and stopped at the nearest. So dark . . . black surrounding a circle of dark, dark blue with specks of white and a glowing moon. It took him a while to orient himself. The perspective seemed to be from the bottom of a well or some kind of hole in the Earth, looking up at a circle of night sky lit with cold, distant stars and a full moon.

But not our moon.

Same size, same color, but the familiar mares and ridges and pocks that made up the friendly Man in the Moon were gone, replaced by stark, foreign contours. For all he knew, the real moon might have turned its back and was showing its so-called dark side.

He moved on to what appeared to be a desert at night, but the dunes formed strange angles, and the moon overhead—the same alien moon as in the first painting—shed much less light than it should have.

Junie was right. These weren't Gia. Or at least not like the chiaroscuro roofscapes she'd been painting before the accident.

Next, a cityscape, but a ruined city, with that same moon overhead. He bent closer. He had a feeling that things were flying in that night sky, obscuring stars as they passed, but he couldn't be sure.

Then a succession of dark landscapes with strangely curving horizons and distant mountain ranges that seemed to reach into the stratosphere.

He turned finally to the work in progress on the easel. He stared, trying to find structure, something to latch on to. It seemed to be a swirling blackness seeded with faint, blurry, yellow-gray blotches—like internal flashes of lightning within a black storm cloud.

Jack stepped back. What had happened to her? He could find nothing welcoming in any of them. They looked . . . felt . . . *dangerous*. He was getting a Pickman's-model vibe—could she have seen these places in her coma when her swollen brain was inching her through death's door? She'd never mentioned seeing anything like what she'd put on canvas. She might have no conscious memories, but her unconscious couldn't forget. Maybe it was trying to vomit them up.

All because of me, he thought as he stepped back into the hall and closed the door behind him. All my fault.

2

Using a one-handed grip, Hank Thompson stood in the center of his room and swung the sword back and forth in a figure eight.

Cool.

It looked like crap, but he couldn't help loving the feel of it, the balance. It almost seemed to move on its own. He'd never held a sword—wait, not a *sword*, this was called a *katana*. Had to remember that. Much cooler sounding than "sword."

He stopped swinging and stared at it. Darryl had brought it to him last night, and bingo—for the first time this week, no dream of the Kicker Man and the katana.

What was it with Darryl and always being in the right place at the right time? He'd seemed like such a nobody at first, but obviously he was tuned into something. Maybe the same something that was broadcasting to Hank's internal antenna.

Whatever was going on, it seemed obvious that this blade was important and somehow connected to the future of Kicker Evolution. Something wanted him to have it.

What something? The something out there whose signals he was picking up? The "Others" on the outside that wanted to be on the inside? They must have wanted him to have this sword real bad because, if Darryl was to be believed, it literally dropped into his hands.

Okay. So he had it. Now what?

He didn't know. Only time would tell, and he wasn't about to waste a lot of time pondering it. He had other, more important matters on his mind. And Dawn Pickering topped the list.

Menck had tracked down the cabbie and found out where she'd been picked up: an abortion clinic.

Hank had almost lost it right there in front of Menck and the others. But he'd hung on to his cool and called the place. To his enormous relief he'd learned that you couldn't just walk in and get an abortion—at least at this place. They required a few blood tests before they put you on the table and did the deed.

So Hank now had two teams on the street—one watching the Milford, and the other out front of the clinic. One way or another, Dawn Pickering was not getting through that clinic door.

He hefted the katana and started swinging his figure eight again. He was just getting into a rhythm when he heard a knock on his door. He ignored it. But when it came again, he reluctantly laid the katana on his bed and answered.

He found a tall, thin, hawk-faced man in a white suit. He had a hook nose and graying hair slicked straight back. He carried a cane wrapped in some sort of dark hide. He extended a business card, trapped between the tips of his index and middle finger. Hank checked it out.

Ernst Drexler II
Actuator
ASFO

"What can I do for you, Mister Drexler?"

"Mister Thompson, we have a problem." His voice carried a hint of a German accent. His icy-blue stare made Hank uncomfortable, but he couldn't show that.

"Oh? Who's 'we'?"

"You and I. The Council of Seven sent me to inspect the premises."

Council of Seven . . . that meant the high-ups of the Ancient Septimus Fraternal Order. Had to play nice-nice with them. They'd opened this lodge building to Hank as a headquarters of sorts for him. The place had a bunch of small, empty storerooms on its second floor. Hank had had these converted to bedrooms for himself and a few choice Kickers.

A great setup. With its deeply recessed windows and solid granite walls, the place looked like a fortress. It offered him a secure Lower East Side location with a room overlooking the street.

So whatever problem this Drexler guy was having, Hank wanted it fixed.

He crooked a finger at Hank. "I want you to see something."

He led Hank down the wide stone stairway to the main hall where he pointed to the ten-foot seal of carved stone suspended on the far wall.

"Okay," Hank said slowly. "I see the Septimus Lodge seal. What am I—?"

"It's called a sigil, Mister Thompson. A *sigil*."

"Right. A sigil. Sorry." What the hell was a sigil, anyway? "But I don't under—oh, shit."

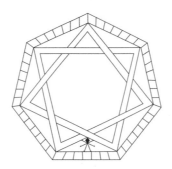

Some asshole had spray-painted a little Kicker Man on the stone.

Hank ground his teeth. The Kicker Evolution attracted people from all walks of life, all the social strata, but the majority seemed to come from the low end. A fair number had criminal records. Lowlifes, some might call them. Yeah, well, maybe they were. But they were Hank's lowlifes.

Trouble was, they pulled shithead pranks like this. He didn't care that they tagged the Kicker Man all over the city—that was advertising of sorts. But you don't piss where you sleep.

Problem was, the guy who did this probably wasn't one of the ones bunking here. And with all the various Kickers wandering in and out during the day, Hank would never be able to track him down.

"Sorry about that."

"Sorry isn't enough. The Septimus sigil is immensely important to the Order. We are an ancient brotherhood, and that sigil is far, far older. This will not be tolerated."

"I'll take care of it."

"That is not enough." Drexler's voice was calm, cool. Maybe too cool. "The Council has taken a step unprecedented in the history of the Order by opening its doors to nonmembers."

"Why us?" Hank said. The question had been bugging him.

Receiving only a cold look from Drexler, Hank went on.

"I mean, the Septimus Lodge goes back, what, a couple hundred years?"

"A couple of hundred? Mister Thompson, it goes back much, much further than that."

"Okay, much further. So if in all that time you've never let in nonmembers, why the sudden change of heart? And why us? And you didn't just let us in, you *invited* us."

"The local members received a directive."

"Yeah? Where from?"

"The worldwide High Council of the Seven. They rule the Ancient Septimus Fraternal Order. When they speak, the Lodges obey."

"Don't think we're not grateful, we are. But what about the rest of the question: Why us?"

"The Council doesn't explain its decisions."

Hank sensed this guy knew more than he was saying. Lots more.

"Well, Mister Drexler. Since the Council entrusts you with inspecting this place, I imagine you're wired in. You've gotta have *some* idea."

A humorless smile played around Drexler's thin lips as he glanced at the Kicker Man graffito, then back to Hank.

"It could be that they think you and your followers—"

Hank wagged a finger. "Not 'followers.' That would make me their leader, and I'm not. Kickers recognize no leaders. We're all simply fellow Kickers."

At least that was the line he made a point of pushing every chance he got: *I'm not your leader. We're all just Kickers.* He figured the more he denied it, the more he'd be identified in their heads as the leader he said he wasn't.

"If you say so," Drexler said, obviously not buying it. "It could be that the Council recognizes a common bond between your Kickers and the Septimus order."

"Which would be what?"

Drexler shrugged. "Who is to say? The Council is wise and it keeps its own counsel."

Yeah. Okay. Maybe they did tell him, maybe they didn't. But either way, he'd bet this guy had a pretty good idea of the *why* part of the question.

"But be that as it may," Drexler intoned, pointing to the Kicker Man graffito, "their hospitality does not extend to *this*."

Hank found himself eyeing Drexler's neck and thinking of the katana. He'd bet one good chop would send his head flying. Did he dare? He had a feeling he'd have to strike fast and hard and not miss. Because this Drexler guy did not look like someone he'd want to mess with.

He shook off the thought and focused on the present.

"I'll have one of the men clean it up. Then we'll track down the one who did this and make certain he never does anything like this again."

Drexler brushed his hands together, as if dusting off dirt. "See to it immediately."

As he walked away, Hank again envisioned the katana biting into his neck. A delightful sight.

3

"Tell me again why that article was never published?" P. Frank Winslow said as they waited for their food.

Jack had called him this morning, pretending to be the same *Trenton Times* reporter who had interviewed him last month. He needed to talk to Winslow and the writer seemed anxious to comply. They arranged to meet for breakfast in the same spot as last time: a bustling lower Second Avenue deli named Moishe's.

Winslow's work had shocked Jack when he'd stumbled upon it. The plots of his novels *Rakshasa!* and *Berzerk!*—both based on dreams—were bizarrely similar to events in Jack's life. When Jack had interviewed him he'd mentioned other dreams his editor hadn't deemed novel-worthy that also seemed plucked from Jack's life.

"My editor thought it was too blah," Jack said.

Winslow reacted like a mother who'd just heard someone say her baby was ugly. "Blah? Jake Fixx is *blah*? What's he, nuts? How can a freakin' ex–Navy SEAL and former CIA black-ops specialist be blah?"

Thirtyish, with a skinny bod, big nose, and thin face, Winslow was a far cry from the burly, brawny hero of his series.

Jack shrugged. "Who can explain editors?"

"I hear ya. Mine's a piece of work. Sounds like yours is too."

Jack knew a couple of authors and a few wannabes. They all loved to bitch about editors. Jack played it up.

"Guy's a clown. Doesn't know squat about good journalism. I fought for the article, but he wouldn't budge. Said I had to find a hook for it or forget about it."

Winslow's hazel eyes stared at him over his coffee cup. "Hook? Isn't Jake himself a hook?"

Jack shook his head. "I guess not. I mean, for me he is. I'm a big fan of the character. Your books are super."

He saw Winslow swell with delight. Authors were so needy.

"Yeah, well, I like him too. I—"

"Here's your food, gents," said a cracked voice.

Sally, their ancient, orange-haired, dowager-humped waitress had materialized tableside carrying their plates. Winslow had the same as last time: eggs over easy with corned beef hash; Jack had opted for the western omelet.

As Winslow chopped up his runny eggs and mixed them into the hash, he said, "What kind of hook does he want?"

"You don't think he'd actually tell me, do you? That would take some original thought on his part. But I do have an idea."

Winslow looked up. "Like what?"

"These dreams you base the books on. What if they're not dreams? What if your unconscious mind has somehow tapped into the life of a real Jake Fixx?"

He took a bite of the yolky hash. "You're not telling me you think that's possible, are you?"

"Course not. But that could be my hook: *Who is the real Jake Fixx?* or *Is there a real Jake Fixx?*"

Winslow nodded. "Ooh, I like that."

"I do too. But I'm going to have to sort of catalogue your Jake Fixx dreams, even the ones you don't use."

"No problem."

"Let's start with the latest." Here was what Jack had come for. "What's happening?"

"Really weird. About this cruddy Japanese sword that everyone wants. I—" He stopped, staring at Jack's face. "What's wrong?"

"Nothing." The idea of this guy looking over his shoulder via his dreams made him queasy. "Go on."

"Well, I can't use it all crudded up, but I can clean it up, make it super shiny—maybe even make it glow a little—and super sharp. You know, sharp enough to cut through a rifle barrel."

"Why not make it sing, too?"

"Hmmm?"

"Never mind."

"And of course I'll have to add a back story where Jake took dueling lessons from a master samurai while he was in the CIA."

"Of course." Fixx was an expert in everything. God forbid he'd actually have to *learn* something. "So how does the dream end?"

"It hasn't yet. Like I told you before, I dream in chapters."

"Well, has he got the sword yet?"

"Got it and lost it."

"Does he get it back again?"

Winslow shrugged. "Haven't dreamed that yet, but no matter how the dream turns out, I guarantee in my book Jake'll get the sword back and use it to cut a swath through the bad guys."

"Who are?"

"Don't really know. Some sort of cult. I'll probably make them members of that Aum Shinrikyo cult—you know, the ones who released sarin gas in Tokyo's subway."

A cult . . . could the yakuza types he'd run into be part of a cult? Didn't strike him as the type. The Kickers could be considered a cult, but they weren't Japanese. That left Naka Slater—if that was his true name. Was he part of a cult?

None of this made sense. Maybe the second Naka Slater would have some answers.

"So you don't know how it ends yet."

"I just told you: Jake gets the sword and—"

"I meant the dreams."

He shrugged. "Doesn't matter. I've got my ending."

Swell. But Jack didn't have his.

4

Dawn jumped and let out a little yelp when the phone rang. But unlike the last time, it kept ringing.

She'd totally hated telling the abortion clinic where she was staying, but didn't have much choice. Mr. Osala had confiscated her cell phone as soon as she'd entered his house. She hadn't dared to stop and get a replacement while she'd been out yesterday.

The clinic had done blood tests and a black woman doctor with an African accent had done a pelvic exam. They'd said they'd call her today with the results. If everything was okay, they'd set up a time for the actual abortion.

She picked up on the fourth ring.

"Y-yes?"

"Ms. Pickering?" said a woman's voice. *"This is Grace from the Sitchin Clinic."*

Relief. She felt her drum-tight muscles relax.

"Is everything okay?"

"Everything is fine. You are eight weeks pregnant and in excellent health. You are an excellent candidate for the procedure."

"When?"

"How does three o'clock tomorrow sound?"

"Tomorrow? Can't I get it done today?"

"I'm sorry. We can schedule only so many a day and today is booked."

Damn. That meant another night alone in this room. She wanted this done with.

"Okay, I guess. Yeah. Put me down for three."

"Excellent. I understand you're paying cash?"

"Yes. Is that a problem?"

"You will be expected to pay in full in advance."

They'd told her this yesterday and she'd agreed. The fee was stiff but she had it, and she couldn't think of anything better to spend it on.

"That's okay. I've got it."

"Excellent. Please be here sharply at three. Have a nice day."

"Yeah. You too."

As she hung up she thought she should pump a fist or something, but she felt no sense of triumph. She'd be totally free of this baby, yeah, but she wouldn't be free of Jerry Bethlehem. He'd still be out there looking for her. And he'd totally kill her if he found out she'd rid herself of his precious Key to the Future.

By four o'clock tomorrow the baby would be gone. Then what? Where would she go from there?

The only place she could think of was Mr. Osala's.

She'd show up at his door saying how sorry she was for running away, and how she didn't know what had come over her—maybe she'd gone a little crazy from being cooped up—and how she'd totally never ever do it again.

What she would so not tell him was that she was no longer pregnant. He'd said the baby was her life insurance policy where Jerry was concerned, and he might get mad if he knew she'd totally ignored his advice.

Well, what he didn't know wouldn't hurt him. And maybe when he was away on his next trip she'd pretend to have a miscarriage.

Meanwhile she'd be safe and comfortable.

Feeling suddenly rotten, she dropped onto the unmade bed.

Listen to me. I sound like a totally gold-plated conniving bitch.

She'd never been like this. Never lied, never cheated. Maybe what she'd gone through—was *still* going through—had changed her. She hoped it was temporary, that when it was over she could get a grip and totally change back. Well, maybe not totally—all this had to leave scars.

But what if this was the real her—the real Dawn who'd been hiding just below the surface of the other Dawn? What if Mom's murder and the knowledge that she'd been screwing the man who not only had killed her mother but was also—

She didn't want to think about that. Every time she did, it made her totally want to hurl.

Maybe that was it. She felt dirty, and totally worthless. So low she wouldn't mind being dead. And when you felt that low, all sorts of things you never thought possible suddenly were easy—like lying and cheating and trading sex for favors.

She had to climb out of this hole. And the first step up and back to her old self was to be rid of this baby. Because the old Dawn hadn't been pregnant.

Tomorrow . . . at three P.M. . . . she'd take that step.

5

Jack waited inside the Ear this time—same table, same back-to-the-wall seat under the perils-of-drink poster. The place was only a quarter full, the kitchen just getting up to speed.

He'd worn the arm sling on the subway ride down. Didn't like the feel but it did seem to make people give him a slightly wider berth. As he'd seated himself here he glommed on an unconventional use for it. He pulled his Kel-Tec backup from its ankle holster and sneaked it into the sling where it could rest unseen, just inches from his fingers.

He liked that so much he thought about making a sling a regular accessory, then decided against it. Put ten guys in a crowded room, one with a sling, nine without: Who would people remember?

No, save it for special occasions.

He thought about his trip to the hospital earlier this morning, right after his breakfast with Winslow. The guy calling himself Naka Slater had been taken down to Roosevelt on 59th Street. Jack had inquired at the ER about an auto accident victim brought in last night. After much wheedling and cajoling he'd been told that they'd admitted an Asian John Doe who'd refused to give his name.

Still alive . . . good.

Jack said he wondered if the guy could be his good buddy, Ishiro Honda. Could he maybe just go up and see if it was really him?

She had to check with the higher-ups to see if that would be okay. Ten minutes later she'd returned to say the higher-ups needed to talk to the hospital attorneys—concerns about hippo regulations or something like that.

He'd told her he'd be back. He wanted to talk to this guy, find out what he was up to, why he'd tried to kill him. But first . . . the new Naka Slater.

He snagged a copy of the *Post* from a neighboring table where one of the help had left it. The Staten Island thing still dominated the front page: an aerial photo of the dead area of woods under a huge headline:

EVEN THE COOTIES
CROAKED!

If the Pulitzer folks awarded a prize for headlines, the *Post* would win every year.

He skimmed the page three article. It reported how tests had shown that even bacteria and mold spores had been killed. The consensus was some sort of toxin, but nobody knew what particular toxin. Whatever it was, this stuff killed *everything*.

Just then a vaguely Asian guy stepped in and looked around. He wore khaki slacks and a long-sleeve, blue-and-white-striped rugby shirt. As his gaze settled on Jack, he raised his eyebrows and pointed. Jack nodded.

The guy wound through the tables and offered his hand when he reached Jack's. "Nakanaori Slater. But you can call me—"

"Naka," Jack said, shaking his hand. Good grip. He pointed to the other chair. "Yeah, I know."

Close up now Jack could see the Caucasian influence in his skin tone and features. Unlike his predecessor, this guy looked like the genuine off-spring of a Japanese and an American. He also looked older than his predecessor—Jack guessed a well-preserved sixty, or maybe younger—and a lot more relaxed. His black hair was streaked with gray, and he too wore it combed down over the left half of his forehead.

"Moki's friend must have told you," he said, smiling as he seated himself. "What else did she tell you?"

His smooth English said he'd been raised in an English-speaking household.

"Nothing. I have no idea who she is."

He frowned. "Then how—?"

"Let me tell you a story, see if it rings a bell. Four days ago, right here at this table, I met with an Asian dude who also called himself Nakanaori Slater. He gave me a middle name too but—"

"Okumo?" Slater's face lightened a few shades. "He said he was Nakanaori Okumo Slater?"

"Yeah. Quite a mouthful. So I was glad for the just-call-me-Naka part."
He looked baffled. "But I'm—"

The waitress arrived then. Older than the one last time. Jack ordered a
Hoegaarden, then waited to see what Slater would do.

"A double Jack Daniel's on the rocks."

Jack realized in the case of Naka One he should have heeded W. C.
Fields's warning about never trusting a man who doesn't drink. Naka Two
drank Jack Daniel's before lunch. Did that earn extra trust points?

He caught Jack studying him. "I need a double after what you just told
me."

"Don't have to explain to me."

"Describe this 'Naka,'" he said.

"Japanese—*all* Japanese from the look of him, though he said he had
an American father." He pointed to the dippity-do over Slater's left forehead. "Same hairstyle too."

Slater lifted his hair, revealing the rest of his forehead. "Did he have
this?"

Jack stared at what looked like a red wine stain spreading from his hairline almost to his eyebrow. He tried to picture Naka Slater Number One's
face and couldn't recall ever getting a peek under the dip.

"Couldn't say."

"My dad called it the Slater Stain. All the Slater men have something
like it." He released the handful of hair, letting it drop back into place.
"He had it, and both my sons have it, though thankfully to a lesser degree
than I." He leaned forward, his onyx eyes intent. "What else did he tell
you?"

Jack gave him a condensed version: Heirloom katana blade stolen from
his Maui plantation, traced to New York, woman living with artist friend
gives him Jack's name, so Naka Slater comes to New York to hire Jack to
find the blade.

Slater's face was even paler than before. "That's incredible! It's all true
except that *I'm* Naka Slater, but I didn't get to New York until yesterday. He
didn't happen to mention any scrolls, did he?"

"No, nothing about scrolls."

"A bunch of ancient scrolls my father and Matsuo confiscated from—"

"'Confiscated.' I like that."

"Okay, stole. They were stolen from me along with the katana, and I've
recovered neither. I don't care about the scrolls—have no idea what's on
them and couldn't care less—but that katana . . ."

The drinks arrived. Even though he wasn't all that hungry after the earlier omelet, Jack ordered the burger with cheddar cheese and bacon. Couldn't pass up an Ear burger. Slater ordered the same.

Naka Two was starting out a lot easier to like than One.

As the waitress was leaving, he tapped her arm and rattled the ice in his near-empty glass. "Another of these?" He pointed to the barely sipped Hoegaarden but Jack shook his head.

Not yet.

Slater drained his sour mash and said, "Another Slater trait: a fondness for booze and a very efficient liver." He put down the glass and stared at Jack. "Now the all-important question: Did you find the blade?"

Jack gave a reluctant nod. Slater must have noticed the reluctance because he stiffened in his seat.

"Oh, God. Don't tell me—"

Jack nodded again.

He slammed his fist on the table. *"Kokami!"*

"Pardon?"

"A Hawaiian term of endearment. Any way of tracking it down?"

Leaving out the deaths and the yakuza and what he'd had to go through to get the sword, Jack told him about the attempted exchange, Naka One's attempt to kill him, the subsequent accident, and the disappearing sword.

Slater squeezed his eyes shut. "So, it's literally a dead end."

"Very literally. Very dead."

Slater's second JD arrived. As he scooped it up and sipped, Jack remembered something.

"Roll up your sleeves."

"Why?"

"The other Naka was younger, but otherwise copied you down to the hair comb. I wonder if his tattoo was part of that."

Slater showed Jack a pair of bare forearms. "I don't have any tattoos. As someone said, why decorate your body with drawings you wouldn't hang on your wall?"

"Okay. This other guy had some sort of hexagon or something tattooed above his left wrist."

Slater frowned as he pulled down his sleeves. "Hexagon? That's it? No dragons or hibiscus or carp or any of the usual Japanese design salad?"

"No." Jack tried to picture the dead man's arm. "Just a hollow hexagon with a bunch of crisscrossing lines. Like hatch marks." He glanced at Slater and found him staring at him. "What?"

"You're pulling my leg, right?"

"No."

He signaled to the waitress. "Can I borrow your pen?"

She handed it to him and he began scribbling on the butcher-paper tablecloth. When he'd finished, he pointed to it.

"Did it look anything like that?"

Jack looked. "Exactly."

"It can't be." He slammed the pen down. "Impossible."

"If you say so. But for curiosity's sake—let's just assume I'm not lying—what's it supposed to mean?"

Slater was silent a long time. Finally . . .

"Sorry. I'm not calling you a liar. It's just . . . that was one of the symbols used by an ancient Japanese cult of self-mutilating monks. They—"

"Whoa." A cult? Winslow had mentioned a cult. "And did you say self-mutilating?"

Slater nodded. "Well, not *self*-mutilating in the strictest sense. They mutilated each other."

"Swell."

"Once they'd gone through acolyte stages and reached the inner circles, they'd cut little flaps in their facial skin to hold a cloth mask in place, leaving only the eyes visible. Then they started giving up their senses, one at a time: sight, smell, taste, hearing, touch."

"Touch? How do you give up touch? Unless you cut off your skin."

"They had a slower method. One limb at a time. The final cut was high on the spinal cord, severing all sensation from the body but not so high as to affect the diaphragm. They were left floating in a black, silent void, seeing the thing they'd suffered for: the Kakureta Kao."

"Which means . . . ?"

Slater pointed to his drawing and ran his finger along the outline of the hexagon. "See this? That represents a head." Then he tapped the hatch-marked center. "What sort of face do you see here?"

"None. Just a bunch of lines."

"Exactly. Originally, when the tattoo was in progress, the artist would draw a rudimentary face inside and then obscure it with all those crisscrossing lines. Hiding it. That's what Kakureta Kao means: They were called the Order of the Hidden Face."

"And what happens when they see this Hidden Face?"

"Then they knew the meaning of everything. They died happy and ful-filled, and joined it in its eternal void."

Jack had noticed something. "You keep using the past tense."

"That's because the last surviving members of the sole remaining en-clave were incinerated by Little Boy on August sixth, 1945."

6

"I hurt, *sensei*."

Wearing a surgeon's mask and a stolen lab coat, Toru Akechi stared down at the man in the hospital bed and grieved. Poor Tadasu. Had he suc-ceeded in his mission he would have been admitted to the Inner Circles.

But he had failed.

Tadasu lay in the bed like a broken marionette—legs suspended on wires, both arms in casts, his neck sheathed in a hard plastic brace.

Toru nodded toward the clear plastic bag suspended over the side of the bed. When he spoke, the surgical mask he wore muffled his voice more than the traditional mask worn in the temple.

"They give you painkillers."

"The pain is in my heart, *sensei*. The pain of failure."

Toru controlled a sudden burst of fury. He wanted to say, You *should* feel pain, Tadasu Fumihiro. In your heart and everywhere else. You deserve intractable pain for such miserable failure.

For although Tadasu had to answer to him, Toru had to answer to others.

But he modulated his response. "You made many mistakes, Tadasu. The first was in choosing the thief."

The younger man looked as if he was about to speak, but instead pressed his lips tightly together and nodded as best he could within his neck brace. He knew better than to mention that his *sensei* had approved the choice of Hugh Gerrish for the job.

It had seemed a good choice at the time: Better to deal with a known quantity here in New York, where they had the temple, and fly him out to Maui rather than try to find someone in Hawaii.

But Gerrish had betrayed them.

"At least we have the scrolls," Tadasu said.

Yes . . . the Kuroikaze scrolls once again belonged to the Kakureta Kao. And that was good. Gerrish had delivered them as promised, but had reneged on the katana. Instead of turning it over, he had fled home with it. The Order's reach was limited here in this barbaric land, and it had been unable to locate him. So they had turned to the man they had overheard recommended to that mongrel, Nakanaori Slater.

At least that had been a good decision: The man had tracked down the katana.

"How could you have failed in the last act of the task? You were to sever all links between the katana and yourself, and thus the Order. You are skilled in the use of the katana. You know all the kata. How could you not only fail to kill him but lose the katana as well?"

Tadasu closed his eyes. "I had my moves carefully planned. But when I saw the blade . . . when I touched it . . . I could not help myself. I dropped my plan and flew into action without thinking."

"That is very unlike you, Tadasu. How could you be so reckless?"

"I don't know, *sensei*. I had this sudden, overwhelming urge. I didn't give in to it. It . . . took over."

"And now, because of your foolish surrender to impulse, because of your weakness, the sword remains lost to us. It could be anywhere. Anyone could have picked it up."

"I saw him, *sensei*."

"You did?" Toru felt a jolt of hope suffuse his heart. Here was a chance to set this right. "Why didn't you tell me? What does he look like?"

"I saw only part of him—just his hand."

"His hand?" The excitement withered. "Of what value—?"

"He had a tattoo, *sensei*."

That might be useful.

"What did it look like?"

"It was the strange man-figure that I have been seeing painted on walls throughout the city."

A man-figure graffito? The necessity of hiding his face—certain to raise alarms in post-9/11 New York—kept Toru from leaving the temple often, but on a recent trip, sealed behind tinted windows, he thought he had seen the figure Tadasu was talking about.

He'd noticed a pen jutting from the breast pocket of the lab coat he'd borrowed. He went to hand it to Tadasu, then stopped as he realized both arms were in casts.

He looked around and found no paper, so he pulled back Tadasu's top sheet and began to draw. When finished he held it up where Tadasu could see it.

"Is this it?"

Tadasu gave another restricted nod. "Yes, *sensei*. That was on his hand."

Toru had no idea what it meant, but he would find out. He would learn everything there was to know about this figure.

But now it was time to deal with temple guard Tadasu Fumihiro. He would be undergoing multiple surgeries. Who knew what he might say under the effects of anesthesia? The Kakureta Kao could not risk exposure.

From a pocket of the silk tunic he wore beneath the lab coat, Toru withdrew the small ebony case of *doku-ippen*. He opened it and chose one of the deadly black-ringed slivers. When he looked up he found Tadasu staring at the box with bulging eyes.

"*Sensei*, this is not necessary."

"Do you question me, Tadasu?"

"No, *sensei*. But—"

"Accept your fate. It is a kind death I offer. One prick of the skin and all your pain—in your heart and body—as well as the shame of your failure will be gone. It is for the Order, Tadasu."

The acolyte closed his eyes. Tears found their way between the lids.

"I shall never see the Hidden Face."

"No, but in making this sacrifice for the Order, you will make that possible for others."

Eyes still closed, Tadasu nodded. "For the Order."

Holding the sliver between thumb and forefinger, Toru found a small area of exposed flesh near Tadasu's shoulder and pressed the sharp tip into the skin.

Then he turned and started toward the door, knowing that Tadasu would be dead before he reached the hallway.

7

. . . incinerated by Little Boy . . . August sixth, 1945 . . .

Then Jack realized: "The Hiroshima bomb—same as the sword. Did the katana belong to these kooks?"

Slater shook his head. "It belonged to a Japanese Intelligence officer named Matsuo Okumo who was at ground zero with the sword when Little Boy went off. He died along with that psycho cult."

"Looks like they've risen from the grave."

"Maybe someone started them up again. They've had since forty-five to rebuild."

"If they're back, why doesn't anybody know about them? They're terrific tabloid fodder."

"If they're back, they're laying low. After the war it was discovered they were kidnapping children and mutilating them."

Jack stomach tightened. "Jeez. How do you know so much about them?"

"My father left a posthumous memoir—a balls-to-the-wall tell-all that takes no prisoners. In his will he asked me to get it published, but no one would touch it as a memoir. I did manage to sell it as a novel. I called it *Black Wind*. Didn't sell too well. If you want a copy—"

Thinking of the *Compendium*, Jack waved off the offer. "Thanks, no. Got too much to read as it is."

"As you wish. My father was pretty merciless with himself as well. At times it was tough, as his son, to read about his failures of nerve, but in the end I respected him more than ever."

Jack thought of his own dad, and how close they'd become on their last outing . . . before . . .

He shook it off and said, "Okay, you've been told this Hidden Face thing is extinct, which may or may not be true, but the guy pretending to be you wore the tattoo and knew everything that you knew."

"Someone must have tapped my phone. That's the only way."

"He wanted the sword. Why?"

"It killed a lot of Kakureta Kao members."

"The memoir says so?"

Slater nodded. "Yeah. If they're back, they may want it as some kind of totem. Or to destroy it."

"Good luck. If Little Boy couldn't turn it into a Dalí clock, I don't see how they . . ." A thought occurred to him. "Wait. If they're looking for it, that means they didn't steal it. Which leaves us with the question of who hired Gerrish."

"Gerrish?"

"The name of the thief. A pro—a very dead pro."

"Dead?" Slater's eyes narrowed. "You?"

"No. But he's not the only one. Two others have gone to their greater reward because of that thing." Jack decided not to mention how O'Day had passed. "Almost like it's cursed."

"Maybe it is." He sighed. "My father told me he'd handled the sword a number of times before the bomb and said it felt different afterward . . . changed."

"Well, it took one helluva beating."

"He didn't mean physically. He meant spiritually. Like it had lost its soul."

"Yeah, right." Jack tried to imagine that happening with one of his guns.

Slater shrugged. "You either get it or you don't. How'd you feel when you held it?"

Jack remembered the dark elation while swinging it around in his apartment. And the urge to keep it instead of give it up.

"Let's get back to this Kaka-Kookoo group. If they didn't hire Gerrish, who did?"

Slater shook his head. "Oh, they hired him. The scrolls that disappeared with the katana once belonged to Kakureta Kao. Matsuo Okumo gave them to my father for safekeeping."

"Then why—?"

"Would they hire you to find it? Maybe something went wrong with the plan. Maybe they tried to kill the thief like they did you, and he escaped and ran back here. Or maybe he thought he could get a better price for it elsewhere."

Or maybe decided to keep it, Jack thought, remembering his own vacillations.

"Well, it is, after all, the Gaijin Masamune."

Slater looked baffled. "What's that? I was told it was a Masamune blade, but 'Gaijin' . . . ?"

"Apparently it's a fabled and much sought after collector's item."

"Sought after enough to kill for?"

Jack nodded. "You betcha. Three corpses will attest to that. And I could have been the fourth." As Slater shook his head in dismay, Jack added, "Something else you should know."

"I'm almost afraid to hear."

"There's another player on the field." He raised a hand as Slater opened his mouth. "Don't ask who because I don't know. I do know they're Japanese—underworld types, from the look of them—and ready to kill to get the katana."

Slater leaned back, puffing out his cheeks as he exhaled. "Man. Who'd have dreamed? I'm almost willing to forget the whole thing, except . . ."

"Yeah?"

"It meant so much to my father."

"He stole it from the museum?"

Slater jerked upright. "How the hell did you—?" Then he relaxed. "Oh, yeah. My alter ego must have told you."

"Only that it belonged to the Hiroshima Peace Museum."

The burgers arrived then. Jack and Naka assembled them in silence, then bit in.

Slater let out a groan. "This is amazing. Why can't we get beef like this on the islands?"

They worked on their burgers a little more, then Jack quaffed some Hoegaarden to wash down a big bite.

"So how did the blade get from the museum to your dad's place?"

"The Peace Museum opened in fifty-five, ten years to the day after the bomb. My father was with the Occupation. When he saw the blade he knew it was Matsuo's and figured he had more claim to it than the museum. He too had been an intelligence officer and was owed more than a few favors. He collected on some by persuading a few commandos to sneak in and snatch it for him."

"That's why you can't go to the police."

He shrugged. "I doubt anyone connected with the museum would re-member it now, even if they heard about it, but why take the chance?" He leaned forward. "I need that katana back. Both my parents revered Matsuo's memory. It was all they had left of him. My father made me promise to keep it in the family. So I don't see how I have much choice."

Jack spread his hands. "And I don't see how you have much hope."

"That bad, huh?" His expression was bleak. "You've got no idea at all where it could be?"

"No, but I know where to find the guy I gave it to. He didn't have time to hand it off before he was hit, but maybe one of his Hidden Face buddies was waiting out there and snagged it after our friend and the truck got intimate."

"You've got to make him tell you."

"If he's crazy enough to be in that cult, I seriously doubt he'll be the sharing type. And there's something else you have to consider."

"Your tone says more bad news."

"Maybe he didn't have anyone waiting. Maybe some passerby found it and took off with it. It could be anywhere—even in a Dumpster."

He looked crushed. "Then what do I do?"

"If by some miracle I can squeeze anything useful out of this guy, I'll let you know. But if I come up empty, as I suspect I will, all you can do is advertise—put out flyers and offer a reward. That might bring somebody out of the woodwork."

He banged the table again. "*Ai Kae!*"

The place had gained a few patrons since their arrival and people were giving them curious and concerned looks.

"Another Hawaiian term of endearment?"

"What? Yeah. I can stay here only a day or two. You think you could make up the flyers and—?"

Jack was shaking his head. "Not my kind of work. If I come up empty at the hospital, you do it. Start a voice mail account and put that number on the flyers. Get them spread around. Check the voice mail often. If anything promising comes through, call me and I'll see what I can do."

Jack would be delighted if nothing came through. That sword had nearly killed him twice. Damned if he was about to give it another try.

"Jesus, God!"

Jack looked up and saw that Slater's face had gone white. He was star-ing at the cover of the *Post* on the next table.

"What?"

"The Black Wind! What happened in Staten Island—it never hit me till now. The Kakureta Kao has brought back the Black Wind!"

Despite Slater's ominous tone, it didn't sound particularly threatening to Jack—like something that might occur after a *frijoles negro* burrito.

"And that's bad?"

"Very. I didn't make the connection because I thought they were extinct. But now that you've seen someone with their tattoo, it's all coming together. What happened on Staten Island is exactly the effect of the Black Wind as described by my father. If they're planning to use it on the city . . ."

"But nobody mentioned a wind or wind damage."

"It's been called the Wind-That-Bends-Not-the-Trees."

"Oooookay." Maybe the Jack Daniel's was hitting him.

"I've got to tell someone. But who?"

"Um, try Homeland Security. But don't mention me, okay? Meanwhile, I'm going to check out this Hidden Face guy in the hospital."

He grabbed Jack's arm. "Ask him about the Black Wind. You've got to find out."

8

The Wind-That-Bends-Not-the-Trees, Jack thought as he reentered Roosevelt Hospital. Where do people come up with this stuff?

He was relieved to find the same clerk at the ER admitting desk. Her name tag read KAESHA and she once might have been called Rubenesque, but she'd moved beyond that. The glazed Krispy Kreme donut sitting next to her keyboard hinted at the how and why.

"Hi, Kaesha. Remember me? I was here earlier about the Asian John Doe?"

She gave him a hard look, then her features softened. "You're the one who thought you might know him."

"Right. Have the hospital attorneys cleared me for a look at him?"

"I'm sorry to have to tell you this, but the patient died a few hours ago."

Crap.

"But," she added, "it would be a great service to him and to the hospital if you could identify him. And the police want to talk to you as well."

Jack stiffened inside. "The police?"

"Well, I suppose it's okay to tell you, since he's dead. But he also had a gunshot wound. The police are looking for any information available."

Double crap.

"Sure. I'll help any way I can."

Uh-huh.

"We appreciate it. I'll see about arranging a viewing and let the police know you're here."

"While you're doing that," Jack said, forcing a tremor into his voice, "I think I'll step outside for a breath of air. We were very close. Had a lot of laughs together. He was a real cutup."

She gave him a sympathetic smile. "I understand."

As soon as Jack was out the door, he made a beeline through the banished smokers and began quick-walking up Amsterdam Avenue. He pulled off his sling and shoved it inside his shirt, then ducked into the Lincoln Center parking garage and cut through to Columbus Avenue.

As he mingled with the crowd there he called Naka Slater and told him to print up those flyers and Martin Luther them all over town, because his only info source was dead. The body count had moved up to four.

9

Hank found the perfect spot on Long Island's North Fork.

Somewhere in the tectonic past, Long Island's eastern third split into a pair of peninsulas. While the longer, wider southern division grew crowded and famous for its wealthy Hamptons and remote Montauk, its smaller sister to the north remained fairly rural, becoming the heart of Long Island's wine industry.

Halfway out the fork—shouldn't it be called a tine? he wondered—and a little ways off Middle Road, he came upon a farm with a dozen or so brown-and-white Golden Guernsey cows munching grass in a field adjacent to the road.

He watched them for a moment, then turned and looked at the slim, oblong, blanket-wrapped bundle on the backseat and felt his excitement grow.

This was gonna be good.

He found a spot on the side of the road where his Jeep would be shielded from the farmhouse by an intervening stand of trees.

Perfect.

Except for the wait. Though the sun was well into its slide toward the horizon, the sky was still too bright for what he planned.

So he took a leisurely drive out to Orient Point on the far eastern tip of the fork and parked near the ferry dock. As he stared across the choppy channel to Plum Island, he thought about the strange turns his life had taken since he'd written *Kick*. From manual laborer to backdoor celebrity.

Life had been simpler and maybe even happier back in his slaughterhouse days. He hadn't had to make decisions for other people, not even for himself. He'd been happy to do what he was told. Some days he'd be a "knocker," using a compressed air gun to shoot a steel bolt into the cow's head to knock it out. Other days he'd be assigned as a "sticker," which he tended to prefer. Once the knocker was through with them, the unconscious cows would be hung upside down by a leg from the overhead rail, and then Hank would come along and slit their throats.

Bloody, bloody work, and hot too because of the rubber jacket and pants. But looking back, Hank realized he'd never felt so at peace with himself, not before, not since.

Peace . . . He shook his head. Would he ever know peace? Then he heard himself laugh. Did he even *want* peace again?

Sure as hell not till he'd found the guy who'd stolen the *Compendium of Srem*—right out of his hands, the son of a bitch. The same guy who'd called himself John Tyleski and pretended to be a reporter. He could still see his nothing-special face, with its brown eyes, and his brown hair as he grilled him. Hank would have the Kickers out looking for him but how do you describe a guy who looked like everybody and nobody?

Hank glanced in his rearview and saw the sun nudging the horizon. Time to go.

He drove at the speed limit, trying to time his arrival at the farm with dusk. He needed some light for his plan, but didn't want too much. The closer he got, the more he felt his excitement build, tingling down his back and around to his belly to settle lower, like a horny kid heading out to meet the easiest girl in town, knowing she'd give it up with the barest minimum of persuasion.

As he turned off Middle Road he spotted a puddle. He stopped and rubbed mud on his license plates, then continued to the farm.

The light was perfect when he reached it. He parked in the blind spot and removed the katana from the blanket on the backseat. He held up the blade and saw the dying light reflect dully along its pitted, riddled surface. He found it strangely beautiful, almost . . . mesmerizing . . .

With effort, he pulled his gaze away and hopped the fence. A Guernsey stood about thirty yards away. She looked up at his casual, unhurried approach. Not afraid. Why should she be? The worst any human had done to her was milk her teats. She lowered her head to the grass and resumed grazing.

Hank positioned himself beside her, feet spread, facing her thick neck. As he raised the katana above his head he felt a stirring in his groin.

He needed this . . . really needed this. And he wanted to see what this katana could do . . . wanted to cut all the way through with a single swing.

But he wanted the cow looking at him when this happened.

"Hey!" he called in a soft voice. "Hey, you."

When the cow looked up he saw his reflection in her large dark eye, a man-shaped blotch silhouetted against the fading twilight.

Now . . . do it now.

To add extra force behind the blow, Hank envisioned the fake John Tyleski's bland features against the skin of the neck. With a low cry he raised the blade even higher and swung with all he had.

SATURDAY

1

"Here's an odd story," Abe said, staring down at a newspaper through the reading glasses perched on his nose.

Jack glanced up and saw it was the Long Island paper, *Newsday*. Abe hadn't ventured into the wilds of Long Island since he'd had a full head of hair, but that didn't keep him from *Newsday*.

"Odd how? Like congress has impeached itself for high crimes and misdemeanors odd, or two-headed-cow odd?"

"A cow he mentions. You're psychic maybe?"

"Call me Criswell. Another moon-jumping incident?"

"Not quite. Someone killed a cow on a farm out Peconic way."

"That's not odd, that's the first step toward a Big Mac. Hard to get ground beef with the cow still alive."

"This one wasn't killed by its owner."

"Those pesky aliens again? Mutilated?"

"Beheaded."

That brought Jack up short. He looked up at Abe and saw he wasn't kidding. The thought of someone hacking away at some poor dumb animal's neck until the head fell off made him queasy.

"Jeez."

"There's more. It seems to have been done with a single blow."

"To a cow? Behead a cow with a single cut? What'd he use—a chainsaw?"

"They think it was a sword."

Ah . . . so this was why he'd brought it up. Jack had told Abe about the

Gaijin Masamune, and how it had sliced through his shoulder like a hot
Ginsu through butter—no, make that soft margarine.

But could it be the Gaijin? Maybe. It had cut through the barrel of his
Glock, yes, but was *any* sword sharp enough to do a cow like that?

Could it have been the katana?

"You think there's a connection?"

Abe gave one of his shrugs. "A sword maven I'm not. But you yourself
just told me this blade was very sharp. But then it disappears and what happens: The next night—the very next night—a cow is beheaded with a very
sharp, swordlike object." His Norman Mailer eyebrows oscillated like cater-
pillars in heat. "Coincidence?"

Last year Jack had been given the chilling message that there'd be no
more coincidences in his life. But that cow wasn't a part of his life, so why
couldn't this be a coincidence?

"Do you believe that?"

Abe shook his head. "No."

"Neither do I."

Crap.

And then he remembered a passage from *Kick* where Hank Thompson
mentioned his years of working in a slaughterhouse.

Could it be?

If so, it would be another in a long chain of noncoincidences.

But he had no way of knowing, so he let it go.

"If it was the same sword, the story could have been about your head
being separated from its body."

"Tell me about it. That thing is *sharp*. Barely felt it cut me."

"Speaking of cuts, how did you explain yours to Gia?"

Jack glanced at his shoulder. He hadn't worn the sling today and hadn't
missed it. His deltoid throbbed, but nothing he couldn't ignore.

"Haven't had to. Haven't seen her since it happened."

"What are you going to tell her?"

Jack shrugged. "The truth. No biggie."

"And when are you going to tell her the truth about the accident that
was no accident?"

He shook his head. "Wish I knew, Abe."

"The longer you wait, the harder it will be."

"She needs a little more distance from the acc—from what happened."

Abe looked dubious. "If you say so." He tapped the newspaper. "And
this sword? What are you going to do?"

"Nothing until I hear from Slater."

"I see the flyers up already. You may be hearing soon."

Jack had referred Naka to one of his old customers, a guy with a print shop who, for an added fee, would farm out the distribution work to guys who could use the extra cash and had nothing better to do.

"Even then, I may opt out."

"You're saying you're going to stop looking? You?" He shook his head. "Such little self-awareness. You know you're not."

"Am too. Going to wait for that katana to come to me."

Abe frowned. "That'll happen, you think?"

Jack nodded resignedly. "Yeah. Got a feeling it will. A bad feeling."

2

Hank waved one of the flyers and shouted, "I want these *down*! I want them *gone*!"

Darryl and Menck looked a little cowed as he paced back and forth across a corner of the Lodge basement. Well, they should be. He was pissed. When Darryl had brought it in to show him, he'd exploded.

He'd awakened this morning still high from last night. The air had seemed a little cleaner, the sun a little brighter.

Doing the cow had had something to do with it. Though he'd tried to avoid it, he couldn't help getting splattered with her hot blood. Messy, but it had felt *good*.

And then the dream. The Kicker Man was back again with the baby, cradling it in his lower right arm. But this time he was brandishing the katana in his lower left, while he held his two upper arms high in a *V* for victory.

The meaning was unmistakable: With the sword and the baby in his possession, nothing could stop the Kicker Evolution.

Well, he had the sword, and Dawn had been located. Only a matter of time before she and her baby were under his roof. Despite some rough spots along the way, everything was working out.

Then this flyer. What a bring-down.

Five thousand bucks for information leading to the sword. He wondered about the amount . . . a coincidence that it was the same reward he'd been offering for Dawn? Or a challenge?

"You've already got the sword," Menck said. "Ain't nobody else gonna get it."

"How do you know that? Whoever this guy is, he's offering a five-grand reward. We've got a lot of people moving in and out of this building, and although they're not allowed on the second floor, and although they have Kicker Man tattoos, some of them would sell their mother for half that."

Darryl said, "But—"

"But nothin! Somebody may have seen you pick it up. That someone may connect you with me. I can think of a million scenarios where this could go south. So I want those flyers down and Dumpstered. Got it?"

They nodded and spoke in unison.

"Got it."

3

Jack spotted him the minute he stepped through the door. Someone was sitting at his table.

"He say he waitin for you, meng," Julio said in a low voice as he met him at the door. "I saw you with him the other night so I figure 'sokay. 'Sokay?"

The guy had his back to the room, but the broad shoulders and gray hair gave him away.

Glaeken—no, make that Mr. Veilleur.

" 'Sokay."

Jack walked over and said, "Mind if I join you?"

Veilleur lifted his glass of stout in a toast and smiled up at him. "Jack.

I was hoping you'd stop by." He gestured to the chair against the wall. "I saved your seat."

Julio came over as Jack sat.

"Usual?"

After two visits to the Ear in one week, Jack had developed a taste for *witbier*.

"Too bad you don't have any Hoegaarden on tap."

Julio made a face. "That yuppie-hippie-emo piss? You kiddin me, meng?"

Jack sighed. "The usual."

As Julio left, Jack turned to Veilleur and noticed a flyer on the table. He turned it around and recognized a photo of the katana. Naka had wasted no time.

"Where'd you get this?"

Veilleur shrugged. "A man handed it to me on my way over. A very interesting sword."

Jack debated whether to say anything about it, then decided why not.

"Supposedly it's called the Gaijin Masamune."

Veilleur's head snapped up. "The what?"

Jack wondered at his reaction. "You've heard of it?"

"No. But I've heard of Masamune and I know what *gaijin* means. It's really a Masamune?"

Jack's turn to shrug. "So I've been told. He didn't sign it, so who's to say?"

Veilleur's gaze was fixed on the flyer. "What else do you know about it?"

Jack didn't want to talk about the katana—would rather not even think about it. He was far more interested in learning more about the Taint. But he had to give the guy an answer so he told him the Cliff Notes version of the story as he'd got it from O'Day—from the meeting between Masamune and the *gaijin* to Hiroshima and the bomb.

In closing he tapped the flyer. "It was stolen from this guy. He asked me to find it for him. I told him flyers were the best way to go."

"Will you know if he succeeds?"

"I promised I'd look into any leads if he wants me to."

Veilleur was staring at the flyer again. "Well, if you come into possession of it, I'd be very interested in seeing it."

He'd be delighted never to see it again, but he said, "Sure. But enough of the katana. Let's talk about the Taint."

"Of course. But first I'd like something to eat. I don't suppose Julio serves food?"

"Serves foodlike substances."

Veilleur frowned. "That doesn't sound very appetizing. Does he have a menu?"

Jack shook his head and pointed to the blackboard over the bar. "Just that."

Glaeken squinted at it. "The writing is very faint."

"That's because it's been there forever. He never changes it."

He looked around. "The place looks too small to have a kitchen."

"Not if you call a freezer and a microwave a kitchen."

Still squinting at the sign, Veilleur started to rise from his chair. "I'll have to move closer—"

Jack grabbed his arm. "I haven't known you long enough to call you a friend, but let me tell you: Friends don't let friends eat at Julio's."

The old man dropped back into his seat. "Thank you. You wouldn't believe some of the things I've eaten in my life, but my stomach's not what it used to be."

"Purely selfish on my part: I don't want you grabbing your gut and running out of here before you've told me a few things."

He laughed. "A practical man, and straightforward about it too. I like that." He sipped his stout. "You want to know more about the Taint."

Jack leaned forward. "Bingo. And maybe throw in a little info about Jonah Stevens while you're at it."

"If we have time."

Julio arrived with a mug of Yuengling for Jack and pointed to Veilleur's stout. "Get you another?"

"I believe so."

"You wanna eat?" When Veilleur glanced at Jack, Julio added, "Don' look at him. He wouldn't know good food if it bit him."

Jack said, "One of your burritos did bite me—right on the stomach lining."

"Don' listen to him. You hungry? You wanna cube steak? We got delicious stuffed cube steak."

Veilleur gave him a wan smile and shook his head. "I'm cutting back on stuffed cube steak."

When he was gone, Veilleur said, "I almost feel obligated to order something, even if I don't eat it."

"The Taint?" Jack said.

"Single-minded, aren't we?"

"So I've been told."

Veilleur leaned back. "To understand the Taint you need to know some of the Secret History of the World."

That phrase again. "When I was a kid, I had a good friend who used to talk about a Secret History of the World."

"The conspiracy crowd believes in a secret history and has countless scenarios for it, mostly wrong. But they're right about one thing: The world has a history known to only a few. It was codified once in a book that I hid away for safekeeping with other so-called forbidden texts, but they've all disappeared."

Jack had a flash. "That wouldn't be the *Compendium of Srem*, would it?"

Veilleur straightened in his chair. "You've heard of it?"

"Heard of it? It's sitting in my apartment."

"Amazing. Well then, why do you need me to tell you the Secret History when it's at your fingertips?"

Jack drummed those fingertips on the table. "It's not exactly an easy read, what with the pages changing every time you turn around."

Veilleur frowned. "Is that so? I guess Srem wound up with a multi-volume work that she had to fit into a single book."

"*She?*"

"Yes. Srem was an ancient, ancient Cassandra who saw the cataclysm coming and wanted to preserve a record of her times before everything was destroyed."

"Cataclysm?"

"We'll get to that. But—"

"Wait-wait-wait." Something wasn't right here. "You said you owned the book. So how come you didn't know how the text keeps changing?"

Veilleur shrugged. "I owned it but I never opened it. Her history was no secret to me. I didn't need to read about it—I'd lived it."

Okay. Jack could buy that.

"But what good is a book that keeps changing?"

He scratched his beard. "Not much. Something must have gone wrong. That sort of book was designed to have a finite number of sheets but a virtually infinite number of pages."

Jack stared at him. "I will add what you just said to my list of Things That Make Me Go, '*Huh?*'"

"It's simple, really. If you have one hundred sheets in a book, you will have two hundred pages, correct?"

"One on each side of a sheet. Right."

"But in this sort of book, when you turn the one-hundredth sheet—notice

I didn't say 'last'—you find another waiting for you. And another after that and another after that."

"But then you've got extra sheets."

Veilleur shook his head. "No. Because sheets are disappearing at the beginning of the book. If you flip back, you will find them again, but the sheet count remains constant."

Jack stared at him. He didn't seem to be pulling his leg.

"You're serious?"

"Of course. It's a lost art."

He realized that, after all he'd seen, he shouldn't be surprised by anything anymore, but this seemed straight out of Harry Potter.

"All well and good, but that's not what's happening. Pages are disappearing here and there about the book and being replaced by ones I've never seen that have nothing to do with what precedes or follows them."

"I imagine that would make comprehension very difficult."

"Tell me about it."

"Something must have gone wrong somewhere along the millennia. Too bad. The text would have explained everything."

At least Jack had an explanation of what was going on with that damn book—if you could call that an explanation.

Yeah. Too bad.

"So now the job falls to you."

"So it seems. Very well. To understand, you have to go back to the First Age, when the Adversary and I were born, and the war between the Ally and the Otherness was more out in the open. The laws of physics and chemistry and matter and energy were more pliable back then. Some people could perform what might seem like magic to you."

"Like Srem?"

"Like Srem. Anyway, I'd already defeated the Adversary—I was a mercenary in those days and did it for money—and it appeared I'd killed him. Because of that, the Ally chose me as one of its paladins."

"*One* of them?"

"There were a number of us back then, and the Adversary had his fellow plotters as well."

"But now it's just the two of you?"

"We're the only two to survive—for different reasons."

"You said you thought you'd killed him."

"Yes, but he managed a rebirth—"

"Besides the one in sixty-eight?"

A nod. "He's resourceful and resilient. We battled for centuries across surreal landscapes that would now be called dreamlike—or nightmarish. Neither side could gain the advantage. In a desperate move, the Otherness created the q'qr race."

"Cooker? You mean Kicker?"

"No. Kicker is Thompson's mangling of an ancient word." He spelled it for Jack, then pronounced it again.

Jack almost leaped from his seat. "Q'qr! I saw that in the *Compendium*. It called the Kicker Man 'the sign of the q'qr.' And under that it had some sort of poem about the q'qr."

" 'The Q'qr died yet lived on . . . the Q'qr is gone yet remains.' Something like that?"

"Yeah. That and more."

" 'The Song of the Q'qr.' A cautionary tale."

"Well, it's hard to be cautioned when you don't know what they're talking about."

Like much of what Jack had read in the *Compendium*, it assumed the reader shared the same reference base.

"The Otherness took a horde of its followers and inserted something of itself into their DNA."

"Did you even know about DNA back then?"

"We called it something else. Our life sciences were advanced, but the Otherness and the Ally blocked advances in weaponry, leaving us with only points and edges to fight with. Which often were not enough against waves of creatures part human and part Otherness."

"Like a rakosh?"

Veilleur shook his head. "The rakoshi were built from the ground up, so to speak; the q'qr were, in the current parlance, retrofitted. They were savage, vicious, their appearance fearsome—large and hairy, with fanged snouts. But their most terrifying feature was their two extra limbs."

"Four arms—the Kicker Man."

"Yes. But their extra limbs were boneless, tentacular, which made them all the more terrifying. What you call the Kicker Man was their symbol. They would draw it in blood wherever they had slaughtered humans—an almost continuous occurrence. They lived to kill and breed, and were prolific at both."

"How'd you stop them?"

"As I said, First Age weaponry was primitive, but our life sciences were advanced. The adepts began searching for an infection that would kill q'qr and spare humans. They were half successful: They created an agent that turned out to be deadly only to q'qr females."

Jack winced at what he saw coming. "With no females around, the q'qr males must have gone after human women."

"An unforeseen consequence. The males would tear through villages and towns, killing all the men and children and raping the women, hoping for at least some half-breeds to add to their ranks. But only a q'qr female could give birth to q'qr children. The raped women gave birth to human children—at least they looked human. Their mothers' DNA had commingled with the remnants of human DNA in the q'qr, but had quarantined the Otherness-created genes. The children seemed fully human but they carried what came to be known as the Taint. After the q'qr were defeated, the Taints were segregated—given their own land apart from the untainted population."

"But if they were segregated, how did the Taint spread?"

"The cataclysm. When its q'qr strategy failed, the Otherness lashed out at humanity, causing global geological and climatological upheavals that wiped out First Age civilization and most of humanity along with it. The surviving humans—pure-blood and Taint alike—huddled together and interbred, and spread out from there."

Jack shook his head. "This sounds like Velikovsky stuff. I mean, I used to be into anthropology and this goes against all the accepted theories."

Veilleur seemed unperturbed. "I imagine it does. But that's why it's called the *Secret* History of the World."

"Come on. There's gotta be some trace of the First Age *somewhere*."

Jack remembered a strange object he'd found in the Pine Barrens as a kid, possibly a leftover from that time. But it had disappeared.

"I'm sure there is, but not much. The upheavals were colossal and extensive. The Adversary and I barely escaped with our lives—all my fellow paladins perished. So whatever little is left is buried deep." He paused. "And yet . . . not so deep. Every human religion from the Sumerians to the Babylonians to the Jews has a cleansing cataclysm in its mythology—usually a flood. And even the q'qr live on in a way. Look at Hinduism—arguably the oldest established religion. Its pantheon includes gods like Shiva the Destroyer, Indra the god of lightning, Yama the god of the dead, and the most fearsome of all, Kali the blood queen. And what do they have in common?"

Jack didn't know Indra and Yama, but had seen pictures of Shiva, and knew Kali all too well. The answer gave him a chill.

"Four arms."

"Exactly."

They sat in silence for a while. Jack didn't know what Veilleur was thinking, but his own thoughts were awhirl. Finally . . .

"So we all carry this Taint."

Veilleur shrugged. "I suppose the laws of probability dictate that some people must be Taint free, but you can't tell by looking at them."

"Can you think of any purpose for a super-tainted baby?"

He shook his head. "Not one."

"Then why did Jonah Stevens—" Jack suddenly remembered something. "Wait . . . the other night . . . you seemed to recognize his name."

"I do. He was the Preparer of the Way for the Adversary's rebirth. And after he was born, Jonah protected him while his mother raised him."

Jack slapped the table. "Then Ras—I mean the Adversary must be behind the baby."

Another head shake. "I don't think so. I believe the Adversary murdered Jonah not too long after he'd set his plan in motion."

"Murdered? I heard it was an accident."

"Accidents can be arranged. I believe Jonah Stevens had it in his head that his super-tainted offspring could take the Adversary's place. The Adversary found out and eliminated him."

"Then I guess that now that the baby is on its way, he'll want to eliminate it as well."

That meant even more competition in the hunt for Dawn Pickering and her unborn child. First Hank and his crew, and now maybe Rasalom as well.

A teenage girl with no idea what she's carrying, clueless as to all the wheels she's set in motion.

Dawn—Dawn—Dawn . . . Where the hell are you?

4

"A woman!" cried the Seer. "A woman with child!"

Toru Akechi chewed his upper lip in worry as he watched the legless, half-naked Seer writhing on the futon. His anxiety stemmed from his elimination of Tadasu yesterday. As one of the Order's *sensei,* he had great latitude with his charges, but that stopped well short of pronouncing a death sentence. He had done what he had done for the good of the Order, but he had not had the approval of the Elders. No member of the Order could be eliminated without that.

He worried that the Seer might learn of it and tell the Elders assembled here. As far as Toru knew, the Sighting potion allowed only visions of the future, but still . . .

The Seer sat up, swiveling his eyeless face back and forth.

"A woman with child!" he cried again. "I see her face everywhere, staring back at me. She is important only for the child she carries. Her child, her child, her child . . . it will change the world. Who controls the child controls the future. The Order must control the child. It must!"

He loosed a guttural sound as he went through another bout of writhing and thrashing. And then he stopped, looking once again at nothing.

"The blade! The blade is with the woman! No! It is with her child! I see the child wielding the blade. The blade and child are together now and will be so again in the future. Her child and the katana are linked to the destiny of the world!"

And then he fainted, falling backward. His head hit the floor with a meaty *thunk.*

A pregnant woman whose face was everywhere. Everywhere . . . a film star? A cover model?

He and the Elders would divine its meaning and hunt down this woman with child and bring her under the Order's wing.

Who controls the child controls the future.

Toru wanted that child for the Order.

But then the second half of the Seeing: *The blade and child are together now and will be so again in the future.*

What else could that mean but that the katana was with the pregnant woman? Find one and they would find the other.

Her child and the katana are linked to the destiny of the world.

The future of the Kakureta Kao was linked to the destiny of the world as well.

He would start the hunt immediately.

5

"Takita-san!"

Hideo looked up and saw Kenji rushing into the room, waving a pink sheet of paper.

"Look at this!"

Hideo took the sheet and froze as he recognized the katana in the photo. And then he was out of his seat and in Kenji's face.

"Where did you get this?"

"Taped to the front door. They're all over."

Hideo stared at the sheet. What did it mean?

Acting on his theory that the owner from Hawaii had hired the *ronin* to find the katana, Hideo had spent all yesterday searching for an urban mercenary. He'd found mercenaries—plenty of them. They advertised in magazines like *Soldier of Fortune* and on various Web sites, but none of them fit the profile of the man he was looking for.

And now this flyer. Who but the owner from Hawaii would be offering such a reward? If so, it meant he had not yet reclaimed the katana.

He had to speak to this man. He was a living link to the sword—the only one within reach—and Hideo needed to learn what he knew. Perhaps he could provide a direction. He needed something, anything. He was floundering about. He felt as if he was drowning.

He grabbed the receiver from his desk phone and began to punch in the number listed on the sheet.

Halfway through, he stopped.

What was he going to say? He would have to choose his words carefully. The last thing he wanted was to raise suspicion, so everything he said had to have a basis in fact. He must assume that this man knew about the deaths of Gerrish and O'Day. He would be on his guard. Hideo did not want to frighten him off. No, he must lure him in and take control of him.

He sat and began making notes in preparation for his call.

6

After Veilleur left for home, Jack lingered at Julio's, kibitzing with some of the regulars. When he finally headed out he found himself walking behind a scruffy guy carrying a handful of pink sheets—the same shade as the one Veilleur had brought to the table. No doubt one of the guys Naka's printer had hired for dissemination.

But to Jack's surprise, the guy stopped at a pole where one of those pink flyers had been stapled and ripped it off. He added it to the stack in his hand and moved on.

He didn't appear to be the civic-minded type to go around decluttering and prettifying the neighborhood. And Jack confirmed this as the guy passed by a pole with one of the HAVE YOU SEEN THIS GIRL? flyers with Dawn's picture. Pretty selective in his cleanup.

Interesting.

Jack picked up his pace and closed the distance between them. When the guy stopped at another pole that carried both flyers, he was practically on top of him.

As the guy ripped off Naka's poster, Jack noticed the Kicker Man tattoo on his thumb web.

Even more interesting. Maybe even verging on fascinating.

Jack reached past him and tugged the Dawn flyer free and crumpled it into a ball.

The Kicker whirled on him. "Hey! You outta your head? Whatcha think you're doin?"

Jack put on a surprised look. "Why, same as you. Cleaning up these unsightly flyers. Aren't they just the worst nuisance?"

"You mind your own goddamn business."

"You mean you don't want help?"

"Help?" He waved the pink flyers in Jack's face. "You wanna get rid of these, fine." He snatched the Dawn flyer from Jack's hand. "But you leave these alone."

"Why? They're just as ugly."

That seemed to stump him, but only for a few seconds.

"No, they ain't. And besides, these here are trying to help find a missing girl. These others are trying to find a crummy-looking sword . . . a . . . a weapon of death. Yeah, a weapon of death."

"Hmmm." Jack pretended to give this serious consideration. "I see your point. But who is this missing girl and who are the people looking for her? Her family?"

"Yeah. Her family. That's it. She ran away from home and nobody knows where she went. They want her back real bad."

"How do we know they weren't abusing her?"

"Listen up, asshole." The Kicker's expression became menacing as he leaned close to Jack. His breath stank. "Stop asking so many questions. If you don't know where she is, then shuddup and move on. 'Cause if you ain't part of the solution, you're part of the problem. Get that? Move on and keep your mitts off the girl flyers."

"Did something die in your mouth?"

The guy's faced contorted. He half raised a fist, then seemed to think better of it. Instead he pointed his finger in Jack's face.

"You just remember what I told you or some bad shit's gonna come down and you're gonna be right under it. Unnastand?"

"Perfectly."

"Good."

With that he turned and stomped away. As he passed a trash can he tossed in all the flyers, including Dawn's.

So . . . the Kickers—Hank Thompson, in other words—were encouraging people to look for Dawn, but didn't want anyone looking for the katana. Because he already had it and didn't want anyone else looking for it?

That meant a fourth player was in the mix.

Naka Slater, the people behind the fake Naka, the yakuza, and now the Kickers.

This was crazy. What was it about that thing?

Well, he was out of it. From the start the chances that Slater would get a hit from those flyers had been slim at best. Now, with the Kickers combing the town and removing them, chances approached zero.

Yeah. Out of it.

So why didn't he feel relieved?

Jack knew the answer. Because the Kickers were interested in the sword. He didn't know what that meant, but the Kicker-Otherness connection said it couldn't be a good thing.

He'd sensed something strange about that sword, but what use could it be to Hank Thompson? Whatever it was, he doubted it was for a good purpose. Maybe he should—

Stop it, he told himself. You're out of it. Forget about it.

And then his cell rang. Slater was on the other end.

"Jack? I think we've got a hit."

Swell.

7

Naka Slater looked both excited and worried as they sat on a park bench near the center of Madison Square Park. Jack sat next to him, munching on a hot dog with peppers and onions from the Shake Shack on the downtown end near 23rd Street. The bench offered a good view of the ornate wedge of the Flatiron Building. The trees were in full bloom, their branches undulating in a gentle breeze. Schoolkids, old folks, secretaries, suits, hipsters, and bag ladies paraded along the crisscrossing paths.

Jack remembered when the only folks who'd enter this park were junkies, pushers, and clueless tourists.

"No one will listen to me," Slater said.

"Who-what?"

"Neither Homeland Security nor the NYPD. I told them about the Kakureta Kao and the Black Wind but I could tell they thought I was nuts."

"Imagine that."

"You think I'm nuts too, don't you."

"I came here about the call, remember? We're after the katana, right?"

"Yeah, but—"

"The call?"

He sighed and handed his cell phone to Jack. "Okay, okay. I've already entered the service number. Listen to the voice as well as the content."

Jack hit the SEND button, punched in the code Slater gave him, and listened.

"Hello. My name is James and I saw your flyer. I have the sword you seek and I know it's a Masamune. So I want more than five thousand for it. I'll need twice that. Call me back if that is acceptable. If not, I will keep it for myself."

Jack pressed the 1 button to replay the message.

Something familiar about that voice.

"Hear those inflections?" Slater said. "He's Japanese."

"You're sure?"

"I speak both languages—very well, I might add. I learned them at a very early age, but Japanese came first, and certain rhythms and inflections bleed through to the trained ear. This fellow speaks nearly flawless English, but there's no question in my mind that Japanese was his first language."

And then it clicked: the leader of the yakuza. He'd spoken—at least to Jack's ear—flawless English.

Red flags flew up all over his brain.

Slater said, "Do you think I should meet his demand? I mean, I can afford ten thousand, but—"

"Agree to it, but let me handle it."

Slater's eyebrows lifted. "You think he's lying? He knew it was a Masamune. That says a lot, don't you think?"

"Doesn't mean he has it. Might just as easily mean he's planning to scam you, or he's looking for it too."

"But he must realize I don't have it. I'd hardly be offering a reward for something I already had."

"Might think—correctly, I assume—that you know more about it than he." He hesitated. He didn't want to mention the Kickers' involvement, but he'd already mentioned a third party, so . . . "I think he's that other player in this sword quest."

Slater's eyes widened. "The yakuza? Do you think they've got it?"

"Not sure, but I'd lay odds they don't. I *will* bet they've scoped you out as the original owner. So if they're looking for the sword and want to know more about it, you da man."

"So what do I do?"

"Give me his number and I'll call him back. I'll agree to the extra money, and set up a meet ASAP—preferably here, preferably today."

Slater looked around. "Do you really think it's safe to carry that much cash around here?"

Jack gave him a look. "You kidding? Nobody's carrying cash anywhere. You're staying in your hotel room and I'm going to check out whoever shows up."

"You think they'll try something sneaky?"

Sneaky . . . how quaint.

"Yeah. Maybe even . . . deceitful."

8

"I grieve over Tadasu-san," Shiro told his *sensei,* and meant it. He would miss him.

They sat in the classroom.

Akechi-*sensei* nodded gravely. "Yes, the Order is poorer for his passing. But he died serving the Order, something we all must be ready to do at any moment."

"I am ready, *sensei.*"

He was also ready to ascend from acolyte to temple guard. He hated to think about it, but Tadasu's passing left an opening in the guard. Perhaps he would be assigned . . .

Shiro hesitated to bring up the subject, but he needed confirmation of a rumor.

"Is it true what I am hearing, *sensei?*"

"And what would that be?"

"That the Order is looking for a pregnant woman?"

Akechi-*sensei* said nothing at first. With his teacher's face forever hidden from him, Shiro had learned to read his eyes. He was relieved to see that they appeared . . . amused.

"There are no secrets in the temple, are there."

Shiro bowed his head. "Not about what happens in the Sighting room."

"It is true, Shiro. The Seer saw a pregnant woman. Just so you won't have to rely on rumor, I shall tell you his exact words: 'A woman with child . . . I see her face everywhere, staring back at me. She is important only for the child she carries. Her child, her child, her child . . . it will change the world. Who controls the child controls the future. The Order must control the child. It must.' The elders are working on an interpretation."

"There are so many pregnant women, *sensei.*"

"Yes, but how many with 'her face everywhere, staring back'? That is the keystone of the vision. It must be someone famous, some woman on billboards or television or magazine covers."

"A pregnant celebrity . . ." That narrowed it down quite a bit, but still . . . how would they possess someone so well known? "I have heard there was another vision about the katana."

His *sensei* nodded. He said, 'The blade is with the woman . . . the blade and child are together now and will be so again in the future.'"

The blade is with the woman . . . the realization struck Shiro like a *bo*.

"The katana is in New York, *sensei*. We know that. So that must mean the woman is in New York!"

His *sensei* stared at him a moment in silence, then his eyes crinkled within the mask and he clapped his hands once.

"Truly, the Face is with you."

And then Shiro experienced what he could only call a vision of his own.

A face . . . a young blond woman's face staring back from every flat surface in the city.

He told Akechi-*sensei* about the flyers.

His teacher nodded slowly. "Possibly . . . possibly."

"But if so many are searching for her without success—I assume no success because new flyers go up every day—how are we to find her?"

His *sensei* thought a moment. When he spoke, Shiro could sense the excitement in his voice.

"Because the Seer said she is with the katana, and before he died, Tadasu told me that the katana is with someone who wears a tattoo like this."

He grabbed a piece of rice paper and a kanji brush from a nearby desk and began to drawn. He turned the page and showed Shiro.

"Have you ever seen this figure before?"

Of course he had—as ubiquitous as the flyers with the girl's face.

Members of the Inner Circles rarely if ever left the temple. Errands for food and medical supplies were left to those of the Order who could show their faces to the public. Consequently, the Inner Circles were ignorant—sometimes blissfully so, he imagined—of what was happening on the teeming streets of the city around them.

"It's the symbol for a group—a subculture, one might say—growing within the city. They call themselves 'Kickers,' *sensei*."

"Who is their leader?"

Shiro shook his head. "I don't know, *sensei*. But I can find out."

And then another vision. Akechi-*sensei* had sent him out with a list of rare herbs and odd ingredients that he was to search out and bring back to the temple. All the acolytes had been given such lists. During his wanderings through the back streets of Lower Manhattan he had seen something he'd paid scant attention to at the time, but now it bloomed in significance.

He clapped his hands once in respectful imitation of his teacher. "I think I know where to look. Last week I saw a strange banner hanging outside an old, old building . . . a banner with a giant stick figure like this one."

After a moment of silence Akechi-*sensei* said, "I will speak to the El-ders. We must put this building under constant surveillance. Immediately." He placed a hand on Shiro's shoulder. "You have done well, my *oshiego*. I am proud of you."

Shiro felt dizzy. He had never seen Akechi-*sensei* touch anyone, or give praise like this. He thought his heart might burst with pride.

9

Dawn leaned against the rear wall of the Milford Plaza elevator. Though she'd showered and scrubbed herself down just half an hour ago, she felt to-tally scuzzy. Three days now with the same clothes.

Yuck.

She'd thought about washing them in the tub but figured they'd never dry, even overnight. She could have sent them out for cleaning, but that meant she'd have to hang around the room totally naked.

Uh-uh.

And she was so not risking a trip outside just to buy new stuff.

Double—no, *triple* uh-uh. She was almost home free now. She could put up with funky clothes for another day or two before going back to Mr. Osala's.

So if she smelled, too bad. Nothing she could do about it. She looked around at the people on the elevator with her and thought, Sorry, folks. You'll have to deal.

At least the short hair was easy to care for, and dried so much more quickly than the length she'd arrived with.

As she stepped out of the elevator she looked around for the time. For a couple of years now she'd totally used her cell phone as her watch, but Mr. Osala had taken that. She spotted a clock behind the registration desk: 2:35. Plenty of time to cab seventeen blocks. She'd be early.

Dawn felt her insides tense as she approached the front entrance onto Eighth Avenue. Tons of people passing by out there . . .

One of whom might be Jerry.

No, she wouldn't let herself think like that. No one could snatch her in front of that crowd. She'd done this two days ago. She could do it again today.

She adjusted her sunglasses, took a breath, and stepped outside. She signaled the doorman, who rushed over. She'd tipped him ten dollars the other day because she wanted him to totally remember her and stay close by.

"Cab, ma'am?"

She gave him the address on West 63rd. He signaled for the next taxi waiting in line, opened the door for her, and told the cabbie where she was going. She handed him another ten.

"Thank you, ma'am." He tipped his hat. "You have a nice day."

I will, she thought, locking both rear doors as the cab lurched into motion. *I'm going to have a great day.*

Sighing, she leaned back. No, she wasn't. She was going to kill the life growing within her. A life that hadn't asked to be conceived. A life that had no control of who had fathered it. An innocent life. How could she . . . ?

She straightened, crying, "No-no-no-no-NO!" as she pounded on the seat cushion.

Over his shoulder the driver gave her a concerned look.

She gave him the *okay* wave. "Sorry."

Leaning back again she told herself not to sentimentalize this. She was doing what had to be done and that was that. No cold feet beforehand, and no looking back afterward.

Like the Nike ads said: Just do it . . .

"We are here, miss."

The cabbie's voice jarred her from a reverie of life regrets, virtually all from just the past year. She looked out the window at the clinic entrance. A man stood by the door with a crude, hand-lettered sign:

Abortion Kills!

Well, *duh.*

She hesitated getting out, not liking the idea of passing him. But who said she even had to look at him? She paid the driver, gave him a nice tip, then slid out.

"Are you coming here?" the man said.

He was clean shaven and neatly dressed in a dark blue golf shirt and jeans. He looked totally harmless. Yet you never knew with these religious nuts. Outside normal, inside a bunch of quotes from the Bible that gave them permission to do just about anything in the name of the Lord.

Behind her the cab pulled away, leaving her alone on the curb.

Averting her eyes, she stepped toward the door.

"You are! You *are* going in! Please don't! Think of your baby and how it will feel to be torn apart!"

She heard engine noise behind her and turned to see a gray panel truck pulling up to the curb. If it had been a cab she might have been tempted to take it away from here, from this nut.

But no, she was seeing this through.

When she continued forward he stepped between her and the door, blocking her way.

"Please think of your baby!"

Behind her she heard a door sliding open as she forced herself to make eye contact with the man.

"Get out of my—"

Terror spiked through her gut as she felt a gloved hand clamp over her mouth. As she lifted her hands to pull it off and scream, an arm snaked around her chest and she was yanked off her feet, spun around, and pushed through the side door of the panel truck. Someone within pulled her inside and for an instant her mouth was free but he clamped his hand across her face before she could scream. She bit him but all she got was leather glove. Panicked, she began twisting and kicking and trying to writhe free as the first man leaped in behind her and slid the door closed. He grabbed her legs and steadied them as the van began to move.

"Easy, Dawn, easy," he said in a tone he probably thought soothing but was not. "No one's gonna hurt you. That's the last thing we want. In fact, you're gonna be safer now than you've ever been in your life."

He knew her name! And then she saw that weird little stick figure on all their hands.

Oh, God, these were Jerry's people!

10

Jack had dressed in wino casual—ripped dirty jeans, fatigue jacket, stomped-on fedora pulled down to his ears and eyebrows, unlaced sneakers three sizes too big for him, and a grime-smudged face. He'd accessorized with yellow rubber kitchen gloves, a pair of women's sunglasses, and a stuffed black garbage bag that supposedly held his worldly belongings but in reality contained nothing but wadded-up newspaper. He waved his free arm in the air as he conversed with no one.

A useful getup: No one except maybe god-squad types ever made eye contact with his type.

When he'd called the number from the voice mail he'd played anxious to get back the katana, but sounded suspicious and wanted a public place. Whoever he spoke to countered by saying surely he'd want to examine the blade and couldn't very well do that in Times Square. Jack insisted on public, specifically Madison Square Park. It had traffic but everyone pretty much minded their own business.

He arrived a little after three—almost an hour early—and began picking through the trash bins, adding an occasional aluminum can or plastic bottle to his bag. Then he chose an empty bench with a clear view of the Admiral Farragut statue and the meeting spot. He began a muttered but heartfelt conversation with himself interspersed with scatological references to passersby.

Eventually a slim, nervous-looking black guy in horn-rimmed glasses appeared, carrying an oblong object wrapped in what looked like a drop cloth. As instructed, he found a bench in the northeast corner of the park and took a seat. Jack rose and began to make another round of the trash cans.

He spotted the heavy yakuza on line at the Shake Shack.

Jack allowed himself a pat on the back. He'd been right.

The Shake Shack made a perfect cover for the big guy. He looked like he liked to eat. Jack was tempted to see if he tried to order tempura or sashimi, but needed to keep moving.

Found one of the others at the park's northwest corner, near Fifth and 26th. Farther along the street he spotted the third loitering outside a sidewalk café on the far side of Madison.

Where was Mr. Boss Man? Had to be somewhere nearby, most likely in that Lincoln Town Car, idling, watching. His men had the exits covered. They could snatch Slater as he left the park, or the boss could follow him if he made it to a cab.

Jack wandered to the downtown end of the park and found a bench with a good view of Big Guy. He pretended to doze but kept watch from behind the sunglasses.

Big Guy hung by the Shake Shack, chomping on a burger, then a hot dog, then an order of fries.

The meeting time came and went. The yakuza had Slater's voice mail number. Jack had told him not to return any calls. Forty-five minutes after the planned meeting time, a Town Car pulled to the curb on 23rd. A driver and the boss man sat in front. Big Guy joined his two buddies in the rear and they took off.

Jack rose and hurried deeper into the park, hoping to catch the decoy before he left.

No worry. The thin black guy was still sitting on the bench with the bundle across his knees. Looked like no one had told him the gig was off. He jumped as Jack plopped down next to him and leaned close.

"The moon is in the seventh house," he whispered.

The guy inched away. "What?"

"The stars are aligning for the End Times. It's all over now."

"Are-are you the one I'm supposed to meet?"

"We'll all meet in the afterlife two thousand light-years from home." He pretended to notice the bundle for the first time. "Hey, is that my Christmas present?"

"Christmas? No—"

Jack raised his voice. "It is, dammit! Santa left it just for me and you took it!"

The guy started to rise but Jack pulled him back and grabbed for the bundle. He pulled it from his grasp, found the edge of the cloth, and shook it out like a sandy towel.

A scabbarded katana fell free. The tip pointed Jack's way so he grabbed it and pulled, baring the blade.

A smooth, unblemished blade.

Jack tossed the scabbard at the guy and jumped to his feet. He clutched his black plastic bag against his chest, stamped his feet, and pointed with his free hand.

"The Sword of Damocles! You're an archangel! I knew it! It's the end times! The End Times! I must prepare myself for sacrifice!"

Now *there's* a mixed bag of references, he thought as he turned and ran screaming from the park.

11

Dawn had no idea how long she'd been in the basement. Not like it was a dungeon or anything. It was warm and well lit; she had a folding chair to sit on. The rest of the furniture consisted of a few long folding tables supporting a bunch of phones, none of which worked—she knew; she'd tried every one of them. But the place had no windows and no clock on the wall, so even though it seemed like days, she knew it had been only hours. How many hours was the question.

No, not *the* question, *one* of the questions.

The big question was who were these people? She'd been hustled out of the truck and into the rear entrance of this ornate old building way downtown. She hadn't seen any women, only men, and not many of those. The place seemed almost totally deserted.

They'd fed her—brought her a Big Mac and fries and a bottle of Aquafina—but they hadn't left her alone. Not for a second. Someone sat by the only exit door at all times. The first had been the guy who'd had the sign outside the clinic. On the heavy side, with short dark hair and a retreating hairline, he'd been called Menck by one of the guys in the truck. He'd tried to make small talk at first but she wasn't interested, and he'd clammed up rather than answer the questions she peppered him with.

She totally recognized the scruffy guy who relieved him: the same guy

she'd run into outside Blume's and in SoHo. She'd know that squint anywhere. They called him Darryl and he must have recognized her downtown
and followed her to the Milford.

She wanted to scream. She'd thought she was breaking free but all she'd
accomplished was trading Mr. Osala's prison for the Milford prison and now
this one, wherever it was.

Was there anyone left in the world who totally didn't want to lock her up?

"How long are you going to keep me here?" she said.

Darryl scratched a bristly cheek. "That's up to the main man."

"You mean Jerry?"

The thought made her heart pound. He'd be royally pissed at her for trying to get an abortion, but he wouldn't hurt her. Not while she still carried
his precious baby. As Mr. Osala had said—why on God's earth hadn't she
stayed with him?—the baby was her insurance policy.

Darryl frowned. "Jerry? Don't know of any Jerry."

He seemed to be telling the truth, but she couldn't think of anyone else
who could be behind this.

"Then who's this main man?"

"He's—" He caught himself. "Probably best if I let him tell you that."

"Well, where is he?"

"You'll see him soon."

Just then the door opened and Menck stuck his head through.

"Bring her upstairs."

Dawn tried to jump to her feet and run—but where? And besides, her
knees were too wobbly. So she just sat there while Menck held the door and
Darryl came over and gripped her upper arm.

"C'mon, gal. Time to see the main man."

Jerry . . . had to be.

She allowed herself to be helped to her feet, then she preceded Darryl to
the door where Menck took her arm and led her up a narrow stairway.

As soon as she hit the first floor she began screaming for help. Her voice
echoed off the stone walls. Darryl and Menck stood by and watched her with
amused expressions. Two other men appeared. She recognized them from
the truck.

"What's her problem?" one of them said.

Darryl grinned. "She thinks there's someone around to hear her."

"There is," said the guy. "Us."

"Someone who cares," Darryl added. He poked her shoulder. "There
ain't."

She stopped. She totally wanted to cry but she'd be damned if she'd break down in front of these jerks.

Menck said, "We called ahead and had the building cleared before you arrived." He tilted his head toward the waiting stairs. "Let's go. Someone on the second floor is waiting to meet you."

She so didn't want to go but they were behind her, pushing. When she reached the top she was out of breath, not from exertion, but fear. They led her down a hall to a half-open door. They guided her through and she stopped cold at the sight of a man she had totally never seen before.

He stood in the middle of the room swinging a sword.

She screamed.

12

As Jack approached the Kicker HQ, he was surprised to see a bunch of them hanging out on the front steps and the sidewalk.

Earlier he'd ditched the rubber gloves and sunglasses, upgrading his look from wino casual to just plain scruffy. He'd traded his torn jeans for ones that were simply well worn. Then he'd stopped over at Gia's where she'd used a Sharpie to draw a faux Kicker Man tattoo in his right thumb web. She'd wanted to know what he was up to but he put her off with a promise of a full explanation later.

He did a quick check on the tat as he approached the throng. Might not pass muster in the light of day, but here in the dark, with only streetlights for illumination, it was perfect.

He stopped by a knot of a half dozen guys and pulled out a pack of Marlboros. Making sure his tat was toward the group, he shook one out and lit up. As anticipated, someone needed a smoke.

"Hey, bro," said a blond guy in a work shirt. "Spare one of those?"

"Sure." Jack extended the box. After the guy had taken his, Jack offered it around. "Anyone else?"

One other guy took him up on it. Jack lent them his lighter to fire up. After a few drags—fake inhaled for fear of coughing—he looked around.

"What's going on? What's everybody doing outside? This a fire drill or something?"

The blond guy grinned. "Damn near. Like three o'clock this afternoon we get the word: Everybody outta the building. Move-move-move. We been out here ever since. I went and grabbed a burger and come back figuring everything'd be back to normal. But no. Still locked out, and no reason why."

A tall, sullen type was eyeing Jack. "Ain't seen you around before."

Jack eyed him right back. "I'm kinda new. Been out all day ripping down those sword flyers. You know they got them posted as far out as Jackson Heights? I mean, what gives with that?"

The blond guy said, "Word is that someone heard just as we were being moved out that the next job would be taking down the girl posters."

Jack stiffened. "You mean those missing Dawn Pickering things we've been plastering all over town? They want them *down*?"

"That's the word." He shrugged. "Don't mean it's true."

"Did they find her?"

The tall guy shrugged. "Don't think so. I been workin the phones these past four weeks and I ain't heard nothin but bullshit comin in. One lie after another, just trying to get a piece of that reward. Sometimes people make me sick, y'know? I think Hank just figured if we ain't found her by now, we ain't gonna find her at all, and he decided to pull the plug."

"You might be right," Jack said.

Like hell. No way Hank would give up on that baby. He and his late unlamented brother Jerry saw Dawn's baby as the Key to the Future. Only three reasons he'd pull the flyers: Dawn was dead, Dawn had gotten an abortion, or Dawn had been found and was under his control.

Clearing out Kicker HQ on such short notice added a lot of weight to number three. If true, she could be inside right now.

"Nice night."

Jack turned away and looked up, pretending to stare at the sky, but really checking for a vantage point that would allow him to see into the building. As he scanned the cornices of the rooftops across the street he spotted a flash of reflection—a double flash, side by side.

As in binoculars.

13

Her scream jolted Hank. Why—?

Oh, yeah. The sword. He'd been swinging it around when she stepped into the room. Must have thought he was going to attack her.

"Hey, it's all right," he said, lowering the blade. "I'm just playing with it."

She stood inside the doorway, trembling, her eyes shifting left and right. "Wh-where's Jerry?"

Jerry? Did she think he was still alive?

Of course she did. She'd known him as Jerry Bethlehem. As far as anyone knew, Jerry Bethlehem was a murder suspect on the run from the law. But that had been an assumed identity. His body had been ID'd and he'd been declared dead under his real identity, Jeremy Bolton. No way Dawn could connect the two.

He studied her. She didn't look pregnant. He barely recognized her. She'd lost weight, and with her blond hair dyed brown and cut short, he might have passed her on the street without recognizing her. Only when he focused on her puggish face did he know for sure it was her.

And he wanted to slug her. Or cut her.

Probably not the best idea to be holding the katana while talking to her, but he liked the way it felt in his hands.

He fumed at the thought of how she'd come within a few feet and a few seconds of killing Jeremy's baby. If she'd set foot inside that clinic, she'd have been out of reach and the Plan would be in ashes right now.

But much as he wanted to, he couldn't hurt her. Not while she carried the Key to the Future.

But after the baby was born . . . a whole new ball game.

Then again, maybe not. She'd be the Mother of the Key, which might make her untouchable.

So Hank bottled his fury while he considered what to say.

She thought Jerry was alive . . . maybe he could use that.

"Jerry's not here at the moment."

"Where is he?"

"Around. He doesn't want to see you yet. He's too mad at you for running off and putting us to all this trouble."

"Us?"

"Him, me, all the Kickers. We've spent a lot of money and a lot of manhours looking for you."

She frowned. "What's in it for you?"

"Why, the welfare of your baby, of course."

She was staring at him as if seeing him for the first time. "You . . . you look like him."

Hank noticed Menck and Darryl still standing in the doorway.

He waved them off. "Close the door behind you." Then he turned to Dawn and said, "Like who?" though he knew exactly who.

"Like *him*. Put a beard on you and—oh, Jesus! You're related!"

"True. Jerry wa—" He caught himself. Almost said *was*. Have to watch that. "Jerry and I had the same father. He's my half brother. And that . . ." He pointed to her midsection ". . . is my nephew."

She grabbed her belly with both hands and backed away until she was pressed against the door.

"Oh, God!"

She began to cry, and he couldn't help feeling a little—just a little—sad for her. After all, she was only eighteen. Just a kid. She hadn't asked for this.

But on the other hand, she wouldn't even exist if not for the Plan, so she *owed* the Plan. Owed it her life. And all the Plan was asking in return was the baby she didn't even want, the baby she was on her way to kill.

He spoke in a soft, soothing tone. "It's not the end of the world, Dawn. It's nine months out of your life. And you're already—what?—almost two months into it. So we're talking maybe seven months here. You see it through, and then, if you don't want the baby, you walk away and spend the rest of your life any way you want to. If you want to stay and help raise him, you'll never want for anything ever again."

She stopped crying and glared at him as she spoke through her gritted teeth.

"I *don't want* this baby! I know who Jerry is and I want this obscene thing out of me! If I could rip it out with my hands I would. It shouldn't even exist. I don't know what you two are up to or what you think this baby's going to be, and I don't care. Find your 'Key to the Future' somewhere else!" Her voice rose to a scream. *"I don't want it!"*

Hank felt heat filling his head. "Well, you're going to have it so get used to it, babes. You can make it easy or you can make it hard, but that's the way it's gonna be."

"Yeah?"

She got a wild look in her eyes, and then suddenly she was charging him. No, not him—for the sword. He pivoted and moved it out of her reach. That was when he realized that she had no interest in him or the sword. She was heading for the window. And at the rate she was moving, it couldn't be just for a look. The window—a single piece of old glass—was down but she looked like she was going to jump right through it.

Hank dropped the sword and dove for her. He tackled her around the knees.

As they hit the floor, he shouted, "Menck! Darryl! Get in here!"

They burst into the room saying "Oh shit!" in unison. They each grabbed Dawn by an arm and hauled her to her feet.

"You can't keep me here! You can't make me a prisoner! It's against the law. I'll kill myself rather than stay here!"

Hank rose to his feet and brushed himself off.

"Take her back to the basement."

He heard her screaming about how they couldn't keep her here all the way down the hall.

Well, she was right about that. This old building in the heart of lower Manhattan was possibly the worst place on the planet to hold her. But he had to keep her somewhere, and preferably close to the city.

He picked up the sword and began swinging it in figure eights again. Where-where-where?

And then the sword gave him the answer—sort of. It reminded him of the North Fork and all the farm country there. Had to be some isolated cabin or old farmhouse for rent.

Yeah.

He tossed the sword onto the bed and headed for the office on the first floor. They had a computer there. He'd start with Craigslist. If he couldn't find anything there, he'd contact some Realtors first thing in the morning.

14

Watching the watcher . . .

Jack kept an eye on the guy with the binocs from behind the rotting boards of a defunct rooftop water tank. He'd sneaked over from the adjoining roof. These old buildings rarely had working alarms on their roof access doors.

At three stories this particular building matched the height of the Lodge across the street. The guy was all in black and his interest seemed particularly focused on one lit window on the second floor. It must have opened into a high-ceilinged room because it was half again as high as a regular window. Still, Jack couldn't see inside from his angle.

Hank had said that the Scientologists and Dormentalists had it in for him because so many of their suckers were defecting to the Kickers. Could this guy be—?

Without warning the watcher leaped to his feet and turned. Jack ducked back and held his breath. Had he made a sound and given himself away? He snaked his hand back and pulled his Glock. A rooftop fight was the last thing he wanted, but if this guy wanted to rumble . . .

But no, he swept on by toward the rooftop entry, yammering on his cell phone as he passed. Light from within bathed him as he opened the door, and Jack got a good look at his face: Japanese.

One of the faux Naka's cult buddies?

When he was gone, Jack moved to the roof edge and looked down to see what was so interesting. He recognized Hank talking to a young woman with short brown hair. He wished he had his Leica along. Then he noticed something long and slim in Hank's hand.

A katana.

Again, binocs would have come in handy to confirm what Jack had already guessed, but this pretty much clinched it: Hank had the Gaijin Masamune.

And that was what had put the watcher on the move. He'd seen the sword and had gone running to tell his boss.

Question was, who was his boss? The suit with the yakuza, or this Order of the Hidden Face Slater had talked about? The answer mattered. One had been ready to kill him and the other had already tried. He knew the location of the yakuzas but not the Hidden Face. If the watcher was one of those crazy, self-mutilating monks, Jack wanted to know where they hung out.

As he was turning away he saw a flurry of motion from within. The woman was diving toward the window. Hank tackled her and brought her down. After a brief struggle, two men came in and hauled her to her feet. Her mouth was open as if she was screaming, but Jack heard nothing. For an instant her face turned his way, giving him a dead-on look. He stiffened as recognition bolted through him. The long blond hair was gone, replaced by short, choppy brown, but no question about who she was.

Dawn Pickering.

All those flyers must have paid off. Someone had spotted her and dropped a dime for the reward.

He leaned back on his haunches, thinking.

He'd found Dawn and the katana in the same place. What were the odds of that? High. High enough to make him uncomfortable. He'd come looking for the katana, but that took a backseat now that he'd found Dawn.

Now he knew why the lower-level Kickers had been kicked out onto the street. Hank and his inner circle had an unwilling guest that they didn't want the hoi polloi to know about.

Despite what Glaeken had said about keeping the katana out of the wrong hands, Jack had made a promise to Christy Pickering to separate her daughter from the man she knew as Jerry Bethlehem.

Okay, not a promise, but he'd taken her money and said he'd do the job. And he had done it. But now she was in Hank's clutches, and that was pretty much like being in Jerry's. So in a way, the fix-it wasn't finished. He felt a duty to Christy to free her daughter.

So the katana could wait. He knew where it was and had a feeling it would never be too far from Hank Thompson. A glance back showed him standing near the window, swinging it in flashing loops.

No, that blade wasn't going anywhere—at least not tonight.

But what about Dawn? He doubted she'd be going anywhere tonight either. He needed a way to get her out of there without endangering her.

His first thought was to call the cops. He could tell them that Dawn Pickering, a person of interest in a Forest Hills murder, was hiding in the

Lodge. A warrant, a search, Dawn is discovered, tells the cops she'd been kidnapped and held prisoner: hot water for Hank and company.

Sounded perfect. The only problem he could see was the pervasiveness of Kickers. The most visible members hailed from the lower rungs of the socioeconomic ladder, but they existed at all levels. Undoubtedly some were in the criminal justice system. And somewhere along the tortuous course of obtaining a search warrant on a building owned by a group as connected as the Septimus Lodge, someone might very well raise a warning flag.

And then Dawn would disappear and Jack would be back to square one.

A one-man assault was out of the question. He needed help—willing or unwilling, witting or unwitting—and had an idea where he might find some.

He peeked over the edge of the roof and saw the watcher step onto the sidewalk below and start toward Allen Street.

Jack jumped up and ran for the roof door. He blasted through, pounded down six flights of stairs and burst onto the sidewalk at a run. He reached Allen Street in time to see the watcher hop into a cab. He spotted another a dozen feet away discharging a fare. He hopped in.

"Hate to say it, but follow that cab."

He expected a remark from the driver, a grizzled fellow with shiny black skin and a curly, gray beard, but he merely turned on the meter and shifted into drive.

The watcher led them to the southbound FDR all the way down to the ferry docks. There he got out and boarded a waiting ferry. Jack followed. It left promptly at ten thirty.

Staten Island, he thought. What the hell's on Staten Island?

The watcher stayed up front, as if urging the boat to go faster, so Jack hung around the stern, watching Lower Manhattan's bright skyline recede in the wake. Two tall, thin structures were missing from the view. Jack had always hated the Twin Towers, considering them irksome, unimaginative, incongruous eyesores. But now that they were gone, he missed them.

Twenty-five minutes later the ferry was nudging into the Staten Island docks. As soon as the gates opened, the watcher hopped off and trotted to one of the waiting cabs. Jack followed to another, and tried a variation on the dreaded phrase.

"See that cab? Follow it."

The driver looked over his shoulder. He was some kind of squat little Asian. His name on the license looked Thai—*Prasopchai Narkhirunkanok.* No way would Jack try to pronounce it. He'd never heard of anyone dislocating his tongue, but that didn't mean it couldn't happen.

"Follow that cab?" he said in accented English. "This is true?"

"That's what I said."

He laughed. "Okay. We follow that cab."

The ferry had landed at the northernmost tip of the island. They followed the watcher's cab along Victory Boulevard to the Staten Island Expressway, which was anything but express, even at this hour. They traveled east to the West Shore Expressway and then south to the landfill where the first cab exited.

The Fresh Kills landfill?

Jack didn't know much about it except that sometime in the middle of the last century New York City declared a couple of thousand acres of Staten Island its dumping ground. Over the ensuing decades it piled up huge mounds of garbage. The landfill closed around the turn of the century, but reopened long enough to accept World Trade Center debris.

"Any idea where he's going?"

The driver nodded. "I saw him. He look Japanese. I fear he is going to bad place."

"Bad place?"

"A temple where Kakureta Kao dwell."

"You've heard of them?"

Another nod. "They once known all over Asia. My grandmother used to scare me by saying she call the Kakureta Kao in Tokyo and they come and take me back to their temple and cut me up. After the war everyone thought they dead, but then they show up here."

"In a landfill?"

"No one want land where they stay. They can be alone there to perform foul rites."

Foul rites . . . he had to mean the self-mutilation Slater had mentioned. But why here? Why in the U.S.?

"There, you see?" he said, pointing ahead. "Kakureta Kao."

Jack saw the watcher's cab stop outside an oblong, two-story box of a building. Not exactly what he'd had in mind when he'd heard the word *temple*.

Someone who looked like a guard let him through the gate in the six-foot stone wall running the perimeter.

Guard?

"Slow down," Jack said. "Let the other cab pull away, then drive by—slowly."

The driver did as he was told. As they passed Jack got a glimpse of the guard in the glow of the single bulb over the gate. He was wearing a kimono and a hakama, like someone out of a chop-socky movie.

"Stop here and turn out your lights," Jack said as they reached the top of a rise.

"I drive you back now, yes?"

Jack dropped a couple of twenties on the front seat.

"Just park here a few minutes. I want to watch the place."

"I do not like it here," he said, but parked and doused his lights.

Jack looked around and could see why. To the west the Hidden Face building stood alone, isolated on a marshy flat. Half a mile or more away in the opposite direction he could see what looked like house lights. Down at the building he spotted a couple of commuter vans parked along the southern flank. Beyond and to the right of the temple rose the dirt-covered hills of the landfill. Like cyclopean burial mounds. In a way they *were* burial mounds—the final resting place of a half century's worth of debris from the urban civilization a few miles to the north.

He pointed to the biggest mound. "How tall do you think that is?"

"As tall as the Statue of Liberty. The Fresh Kills landfill is one of largest man-made structures on Earth. It can be seen from space."

It sounded rehearsed.

"You give tours?"

The driver shrugged. "I learn if I give interesting fact to fares, they give to me bigger tip."

Jack turned his attention back to the temple, trying to imagine what was going on in there. He hoped they were planning a raid on Kicker HQ.

15

Shiro tried to rein in his excitement as he approached the front entrance of the temple. He placed his cell phone in the galvanized, foam-lined, waterproof milk box outside the door. There it would rest among watches and flashlights and other phones.

He found the phone invaluable in the outside world—without it he would not have been able to call Yukio and tell him to maintain surveillance on the Kicker house while he returned to the temple—but useless when he needed to contact the temple. No technology from beyond the sixteenth century—the time of the Order's defeat of the Nobunaga Shogunate—was allowed inside. No radios or TVs or watches or guns. And worst of all, no air conditioners in the summer when the heat and humidity suffused the land-fill area with the reek of old garbage and methane.

But no sacrifice was too great for the Order.

Minutes later Shiro was kneeling in his teacher's sparsely furnished quarters, bowing before him. He raised his head to speak.

"I saw them both, *sensei*—the woman and the sword!"

Akechi-*sensei*'s eyes narrowed to slits within the eyeholes of his mask as he studied Shiro. "You are sure of this? Absolutely sure?"

"She has changed her appearance, but I studied her through my field glasses and I have no doubt that her face is the same as in the photograph on the flyers."

His *sensei* closed his eyes and remained silent for what seemed like an eternity.

"But that does not mean she is the same woman whose face the Seer saw 'everywhere.'"

"But her face *is* everywhere, and she is with the katana—in the same room! The katana and the baby together! Just as the Seer said."

The eyes opened and fixed on Shiro. "Yes. It is indeed as the Seer said. You have done well, Shiro."

The praise warmed him. "Thank you, *sensei*."

"Remember the Seer's words: 'Who controls the child controls the fu-ture.' And, 'Her child and the katana are linked to the destiny of the world.' The katana and the baby are together now, but elsewhere. We must keep them together. *Here*."

Shiro thought about the old stone building and all the men milling around outside it.

"*Sensei*, it will be extremely difficult to steal the sword and make off with the woman."

Akechi-*sensei* nodded. "I am aware of that. If we had only the sword to worry about, we could start a Kuroikaze atop the building, then stand back and wait until everyone inside was dead. When it was safe we could simply walk in and take it."

Shiro thought of the many innocents in the neighborhood who would be dead as well, but didn't mention it. His *sensei* was not the sort to worry about collateral damage.

"But the Kuroikaze would kill the woman and child as well."

"Exactly. So I see no alternative to invasion. Tell me what you know of this place. We shall make a plan and strike."

"When, *sensei*?"

"Why, tonight, of course. You have seen both her and the katana there tonight. Tomorrow it might not be so. We must strike as soon as possible."

Shiro leaped to his feet. "I'll call Yukio and ask him what he sees. I had only one angle on the place. He'll have another."

His *sensei*'s eyes narrowed. "You do not bring the phone in here, I trust."

"No, *sensei*. It is outside."

"Use it then. Ask Yukio if he can find another entrance besides the front door."

"Yes, *sensei*."

Shiro hurried off with his heart pounding. At last! Tonight he would finally be able to put to use all of those years of martial arts training.

He couldn't wait.

16

The driver remained antsy while Jack became bored.

He glanced at his watch: 11:39. He wasn't quite sure what he'd been hoping for. Ideally, the watcher would make his report, and soon after a mob of monks would come charging out, pile into the vans, and head for Kicker HQ.

Jack's plan was to follow and let them launch whatever plan they'd cooked up. And while they were busy trying to retrieve the sword, and the Kickers were engaged trying to keep it, Jack would snoop around during the fracas, find Dawn, and spirit her away. If he had to damage or kill a few

Kickers along the way, so be it. They'd kidnapped her, and if they wanted to get in his way, they'd pay the price.

He hadn't forgotten what Veilleur had said about keeping the katana out of the wrong hands. But the katana was a thing, Dawn was an eighteen-year-old girl. That set the priorities.

But the temple remained quiet—at least that he could see. The piddly security lighting gave him an idea.

"Listen," he said to the cabby. "I'm going down for a look-see. I—"

"No-no! You mustn't!"

"I'll be fine."

"I take you back to ferry now."

Jack pulled a bill from his wallet and tore it in half. He'd seen this in a movie and it seemed like a cool move. He handed one half through the partition.

"Here."

The driver took it and stared at it. "What is this?"

"Half of a fifty. I'm going down for a look. You wait here. If you're still here when I get back, I'll give you the other half. Sound fair?"

"Yes-yes. Most fair."

Jack opened the door and stepped out. "I won't be long."

He circled around through the dark to the north end of the property, then made his way down a slope dotted with clumps of rank grass and skunk cabbage. When he reached the wall he crouched and waited for any sign that he'd been seen.

When none came, he rose and carefully felt along the near edge of the top of the wall. Finding only smooth brick, he did an overhand pull-up and—clenching his teeth against the howl of pain from his left deltoid—scanned the top. No razor wire or broken glass. He checked the walls for security lights. If he found any, he'd head back to the cab. They'd probably be motion activated and would light up as soon as he went over the wall.

But no . . . no lights. No sign of a dog or anyone patrolling the yard. Just that one guard at the gate.

Great.

He hurried around to the west side of the wall where he could put the temple between him and the front gate. He was ready for the pain this time when he levered himself up and over. Landing on the other side he froze in a crouch, listening. A growl or a bark would send him back over that wall in a heartbeat.

All quiet.

Maintaining his crouch, he hurried over to the side of the building and began inching along beneath the windows, listening. He didn't expect anyone to be speaking English, and knew he'd never understand a word. But he was searching for a certain tone of excitement, or the sound of guys gearing up for battle.

He found it near the southwest corner. Loud chatter flowing from an open window, then what sounded like someone giving a pep talk, then cheers and the sound of trampling feet.

As the sound faded he dared a peek over the sill into what looked like some sort of classroom. He spotted the last three guys of the group that had been gathered here, scrambling out through a door. All wore black from head to toe and held knives and nunchaku. They looked like ninjas without hoods.

Jack allowed himself a little smile. He didn't need to understand a word they'd said to know they were on their way to the Lodge to kick some Kicker ass and grab that sword.

And Jack would be right behind them.

He noticed with a start that the room hadn't completely emptied. A lone figure in a hooded blue robe sat statue-still behind a desk, staring into space. At least Jack thought he was staring. Maybe he was meditating. Jack couldn't see his features through the red silk drawn across his face. The mask had eyeholes but Jack's angle didn't allow him to see through.

Definitely creepy. Slater hadn't exaggerated. These were weird dudes.

The head started to swivel toward him so he ducked and moved away from the window. As he heard the van engines rumble to life on the far side of the building, he swung back over the wall and started making his way up the incline. But as he neared the spot where he'd left the cab, he didn't see it. He ran up onto the crumbling pavement and looked around. He was sure—

And then he saw a little piece of paper weighted by a stone at the side of the road where the cab had been. He picked it up.

Half of a fifty-dollar bill.

Gone. The weasel had run off.

Jack stomped around in a circle, calling the little Thai bastard every name he could think of. When he finished he felt a tiny bit better, but he was no closer to Manhattan. He had a phone and he could call a cab, but if this tertiary road had a name, he didn't know it. So where could he tell them to pick him up?

He broke into a run toward the house lights a half mile away. He'd find a street there. Then he'd have an address.

SUNDAY

1

Shiro watched the time on his cell phone, waiting for the 4 of the 1:14 on its screen to advance. He and his three companions, Jun, Fumio, and Koji—two guards and another acolyte—would enter from above, while Yukio and the others would break in through the back.

As he gazed down at the rooftop two stories below, he felt his blood pounding in his ears, his palms slick with sweat. Even though he had company, he felt alone. He and Yukio knew the most about the Kicker building—and not much at that—so they were in charge. Shiro had never been in charge of anything before. His every move since being taken from his fishing village had been directed and guided by the *sensei* of the Order. He found being in charge of his own actions as exhilarating as it was terrifying.

He wished Akechi-*sensei* were at his side now. He could tell that his teacher had wanted to come along, but his vow prevented him from appearing in public without his mask, and they could not risk the attention he would attract if he appeared with it. So they had left him behind in the classroom.

It had taken them almost an hour to reach Lower Manhattan. He had heard that the Staten Island ferry had once transported cars, but no more. So they had been forced to take the Verrazano Bridge into Brooklyn and cross back over via the Manhattan Bridge which left them only a few blocks from their destination. When they arrived at the building, passing it on the street, he had been relieved to see that most of the Kickers who had been milling around on the sidewalk earlier in the evening had drifted away. Only a few remained, clustered on the front steps.

The Kicker building did not adjoin any of its neighbors. It sat unattached on its property, with a narrow alley on its east flank and wider spaces to the west and rear. That was good news for those invading from street level, but not so good for those entering from above.

Using dramatic kicks and throws, Jun and Koji had got into a mock fight near the front of the building. While those on the steps were occupied cheering them on and calling for blood, Yukio had backed the van unseen into the alley on the building's west side. They were waiting below for the agreed-upon moment to invade via the rear entrance.

Success or failure rested in the hands of him and other members of the Order's Outer Circles. Failure was unthinkable. They must succeed.

And the first step to success was reaching the roof.

An interesting roof. Someone had gone to the trouble to create a garden there—flower beds, potted trees, even an area of sod. He wondered who had done it. He could not imagine these Kickers . . .

He shook off the questions and focused on his phone. This was taking—

There! It changed to 1:15. He signaled to the others and they began to rappel down the wall of the building on the east side of the Kicker home. When he reached a point ten feet above roof level he kicked backward with everything he had, swinging away from the wall. He let the rope slide through his gloved hands as he glided through the air to land with a jolt on the Kicker roof, half a foot inside its low parapet. The others landed successfully as well.

Without speaking he pointed to Fumio and then to the western edge of the roof. He would ready a rope there to lower to the van parked below when the time came, then he would stand guard to make sure no Kicker came up on the roof.

Shiro, Jun, and Koji made their way through the potted trees—mostly decorative like cherry and dogwood, and even a delicate five-fingered maple. They reached the door to the floors below and, as expected, found it unlocked. With no adjoining roofs to allow trespassers access, there was no need to lock it.

They crept down the stairs to the third floor and peered along the hallway, dark except for light from an open door that appeared to be a bathroom. It was empty. With luck, the few Kickers who remained in the building were asleep.

Shiro had seen the katana through a second-floor window, so they continued down. Once there, they found it as dark and deserted as the floor above. Shiro led them along the hall to the third door and stopped there. By his calculation, this one opened into the room they wanted.

Now the truly difficult part. They had to enter, subdue whoever might be within, and leave with the katana—all without a sound. Shiro had given it a lot of thought on the way over and had decided on a precipitous entry rather than a stealthy one.

No light shone from under the door, so the room was either empty or its occupant asleep. If empty—easy. If occupied, they had to silence the occupant before he could raise an alarm.

Shiro pulled out a flashlight and turned it on. As he reached for the doorknob he nodded to the others, each gripping a handle of the nunchaku looped over his neck. He knew where the bed was. He'd shine the light on it and Jun and Koji would take care of whoever was in it.

He pushed open the door and glided inside. The man he'd seen with the sword lay in bed. He jolted upright, raising a hand against the light in his eyes.

"What the f—?"

Jun and Koji's nunchaku whipped through the air and cracked against the man's skull. He fell back without a sound and did not move. Blood began to leak onto his pillow.

Shiro flashed the light around and found a katana in a scabbard leaning in a corner. He handed the flashlight to Jun and grabbed it. He pulled the blade free and held it in the flash beam. He had seen the photos so many times, he knew the pattern of holes and defects by heart. This was it. This was the katana the Order sought. Akechi-*sensei* would be so proud.

A strange, vaguely unpleasant feeling coursed through him as he gripped the handle. He couldn't identify it . . . he'd never felt anything like it before. He felt strong . . . powerful . . .

Suddenly a noise at the door and a voice—

"Hey, what's goin on?"

Jun swung the beam, revealing a disheveled man in underwear. Without thinking, Shiro thrust the sword at him and watched with shock as it sank into the left side of his chest.

Immediately he withdrew it and staggered back, horrified. What had he done? He hadn't meant . . . he'd reacted . . . it almost seemed the sword had reacted for him . . . on its own.

The man's eyes went wide, his mouth worked as blood spurted from his chest, then he sagged to his knees and held the worshipful pose for the last beats of his dying heart before slumping back onto the floor.

Shiro looked around and saw Jun and Koji staring at him in awe.

Then Jun bowed. "For the Order."

"For the Order," Koji echoed, bowing as well.

Shiro shook himself. "Yes, for the Order."

But had it been for the Order? He felt as if it might have been for himself . . . or for the katana.

As the other two dragged the body farther into the room, Shiro wiped the blade on the bedsheet, then, with strange reluctance, sheathed it. They closed the door behind them and headed back to the roof.

There they found Yukio waiting with the rope. They lowered themselves to the alley and crawled into the van. The other three were softly congratulating one another and recounting the night's events. Shiro barely heard them. The shocked face of the man he'd killed filled his brain.

2

"Don't look so down in the mouth, girl. No one's gonna hurt you. You're gonna be taken good care of."

Dawn slumped in one of the basement chairs and looked up at the man called Darryl. She totally wanted to scream at him to get out, but she was screamed out. Cried out too. She felt as if she were spiraling down through an endless black void, with nothing to grasp, nothing to break her fall.

Why did they want this baby? What was the *Plan*?

Did it matter now? She was going to have to resign herself to the fact that she was doomed to have this baby. She didn't see any way around it.

So okay. If that was the way it was going to be, she'd have to find a way to make the best of it, find a place in her head to totally retreat to for the next seven months while she waited for the baby. After that she'd get her life back and be on her way.

Giving in . . . surrendering . . . getting all fatalistic. She didn't know if she could do that, didn't know if she could stop looking for an escape route.

She clenched her fists and ground her teeth as she thought about how she had only one person to blame for all this.

Me.

Her mother had totally warned her from the start about Jerry, but did she listen? No way. She had all the answers and Mom had none. She'd let Jerry suck her in with that smooth line about designing video games for women and how she'd be the toast of the gaming world. Total bullshit. But it worked. She let him into her life and into her body, without a clue as to who he really was. And now she carried his baby.

God, if she'd only known . . . she might have set his bed on fire and watched him burn. No, not might have—*would* have.

"Whatsamatter?" Darryl said. "Cat gotcha tongue?"

"When's Jerry coming?"

That was what she dreaded most—facing that sick, perverted son of a bitch, watching him totally gloat over her, telling her she could run but not hide from him.

Darryl frowned. "Jerry? Jerry who?"

So that was how it was going to be—play games with her till he showed up. She stared at the floor. "Leave me alone."

"Hey, don't be mean to me now. We're gonna be seeing a lot of each other. We might as well be friends. It'll make the time go faster and easier, know what I mean?"

She looked up at him. What was he implying? Give him a little something and he'd make things easier for her?

Her stomach turned. Henry had been clean and neat and she'd still had to force herself to do him. This dirty creep . . . God, she'd rather die.

"Could you just leave me alone? I've had—"

Something thumped against the door. Darryl spun.

"Menck? That you?"

Another thump.

He started for the door. "Hey, Menck. Whatta you think—?"

The door burst open and three black-clad figures piled in. They didn't hesitate or break stride as they swarmed toward Darryl. He tried to backpedal but two of them were on him in a second, whacking him with their nunchucks. She knew what they were because some kid at school had split his scalp trying to show off with a set. His head had bled like Darryl's was bleeding now.

She opened her mouth to scream but the third was already in her face, clamping a hand over her mouth.

He looked Japanese—all three did. He had some sort of black scarf wrapped around his head and the lower half of his face, but she could tell he was Japanese.

"Shhh!" He put a finger to his lips in a surprisingly gentle gesture. "We are here to rescue you," he said in thickly accented English.

Rescue? That could only mean Mr. Osala. He must have hired these . . . these ninjas to bring her back.

She was totally ready to go. She'd thought his place was a prison. This was a hundred, a thousand times worse. And he had no agenda beyond keeping her safe from Jerry.

She nodded and pulled the ninja's hand away. "Let's go. Let's get out of here."

He pushed her in front of him and signaled the other two who led the way out. She had to step over Darryl, and then over the one called Menck. She noticed both were still breathing.

Her rescuers guided her up to the ground floor, out a back door, and into a waiting van that held five more of their kind. They all cheered when they saw her. She was squeezed between a couple of them and largely ignored as they yammered away in Japanese. One of them held up a sword and those with her cheered.

As they pulled out of the alley and onto the street, it finally became real that she was free. So easy. These guys had just waltzed in, busted a few heads, and led her out.

Jerry was going to be so totally pissed.

The driver wound this way and that until they came to a parked van just like this one. Half of them switched over, and then her van got rolling again.

"Where's Mister Osala?" she said.

The three surrounding her in the back stared her way but said nothing. Their flat black eyes held no hint that they had any idea what she was talking about.

Maybe it's a language thing, she thought, fighting a twinge of unease. *They don't understand English.*

But when the van turned east onto the ramp to the Manhattan Bridge, the unease bloomed into alarm.

"This isn't the way to Mister Osala's. Where are you taking me?"

They continued to stare and say nothing.

3

Jack found Kicker HQ in chaos.

Obviously too late to sneak in behind the Kakureta Kao's boys and spirit Dawn away.

It had taken half a forever for the cab to show up, and then the guy refused to drive him to Manhattan. Jack had offered him all the cash on him but the driver would take him as far as the ferry and that was it. So he'd had to wait for the ferry, then find a cab to bring him back here.

All for nothing.

Looked like some sort of call had gone out because the Lodge building was crammed with Kickers, all looking shocked and furious. He scanned the crowd and spotted the blond guy in the work shirt who'd bummed a ciggy earlier.

He sidled over and said, "Dude, what happened?"

The guy looked at him like he'd just asked what year it was. "Where've you been?"

Jack shrugged. "Grabbing some food, downing a few beers. I left the place quiet with a few folks outside, now I wander back and find a ton of folks inside. What gives?"

"We were invaded."

Jack let his jaw drop. *"What?"*

He nodded. "Bunch of ninja types worked over Hank and Menck and Darryl, and fucking killed Haber."

"You're putting me on, right?"

"Swear by the Kicker Man."

"What the hell for?"

"Hank's sword. Makes sense: Jap sword, Jap sneak attack, just like Pearl Harbor. Killed Haber with it and disappeared."

"So where are they? The hospital?"

"Nah. Carson's a paramedic so he's sewing up their heads. Says they look worse than they are." He shook his head. "Probably gonna have to call the cops about Haber, though nobody wants to do that." His face reddened. "Man, I ever get my hands on those fuckers—"

"You do, you let me know, 'cause I want a piece of them too."

Jack wound his way through the throng to the front steps where he stood and stared at nothing.

Timing was everything and he'd blown that. The place was packed with Kickers. Even on the outside chance he could find Dawn, he'd never be able to sneak her out.

Something he'd just heard nagged at him.

Man, I ever get my hands on those fuckers . . .

Yeah. No doubt they all felt that way.

He made his way back inside and wove through the first-floor corridors, checking room after room, looking for one with a computer—and for Dawn. Not that he expected to find her. They wouldn't keep her on the first floor—too easy to escape. They'd hold her upstairs or in the basement. And if anyone asked what he was doing, he'd say he was looking for a bathroom.

As expected, no Dawn, but he did find a dark office with a monitor glowing on the desk. He eased in and closed the door behind him. The screensaver was the Septimus Lodge sigil bouncing around a black background.

He wiggled the mouse and looked for Google Earth on the desktop but didn't see it. Checked the program list—not there either. Didn't have time to download it, so he went to Flashearth instead. He typed "staten island, ny" into the little search box and was immediately rewarded with a satellite view.

And yeah, the cabbie had been right—the Fresh Kills landfill was visible from space. He coned down until he found the roof of a rectangular building sitting in an empty area with a clear view of the mounds. Had to be it. He put the crosshairs in the center of the roof and copied the latitude and longitude coordinates down to the second. Then he closed Explorer and rejoined the Kickers.

Now . . . how to get the word out? He couldn't stand here and shout it, because then they'd want to know how he knew. He needed anonymity— like phoning it in. Problem was he didn't have a number for Hank or the Lodge or any Kicker for that matter.

But he knew his own.

He edged over to a side table in the foyer and slipped his TracFone from his pocket. After memorizing a number from his call history, he erased everything and thumbed the volume to max. Then he slipped the phone onto the table and headed for the door.

Once outside, he hurried up toward Allen Street. After cadging some change from an all-night bodega along the way, he found a pay phone. He called his TracFone.

Nearly a dozen rings before someone picked up.

"Yeah?"

"Hey, I know who raided your place and I know where you can find them."

"The fuck is this?"

"The guy who's gonna help you get even with those ninja pricks. I'm gonna tell you zackly where they are, so listen up."

Jack heard the guy yelling away from the phone. *"Hey, everybody shut the fuck up! This could be important."* Then he came back to Jack. *"Whatcha got?"*

"Write this down: They're hiding on Staten Island and I can give you the exact coordinates of where they are."

"Coordinates?"

Jeez.

"Yeah. Numbers you can plug into a car's GPS and it'll take you to their front door. Got a pen and paper?"

Jack heard the guy yelling for paper. After a few seconds he came back. *"Okay. Shoot."*

Jack gave him the coordinates and made him repeat them.

"How do I know you ain't pullin my chain?"

"If I'm lyin I'm dyin. Check with Hank. Suggest he send one guy out there. If he finds a buncha Japs in a two-story building, that's the place. Then you can send out a raiding party for some payback—and Hank's sword."

"The sword's there?"

"Guaranteed."

Jack hung up, then started dialing again.

Might as well make it a party.

4

Hideo awoke with a start. Someone was knocking on his door. He leaped from his bed and opened it to find one of the night security men standing there.

"Sorry to bother you, Takita-san, but someone is on one of the special-use phones asking for the man who wants the katana. I wasn't sure—"

Hideo pushed past him and ran for the stairs. He'd used one of Kaze's pay-as-you-go phones to call the number on the flyer; whoever it was had used that number to call back.

This could be important.

He found the phone sitting apart from the others. He snatched it up. "Hello?"

"Hi. Are you still interested in that ugly, beat-up old katana?"

He recognized the voice. The same as yesterday, the one who set up the meeting in that park. Hideo had suspected he might be the *ronin*, working for the previous owner, but had no way to tell. The voice sounded similar to the man he'd faced in the Gerrish apartment, but not so easy to tell over a cell phone. When no one approached the clerk they had set up with a decoy katana, Hideo suspected that the *ronin* had spied the trap and stayed away.

"It is possible, yes."

"I know where you can find it."

"Why would you wish to tell me? You no longer want it?"

"Let's just say priorities have changed, and maybe I'd rather see you with the blade than the Kakureta Kao."

The unexpected Japanese words stunned Hideo into silence.

Kakureta Kao . . . he hadn't heard them mentioned in a long, long time. How did this *gaijin* know about them?

"The Kakureta Kao no longer exist."

"Wrong. They've got a temple on Staten Island, and in that temple is the crudded-up katana you want so badly. Here are the exact coordinates of the building."

The man read them off twice and Hideo wrote them twice.

"You are sure this—hello? Hello?"

The connection had been cut.

Hideo stared at the coordinates, seeing them as either a gift from Heaven or a trap. He'd set a trap for the *ronin*—and he was now sure that was he on the phone. So was the *ronin* returning the favor with a trap of his own?

And his mention of Kakureta Kao . . . could that be true? The sect reportedly had been wiped out in World War II. But it served no purpose for the *ronin* to lie about such a thing. In fact, how could he even know about them unless . . .

. . . unless they were back.

He turned to his computer and opened Google Earth. He punched in the coordinates and found himself looking down at the roof of an isolated rectangular building.

Could it be?

Assuming the *ronin* had told the truth, what was Kakureta Kao doing here in New York? But more importantly, did the sect have any connection to Kaze? It seemed unlikely, but Kaze Group's tentacles were pervasive, and had a long reach.

The safe and sensible thing to do was to gather information before he and the yakuza paid a visit to this building.

He glanced at the clocks on the wall—one for New York and one for Japan. It was still midafternoon in Tokyo. He should call the home office just to be sure.

5

Dawn shrank back against the wall. She'd have totally pushed herself through it if possible.

"Wh-who are you? What do you want with me?"

The ninja types had removed their scarves or headpieces or whatever and now they looked like young Asian goths. Three of them remained in the room with her. They could have been NYU grad students at some East Village club, except they didn't seem to speak English, or were pretending they didn't. Each was taking a turn swinging the cruddy sword she'd seen with Hank. Why they'd be so happy with a piece of junk was beyond her.

She remembered the growing horror of the ride through Brooklyn and then across to Staten Island as she realized that these men hadn't been sent by Mr. Osala—they had no idea who he was.

They'd brought her to this strange building out near the landfill and stuck her in this candlelit room on the second floor. She didn't know how long she'd been here, but she hadn't had a second alone. She had to go to the bathroom but didn't have the nerve to ask.

"Tell me—*please*! What am I *doing* here?"

One of them glanced at her, then went back to chattering in Japanese with his friends.

Back still against the wall, she slid-sank to a squat and buried her face in her trembling hands.

What had happened to her life? She couldn't call it a nightmare—more like a series of nightmares, each more terrifying than the last. She'd been scared at that Kicker place, but this was downright terrifying.

And then she sensed movement in the room and heard the guys saying something like, "Akechi-*sensei*."

She looked up and saw a tall, thin figure at the door, wrapped in a hooded blue robe with a red silk mask over its face. The young ones bowed

and scraped as he glided into the room. He stopped before her and stood
with his hands folded inside his long sleeves as he stared at her. The black
eyes through the holes of his mask were the only sign that she faced a human. Otherwise he could have been some sort of alien monk.

She tried to rise but her legs wouldn't support her.

Why was all this happening to her? She hadn't been the best person, but
she hadn't been bad. Certainly hadn't been evil.

Why me?

The monk spoke in a high-pitched voice. His English was heavily accented but she understood him.

"You are with child?"

Was that what this was all about? The baby? The *baby* again? Was
everybody crazy? Had the whole world gone insane? What was it with this
baby?

She'd show them.

"Me? Pregnant? No way. I'm a virgin. I'm saving myself for the right
man."

The monk whirled and machine-gunned some gibberish at the younger
ones. Their bland expressions turned concerned—especially the tallish
one who stepped forward. He looked like he'd just been told his dog was
dead.

He bowed and the two of them exchanged a few words, then the monk
pointed a long finger at the doorway and gave an order. The other two hurried out while the tall one stayed behind.

They spoke in low voices, as if afraid she might eavesdrop. Fat chance.
Arigato and *konichiwa*—picked up at a hibachi restaurant—were the extent
of her Japanese.

And then one of the other young ones returned, yammering away.
Everyone stepped aside as some sort of high-sided, wooden, wheelbarrow-
like cart rolled through the door, propelled from behind by the third young
one.

And in the cart . . . another masked monk in a blue robe, but this one
had no legs and—oh, Christ! She hadn't noticed it at first, but now she could
see candlelight flickering off the rear walls of his empty eye sockets. He was
missing his eyes too!

His cart stopped before her. He thrust a gnarled hand in her direction
and clutched at the air just inches away.

Was he trying to touch her? No way!

She frantically crabbed away across the floor but the cart followed until she was backed into a corner. She tried to make herself smaller but his hand kept coming closer and closer . . .

And then the fingertips grazed her skin and like a sprung trap the hand clamped down on her forearm.

Dawn screamed and tried to pull away but the monk's grip was like iron. She twisted and thrashed but still could not break free.

What was he doing? Was he going to grope her?

But just as suddenly as he'd grabbed her arm, he released it and waved his hand in the air, jabbering at the top of his voice.

Whatever he said, it seemed like good news to the others, because the young guys started jabbing their fists in the air and the standing monk's eyes glittered with happiness.

What had the eyeless one said?

As if reading her mind, the tall one stepped closer and leaned over her.

"You may lie to me. You may lie to the others. But you cannot fool the Seer."

Seer? What was he talking about?

"I don't—"

"You are not a virgin and you are with child. You carry the infant we seek."

"Seek for what?"

"That is none of your affair."

His right hand darted out and she felt a sharp sting in the left side of her neck. She flinched and slapped at his hand. As he withdrew it she saw a sliver of wood between his thumb and forefinger. It looked like an oversize toothpick with a blue stripe.

"What—?"

"You will rest now."

"But . . ."

Her lips stopped moving and her eyelids suddenly weighed a ton each. Before they closed she saw one of the young ones approach with Hank's sword. Was he going to cut her with it? She knew she should be afraid but couldn't manage it.

But no worry about that. He laid it at her feet and bowed. And then all the young ones cheered.

She gave up the fight against her eyelids. As she let them close she felt herself drifting. She wanted to ask what they wanted with the baby . . . what were they going to do with it . . . or to it?

Ice pierced her chest. *To* it? They weren't going to hurt it, were they? They couldn't . . .

Listen to me, she thought as her senses fled. Yesterday afternoon I was totally going to abort it and now I'm worried someone's going to hurt it. I am so messed up . . . so-so-*so* messed up . . .

6

Hank pressed his palms against the temples of his throbbing head.

God *damn*!

His sutured scalp would heal and the headache would eventually go away, but the humiliation . . . suckered like that . . . knocked clean out and lying in bed while the katana was stolen and poor Haber was murdered right there in Hank's bedroom.

Shit! He was the leader here, yet he hadn't put up any sort of fight and had to be half carried down here to the basement all rubber-legged and bloody-headed in front of everyone.

How would he ever live that down?

"Hey, boss," a voice said as a hand holding a cell phone appeared a few inches from his nose. "Andy's on the phone for you."

Andy . . . ?

Oh, right. He'd sent him out to check out that cockamamie call about Dawn and the sword being somewhere out on Staten Island. He took the phone.

"This is Hank. Bullshit, right?"

"Uh-uh. I'm ninety-nine percent sure we've got the real deal here."

Hank straightened. "No kidding. What makes you think so?"

"First off, the building's right where he said it would be. Second, it's walled in and there's some guy dressed like a samurai standing guard. I sneaked up and peeked at the building and could swear I heard a girl scream inside."

Dawn . . . what were they doing to her?

All right. Japanese guys after a Japanese sword. He didn't know why they wanted it, but he didn't have to. Maybe they considered it a sacred object or something. Didn't matter. It made some sort of sense.

But Dawn? What the hell could they want with Dawn? And if they hurt that baby . . .

"Good work, my man. You stay there but stay out of sight. We're on our way."

He snapped the phone closed. Suddenly his head didn't hurt so bad. He'd just been handed a chance to redeem his cred with the Kickers—plus get back Dawn and the sword as well—and he wasn't about to waste it.

He jerked to his feet and immediately regretted it. The room tilted and did a three-sixty. He steadied himself with a hand on a table. When everything stabilized, he looked around. Darryl and Menck sat on the far side of the table, still looking dazed. A half dozen others milled around.

"Listen up, everyone. We've found them and we're going after them." A cheer went up. After it died, he added, "Call every Kicker you know and put out the word: Anyone with a car, and anyone who can beg, borrow, or steal one, get it down here. The Kickers are going to Staten Island to kick some Jap ass."

More cheers, and then they got moving.

Hank turned to Darryl and Menck. Under different circumstances he would have been screaming at them for being fuck-ups and letting some Japs get the drop on them. But since the same thing had happened to him, he held his tongue.

"Listen, you guys probably should stay here. You're banged up already and things could get rough out there."

Menck looked up at him. "You going?"

Hank nodded. Of course he was going. He needed to be out with the troops on this one.

Darryl said, "Then we're goin too."

Not exactly what Hank had wanted to hear. He'd hoped they'd stay behind, nursing their wounds so he could be seen out there in the trenches ignoring his.

"Yeah," Menck said. "I need to be busting some of the heads that busted mine."

Busting heads . . . Hank couldn't argue with that. What he'd really like to do was bust into this place with an AK-47 and mow down every one of the bastards.

But no . . . no guns. In the first place, Hank discouraged guns among the Kickers and had banned them from the Lodge. Not because he feared or disliked them—he *loved* guns—but because New York was so anti-gun. Carry permits were nigh impossible to get. Get caught carrying, even a gun you legally owned, and you faced felony charges. Get caught with an illegal piece and you were in even bigger trouble. Hank didn't think many of the Kickers would qualify for legal pieces.

But he had a much more important reason for wanting them left home tonight.

"All right, one more thing," he said to the ones still present. "Get the word out: no guns." Some disappointed groans and protests began. He raised a hand to cut them off. "I'm real serious about this. We don't know what kind of confusion we'll run into. We go in there with guns blazing, shooting up the place, we'll most likely kill as many of our own as the bastards we're shooting at. And worse, we've got no idea what the walls in that place are made of. If they're just drywall, a wild shot can kill someone two rooms away, and that someone might be Dawn." He smiled. "Or even worse, me." This got the laugh he'd hoped for. "So pass the word: no guns."

"What if *they*'ve got guns?"

"Both Darryl and Menck didn't see any. They had knives and nunchucks. If they had guns, they would have brought them. Look, they think they're ninjas or something. And ninjas don't use guns. For our own safety, we can't either. But put a bunch of knives, two-by-fours, chains, crowbars, baseball bats, maybe a few chainsaws into the hands of a bunch of pissed-off Kickers and these gooks won't know what hit them."

A solid cheer this time.

He clapped his hands. "Okay then. Let's start gathering some head-busting equipment."

Hank would carry a crowbar, but he'd also take along the .38 Chief Special he kept hidden in his room. Just in case.

And as for those Japs, the ones who survived tonight would curse the day they messed with Hank Thompson.

7

Jack watched the last of the fleet of cars, vans, and pickups roar off for Staten Island. Three of the Kickers who'd piled in had bandaged heads—Hank was one of them. The rest of them looked like a crowd of movie extras on their way to Castle Frankenstein. All they needed were pitchforks and torches to complete the picture.

When the street was quiet, he stepped from the shadows and hurried toward the Lodge building. He ran up the steps to find the front door open and a couple of Kickers hanging around inside. They gave him suspicious looks and stepped toward him as he entered.

Before they could challenge him, Jack positioned his faux tattoo where they could see it and said, "Am I late?"

The heavier of the two nodded. "Missed them. Just left."

"I got a call and came as soon as I could. Damn." He looked around. "Nobody else heading out?"

The guy shook his head. "Nope."

"Shit." Jack loosed a disappointed sigh. "Well, anything I can do around here till they get back?"

Now he was getting a different kind of look—incredulous. Jack guessed not too many of their peers volunteered.

Finally the thin guy spoke. "You can go upstairs and help Ansari and Stayer clean up the mess in the boss's room."

"Hank's room?" He assumed that was on one of the upper floors—just where he wanted to be. "What happened?"

They glanced at each other. The heavy guy shrugged and said, "Someone got killed."

Jack feigned shock. "No way! I heard something was stolen, but nobody said anything about—"

"We're keeping it quiet for now. Look, you want to help those guys, be our guest. Don't think you'll get an argument from them. They're on the second floor."

"Great."

He headed up the granite steps but passed the second floor and continued to the third. He hurried from room to room—all unlocked, all empty.

Well, he'd seen Dawn through a second-floor window. Maybe he'd find her there.

On the second floor he did another room-to-room search until he came to one with two guys scrubbing a red stain off the floor.

"Is there where Haber bought it?" he said, remembering the name and trying to sound more knowledgeable than he had downstairs.

Ansari and Stayer—he didn't know who was who—looked up at him.

"Who wants to know?"

"The guys downstairs said I should come up and help you. What needs to be done?"

"Well, your timing's fucking great," one of them said. "We're just about through."

Jack decided to go for the gold.

"Where's the girl?"

This earned him instant suspicion.

"What girl?" the other one said.

Jack was flowing toward a kneecapping mood. The Glock was a growing itch against the small of his back.

"The one whose picture I've been hanging all over town for weeks. Word is they found her. They got her here?"

"If you know so much, you should know the slants took her when they grabbed the boss's sword."

Jack didn't try to hide his shock. "They took her too?"

"Yep."

"What the hell for?"

The first one shrugged. "That's the million-dollar question. All we know is that Menck and Darryl was watching her down in the basement, now they've got broken heads and the girl's gone."

Jack stared at them for a few heartbeats as his mind reeled, then he spun and ran back down the hall.

"Hey, where you goin?" said a voice behind him. "I thought you was gonna help."

In your dreams.

He pounded down the stairs.

What the hell? He hadn't seen this coming. The Kakureta Kao had taken Dawn? Why-why-why?

And it didn't sound like a spur-of-the-moment thing, as in taking a hostage for insurance. The sword had been on the second floor, and Dawn in the basement. Taking her couldn't have been happenstance.

Goddamn. He'd thought he was drawing the Kickers away from her when all the time he was sending them to her instead.

He blew through the foyer and out to the street. He needed a cab. He was turning toward Allen Street when he heard a toot. He looked and saw a green Land Rover double-parked in front of the Lodge. A bearded, older man stood beside it.

Veilleur waved. "Need a ride?"

Jack fairly leaped toward him. "How the—?"

"A woman with a dog told me you might need some company." He opened the driver's door. "I suggest you drive."

"The Ladies . . . you know them too?"

A nod. "Very well."

Jack jumped in and started the car. As soon as Glaeken was settled in the passenger seat Jack gunned it toward the Manhattan Bridge.

"But how did she know?" Jack said.

The old man shrugged. "She doesn't know everything that goes on, but she knows quite a bit."

"Who are they?"

"You really don't know?"

"Would I be asking if I did?"

A pause, then, "Perhaps she doesn't think you're ready to know. I think you're more than ready, but the decision is hers."

"Come on. A hint at least."

He shook his head, then said, "All right. You keep saying 'They.' There's only one."

That shocked him. "But I've seen—"

"Only one, but she comes in many shapes and sizes." He waved his hand. "Forget the Lady for now. Let's plan what we'll do when we reach our destination."

Jack forced his thoughts back to Dawn, but they wouldn't leave the Lady entirely.

"Did she at least say why this cult kidnapped Dawn?"

"She's not sure. One thing we agree on is that her baby is important to all the wrong people."

"What about the sword? Why do they want that?"

"Apparently it was instrumental in fulfilling a prophecy that doomed them in the past. They think controlling it will protect their future." He looked at Jack. "It might be best for the world if the Kakureta Kao has no future."

Their eyes locked for a second, then Jack turned back to driving.

"That might already be in the works."

He prayed Dawn wouldn't go down with them.

8

Hank saw the building, saw the wall, saw the gate, saw the guard in his corny kung-fu getup. A big entrance opened in the center. He'd never been here before, but for some reason the place looked familiar.

No matter. They'd arrived.

His blood sang in his ears. He'd counted thirty-seven Kickers, including himself, in nine vehicles. How many of those Japs could be in there? Two dozen, tops. He couldn't see any reason why he wouldn't have Dawn and the sword back in fifteen minutes.

The sooner the better. His head still throbbed and he felt like puking. He just wished he'd seen the guy who'd done this to him. All he remembered was a bright light in his eyes and then nothing. So if he couldn't make the guilty one pay, they'd all pay.

He phoned ahead to Menck in the lead car—the one with the GPS.

"Slow down until we can get one of the pickups in front, and then we'll run that fuckin gate. No talk, no dickin around. We're going in."

He watched a battered old truck make its way to the front, then gun forward. The rest followed in its wake.

The guard stepped out behind the chain-link barrier and waved them to stop. But instead of slowing, the pickup accelerated. The guard dove for cover as the truck hit the barrier dead center, sending the double gates flying back on their hinges.

And then they were all barreling through, one after another, pulling up before the entrance and piling out. No flood or security lights on the outside, and hardly any light inside. Headlights provided all the illumination. As they were milling around, getting organized, the guard from the gate came running up behind them, shouting and waving a sword. A length of chain whirled through the air, catching his knees. He went down and in a flash a dozen guys were on him. Crowbars and two-by-fours rose and fell. When the whooping knot stepped back, the guy lay flat, facedown, unmoving. A grinning Kicker brandished his sword.

This was going to be *easy*.

"Everybody inside!" Hank shouted, waving his crowbar in the air. "Trash the place and everybody in it!"

The Kickers roared and charged the entrance. The big glass doors weren't even locked. Again that sense that he'd seen this place before.

Hank hung back. Menck and Darryl, each carrying two-by-fours, did the same. Their heads must have felt like his.

Much as he'd have liked to, he couldn't wait out here through the whole melee. Had to be among them, pretending to lead them. So when half their number had pressed through the entrance, he checked the reassuring bulk of the .38 in his front pocket, then started forward, motioning Darryl and Menck along.

"Come on. Time for some payback."

They flowed into a big center hallway that ran the length of the building. Opposite them, faintly visible in the dim light, a wide set of stairs ran up to the second floor.

Now he knew why the place looked familiar: just like his old high school. Man, he'd hated that place.

But where were the lights? The only illumination came from some sort of oil lamps strung along the center of the ceiling. He found a bank of light switches and started flipping them.

Nothing. The place didn't seem to have electricity. Why wouldn't—?

A Kicker cried out and clutched his face. Hank gasped as he saw something round and pointy jutting from his eye—a throwing star. Another sliced into his throat.

And then came a hail of the things. Hank dropped to his knees as the stars pierced heads and shoulders and raised hands.

The rain stopped, replaced by shrill cries echoing from both sides as black-clad figures charged out of the dark. Sword blades gleamed in the lamplight.

Their blood up now, the Kickers charged right into them. Some fell victim to the swords but their overwhelming numbers inundated the attackers and crushed them.

Hank counted seven Kickers down. Some looked dead, others—like the guy with the star in his eye—were still mobile but out of the fight. Hank couldn't let these minor losses take the steam out of them.

"Listen up! We knew we wouldn't come through this without a scratch. Yeah, we're bloodied, but we're unbowed. If this is the best these gooks have to throw at us, the battle is won! All we've got to do now is find the sword and the girl. So we're gonna split up."

He used his arm to draw an imaginary line through the group, then pointed to the right.

"This half stays down here with Darryl and Menck. Your job is to search every room on the first floor. The rest of you come upstairs with me. We'll do the same on the second. Those of you who are hurt but still able to get around, help get the others outside." He clapped his hands. "All right! Let's move! And fuck up anyone who tries to stop you!"

They let loose a battle roar and divided.

As Hank's group headed for the stairs, a frantic voice shouting in Japanese echoed down from the second floor. But that was instantly drowned out by the sound of someone starting and revving a chainsaw.

———✦———

Shiro stood watch over the girl and the katana—together, just as the Seer had predicted. Akechi-*sensei* had used a *doku-ippen* on her that caused sleep but would not harm the life she carried.

He was dreaming of the glory in the Order's future when he heard a commotion from below. He looked out the window onto the rear of the property but saw nothing. He padded down the hall to one of the narrow stairways at each end of the building and heard cries of rage and pain—the unmistakable sounds of battle—echoing up the well.

Baffled, he hurried down in time to see some of his brothers fall before the onslaught of an invading rabble.

Kickers! It couldn't be anyone else. They'd come for the girl and the katana.

Shiro's hands patted his sash and his pockets—empty. He was unarmed, but he could remedy that.

He dashed back up to the second floor and ran its length, shouting a warning and a call to arms.

He pounded on his *sensei*'s door.

"Akechi-*sensei*! We're being attacked. They want the katana and the girl!"

The door swung open and Shiro gasped at the sight of his teacher's face. He must have removed his mask and hadn't had time to replace it.

"Arm yourself and guard the katana and the child! Let no one near them! I will guard the sacred scrolls! Hurry!"

Shiro ran to his room and grabbed his katana. He was starting back toward the hall when he spied his bow standing in a corner.

. . . guard the katana and the child! Let no one near them!

How better to do that than thin the ranks of the attackers?

He grabbed his quiver and ran for the stairwell at the end of the hall.

Darryl let one of the big guys without a headache kick in the doors.

The first room was dark and empty save for some bedding—didn't they call it a futon or something like that?—along with some clothes and not much else.

In the second they found a couple of burning candles and an old, bald-headed guy in a blue robe, cowering on his futon. Looked like some sort of monk—like from a kung-fu movie. Then Darryl noticed with a start that he didn't have any legs.

The monk was wailing in Japanese, motioning them to leave.

"What do we do?" a Kicker said to Menck.

Before Menck could answer, another said, "We do like the boss said. We fuck him up."

The monk's wailing and whimpering grew louder as the two of them stepped forward, one with a two-by-four, one with a crowbar. They raised them when they reached him—and suddenly the monk didn't look afraid anymore, and his wailing and whimpering changed to raging screams as he pulled a long sword from beneath his robe and started swinging.

Darryl cried out in surprise and fell back. He watched in horror as the monk opened the first Kicker's thigh, then backhanded a slice deep into the second's knee. They screamed and went down. Fortunately they fell on him, pinning him. A couple of other Kickers rushed in and turned the old dude's skull to mush.

"Shit!" Darryl shouted. "These guys are crazy!"

Menck knelt next to the futon and started tearing strips from the bedding. As he wrapped one around the bleeding thigh he looked up at Darryl.

"I'll take care of these guys. Keep going. Let's find what we came for and get the hell out of this madhouse. And be careful, damn it."

Don't need to tell me, Darryl thought.

He wished he was staying behind with Menck.

"All right, guys. Let's roll. Stick together and keep your eyes open. You see anyone who ain't us, clobber him first and ask questions later."

As he was rejoining the Kickers in the hall, one of them let out a gurgling cry. Darryl watched him sink to the floor clutching at a black arrow shaft sticking out both sides of his neck.

And then another went down with an arrow sticking out of his head—this one didn't come out the other side.

Suddenly everyone wanted into the room. All but one. This bearded mountain of a Kicker Darryl knew only as Jesse picked up a dead Jap in the hall and charged whoever was shooting at them, holding the corpse in front of him as he bellowed at the top of his lungs.

Darryl dropped to his knees and dared a peek down the hall. He saw a skinny guy in black, much like the ones who'd charged him in the Lodge basement, standing by the front entrance and shooting arrow after arrow like a machine. Some of his shots went wide, but a lot of them plowed into the dead monk.

Finally the Jap ran out of arrows. When Jesse saw this, he tossed the monk aside and picked up speed toward the Jap. Now that it was safe to go out, the Kickers around Darryl loosed howls of rage and joined the chase like a pack of baying hounds. Not wanting to be thought of as a coward, Darryl brought up the rear, keeping an eye over his shoulder in case another archer appeared.

Out of arrows and with a mob coming his way, the Jap turned and ran for the far end of the hall. The Kickers were almost even with the entrance when four Japs in suits—suits and *ties*—stepped into view.

Like it had a single mind, the mob changed course and charged toward the newcomers.

"Stop," Hideo said, staring at the building a few hundred yards ahead.

Kenji pulled the car onto the shoulder and looked at him expectantly.

Hideo checked the coordinates. Yes, this was the place. But look at all the vehicles in front of it. That did not seem at all in keeping with the Kakureta Kao's antiquated ways.

He had talked to the home office and had been told that Kaze Group had no dealing with the cult. Hideo was free to do what he wished with them.

He tapped Kenji's shoulder and said, "Turn off the headlamps and proceed to the building. We do not want to announce our presence too early."

Kenji complied and soon they were gliding up to the ruined front gate.

"Park here. We will walk the rest of the way."

A moment later Hideo, Kenji, Goro, and Ryo were standing in a tight circle. The three yakuza were fastening silencers to their pistols. Even Hideo was armed for this trip, but he kept his weapon in the holster strapped to his shoulder. He had no idea what make it was, only that it was loaded with .9mm hollow-point rounds and ready to fire. He felt no need for a silencer, for he had no intention of drawing and firing it unless circumstances became dire. And in that case, he doubted silence and secrecy would be issues.

When the yakuza were satisfied with their weapons, the four of them walked through the gate and toward the main entrance. As they wove through the parked vehicles, they heard groans and voices. They came upon half a dozen or so dead or wounded Caucasians. These were most certainly not Kakureta Kao monks.

One of them with a bloody head looked up and spotted them. He was carrying a crowbar. He lifted it as he rushed them.

"Dirty motherfu—"

Phut!

Kenji shot him in the face. Before the man's body hit the ground, Ryo and Goro were shooting anyone not already dead, and even those who were.

He noticed strange tattoos on the hands of some of the corpses. He'd seen that spidery figure here and there about town.

But the figure didn't bother him a fraction as much as his lack of shock or revulsion at the cold-blooded murder of these men. The prospect of failing in his quest for this strange, elusive katana had changed him. He was now ready to eliminate, by any means necessary, every barrier or impediment to his finding it.

He motioned the yakuza toward the main entrance and they joined up with him. As they pushed through the glass doors they saw a slim young Japanese man dash past, clutching an old-fashioned samurai bow.

A Kakureta Kao member?

They stepped into the hall for a better look and found themselves in the path of a charging crowd of a dozen or so Caucasians. Hideo leaped back while the three yakuza held their ground and opened fire. In five seconds it was over. All the Caucasians were down, screaming, groaning, writhing on the floor.

Goro and Ryo reloaded while Kenji finished those still alive. Then he too reloaded.

Hideo noticed more of the spidery tattoos. Was this some sort of rival cult at war with Kakureta Kao?

No matter. They were all dead. At least he hoped so.

He pointed to Ryo and Goro. "You two search that side." He gestured to Kenji. "We will take this side. Use your flashlights. Search every room. Find that katana."

The first room he entered held an eyeless monk on a futon. Here at last was the Kakureta Kao.

"Where is the katana?" he asked in Japanese.

The monk smiled and shook his head.

Kenji shot him in the leg.

He howled wordlessly and clutched his wound, and Hideo saw no sign of a tongue in his open mouth. Kenji looked at Hideo. Hideo considered the madness of this cult and concluded he would learn nothing from this one, even if he had a tongue. He nodded.

Kenji shot the monk in the head. As they searched the room, Hideo heard pleading cries in English from a room across the hall: "No!" and "Please, no!" Then phut sounds. Then silence.

More of the spider cult dead.

"Keep searching," he said.

He and Kenji joined the others in the hallway and proceeded to the next set of rooms. As Goro and Ryo opened the door to theirs, an aging monk, holding a long tanto high, screamed and leaped at Goro. Hideo saw Ryo's pistol flash up, and Kenji's whip around, but too late: The monk buried the blade to the hilt in Goro's chest.

Goro managed to get off a shot into his belly, and his two fellow yakuza finished the job. Goro swayed, then toppled backward like a felled oak to lie staring blindly at the ceiling.

Ryo and Kenji rushed to him, screamed curses when they confirmed what Hideo already knew. Ryo shot the dead monk twice more in the head, then removed his suit coat and draped it over Goro's head and shoulders.

Watching it all, as if from a great distance, Hideo wondered about his detachment. He'd never seen death before coming to America, and now he was inured to it. Or had his mind and emotions merely stepped back so as not to go mad?

"Let's keep moving," he said.

Hank and his posse reached the second floor and found it empty. And after he signaled to Jantz to turn off his chainsaw, it was quiet.

"Okay," he said. "Here's what we do. Since we have only two flashlights between us, we divide into two groups and check each and every room. You see the girl or you see the sword, you give a holler and—"

"*Aiiiii!*"

The hall around them exploded with cries and movement as a half dozen blue-robed figures burst from doorways with knives and swords held high. Even more startling than their sudden onslaught were the silk masks beneath their hoods.

Even stranger was the fact that two of the monks had only one arm, and another was hopping on one leg.

A couple of Kickers went down immediately, but the rest recovered and fought back. The three amputees went down first, and the other able-bodied types soon followed. But they'd taken out five Kickers—three dead and two wounded.

Hank had the two wounded placed on the stairs. One had a stab wound in his leg, and the other had had his left arm sliced open.

"Wait here. Keep pressure on those wounds. We'll be back for you."

He looked around at his crew, whittled abruptly from fifteen to ten. Hank was shaking inside. He wanted out of here so bad he could taste it. But he needed the girl and the katana—in that order. If it came down to a choice between the two, he'd take Dawn. He needed that baby, needed the Key to the Future more than anything else.

"Change of plans," he said, doing his best to appear calm and in control. "No splitting up. I think we've pretty much wiped them out, but we'll play it safe and all go door to door together."

The nods all around told him that was a popular decision.

The first two rooms they broke into were unoccupied. One looked like a tiny dorm room, but the other was big and set up with a bloodstained table and a bunch of knives and saws that looked like surgical equipment.

He had a feeling some ugly stuff had gone down in there.

In the third room they found a bald old monk with no arms or legs lying on a futon. The socket of his shoulder, where his arm should have started, was freshly sutured. What was wrong with him? Gangrene? Why hadn't they taken him to a hospital?

"What do we do with him?" one of the Kickers said, stepping up to the futon and bending over the monk. "Look. He's smiling. Like he's glad to see us."

Another Kicker stepped over for a look. "Damn. If he ain't."

Hank was debating whether or not to club the guy when the two Kickers cried out in surprise.

"Shit!" one said, pulling something from his neck. "He spit something at me." He held up a red-striped toothpick. "Look at this!"

The other pulled the same from his cheek. "Me too."

That seemed to settle it without a word from Hank. He turned away as they pulped the monk's head.

Hank motioned toward the door. "On to the next."

But as he reached the door he heard two heavy thumps behind him. He turned and saw the two Kickers crumpled on the floor. He stepped over and checked them. Their wide, staring eyes told him they were dead.

He turned to the others. "Those toothpick things must have been poison. All right, that settles it. You see one of these guys, you flatten him."

The next door was heavier than the rest—thick oak planks that resisted their most powerful kicks. A secure room . . . made to safeguard valuables. Valuables like Dawn and the sword, maybe?

Hank turned to Jantz and pointed to his chainsaw. "Fire that thing up again and go to work."

Toru stood in the dark and listened to the futile kicks and thuds against the sturdy door that guarded the scrolls and the *ekisu*. Not only was it thick, but reinforced high and low by heavy crossbars. He had intended to bring the girl and the katana in here, but the barbarians had invaded this level before he had a chance.

Then he heard another sound—the roar of a small gasoline engine.

What—?

When he heard a saw attacking the wood, he knew.

His gut roiled as he tightened his grip on his katana. He knew he would not survive this, but he would make them pay dearly.

An errant thought plagued him. What if they weren't interested in the scrolls and the *ekisu*? What if they were only after the girl and the katana?

He shook it off. No. Who would not want to control the secret of the Kuroikaze?

Perhaps he could make them pay so dearly that they would forget about the Black Wind.

Wood dust peppered him as the saw pierced the door and began a downward cut. He positioned himself so that he would be behind the door when it opened, then closed his eyes behind his mask. Only a matter of time now.

Finally, after cutting through the crossbars and around the lock, the chainsaw was withdrawn. The door burst open, exposing the room to wan light from the hall. Toru held his breath as flashlight beams lit the sawdust motes in the air.

"Empty," someone said as he stepped forward.

Toru acted then, stepping out from cover and slashing toward the man's neck. The blade opened a wildly spraying gash in his throat. As the man went down, Toru delivered an overhead chop to the shoulder of the man behind him, nearly severing the arm from his body, then stabbed at a third man, piercing his rib cage through and through. But when he tried to withdraw the blade, it wouldn't budge—jammed between front and rear ribs.

He ducked as something flashed toward his face but not quickly enough. His head exploded with pain and bright flashes, but he remained aware as he hit the floor and felt each kick and each blow that followed.

"All right! All right!" cried a voice. "Enough!"

"The motherfucker killed Thoren, Hendricks, and Rucker, boss! Ain't no such thing as enough."

"Oh, he's gonna get his. Don't you worry."

Toru became aware of someone leaning close, but his eyes would not focus. He felt a finger poke a broken rib, sending a stab of pain through his chest.

"Where's the girl? Where's the katana? Tell me and I'll let you live."

Live? Did he know what he was saying? How could he go on living if he betrayed the Order?

But as for answering, Toru could not have done so, even had he wished it. He knew from the pain and his inability to move it that his jaw was broken.

The man withdrew. Toru heard his voice as if from down a long corridor.

"You know what? These monks or whatever they are seem to like to cut themselves up. Let's see if we can help this guy along. Whatta ya say, Jantz?"

"Aw*right!*" said a third voice.

Toru heard the chainsaw roar to life again and wanted to scream.

Glock in hand, Jack took the lead as he and Veilleur picked their way through the corpses. He'd expected some bloodshed but not bodies piled up outside the front door. Sort of like Vlad the Impaler warning the Turks.

All Kickers, as far as he could tell, but not all killed the same way.

He whispered, "Some of these guys have been cut, some shot. And this one's got a *shuriken* in his eye. Bet that smarted."

Veilleur nodded. "The work of both the Kakureta Kao and your yakuza friends, I imagine."

Friends. Right. With friends like those . . .

"Looks like the Kickers are getting the worst of it."

"No surprise. They are the least skilled, after all."

"We'd better be careful."

"Thank you," Veilleur said with a smile as he bent and picked up a long, curved crowbar. He hefted it and made a couple of short swings. "A much-needed warning as we stand over seven corpses."

Jack realized it had been kind of a dumb thing to say. But he was used to working alone.

"Just playing Master of the Obvious."

"You have proven yourself worthy of the title." Veilleur gestured toward the entrance. "I think we should find another way in, don't you?"

Jack agreed. They made their way to the north end of the building. They'd heard the sound of a chainsaw as they'd approached, but that had stopped now. They found a fire exit around the corner—unlocked. They slipped through the doors, Jack again in the lead, and found themselves at the bottom of a narrow stairwell.

He eased the door to the hallway open a crack and peeked out. He jerked back, then peeked again.

"What is it?" Veilleur whispered.

"I see dead people."

A slaughterhouse.

Corpses of Kickers and robed cultists littered the floor near the main entrance. Just this side of them, what looked like a dead yakuza—the heavy one—with a jacket over his head.

He narrowed the opening when he caught movement farther down the hall. As he watched, the yakuza—the two remaining gunsels and their boss—exited one room and crossed the hall to another.

He tapped Veilleur's shoulder and pointed up the stairway. The old man nodded and they headed for the second floor.

Fewer bodies up here—a half dozen maybe, all in blue robes. Nothing moving. He motioned Veilleur to follow and started down the hall, peering into the rooms as they passed. He saw two dead Kickers in one, next to the battered body of a limbless monk. Two doors down they came upon a room awash in blood—three dead Kickers plus someone's arm.

Christ, what happened in there?

Jack decided he didn't need to know and was about to move on when Veilleur stopped him.

"Wait. I want to see . . ."

He led Jack inside where they found the source of the arm: another dead limbless monk, only his were freshly severed and strewn around the room. His belly had been ripped open as well. Jack remembered the sound of the chainsaw and turned away.

He felt a little ill. In a way, all this was his doing. He might not have created the conflict between them, but he'd put three vicious pit bulls in the same ring. He hadn't realized how vicious. He'd expected bloodshed, but this had gotten out of hand.

Veilleur seemed unfazed. He'd given the monk's quartered and eviscerated body barely a glance before moving on. He was now picking through a pile of scrolls in the corner, unrolling them a little and shining his flashlight on them.

After looking at three or four he turned to Jack. "Would you get me one of the oil lamps from the hall?"

Jack checked the hall. Voices drifted down from the other end. He stepped out, unhooked the nearest lamp from the ceiling, and ducked back inside.

Veilleur took the lamp and tossed it onto the scrolls.

"This should have been done centuries ago."

"Why?"

"They tell how to create the Kuroikaze—the Black Wind."

Slater had mentioned the same thing.

"What the hell is it?"

"No time to explain here. Suffice to say it's vile and evil. There's enough evil in the world without the Kuroikaze too."

"I need more than that. What's it do?"

Veilleur looked at him. "It kills. It sucks the life out of everything it touches. You read about that incident a few miles from here, I assume. Where everything—plants, rodents, insects, even bacteria—were found dead?"

"The wilt."

"It's no coincidence that it happened not far from the Kakureta Kao building."

"That was a Black Wind?"

Veilleur nodded. "A miniature example. I suspect they were experimenting."

Then Slater hadn't been crazy.

"What for?"

"My guess is revenge. Or simply because they're all even madder than they seem."

The spilling oil soaked into the old paper, setting the pile ablaze. The room began to fill with smoke.

"Are they the only copies?"

"Who can say? I hope so. But at least we know that no one will be using these."

Jack returned to the hall and started to lead the way toward the other end when he heard a voice on the main stairwell asking for Hank.

He and Veilleur ducked into the next room—free of corpses, thank you—and waited.

Darryl cowered behind the door of the empty room, hands pressed against the sides of his throbbing head, waiting. He'd thought he was home free when he'd ducked in here to escape the shoot-out. A few minutes later he thought he was dead—just about peed his pants—when two of those suited gunmen came in. But they hadn't looked behind the door.

For a while now everything had been pretty quiet—except for the sound of a chainsaw somewhere in the distance. Upstairs maybe?

Did he dare take a peek? Didn't see any alternative. Sure as hell couldn't stay here all night.

He crept to the door on hands and knees and peeked out. Bodies every-where. He knew some of those dead faces.

No movement anywhere, no sound. He took a deep breath and made a tiptoe dash to the next room.

Oh, shit. He wasn't alone. The lone, sputtering candle revealed the leg-less monk and the two Kickers he'd stabbed. Except the Kickers had been alive when he'd left them with Menck, and now they were—

Say . . . where was Menck?

"Darryl?"

He almost screamed when he turned and saw the dead monk rising from his bed. But no—the top of his bedding was moving with him. Menck's ban-daged head popped out from under the futon.

"Shit, Menck, you almost gave me a heart attack. What the fuck you do-ing under there?"

"Hiding. When I saw those Japs going room to room after massacring our guys, I dove under here." He pointed to the two dead Kickers. "They shot them up, then left."

Darryl's stomach knotted. "So it's just you and me out of all those guys?"

Menck nodded. "Seems that way. At least down here. Don't know about Hank upstairs."

"Shit! Hank and his no-guns rule. We didn't stand a chance."

"Hey, nobody figured on hit men."

"You think that's what they are?"

"Sure act like it. Stone killers with silencers. That says hit men to me."

Darryl couldn't argue with that. "But who hired them?"

"The fuck *I* know?"

"Yeah. Right. Look, we either gotta get outta here—with Hank if he's alive, without him if he ain't."

Menck shook his head and moved to the window. "Fuck Hank. Probably as dead as these guys." He touched his bandaged scalp. "My head's killing me and I feel like I'm gonna puke. I'm outta here."

Darryl followed him, knowing exactly how he felt. They were on the first floor. If they could get the window open, it was only a short drop to the back-yard. Real tempting.

As Menck started lifting the sash, Darryl checked out the yard. He froze when he saw the lone black figure standing maybe fifty feet away. Couldn't make out any features.

"Someone's out there."

Menck stopped and stared. "The fuck is he?"

"One of the hit men?" Darryl said, but didn't really believe it.

Something about the guy sent a deep chill through Darryl. He didn't seem to be holding a weapon or anything. He just stood there with his head thrown back, his legs spread, and his arms angled out from his body. He looked like he was praying, but for some odd reason he made Darryl think of an antenna—but what kind of signal he was picking up was anyone's guess.

He might be lots worse than one of the hit men.

"Must have put an extra guy outside to make sure no one escapes. They want to kill us all. Shit!"

"We gotta get Hank."

Menck turned from the window and headed for the door. "You get Hank while I get out."

Darryl grabbed his arm. "Hey. We're Kickers, man. We stick together. I'm gonna go find Hank. You want to face him later after you ran out on him, fine. Not me."

Menck looked at the ceiling, then said, "Fuck. All right. Let's find him."

Darryl peeked out the door. Nothing moving. The main staircase was only a few dozen feet down and across the hall.

But the hall was the last place Darryl wanted to be. He wanted to stay in this tiny room till morning, till he and Menck were the only ones left in the building, then sneak away.

But Hank was the man, the boss, the primo Kicker. Darryl had to find him.

"Okay. Let's go!"

Repressing a whimper of terror, he hurried across the hall in a crouch and into the recess of the stairway.

Made it.

With Menck close behind he ran up the first flight but stopped at the bottom of the second. A couple of guys lay sprawled on the stairs. Dead?

Then one of them said, "Darryl? That you?"

A Kicker. He hurried up to them. He didn't know their names, but knew they were hurt.

"Where's Hank?"

The guy jerked a thumb over his shoulder. "Still looking."

Hank alive. Okay. Now to find him.

"How is it up there?"

"I think we got the floor to ourselves now. How's it downstairs?"

Don't ask, Darryl thought, but said, "Quiet. Hey, I'm gonna find Hank. You guys sit tight."

"Like we have a choice?"

He motioned Menck to follow him. They found dead Kickers at the top of the steps and dead monks in the smoky hall, but no sign of Hank. He coughed and looked around. Smoke was pouring from one of the doors down the hall.

"Hank?" he said softly. A little louder: "Hank?"

Someone stepped out of a door near the other end of the hall and waved them forward. By the time they got there, Hank and half a dozen other Kickers, including Jantz and his chainsaw—his very bloody chainsaw—were gathered outside the door, waiting.

"What's burning?" Hank was saying, waving at the smoke as they came up. He smiled at Darryl and Menck. "Hey, guys. We pretty much own the floor, but we need reinforcements."

Menck shook his head. "We're it, I'm afraid."

Hank's eyes widened. "*What?* What happened?"

Darryl gave him a quick rundown about the killer monks and the arrows and the hit men.

"Silencers?" Hank said.

"Yeah." Darryl looked around. "Where're the others?"

Hank looked at him. "Crazy fucking monks." He shook his head. "Shit."

"My sentiments exactly," Menck said. "This whole night has turned to shit. Let's get out of here."

Hank shook his head. "Only two more rooms to search. She's got to be in one of them."

He started across the hall with everyone following him. He kicked open a door, then stepped back.

"Finally!" he said.

Darryl looked over his shoulder and saw Dawn lying on the floor. Four candles burned around her, and on the floor before her lay a Japanese sword. Darryl couldn't tell if it was *the* sword because it was sheathed in a curved scabbard.

Hank checked behind the door through the hinge space before stepping in. He went straight to the sword and half pulled it from its scabbard. Darryl saw the moth-eaten metal and knew they'd found it.

"Bingo," Hank said.

He slammed it back into the scabbard and tossed it to Menck. He knelt next to Dawn and scooped her up in his arms, then hoisted her over his shoulder where she hung like a rag doll. When he turned to them, his face was grim.

"They better not have hurt this baby."

Or what? Darryl thought. They're all dead.

But he said nothing.

"We're going home," Hank said when he reached the hall—which was smokier than ever.

Darryl didn't know if he'd ever heard sweeter words. But they still had to get by the hit men.

Hank nodded to Jantz. "You and the others take point, see if we're clear ahead. Darryl—you and Menck cover the rear."

As Jantz and the rest moved off toward the staircase, Hank reached into one of his pockets and pulled out a pistol. He handed it to Darryl.

"Know how to use this?"

Darryl had done some hunting in his day, but with a rifle, never a pistol. Still, with all the shit that was going down here, he wasn't about to let a gun slip through his fingers.

"You betcha."

He took it. A snub-nose, six-shot revolver. He didn't know what caliber, and didn't care. All that mattered was that it fired when he pulled the trigger.

Down the hall, flames were licking from one of the doorways, and the smoke was getting worse. Jantz and the rest were already at the stairs. Hank started after them with Dawn. Darryl and Menck followed Hank.

"All we gotta do, man," he whispered to Menck, "is make it through the front door and we're home free."

Menck had the sword on his shoulder like a rifle. "We ain't there yet, my man. Not until—"

His words cut off in a gurgle. Darryl whipped around and saw Menck's mouth wide open and his arms spread like he was belting out the last note of a song. But the sword was flying through the air, his eyes were bulging, and it looked like he had a second mouth under his chin, wide open, and spitting blood.

And behind him, a shadow in black, pulling a bloody knife away from Menck's throat.

"Fuck!" Darryl shouted, raising the pistol and firing as Menck's knees gave way.

The Jap's head jerked back in a spray of red and he went down.

I hit him! Darryl thought. God damn, first time I ever shot a pistol and I hit the fucker!

But Menck—poor Menck was a goner. Menck was *gone*.

"What the fuck?" Hank had stopped and turned. He looked at Darryl, then Menck, then Darryl again. "Shit! Keep moving!"

Leave Menck—just like that?

"But—"

"We can't help him. Cover me, Darryl." He looked around. "Hey, where's the sword?"

He pointed toward the dim smoky hall behind them. "Back there somewhere. Want me to—?"

"Leave it for now. We'll send somebody back. Just cover my ass till we get out of here."

Darryl did just that, walking backward, gun swinging left and right, all the way to the stairway. They found Jantz waiting at the bottom with the two wounded and the rest.

Hank said, "Jantz—the sword's still up there, in the hall. Take someone and go get it. Don't worry. Nothing moving up there. The rest of you come with me."

As Jantz and another Kicker hurried upstairs, Darryl peeked up and down the hall, then longingly at the entrance directly across from them. Twenty feet of exposure and they were outta here.

He thought he saw a flicker of movement in one of the doorways but it didn't repeat.

He motioned to Hank and the others behind him. "All clear. Let's move!"

Holding his breath, waiting for the silent bullet that would end everything, he scurried across the hall and into the entrance recess.

Made it!

The rest made it as well. He held the door for Hank and Dawn, then started for the cars. They all stopped when they saw the bodies. All the guys who had been wounded in the first attack were dead.

"Shit!" Hank said. "Shot down like dogs."

Darryl couldn't look. He made a beeline for the cars.

"Find us some wheels and make tracks," Hank said behind him. "Jantz can follow."

Don't have to tell me twice, Darryl thought.

It must be on the second floor, Hideo thought. If it is here at all.

No—no negative thinking. The caller had been correct about the Kakureta Kao, and he would be correct about the katana as well. They simply had to find it. Only a matter of time.

He stood in the last room at the end of the first-floor hallway with Kenji and Ryo. They had run into no more opposition since Goro's death. Now it was time to move upstairs. Who knew what they would find there?

He was stepping out into the hall when he caught a flash of movement by the main stairs. Monks or members of the rival cult, he could not say. He stepped back and motioned the yakuza to be still.

And then he clearly heard someone say in English: ". . . the sword's still up there, in the hall. Take someone and go get it. Don't worry. Nothing moving up there. The rest of you come with me."

His heart leaped. *Still up there . . .* The katana was almost within his grasp.

He repressed the urge to lead a charge down the hall. Better to learn how many they were, and how well armed.

He peeked again and saw a knot of them—some scurrying, some limping, one carrying a woman—cross the hall and disappear through the entrance.

Take someone and go get it. Don't worry. Nothing moving up there. The rest of you come with me.

Hideo could take that only one way: Deal with these two remaining members of the rival cult and the katana would be his.

He stepped out into the hall and motioned the yakuza to follow. They passed a bloody chainsaw lying on the steps, and found the second floor full of smoke. To his left he heard a cough and a hoarse voice.

"Where *is* the fucking thing? I can't see shit."

He pointed the yakuza in the direction of the voice. They disappeared into the smoke. Hideo heard cries of surprise, a number of *phuts*, cries of pain, more *phuts*, then silence. When he arrived at the scene he found the yakuza standing over a pair of bodies.

Now to find the katana. The smoke would make it more difficult, but they had time.

"He said it was in the hall. Search the floor and—"

He caught a hint of motion in the flickering light from a nearby doorway. He pointed the yakuza toward it and the three of them approached with caution. The man downstairs had said there was "nothing moving" up here, but he could have been wrong.

They moved opposite the opening and peered in. Hideo blinked at the sight of a bearded old man holding the katana by its handle and calmly examining the blade. He waved it in the air, then glanced at them. Hideo flinched when he spoke in archaic-sounding Japanese.

"Despite all it's been through, the balance is still excellent."

The yakuza had their pistols pointed at him but didn't fire as they might have with anyone else. Hideo understood. Something about this man. Though old, he possessed a powerful-looking frame. But that wasn't it. He had a . . . presence that seemed to fill the room and pour out into the hallway.

"Give me the katana," Hideo said, "and you shall live."

He didn't know why he'd said that. A feeling he had . . . as if the world would be a poorer, darker place with this man's passing.

"This? Masamune-san made it for me, but I don't think I want it."

Wondering what he meant by that absurd statement, Hideo gestured the yakuza into the room and followed.

"A wise choice. I am a man of my word. If you will hand me the sword, we will take our leave and—"

Something hard jammed against his left ear and a voice said, "I'd like to have something to say about that."

The yakuza whirled and reacted with shock. As they aimed their pistols the voice said, "Uh-uh-uh. Hair trigger. One twitch and his brains will Jackson Pollock the wall."

Hideo knew Kenji's English was good enough for him to understand, but he didn't know about Ryo, so he translated.

They turned as one and retrained their weapons on the old man who still held the katana poised before him.

"Looks like we've got a John Woo situation here," the voice said.

Hideo was almost sure now that it was the *ronin*. A slight turn of his head confirmed it.

"Who is John Woo?" the old man said.

"Never mind."

But Hideo knew what he meant, and he was wrong. He felt sweat gathering on his brow and under his arms. His knew his life depended on convincing the *ronin* of the futility of this.

"This is not the standoff you think it is," he said. "We were sent to return the katana to Japan."

"By whom?"

"That is not important. What matters is that we were charged with the task and we will see it through no matter what the cost. If you do not hand over the katana within the next few seconds, they will kill your friend and then—"

"And then that'll be the end of you."

"You must understand that they do not care about me. They will kill your friend and you will kill me and they will kill you. So you see, no matter what happens here, the katana will be returned to Japan."

"Perhaps there's been enough killing, Jack," the old man said.

Jack . . . the *ronin*'s name was Jack.

"Listen to him, Jack. With age comes wisdom."

The old man said, "Should we give it to him?"

Jack said, "I kind of promised it to someone else."

Hideo shuddered. "Then what happens next is on your head."

The muzzle pressed harder against his ear.

"And *in* yours."

The old man sighed. "You don't leave me much choice. No more killing. I wish I could say the same for bloodshed."

Hideo was sagging with relief when he saw the blade of the katana flicker—or seem to. And then he heard Kenji and Ryo grunt and drop their guns.

The shock of wondering *why* was replaced by the horror of realizing that they were dropping hands along with the guns.

"Good Christ!" Jack said.

Kenji and Ryo started screaming then, each gaping at the spurting stump where a hand had been. They dropped to their knees—first Ryo, then Kenji—and knelt there squeezing their wrists to stanch the flow.

Hideo looked at the old man who was again calmly examining the blade, now slightly smeared with red.

"Quite an edge. Masamune-san certainly knew his trade."

Hideo was still trying to comprehend what had happened. He hadn't seen the katana move. Could this old man have struck so swiftly that the blade had seemed only to flicker?

Hideo slowly slipped his hand inside his coat, edging toward his pistol. But the *ronin* grabbed his wrist.

"Don't be stupid now."

He reached in and pulled Hideo's weapon from its holster.

"H and K," he said, holding it up. "Nice."

He dropped it, then stepped away. Hideo turned to face him.

"What now? Are you going to execute me like you did my brother?"

The *ronin* looked puzzled. "What?"

"You killed my brother."

"Your James Cagney is lousy. Do you mean Yoshio?"

Hideo closed his eyes. He *did* remember.

"I'm his brother."

Jack smiled and said, "Despite the fact that he once had a gun pressed against the back of my head, I liked him."

"Then why did you kill him?"

"I didn't. A man named Baker did. He's dead."

"How? You?"

Jack shook his head. "I sure as hell tried, but someone beat me to it." He stared at Hideo. "So, do you and your brother work for the same organization?"

Hideo stiffened. "What did he tell you?"

"Nothing. Just curious. He died trying to unravel a secret, and I knew he wasn't doing it for himself."

Yoshio had died in the course of duty. His honor was intact.

Jack said, "Did you happen to come across an eighteen-year-old girl in your travels?"

"I saw a man carrying a young woman out of the building."

He looked at the old man. "Dawn."

Hideo did not care about the girl. To restore honor to his family name he needed what the old man was holding.

"I must have the katana."

Jack shook his head. "The owner hired me to find it. He gets first dibs."

"I could make a case for being the rightful owner," the old man said, still holding the katana. "I'm the *gaijin* who gave Masamune-san the short sword to refashion into something more graceful."

"I kind of suspected that," Jack said.

The old man stared at the blade, then shook his head. "But by the time I returned to pay him and claim it, he was dead and the blade was gone." He shook his head. "Time passes too quickly sometimes."

Hideo glanced at Jack and saw calm acceptance in his expression. Surely the old man was mad—claiming to be seven hundred years old—but the *ronin* too?

Then again, feeling the old one's presence, he might be telling the truth.

He shook himself. What am I thinking?

"Well," Jack said, "if you didn't pay for it and never took possession, I can make as good a case for you *not* being the rightful owner."

The old man sighed. "I suppose so."

Hideo looked over at the yakuza. Kenji still knelt, but Ryo lay on his side. Both looked pale and weak and ill. But by applying constant pressure, they had stopped the blood loss from their wrists. They would survive, but they were of no use to him now.

Hideo did something then that he'd never done in his life: He dropped to his knees and folded his hands in supplication.

"Please give me the sword. My family honor depends on it."

Jack's expression hardened. "You and your goons were ready to Swiss-cheese me at Gerrish's place. Instead of gabbing I should be kneecapping you. Shove your family honor, pal."

He bent and picked up the scabbard, then tossed it to the old man.

"We need to get back to the city."

He kicked Kenji's and Ryo's pistols—still gripped in their hands—into the hallway, then did the same with Hideo's.

Without a word, the old man sheathed the sword and handed it to Jack, then walked out of the room. The *ronin* followed, leaving Hideo on his knees.

"Don't do anything stupid."

Hideo rose on wobbly legs. He had failed Sasaki-san. He could not return without the katana. And he could not stay here.

He staggered out into the hall. The *ronin* and the old man had disappeared into the smoke but he heard their footsteps on the stairway. He found his pistol and hefted it. His first impulse was to stick the barrel in his mouth and pull the trigger. But he didn't know if he could do that.

Perhaps later he would find out, but as for now . . .

He hurried for the stairs. He would have the katana or die trying.

He was down the first flight and rounding the bend when he came to a sudden stop as he felt something jab against his chest. The *ronin* stood before him with the muzzle of his pistol pressed over Hideo's heart.

"I warned you about being stupid."

Hideo's pistol was down, against his thigh. He began to raise it.

"Don't," the *ronin* said. "Your brother was a good guy, a brave man. I'm sure you're just as brave, and I know you think you're doing what you have to do, and I respect that, but you're trading brave for stupid now. Do that and this can end only one way."

Hideo didn't stop the upward movement of his weapon. Honor demanded he resolve this, one way or another.

He heard a sudden, almost deafening sound as something smashed into his chest, half turning his body as it tumbled backward. He landed on his shoulder, then flopped onto his back where he stared at the cracked ceiling and listened to the death cries of his punctured heart.

"Aw, jeez," he heard the *ronin* say. "Why'd he have to do that?"

The old man said, "I think he was using you to do something he couldn't do himself."

"Swell."

The voices faded away, the ceiling faded to black, quickly followed by everything else.

Shiro had been drifting in a twilight of consciousness, vaguely aware that he should be up and doing something . . . but not knowing what . . . and even if he knew, he lacked the will to rouse himself from the twilight.

And then he started at the sound of a shot and came fully awake.

Raising his head sparked an explosion of pain, and with it the memory of what had happened.

. . . cutting the throat of the man with the sword . . . the katana tumbling away into the smoke . . . the pistol pointed at his face . . . ducking . . . the crushing impact against his head . . .

He struggled to his hands and knees, then, using the nearest wall for support, made it to his feet. His eyes stung from the smoke. He coughed, sending another jolt of pain through his head. He touched his scalp and felt the wet, congealing blood there. He did not know how badly he was wounded and did not have time to worry about himself.

Where were his brothers of the Order, where was the sound of battle?

He stumbled down the hallway in a fruitless search for the katana, going from room to room, finding dead brother monks in some, others slumped on the floor, and flames . . . flames coming from the scroll room.

"*Sensei!*"

He hurried toward the room and found much of it aflame. The scrolls—destroyed, gone forever. Holding an arm across his face, he braved the heat and stepped inside. Where—?

He found Akechi-*sensei* on the floor, and gagged when he saw the ghastly wounds where his limbs had been severed from his body, his belly opened. He fought the urge to drop to his knees and sob and die alongside his teacher.

But such a luxury was denied him. Vengeance called.

The Kickers . . . one of them had carried a chainsaw . . . they did this. They slaughtered his brothers and destroyed the Order.

No . . . not completely destroyed. Shiro remained.

He turned to the shelves on the far side of the room. The flames had yet to reach the vials there.

The *ekizu*.

Fighting the heat, he grabbed a vial and ducked back into the hall.

The blue glass felt hot but not too hot to hold. He prayed the *ekizu* hadn't been ruined. Because tonight he intended to let the Kickers feel the full fury of the Black Wind.

9

"You get the feeling we were set up?" Darryl said as he drove them across the Manhattan Bridge.

Hank looked at him and realized he did have that feeling, had sensed it soon after they'd walked into the place. He simply hadn't pinned it down.

He glanced back at Dawn, stretched out on the rear seat, still unconscious—was she ever going to wake up?—then out the rear window at the two cars carrying the few survivors of the three dozen or so Kickers who'd started out earlier.

What a catastrophe.

"Yeah, I kind of do. But who? And why?"

"The guy who called and told us where we could find the sword."

"Yeah, but who *is* he?"

"One of those Enemies you talk about?"

The Enemy . . . out to destroy the Plan. But they'd be after Dawn, and the last thing they'd want to tell him would be where to find her.

"No, not them." He shook his head. "I don't understand any of this.

What did those sicko monks want with Dawn? And those hit men. Who were they sent to hit? Us or the monks?"

"I think they were looking for the sword."

"The hit men? Why the hell—?"

Darryl shrugged. "Don't know. But didn't you tell me that sword's called a katana."

"Yeah."

"Well, while I was hiding, I heard one of the hit men say it twice. Didn't understand anything else in their jibber-jabber, but I know I heard that word."

"They must have been the ones behind those flyers."

"Maybe. Still, three bunches of folks all after the same thing winding up in the same place at the same time . . . if that don't smack of a set-up, I don't know what does."

Darryl might not be the brightest bulb in the box, but Hank had to admit he had something there.

"Whatever, the important thing is the Kickers came away with Dawn and the sword."

"Hope so. Hope we didn't lose Menck and the others for just half the prize."

Hank's neck tightened. "What do you mean, 'half'?"

Darryl looked in the rearview. "Well, I ain't seen no sign of Jantz."

"We had too much of a lead, that's all."

"Hope so."

So did Hank.

10

Hank eased Dawn onto the bed and pulled a sheet up to her neck.

He figured the basement was still the best place for her, so he'd called ahead to have a bed moved in from upstairs.

He stared down at her and shook his head, thinking, You've been one hell of a lot of trouble, girl. Thirty-some guys just died for you. Hope to hell you're worth it.

"What do we do now?" Darryl said.

Hank turned and saw him standing there with Ansari.

Good old Darryl. He'd hung in there. He'd always seemed like a loser, but the guy had guts.

"We heal our wounds and go on like before. One thing we won't have to worry about is those crazy Jap monks."

"But what about the hit men?" Darryl said.

Good question. Hank didn't have an answer, but figured he should look like he did.

"They come here, they'll be on our turf, and we'll know how to deal with them." He frowned. "Where's Jantz? He should be here by now." He pointed to Ansari. "Go upstairs and check. If he's here, have him bring me the sword."

As the door closed behind Ansari, Hank jumped at the sound of a strange voice.

"I don't think you'll be seeing the katana again."

Hank whirled and found himself face-to-face with a stranger.

"Who the fuck are you?"

The guy looked young, slim, maybe five ten, with Latino-ish skin. He was working on a mustache. Reminded Hank of Prince, but not so foppish or faggy. He wore a long-sleeve black shirt and black pants. Seemed like a guy going for either the Latin lover or the Zorro look.

And then suddenly his face changed. It didn't rearrange itself, just . . . changed. Almost like a shift in the lighting. But his eyes . . . whatever they'd been hiding behind was gone and now they were bared for all to see.

Hank had seen eyes like those in his dreams, black holes spiraling down into a place where light was a legend, a myth.

"For now, you may call me Rafe."

"Well, listen, Rafe. You've got no business here."

"Yes, I do. I'm taking the girl."

"The fuck you are!" Darryl said.

Hank watched him start to pull the .38 he'd lent him from his pocket, but it never made it out.

"What the—?" he said.

He seemed to be frozen. Hank reached to grab the gun but couldn't move anything but his head.

What's going on?

"You . . ." Darryl said, looking at Rafe. "You were out back of that building tonight. You're the one I saw."

The man nodded. "I must thank you and your followers for a most gratifying and satisfying evening. The slaughter was quite tasty."

What was he talking about?

Hank found his voice. "What do you know about the sword? Do you have it?"

He shook his head. "I don't know who ended up with it. Most likely the corporate hireling from Japan. But no matter, now that I know it exists, I can find it whenever I need it. I would have stayed around until the finish but I was forced to follow you to keep an eye on Dawn."

"Are you one of the Enemy?"

He laughed—a chilling sound. "You mean as in *Enemy* with a capital 'E'? How typical of Jonah."

Jonah?

"You've heard of my father?"

"*Heard* of Jonah Stevens? I knew him. I knew him well. Too well."

"You're not old enough."

"Is that so?"

"Are you or are you not one of the Enemy?"

He smiled a smile women probably would find sexy. "There's no easy answer to that. No, I'm not the Enemy he was referring to—for that enemy is my enemy as well—but I certainly was not his ally."

"I don't understand."

"What makes you think you should? By the way, I was with him when he died."

"How? How did he die? The Enemy?"

Was that why his father had stopped coming around? Hank had guessed that but never known for sure. He'd paid regular visits as Hank was growing up, telling him about the Plan, about his destiny, and then when Hank was around seven he stopped coming around altogether. The question of why had plagued him ever since.

"Jonah was crushed in an elevator shaft. A slow, painful death. Took him hours to die."

"You were there? Didn't you help him?"

The man raised his eyebrows. "Help? Why would I do that? I'm the one who put him in there. I stayed to sup."

Hank let out a roar of rage and struggled to break free of whatever was holding him back, but couldn't budge a muscle. What kind of power did this bastard have? Had he hypnotized them into thinking they couldn't move? Had he drugged them?

"What's he talking about, Hank?" Darryl said.

"Just shut up for a minute, okay?" He turned to Rafe or whoever he was. "Why? Why'd you kill him? What he ever do to you?"

"He forgot his place. He began to think he could supplant me."

"'Supplant' you? Why would he want to do that? I mean, who the fuck are *you*?"

"I am the One. Jonah forgot that. He conspired against me. You were part of that conspiracy." He pointed to Dawn. "As was she, but most especially the child she carries. That was the ultimate goal—to concentrate his bloodline in a child he could use to replace me." He smiled as he shook his head. "It never would have worked, but the very fact that he was thinking along those lines made him an unfit guardian. He was supposed to be my protector, but instead he plotted against me. I could not allow that."

An awful thought plowed into Hank like a runaway train.

"You're not going to hurt the baby, are you?"

The man shook his head as he stared down at Dawn. "No. I sensed the child's existence upon its conception, and I must say my first impulse was to eradicate it. But as I became aware of other things, I decided the child might prove useful."

Hank's panic throttled down to cold unease. "Useful how?"

"I can foresee a circumstance where the child might indeed act as the Key to the Future, though not quite in the way your father intended."

The Key to the Future . . .

"You know about that? You were listening?"

Another laugh, colder than the first. "You mean did I eavesdrop on his paternal maunderings? I didn't have to. He told me. He told me everything before he died. Everything."

Hank wanted to rip his throat out but still couldn't budge.

The man added, "I also see that I might have use for you and your followers in the near future."

"In your dreams, asshole."

"Don't be too hasty. Our ends coincide. I might prove as useful to you as you to me."

"Like how?"

"Dissimilation . . . I believe that's what you call it, correct?"

Hank nodded, though he didn't like his words thrown back at him. "Yeah. What about it?"

"Wouldn't you like to see everyone on the planet dissimilated—every man, woman, and child an island?"

"That's the idea," he said slowly. "Break from the crowd."

Where was this going?

"That works into my plans as well. I may be able to assist you toward that end. But not tonight."

Hank felt his gut twist as he watched the man step over to the bed and lift Dawn into his arms as if she weighed nothing.

"Where are you taking her?"

"Someplace safe—safer than here. A place she will not escape from again."

That shocked Hank. "She's been with you? And she got away?"

"An unfortunate lapse by one of my employees. It will not happen again." He looked up, as if watching the sky through all the floors and ceilings overhead. "I suggest that if you want to be present for any future mass dissimilation, you leave the city at once. An ill wind is about to blow."

"Wind?"

He smiled. "An ill wind that blows nobody good—except me. You'd best leave now."

Hank had no idea what this loon was talking about, so he shook his head. "No way."

Like he was letting this wimpy-looking dude or anyone else—no matter what his eyes looked like—tell him to get out of town.

"As you wish."

And then the man carried Dawn out the door and up the steps to the first floor. Hank waited to hear some sort of commotion from above but all stayed quiet. Was everyone else in the building frozen too?

Suddenly he was stumbling forward, able to move again. Free. He grabbed the .38 from Darryl's hand and ran up to the first floor where he found the foyer deserted.

"Hey, boss."

Hank started and turned to see Ansari strolling in. "Where the hell is everybody?"

"Stayer thought he heard something on the roof so we went up. We found out how they got in: Scaled down ropes from next door. We never thought to keep watch on the roof."

"We will now."

"Damn right. Stayer's up there doing the first shift. We'll rotate till we can find a way to alarm that door."

Hank looked around. "You see anyone come through here who didn't belong?"

"Like who?"

"Never mind."

The guy had slipped out with Dawn. Maybe that wasn't such a bad thing. He'd told them he'd take good care of her. He seemed as interested in the baby as Hank.

I can foresee a circumstance where the child might indeed act as the Key to the Future, though not quite in the way your father intended.

Hank wasn't sure what that meant, but it sounded good. And the guy had been holding all the high cards when he'd said it, so no need to lie.

Hank couldn't help feeling an odd sense of relief. Keeping Dawn and her baby locked away and healthy had looked to be an almost impossible task. Now it was out of his hands.

But once the baby was born—he and Jeremy had figured that would be next January—he'd go looking. His dreams had led him to Dawn, so he was sure they'd lead him to the baby. He didn't want to go one-on-one with that weird dude, but with a bunch of Kickers behind him . . . different story.

He looked at Ansari. "Jantz ever show up?"

He shook his head. "No sign of him, no call, no nothin."

Not good. He should have been here by now . . . unless he ran into the hit men.

Oh well, his dreams had also led him to the sword . . . or rather the sword to him. It would happen again.

The weird guy's parting words came back to him: *I suggest that if you want to be present for any future mass dissimilation, you leave the city at once.*

Get out of Dodge? Fat chance. This was Hank's town now.

11

Shiro unfolded himself from the tiny space between three large potted trees.

He'd stumbled as he'd swung onto the roof. Someone below must have heard because in less than a minute four Kickers arrived. They did a quick, cursory search and then spent the rest of the time looking at the ropes Shiro and his now dead brothers had left dangling from the neighboring rooftop.

Finally three of them returned below, leaving the fourth as guard. He immediately set a chair by the door and lit up a cigarette. Shiro watched from his hiding place, waiting for his chance. From the way he was drawing and holding the smoke, Shiro suspected it was cannabis.

Good. It would slow his response time, dull his senses, give him a false sense of well-being.

After a while the sentry's head drooped—just what Shiro had been waiting for. He padded up behind him, wrapped an arm around his head and dragged his tanto across his throat—just as he had done with the Kicker carrying the katana back at the temple.

Leaving the gushing, twitching body in the chair, Shiro walked to the center of the roof and sat. He pulled the vial of *ekisu* from his pocket and removed the stopper. He raised it toward his mouth but stopped midway.

He was afraid . . . afraid of what it would do to him . . . afraid of seeing the Hidden Face before he was ready.

And yet, what had he to live for? His brother acolytes and the elder monks were dead, his *sensei* butchered, the sacred Kuroikaze scrolls turned to ash.

The Order of the Kakureta Kao was, in almost every sense, extinct. Only he survived to exact vengeance. He could go below and slay many of them, but they would overcome him and the Kickers would go on.

But not if their leader died.

He knew Hank Thompson lived below. A Black Wind starting here would kill everyone in the building, and in the buildings for many blocks around. Shiro's head had been injured, but his body remained strong. He would take a long time dying, and the longer he held on, the greater and stronger his Kuroikaze. It might spread for a mile or more.

He realized then that no one in the world would ever forget tonight. The Trade Towers' death toll would pale before Shiro's Black Wind. And all would know it began here, with the Kickers. They would be shunned and reviled and hounded across the land.

An eye for an eye, brothers for brothers.

His fear faded. He titled the vial to his lips and downed the *ekizu* in one bitter gulp. Then he lay back and waited.

It took effect more quickly than he'd expected. In a matter of seconds he felt his skin begin to tingle as the extract coursed through his capillaries. Then the tingling faded, replaced by no sensation at all. He no longer felt the roof beneath him. He could have been floating a few inches above it— naked, because he could not feel the clothes against his skin, nor the saliva against his tongue. Did he still have saliva?

The carbon monoxide tang of the air faded along with the sight of the stars and the incessant Manhattan rumble.

He spread his arms—or at least tried to. Did he even have arms? Or a body?

Shiro began to tumble through an endless, featureless void with no up or down or left or right. Panicked by the perfect disorientation, he screamed. Or tried to. He had become pure consciousness in a starless cosmos without light or matter, a black, seething chaos without form or substance.

And then something ahead, faintly luminous, coming his way . . . or was it stationary and he approaching it? Without asking how he could see without eyes, his crumbling mind grasped at it, clung to it as the only reference point in this endless void.

As he neared, it started to take form . . . slowly he began to make out its shape . . . and when finally its features became clear . . . he did not understand what he was seeing . . . and as his consciousness tried to comprehend the incomprehensible . . .

. . . it shattered.

12

Jack led Glaeken up to the roof across the street from the Lodge. He felt stained by the carnage they'd left behind, and wanted to shower. He knew the residue lay beneath his skin and had no illusions that he could wash it off, but a cleansing ritual couldn't hurt.

He felt bad about Yoshio's brother—didn't even know his name. His death had been so unnecessary. And then again, maybe not. In retrospect it almost seemed as if he were playing a role in a tragedy that could end only one way.

They arrived in time to see four Kickers wandering around their rooftop.

"Wonder what they're looking for?" Jack said. When Veilleur, standing stiffly beside him, didn't answer, he nudged him. "You with us?"

"He's near."

"Who?"

"The Adversary. I thought I sensed him at the Kakureta Kao building, but with all the chaos around us I couldn't be sure. But here, now, in the quiet, I can feel him."

"Where?"

"Down there somewhere, no more than a block away, I'd say."

As Jack scanned the street below, not sure what he was looking for, a question formed.

"If you can sense him, can't he sense you?"

Veilleur shook his head. "I think he has a vague sense of where I am. I'm sure he knows I'm in New York City, but nothing more specific than that. I'm not who or what I used to be, you know. To him, for the most part, I'm simply another mortal."

"Why would he have been on Staten Island?"

"To sup on the slaughter. He feeds on death and fear and human carnage."

"And misery. Yeah, I know."

He remembered his last meeting with Rasalom, back in January, when he was feeding on Jack's misery and despair.

"He certainly feasted tonight, but I wonder . . ."

"What?"

"Might he have been there because of Dawn as well?"

Jack thought on that, but it didn't gel.

"He's already holding most of the marbles. What good can Dawn and her baby do for him?"

"I can't imagine. Perhaps I'm wrong."

"You wrong often?"

Veilleur shrugged. "It happens."

Jack watched the Kickers on the roof mill around some, then three of them left. The remaining one seemed to be playing guard, but without much gusto. Jack trained his attention on Hank Thompson's window, hoping to catch a glimpse of Dawn as he had before.

Movement on the roof drew his attention there in time to see a dark figure slip from the shadows and slit the throat of the Kicker on guard.

"Did you catch that?"

Veilleur nodded. "One of the Kakureta Kao, I'd guess. I didn't think there were any left."

The figure seated himself in the center of the roof, drank something, and lay back.

"What's he up to?"

"Kuroikaze!" Veilleur grabbed his shoulder and squeezed. "He's sacrificing himself to create a Black Wind! This explains the Adversary's presence. He must have known this was coming."

"Well, if it kills everything, even bacteria, won't it kill him too?"

"Kill him? He'll suck it in. Depending on how far it spreads, he'll feed as he's never fed before. The fear, the misery, the hopelessness a Kuroikaze engenders will bloat him, but the aftermath . . ." He shook his head. "Remember the panic in the city after nine-eleven? This will be much worse. The Kuroikaze will be called a terrorist attack—and believe me, more than three thousand will die tonight—and since no one will know what caused it, no one will know how to defend against it. Homeland Security will look useless. Imagine the terror. Imagine the Adversary's joy." He turned to Jack. "You've got to stop that *shoten*."

"Me? How? I don't exactly have a sniper rifle handy, and that's one hell of a pistol shot from here."

"Then you'll have to go over there."

"Swell."

"I'd go myself, but I'm no longer up to it."

"Okay, let's just say I get there. How do I stop it?"

Veilleur looked at him. "There's only one way to stop a Kuroikaze: kill the *shoten*—the focus."

Jack nodded toward the rooftop. "Him?"

"Him."

Jack didn't feature entering that place and fighting his way to the roof for nothing.

"We don't even know if there's even going to *be* a Black Wind."

The words had no sooner passed his lips when something changed in the air above the Lodge.

A shadow had formed. No, shadow wasn't right. More like a cloud . . . a black cloud the size of a stretch limo, lying low and flat atop the roof. The blackest cloud Jack had ever seen, a black like no cloud should be, twisting and contorting as if boiling from within as it expanded. It had doubled in length since he'd spotted it and continued to grow as he watched.

Jack felt his saliva dry as every neuron in the self-preservation centers of his brain screamed at him to *run*.

"Is that what I think it is?"

"I've never seen one," Veilleur said, "only heard about them. But I can't imagine it being anything else."

The space around the Lodge darkened as the cloud seemed to be sucking the light from the air. Jack didn't know if it was real or imagined, but he thought he could see faintly glowing wisps of light streaming toward the ever-enlarging cloud.

The cloud now overhung the entire Lodge, rising as it continued to expand.

"The Kickers inside are beginning to feel the wind and its effects by now, losing strength, losing hope, losing the will to live. And soon they will simply stop living."

"How do you know so much about it?"

"It's a holdover from the First Age—Otherness inspired. You can read about it in the *Compendium of Srem*. But right now that cloud is going to keep expanding, and the winds will expand with it, until the *shoten* himself dies."

"How long will that take?"

"Depends on the vitality of the *shoten*. With a strong young man such as we just saw . . . long enough for the winds to reach Sutton Square and beyond."

The words jolted Jack. "You're a bastard, you know that."

"Only stating a fact."

Jack looked again at the cloud, feeling every instinct begging him not to go there.

"I'd better get moving then."

"Yes. And quickly. Keep moving as fast as you can. It's called The-Wind-That-Bends-Not-the-Trees. Legend says it blows through the human soul. It's felt only by humans, but it sucks the life from everything. First it robs your resolve, steals any hope of success, stifles your will to go on, to live. Be prepared for that and fight it."

As Jack turned to go, wondering how he was going to pull this off, Veilleur thrust the katana at him.

"Take this."

Jack patted the Glock at the small of his back. "I'm okay."

Veilleur pushed it on him. "You may need it."

Jack couldn't see a downside so he grabbed it and ran.

13

"Did the lights just fade?" Darryl said.

Hank looked up, annoyed. Couldn't Darryl ever keep quiet?

"Looks the same to me."

He felt like crap. So crappy he couldn't muster the will to do much of anything. Not even sleep, though he was dead on his feet.

Somehow he and Darryl had wound up back in the basement. Neither had spoken much, just sat and stared at the wall or the floor or the backs of their eyelids. He was staring at the floor now and thinking.

Sometime during the next day, probably less, someone was going to discover that bloodbath on Staten Island, and thirty-some of his guys, most of them with Kicker tattoos, would be found among the bodies. The police and the media would want answers and they'd be all over him. He needed a story that would—

The light dimmed.

He looked up at Darryl, who said, "Don't tell me you didn't notice that."

Hank nodded. "Probably some sort of brownout going—"

A chill ran across his nape. He tried to shake it off but it turned to a prickling that moved across his shoulders and down his spine. The sudden breeze spread it all across his body.

Breeze?

Hank looked around. He hadn't heard the door open. It wasn't. It was closed tight. So where—?

The breeze picked up as the light dimmed further.

"Hank? What's happening, Hank?"

"I don't know."

"Where's this wind coming from?" He could hear terror edging into Darryl's voice. "We're in a basement, Hank. How do you get wind in a basement with no windows and the door closed?"

The light kept dimming. The overhead bulbs were burning but something seemed to be eating the light out of the air. And the wind—the wind seemed to be coming out of the walls. It swirled around him, making him feel as if he was at the center of a miniature tornado.

He glanced over at Darryl and saw him stagger to his feet. He held an arm across his face to shield his eyes from the blasts of air.

And not clean air. It had a damp feel and carried a musty odor, as if it were blowing from the floor of a black abyss that had been sealed since the dawn of man.

"I'm getting out of here."

Exactly what Hank was thinking. As he struggled to get up he spotted a pile of leftover Dawn flyers on a nearby table. The flyers should have been flying—swirling all around the room—but they simply sat there undisturbed.

What the—?

The light had faded to the point where he could barely make out Darryl. He watched him struggle toward the door against the wind and noticed his clothes weren't blowing. They hung on him without a ripple.

And then Darryl stopped fighting and dropped into a chair.

Hank could barely hear him above the roar of this ghost wind, but it sounded like he said, "What's the use?"

Hank realized that was just how he felt. No use trying—anything. All was lost, all was hopeless, and it would all be over soon.

Hank sat down to wait.

14

"Stop here, Georges."

"*Oui, monsieur.*"

Dawn opened her eyes and totally panicked as memories of the night cascaded around her.

Abducted by Kickers—Jerry's brother—ninjas—eyeless, limbless, masked Japanese monks—

But she was in the back of a car now, with two silhouetted figures in the front seat. It slowed to a stop on a dark city street. She recognized one of the voices.

Mr. Osala?

She tried to sit up but her body wouldn't respond. Neither would her voice when she tried to speak. She could blink and move her eyes, but that was it. Whatever those monks had drugged her with was still working. How long before it wore off? What if it *never* wore off or left her permanently mute and totally paralyzed?

Panic surged again. She wanted to scream but couldn't even whimper.

Above her she saw the moon roof sliding open. To her shock, the figure in the passenger seat, the one who sounded like Mr. Osala, rose and slid through onto the roof. She saw him stand and spread his feet as he positioned himself in front of the opening. He faced ahead and raised his arms like she'd seen some born-again Christians do when they prayed.

But he didn't seem to be praying.

Dawn angled her gaze down and through the windshield and would have totally gasped if she could have. An ugly black cloud was spreading over the rooftops down the street. Whatever Mr. Osala was up to, it seemed to involve that cloud.

15

As soon as Jack hit the street, his skin began to prickle and tingle as if the air were full of static electricity. But it was full of wind instead—wind that seemed to come from all directions. He looked up and saw that the cloud was bigger than before, blocking the stars.

Stifling a tsunami of nausea, he ran across the street and pulled his Glock as he dashed up the Lodge front steps, prepared to shoot his way through anyone who tried to stop him. The wind was even worse inside. The two Kickers who'd been watching the front area on his last trip were still there, but one lay slumped in a corner while the other sprawled in a chair. They looked up as he came through. The one in the chair started to raise a hand as if to stop him, but let it fall limp at his side. His eyes looked frightened, hopeless, lost.

Jack started for the stairs at a run, but the cold, musty gale roaring from the stairwell slowed him. He had to holster his pistol and stick the katana through his belt, then put his head down and pull and claw his way up the steps.

By the time he reached the second floor, he was tired. The wind seemed to be blowing through him as well as at him. As he forced his way toward the third floor, the blast increased its ferocity, but its roar changed to a heart-breaking moan of despair that brought tears to his eyes.

By the third floor he was so tired he didn't know if he could make it. In fact he doubted very much that he would make it. And so what if he didn't? Wasn't going to matter in the long run anyway.

Veilleur's words echoed through the wind.

. . . it sucks the life from everything. First it robs your resolve, steals any hope of success, stifles your will to go on, to live . . .

Was that what was happening here?

He pulled out his Spyderco, flipped open the blade, and jabbed the point through his jeans and an inch into his thigh. He grunted with the pain, and then his breath whistled through his clenched teeth as he twisted the blade.

Focusing on the pain, he started up the final flights to the roof. But even the pain couldn't fully distract him from the alien emotions swirling around him.

Existence is empty, futile. Why go on? Why prolong it?

He punched the wound in his thigh and gasped with the shock of pain.

Yes, pain . . . pain is real, the only real thing, and it's all around. Why suffer when you don't have to?

No . . . one step after another . . . after another . . . he forced himself to keep moving until he reached the roof door. He leaned hard against it, expecting resistance, but it fell open and he landed on his hands and knees.

Of course. *It's felt only by humans . . .*

That was confirmed by the rooftop garden around him—not a single leaf so much as fluttered. But they were brown and drooping.

He tried to regain his feet but found it impossible. The wind was colder and stronger than ever here, and he was too tired. Exhausted was more like it. Out of strength, out of will . . .

Through a fog of ever-growing darkness he made out the so-called *shoten* lying on his back maybe thirty feet away. His jaw hung open and a slim, twisting, undulating wisp of blackness spun like a miniature tornado from his mouth to the roiling cloud high above.

Thirty feet . . . might as well have been a mile. He'd never make it. Why even try?

. . . enough for the winds to reach Sutton Square . . .

Jack dragged himself forward, trying to ignore the dark emotions tugging on him, weighing him down . . . barren desolation . . . eternal, abysmal longing . . . infinite hopelessness . . .

The pain in his leg no longer distracted him, but simply added to the misery seeping through him.

Twenty-five feet . . . twenty . . . fifteen . . .

What was he going to do when he reached the *shoten*?

His Glock. All the misery swirling around him had driven it from his mind. He pulled it out, sighted on the *shoten*'s head, and pulled the trigger.

He felt rather than heard the hammer hit home, but no report followed. Dead cartridge? Bad primer? He ejected it, took aim, and the same thing happened. Something wrong with the Glock? Hard to believe. The damn things were so reliable.

But in the long run, nothing is reliable, nothing is worthy of trust.

He dropped the Glock, pulled the Kel-Tec from its ankle holster, aimed, pulled the trigger.

Nothing.

He tossed that aside and continued his crawl. He'd strangle the son of bitch.

But as he closed on him he felt a formless wave of fear and horror emanating from the *shoten*. If it was bad out here, what must it be like inside him?

"It's just no use," he heard himself say. He'd never reach him. "Just no use."

He forced his arms to slide forward, stretching them to their limits, but they fell half a foot short. Needed to move closer, but the wind was so strong here Jack's sapped muscles could not push him forward another inch.

. . . you may need it . . .

The katana.

He reached back and struggled it free of its scabbard. The wind howled louder, blew harder, but he edged the blade forward until its point rested against the side of the *shoten*'s throat. And then, with the last of his strength, he rammed it home.

As he saw a jet of blood arc toward the cloud, he released the handle and let his head drop against the roof.

16

"*No!*" Dawn heard Mr. Osala scream. "No! Not yet!"

Way down the street she saw the weird black cloud begin to shrink.

"What's happening?" he shouted to the sky.

As the streetlights began to brighten again, he lowered himself back into the car and sat silent and staring through the windshield.

Dawn tried again to move and found she could sit up.

"Mister Osala?"

The figure in the passenger seat turned and flipped on the overhead courtesy light.

"Finally awake, I see." His expression wasn't exactly welcoming. "I'm not in the mood for you now."

"Sorry."

Something about his face . . . changed, and yet the same . . . more than the start of a mustache . . . somehow he looked younger . . . softer . . . sexier.

Sexier? Mr. Osala? Sexy was so not the word she'd ever have associated with him, but looking at him now caused a stir within.

"Do you see now why I wanted you to stay off the streets and out of sight?"

She nodded meekly. "Yes."

"I'm sure you thought I was being overprotective and exaggerating the risk. But I've been proven right, haven't I? Consider what has happened to you since you escaped Henry. You have been living a nightmare, am I correct?"

Dawn bowed her head. Had she ever.

"Totally."

"Home, Georges," he said.

That reminded her. She looked up. "Where . . . where's Henry?"

"Henry has been . . . sacked. Discharged for dereliction of duty."

"But it was totally my fault. I—"

"No"—his voice turned to ice, taking on a tone that pressed her back into her seat—"it was not. He made choices. Bad ones. You will never see him again." His tone softened, just barely. "You almost had the baby aborted, didn't you."

The car glided uptown.

He wasn't asking a question. Obviously he knew the answer, so she simply nodded.

"Do you realize that you might very well be dead now if you'd succeeded? You'd have been no further use to Bethlehem and he would have killed you."

"I never saw him."

"Then he would have ordered you killed. And his equally vicious and deranged brother would have done it."

Speaking of deranged . . .

"Who were those monks and why did they kidnap me? I totally thought you'd sent them to rescue me."

A cold smile flickered. "Me? Send them? I hardly think so."

"But how did you get me out?"

"Bethlehem's people came to steal you back, and while they were all otherwise engaged, I simply carried you to my car and we drove away. Isn't that right, Georges."

"Correct, Master."

Master, she thought. Here we go again.

"Was Jerry there?"

Mr. Osala shook his head. "Unfortunately not. A fair number of his brother's followers were killed, but he was not among them. You can read the details in the paper tomorrow."

"But what were you doing on the roof of the car?"

He reached up and turned out the courtesy light. "Be still now. I wish to be alone with my thoughts."

He turned and stared out the windshield as the car moved uptown.

Dawn hugged her arms around her. Back to Mr. Osala's penthouse. Another sort of prison, but at least it was safe.

And safety had a lot going for it right now.

17

Still.

Jack lifted his head and looked around. The wind had died and the night was brighter. Stars shone and the cloud was gone as if it had never been.

His left fingers felt wet. He looked and saw that a pool of blood from the dead *shoten*'s throat had spread to his hand. He struggled to his knees and waited until the roof steadied and the stars stopped spinning. Then he wiped his fingers on the dead man's pants leg, and did the same with the sword.

He forced himself to his feet and sheathed the blade. As he staggered toward the roof exit he picked up his Glock and Kel-Tec.

Had to get downstairs and find Dawn, then get the hell out of this building.

He made it to the first floor, almost falling a couple of times along the way. The first sign of life he saw was the two pseudoguards in the front foyer. They looked dead at first, then he saw their chests move. Alive, but barely.

Why was he up and about? Less exposure?

Whatever. They'd stashed Dawn in the basement before, so that was probably where they had her now. Trouble was, how was he going to get her out? If she was in any shape similar to those two in the foyer, he was going to have to carry her, and he could barely stand.

As he approached the basement door it opened. He stopped, pulled his Glock, and waited.

For a few heartbeats, nothing happened. And then a shaggy, bandaged head appeared near the bottom of the opening, gradually followed by the rest of a Kicker crawling out on his hands and knees.

Jack put a foot on his back and pushed him down.

"Hey!" His voice was barely audible.

"Where's the girl?"

"Gotta get help for Hank." His face was against the floor. "He's in a bad way."

Jack pressed harder. "The girl—she in there?"

"No. Scary guy took her." It seemed to take all his energy to talk.

"Who?"

"Guy with scary eyes."

Jack had a feeling he knew who he meant.

"And you just let him take her?"

"Paralyzed us."

No doubt about it now.

Rasalom.

Shit. What did he want with her?

No use in hanging around. He pushed his way back up the steps. The guys in the foyer were starting to twitch. Jack reeled past them and out into the night where he found Veilleur's car idling at the curb.

Jack dropped into the passenger seat.

"The girl?" Veilleur said.

"Gone. Your old friend took her."

When Veilleur said nothing Jack glanced at him and saw a worried look on his face.

"What?"

The old man shook his head. "I don't like this."

"Yeah, well, you can see him being drawn to a super oDNA being, I guess, being filled with a sort of Otherness and all, but what can he do with it?"

Veilleur's expression turned grim. "I don't know, but I can guarantee without hesitation that, whatever his plan, it is grim tidings for the rest of us."

18

"You're sure you're all right?" Veilleur said as he pulled to a stop on Sutton Square.

Beyond the East River, dawn was pinking the sky over Queens. The yellow front of Gia's townhouse beckoned.

Jack nodded. "Yeah." Then shook his head. "No. But I will be after I get inside."

Strengthwise he was maybe eighty percent, but emotionally he remained spent. The Kuroikaze had sucked something out of him and he knew of only one place where it could be replenished.

But that wasn't why he'd told Veilleur to drop him here. He wanted to make sure they were okay.

Veilleur sighed. "Count your blessings. It's wonderful to have people you love to turn to."

"You mentioned a wife . . ."

He nodded sadly. "Perhaps I should have said, People you love who recognize you when you step into the room."

So that was it. Poor guy.

"I guess tonight got to you after all then."

Veilleur looked at him. "Got to me?"

"You know—all the blood, death, and dismemberment. It looked like it was just rolling off your back."

"Why shouldn't it? This was nothing, Jack. Compared to what I've seen, this was a pinprick on a whale's hide. You have no idea, you cannot conceive of the atrocities Ra—the Adversary has perpetrated down the millennia. Too often I've had to wade through the aftermath, looking for him. Multiply what you saw tonight millions of times and you'll have the barest inkling of what we can expect if the Otherness is allowed in."

Dismayed, Jack shook his head. "You're a buzzkill even when there's no buzz."

Jack offered his hand and they shook.

"Thanks for the lift."

He got out with the katana and watched Glaeken drive off. Then he let himself into the townhouse as quietly as he could. As he closed the door and put the katana in the umbrella stand he heard someone crying upstairs.

"Vicky?"

He dashed up to the second floor where he found a terrified-looking Gia cringing on the bed with Vicky. She was wearing an oversized Iowa State T-shirt and little else; Vicky wore shorty pajamas.

"Jesus, Jack! You should have let me know it was you."

"Sorry. I thought everybody'd be asleep, and then I heard Vicky crying."

"She woke up screaming from a nightmare half an hour ago and she's just now calming down."

Jack knelt beside her. "What was it about, Vicks?"

"I don't know!" A sniff and a sob. "I was just sc-sc-scared!"

"The weird thing is," Gia said, "when her screams woke me up, I was in the middle of some horrible nightmare myself."

Half an hour ago . . . The Kuroikaze had been going strong then. Could it be . . . ?

Yeah. Most likely.

He put an arm around Vicky's shoulders. "It's okay, Vicks. I'm here. I won't let anything scare you. Got that?"

She nodded and sniffed; her sobs seemed to have passed.

"Jack?"

"Yeah, Vicks?"

"You sorta kinda like smell bad."

He had to laugh. "Yeah, I probably do. One hot shower coming up."

19

"You do smell better," Gia murmured as Jack spooned against her in the bed.

"Rough night."

"Do I want to know?"

"No way."

"Then don't tell me."

He snuggled closer, pressing the fronts of his thighs against the backs of hers.

"Let's just sleep, Jack. I'm really tired."

She was tired? All he wanted was to be close enough to feel clean again. Or at least cleaner. With what he knew floated in his DNA, he'd never feel completely clean.

She hadn't a clue as to what had happened downtown a little while ago. That would change in the morning.

"I'm more tired than you. I could sleep for a week."

"Oh, yeah? I could sleep for a *month*."

"Really? I could sleep for a *year*"—he tried to think of the loudest thrash-metal band he knew—"at a Polio concert."

She laughed. "Okay. You win. You're more tired." She pushed her butt back against him. "See you in the morning."

"Love ya."

"Love ya too."

20

"Like a zombie, you look," Abe said as Jack approached the rear counter.

Which meant he looked lots better than he felt.

Jack leaned the katana, wrapped now in one of Gia's paint-stained drop cloths, against the base of the counter and slumped onto a stool.

"Coffeeeeeee . . . coffeeeeeeee."

God, he needed sleep. Usually he could go days on a few hours, but he couldn't seem to shake the effects of the Kuroikaze. And every time he'd dozed off, images from the abattoir the Kakureta Kao temple had become would flash through his head, waking him.

As Abe turned to fill a cup from his bottomless coffee pot, Jack glanced at the screaming headlines on the front pages of the morning papers. The *Daily News*:

SLAUGHTER ON
STATEN ISLAND!

And the *Post*:

KILLINGS IN
THE KILLS!

Abe handed Jack a steaming cup. He took it and sipped. He'd already had four cups but they hadn't helped.

"You've read?" Abe said, pointing to the *Post*.

Jack shook his head.

He held it up. "You want?"

Another shake.

He snorted. "You want I should read it to you?"

"No, thanks."

Abe's eyebrows rose, ridging his forehead and part of the infinity pool of his bare scalp.

"I don't get it. You love stories like this. All the details, you want. You . . ." His voice trailed off as he looked down at the headline, then back at Jack. "They say almost fifty bodies were found by press time and probably more to come. That dwarfs even the number found in the Red Hook warehouse." His expression slackened. "Oy! You again?"

Jack shrugged. "Mostly as a nonparticipant."

Unlike Red Hook.

"Mostly?"

Jack shrugged. "Would've been completely non if someone had given me a choice at the end."

Abe looked worried. "What set you off? Please tell me Gia and Vicky are—"

Jack raised a hand to stop him. He didn't want to go there—didn't want even to consider the slightest possibility of anything happening to Gia and Vicky again.

"They're fine. I told you: nonparticipant. I was simply the party planner. Not my fault if the crowd got rowdy."

Abe turned his hands palm up and waggled his pudgy, stubby fingers. "Give-give."

Jack didn't feel like talking about it, so he pointed to the giant soft pretzel on the counter. From the amount of crumbs—Abe's parakeet Parabellum was swiftly diminishing their number—he figured Abe had started out with more than one.

"Pretzels for breakfast?"

"Breakfast was hours ago. This is lunch."

"Oh. Right."

He tore off a loop and bit into it. The salt tasted good. He was hungrier than he'd thought.

"Last night?"

"Okay, okay."

Jack gave him a moderately detailed account of what went down up to the point where he regained the katana.

"All this for a rotten old sword?" Abe said.

"And a pregnant teenager. Everybody wants her baby. Damned if I know why."

"Where is she now?"

"That's another story."

"There's more?" He rubbed his hands together. "Goody."

So Jack gave him a rundown of the Kuroikaze and Rasalom ending up with Dawn.

"A busy night you had." Abe opened the *Post* and began flipping pages. "So *that*'s what happened downtown."

Jack broke off another piece of pretzel.

"What does it say?"

"First page it would have made if not for your party. They're blaming some 'yet-to-be-identified toxin' that made people weak and sick. Might be related to a strange cloud a few folks saw, might not."

"Any deaths?"

"A couple. They don't know how many yet. They were still canvassing at press time. They say the dead folks were old, so it could have been natural."

"Or accelerated by the Kuroikaze."

"After what you say it was like, I shouldn't be surprised." He looked up. "What now?"

Jack lifted the katana and hefted it.

"In a little less than an hour I'm meeting with the guy who hired me to find it. I'm going to hand it to him and say, 'Sayonara.' If I knew how to say 'good riddance' in Japanese, I'd say that instead. This thing has been nothing but trouble."

21

"There's a guy here says you want to meet with him."

Rage bloomed in Hank as he looked up to see Darryl standing at the door to his room.

"*I* want to meet him? Didn't I tell you I didn't want to see anyone? *Any-one?*"

"Yeah, I know, but it's that weird Lodge guy and he won't take no for an answer. Says he can help us out of this mess."

"Which one?" Hank could think of so many.

Darryl pointed to the window. "That one."

Hank didn't need the window to know what was out there, but he forced himself to his feet and made his way over to peek around the edge of the shade.

Below, the near and far sidewalks were packed with reporters. They'd have been blocking the street if not for the cops there.

He staggered back to the bed and sat, cradling his head in his hands. He just wanted to be alone, but he couldn't stiff the Septimus Order's point man—its "actuator." Couldn't risk getting kicked out of this place.

"Send him up."

"He's got someone with him."

"Send them both up, but it turns out the other guy's a reporter, your ass is grass."

As Darryl left, Hank closed his eyes and swallowed against a rising gorge. He felt like a warmed-over cow pie. Wanted to puke so bad, but had nothing left in his gut. What had happened last night? That wind, those feelings of hopelessness and helplessness . . . they went entirely against the take-control message of the Kicker Evolution.

The only good thing was it was gone and it hadn't sucked all the life out of him. Just some.

His thoughts drifted further back, to that insane building on Staten Island and all the men he'd led into it—well, not *into*, but *to*—who wouldn't be coming back. They'd given as good as they'd got until those hit men showed up.

Thirty men gone . . . and what had he to show for it? Not a goddamn thing. The hit men probably had the sword, and the guy with the infinity eyes had Dawn.

Thirty dead Kickers, and the cops and the press wanted to know how and why. Hank hadn't the faintest idea what to tell them.

A vaguely accented voice from the doorway: "Mister Thompson?"

Hank looked up and saw a hawk-faced Ernst Drexler. The white of his suit in the morning light hurt his eyes. Hadn't Darryl said he had someone with him? Hank didn't see anyone else.

"Come in, Mister Drexler. What can I do for you?"

Drexler glided to the window and tapped it with the silver head of his black cane.

"It's more a matter of what I can do for you."

"In particular?"

"We have people."

When Drexler didn't go on, Hank said, "So do I."

"Not the kind of people we have. Allow me to introduce Mr. Terrence McCabe."

Hank turned as a true-blue, briefcase-toting suit came through the doorway. A gray business suit, black shoes, white shirt, and striped tie. The guy inside it all was short, with shiny black hair, a round face, and a rounder body. He reminded Hank of an actor he liked . . . from a movie about a giant alligator. Oliver somebody.

He strode forward, hand extended. The guy seemed to fill the room.

"An honor to meet you, sir," he said in a booming voice

Remaining seated on the bed, Hank raised his hand and shook. McCabe's grip was like a vise.

"Don't call me 'sir.' It's Hank."

"Very well. Calling a man I admire by his first name . . . that won't be easy."

"Work on it. Just not so loud. Lower the volume." McCabe's voice was worsening the pounding ache in his head. "So who are you?"

"I have a law degree and I'm a member of the bar, but my work—my forte, you might say—is public relations. A famous director gets caught DUI, a big-name actor gets caught with an underage fan, a country singer gets caught with his best friend's wife—or worse yet, his best friend—who do they call?" He jabbed a thumb against his chest. "Yours truly. Because my subspecialty in PR is damage control."

Damage control . . . Hank had known he'd needed it but hadn't wanted to think about it now, hadn't wanted to think about anything. But somebody had to, and he'd been it.

Until now.

"And you want me to hire you?"

He grinned. "No need. The rest of the world pays an arm, a leg, and rights to all earnings of their firstborn. For you, it's all taken care of."

"Yeah? Who by?"

McCabe glanced at Drexler.

Drexler said, "We have a wealthy sponsor who's willing to do that."

"Who?"

"He wishes to remain anonymous for now."

Hank looked at McCabe. "And how are you going to control all this damage?"

"Spin, Hank. I'm going to spin it in another direction."

Spin . . . yeah, what had happened since midnight was going to need major, major spin. But . . .

"I'm not a spin guy. *It is what it is*—that pretty well sums up my approach."

"And it's an admirable approach, Hank, but the Kicker Evolution has grown too big for that, and it's growing bigger by the day. 'It is what it is' isn't going to work in this case because everyone can see what it is, and what they see isn't good. I'm going to get them looking the other way."

"I was thinking of playing dumb," Hank said. "I mean, I can truthfully say that I don't keep track of every Kicker's every move. They're all free men and women who act on their own, and what led them to become involved in this terrible tragedy is anyone's guess. I'll say I'm just praying the perpetrators will be brought to justice."

"Lack of firsthand knowledge will definitely be part of the game plan, but we need more. We need to play the blame game as well. We must paint your fallen followers as victims. Any idea as to whom we may point to?"

"Well, the Dormentalists and Scientologists have it in for me." In fact, the three groups were waging an Internet war, crashing each other's sites and all. "They're losing members left and right to the Kicker Evolution and—"

McCabe jabbed a finger in his direction. "Perfect! Perfect!"

He started wandering around the room, waving his arms in the air as he riffed about older, more established, more organized belief systems—little more than corporatized cults, really—becoming increasingly jealous and finally desperate as their numbers dwindled. . . .

As Hank listened he remembered how he'd been feeling the need for a right-hand man, a smart, loyal second in command. Darryl fit the loyal part and, despite appearances, was no dummy, but he'd never cut it. He needed someone who was into spin and details. Hank hated details. He was a big-picture guy.

And in walks Terrence McCabe, a detail man and spinmeister if he ever saw one. He had a feeling Terry was going to work out just fine. Not just in spin, but in cleaning up the Kicker image, and maybe getting things in order, getting operations organized. Right now everything was helter-skelter.

Yeah. Terrence McCabe was just what the Kicker Evolution needed.

He glanced at Drexler and found the man's piercing blue gaze fixed on him.

"Excuse me, Terry," Hank said, holding up a hand. "But I'd like to ask Drexler here what's his angle in all this?"

Drexler smiled—sort of. "As I've mentioned in the past, the Order's Council of Seven senses a certain commonality of interests. We wish to explore that further. But to do so we first must remove your organization from the limelight. Once that is done, we shall initiate certain ventures that will be to our mutual benefit."

"Like what?"

"We shall discuss them soon. I assure you they will be in line with the tenets of the Kicker movement. And they will happen. I shall see to it."

He seemed pretty confident. But then his card said he was an "actuator." Wasn't that what an actuator did—made things happen?

He had awakened with the future looking pretty grim. It had brightened quite a bit in the past few minutes.

Thanks to Drexler . . . and his bosses in the Septimus Order.

Strange how things happened. Almost as if there was a plan. Daddy had had his Plan, but this seemed bigger. Much bigger.

But who was behind it? The Septimus Order, obviously. But who or what was behind the Order?

22

Naka Slater was staying at the Grand Hyatt on 42nd. The taxi took the high road and dropped Jack off at the Park Avenue entrance that admitted him onto one of the mezzanine levels. He looked around, spotted some elevators, and headed that way.

"Hey, honey," said a sultry voice. "Is that a sword or are you just glad to see me?"

He stopped and turned to find himself facing a sultry, eye-poppingly proportioned redhead in a scarlet minidress and black stockings. She'd draped a silk scarf over her bare shoulders. The red of her lips matched the scarf and dress. Perfectly.

Jack waved her off. "No time now."

But as he started to turn away he spotted the snow-white miniature poodle peeking from her shoulder bag.

A woman. With a dog.

"Are you her?"

She pivoted and lowered the scarf to reveal the crisscrossing lines and open sores on her back. That clinched it.

He said, "Any particular reason for the Jessica Rabbit look?"

She smiled and shrugged. "It's Forty-second Street, and I remember the good old days." Her smile faded. "We need to talk."

He held up the wrapped katana. "About this, I presume."

A nod. She pointed to the railing overlooking a wide-open space. "Let's go over there."

She led the way. They leaned on the railing for a moment and watched the comings and goings in the large, bustling lobby one level below. To the right an escalator led down from the lobby to the marble pool-and-fountain-lined entrance that opened onto 42nd Street.

The poodle watched from her bag, pink tongue out, panting.

"Before we go any further," he said, "who are you?"

She shook her head. "How many times must I tell you: I am your mother."

"You're not getting off that easy this time. Who or what are you?"

Her green eyes fixed on his. "I think you know. You tell me."

"I . . ." This sounded so crazy. "I think you're Mother Earth."

She smiled. "Would it were that simple, but it's much more compli-cated. Too complicated to go into right now."

"But—"

"Some other time." She touched the katana. "This is of more immediate concern."

Something in her tone convinced Jack that arguing would be futile.

"Okay. What about it? In five minutes it's going to be in someone else's hot little hands and probably by tomorrow it will be on its way back to Maui."

"Instead of giving it to this man, it might be better if you took a boat out past the continental ridge and dropped it into the Hudson Canyon."

He glanced at the katana, then back at her.

"You're telling me it's evil?"

"Good and evil are difficult to apply to weapons. They can be a means to either end. But this blade . . . I sense something significant, something of great import about it . . . that it will be a means to a momentous end."

"A good end or a bad end?"

"I wish I could say."

"Didn't we have this conversation about a certain unborn baby?"

She nodded. "They are somehow linked. The baby is all potential with no history. But this . . ." She pointed to the katana. "It has been used for both good and ill throughout its existence. Its last act before the fire was fratricide—a terrible thing, yet done for good reason for a good end. Immediately after that came the fire."

Before the fire . . .

"The bomb?"

She nodded. "The nuclear fire changed it. It is now something less, in that it has lost some of the steel its fashioner gave it. But it is also something more."

"More how?"

"I wish I knew. It might now be a weapon only for good, or only for evil. Or, like any blade, it might cut either way, depending on who wields it. But it *will* be used for something momentous."

"So you'd rather have it used for nothing at all."

She shrugged. "Just an instinct. No one can tell the future."

"Trouble is, it's not my decision. Maybe you can talk to Slater, convince him to give it to you or drop it in the ocean off Maui. I'll introduce you . . ."
Her stare stopped him. "What?"

"You're going to return it to him."

"Yeah. We have a deal."

"Even after what I said about its momentous potential."

"Look, he paid me. I said I'd look for his katana and if I found it I'd return it to him. We shook hands on it. I gave my word."

She nodded. "Your code. Is that more important?"

Jack sighed. He didn't like to get all philosophical and look too deeply into these things. He tended to follow his gut. He'd learned to trust it.

He shrugged. "My word is my word."

"And you've never broken it?"

Yes, he had. He thought of his final facedown with Kusum. But Vicky's life had been at stake there. Where Gia and Vicky were concerned, he also listened to his gut, and in that situation his gut had said, *Fuck the code, waste him.*

And he had.

But the odd thing was, despite the unquestionable necessity, it had bothered him for a long time after. Still bothered him.

"It's like being the little kid with his finger in the leak in the dike. If he pulls it out because it starts to feel a little uncomfortable, he may not be able to get it back in. And then more and more of the sea will flow through, widening the hole until the dike fails and drowns him." He hated verbalizing this stuff. He shrugged. "Am I making any sense? Do you see what I'm saying?"

"You're saying you're going to return the blade."

"Well, given a choice between my word and a big fat maybe, yeah, I'm returning the blade."

"I hope it's the right decision."

"As far as I can see, it's the only decision."

But he'd rather someone else be making it.

23

A smiling Naka Slater opened the door and stepped back, his eyes on the package in Jack's hand.

"At last. The prodigal sword returns to the fold."

Jack figured that mix of metaphors beat his own from the park yesterday, but didn't congratulate him. Instead he added to the mix.

"Wrapped in a coat of many colors." Closing the door behind him, Jack handed it over. "All yours."

And good riddance.

But the Lady's words haunted him.

. . . it will be used for something momentous . . .

Was this chubby sixty-something plantation owner going to be the one to wield it? Hard to believe.

"How did you ever track it down?"

"Crack detective work."

"And you didn't have to buy it back? Because I'll reimburse—"

"No need. Reasoned discourse carried the day."

He carried it to the bed where he began to unwind the drop cloth.

"Would you believe this is the first time I've ever handled it? At least that I recall."

"You mean it was sitting in your house and you were never tempted to play samurai with it?"

"Tempted like crazy. But it was displayed in a sealed glass case for just that reason."

The grip end came free first.

"You've added a handle and a hilt."

"Not me. Someone along the way."

When he revealed the rest he grinned like a little boy with his first puppy.

"A scabbard too!"

As Slater grabbed the scabbard and pulled the blade free, Jack stepped back and slipped his hand to the Glock under the back of his loose T-shirt. He'd already played this scene once and had come away with a sliced-up shoulder. Not taking any chances this time.

Slater stayed bedside, however, swinging the blade back and forth. But as he swung it his smile faded to a frown, and then a grimace of distaste. He stopped swinging it and dropped it on the bed.

Jack stared at him. "This isn't where you try to tell me that isn't the right sword, is it?"

He shook his head. "No. I'd recognize those defects anywhere. But there's something *wrong* with that thing."

"Maybe the handle changes the balance or—"

"No-no. I mean something wrong *inside* it. The legends say that Masamune put a little of his gentle soul into each of his katana so that it would not be used for indiscriminate killing. It would sever an evil man's head but not cut a passing butterfly."

Buuuullshit . . . buuuullshit . . .

"So you're saying it's not a true Masamune?"

"I'm not enough of an expert to tell. Maybe it is, and maybe the Hiroshima bomb burned away whatever of Masamune was in there. I don't know. But I do know I don't want that thing in my house."

"You kidding me? It's been in your house all your life."

"Yes, two houses and two countries. Maybe I touched the katana when I was little. Maybe a part of me recognizes the difference. I don't like what it's become. I don't want it." He sheathed the blade and held out the katana to Jack. "Here. You take it."

"Hell no. What am I going to do with—?"

He grabbed the drop cloth, shoved it and the katana into Jack's hands, then hurried to the dresser. He returned with an envelope and gave that to Jack as well.

"Here—the rest of your fee." He then stepped to the door and opened it. "Please. Take it. Do whatever you want with it."

Nonplussed, Jack stepped back into the hall. "You're sure?"

"Absolutely. You did a wonderful job, but I've changed my mind. Are we square?"

"If you say so."

"Then it's a done deal. Thank you. Good-bye."

He closed the door.

"Yeah. Good-bye."

Jack looked down at the katana. Now what?

24

1:06.

Dawn blinked at the display on her bedside clock radio: P.M.? Couldn't be.

Clad only in panties, she dragged herself from under the covers and stepped to her bedroom window. She pulled aside the heavy drapes and cringed in the bright light. The sun was high, and Fifth Avenue and Central Park bustled below.

Right back where I started.

Or had she ever left? The events of the past few days seemed too totally fantastic to be real.

Shadowed around the city, abducted in broad daylight, Kickers, Jerry's brother swinging some weird sword, then kidnapped by ninjas, drugged by Japanese monks, rescued by Mr. Osala—who, it seems, likes to stand on the roof of his car during a storm—and now back to the penthouse.

Had she dreamed it all?

She went to her closet and pulled out a robe. She'd totally never worn one before she came here. After all, she'd been able to walk around her house in pretty much any state of undress she pleased. But this wasn't her house. So when she didn't feel like getting dressed—like now—she threw on one of these things.

She stepped out into the hall. The marble floor was cold on her feet as she padded to the kitchen hoping to find some coffee. But the kitchen was empty, just like the coffeepot. She'd make some herself if she knew where anything was, but this was Gilda's domain and she ruled it like a jealous queen.

Dawn realized she needed more than coffee. She was starving. She'd have to track down Gilda and have her whip up some breakfast. Or lunch. Or whatever.

She found her in the hall carrying an armful of men's clothing. They looked like . . .

"Are those Henry's?"

Gilda didn't look at her. "Yes."

"Then Mister Osala really did fire him?"

Gilda said nothing, just kept on moving toward the foyer. Dawn followed in a daze. Then it was true . . . all true . . . the nightmare had been real . . . and Henry had been fired because of her.

"I'm sorry about what happened. I—"

Gilda's cold look cut her off as she stopped and turned. "You should be ashamed. He was only trying to make you happy, and you betrayed him."

The truth of her words struck like a slap in the face. Yes, she'd totally betrayed him.

"But don't you see? I didn't want to stay here. I wanted to get away and none of you would let me."

"We are here to protect you."

"I know that, and after all that happened, I know this is the safest place to be. But I didn't see it that way then. I didn't mean to cause any trouble."

The ice remained in her tone. "Well, you did."

She turned and continued toward the foyer where she laid the pile by the door.

"Is Henry coming to pick them up?"

She wanted to tell him how sorry she was, but didn't know if she could face him.

Another cold look from Gilda. "Henry is never coming back."

"Then why are you putting his clothes out?"

"They are to be burned."

"Burned?" She didn't get it. "But he was only fired. You talk about him like he's dead."

Gilda turned away and headed in the direction of the kitchen.

"I will make you some lunch."

But Dawn was no longer hungry. She stared at that forlorn pile of clothing, thinking it couldn't be . . . it totally couldn't be.

Henry was out there in the city, totally alive and looking for another job. He had to be . . .

But what she'd seen in Gilda's eyes just before she'd turned away said otherwise.

She felt her blood turning to ice.

Dead? But that could only mean that Mr. Osala had . . .

What have I *done*? Who are these people? What have I gotten myself into?

25

Jack entered his apartment with the katana.

The Lady's words had haunted him.

It might now be a weapon only for good, or only for evil. Or, like any blade, it might cut either way, depending on who wields it. But it will be used for something momentous.

She'd wanted him to dump it in the ocean but had not offered a clear reason why.

. . . something momentous . . .

Momentous good or momentous evil?

If the latter, then yeah, dump it in the Mariana Trench, where no one, not even Rasalom, could reach it.

But if at some crucial moment in the coming showdown it could tip the scale against the Otherness, Jack didn't want it under seven miles of ocean.

. . . it might cut either way, depending on who wields it . . .

O'Day had killed Gerrish with it, and Jack guessed that would be considered an ill use of the weapon. But Glaeken had used it defensively, and nonlethally at that.

Yeah . . . so it depended on who wielded it.

He'd given it a lot of thought, leaning this way and that. The tipping point had come when he remembered what Veilleur had said about Rasalom being at the Kakureta Kao temple. If so, he could have gone after Dawn or the katana. The fact that he'd chosen Dawn told Jack that the katana wasn't all that important to him.

Jack decided to keep it, figuring he could dispose of it at any time if he changed his mind. But if he ditched it now, there was no going back.

It wouldn't fit in the false back of the secretary with the rest of his goodies, so he found a spot on the top shelf of one of his closets. It was too long to lie flat so he leaned it at an angle.

He stared at it for a moment, wondering if he was doing the right thing.

Don't make me regret this, he thought, then shut the closet door.

www.repairmanjack.com

THE SECRET HISTORY OF THE WORLD

The preponderance of my work deals with a history of the world that remains undiscovered, unexplored, and unknown to most of humanity. Some of this secret history has been revealed in the Adversary Cycle, some in the Repairman Jack novels, and bits and pieces in other, seemingly unconnected works. Taken together, even these millions of words barely scratch the surface of what has been going on behind the scenes, hidden from the workaday world. I've listed these works below in the chronological order in which the events in them occur.

Note: "Year Zero" is the end of civilization as we know it; "Year Zero Minus One" is the year preceding it, etc.

THE PAST
"Demonsong" (prehistory)
"Aryans and Absinthe" (1923–1924)
Black Wind (1926–1945)
The Keep (1941)
Reborn (February–March 1968)
"Dat Tay Vao" (March 1968)
Jack: Secret Histories (1983)

YEAR ZERO MINUS THREE
Sibs (February)
"Faces" (early summer)
The Tomb (summer)
"The Barrens"* (ends in September)
"A Day in the Life"* (October)
"The Long Way Home"
Legacies (December)

YEAR ZERO MINUS TWO
Conspiracies (April) (includes "Home Repairs")
"Interlude at Duane's" (April)
All the Rage (May) (includes "The Last Rakosh")

Hosts (June)
The Haunted Air (August)
Gateways (September)
Crisscross (November)
Infernal (December)

YEAR ZERO MINUS ONE

Harbingers (January)
Bloodline (April)
By the Sword (May)
The Touch (ends in August)
The Peabody-Ozymandias Traveling Circus & Oddity Emporium (ends in September)
"Tenants"*
yet-to-be-written Repairman Jack novels

YEAR ZERO

"Pelts"*
Reprisal (ends in February)
the last Repairman Jack novel (will end in April)
Nightworld (starts in May)

Reborn, The Touch, and *Reprisal* will be back in print before too long. I'm planning a total of sixteen or seventeen Repairman Jack novels (not counting the young adult titles), ending the Secret History with the publication of a heavily revised *Nightworld.*

*available in *The Barrens and Others*